Colin turned sharply on his heel and glared at this woman who wouldn't take a hint.

"Lady—"

"Miranda," she prompted.

"Miranda," Colin echoed between gritted teeth. "You are a royal pain, you know that?"

Miranda always tried to glean something positive out of every situation, no matter how bleak it might appear. "Does that mean you'll look for her?" she asked him hopefully.

He blew out an angry breath. "That means you're a royal pain," he repeated.

With nothing to lose, Miranda went out on a limb. "Please? I can give you a description of Lily's mother." And then she thought of something even better. "And if you come with me, I can get you a picture of her that'll be useful."

He had a feeling that the woman just wasn't going to give up unless he agreed to help her. Although it irritated him beyond description, there was a very small part of him that did admire her tenacity.

* * *

CHRISTMASTIME COURTSHIP

BY
MARIE FERRARELLA

HarperCollins
P U B L I S H E R S
Since 1817

First Published in Great Britain 2017
By Mills & Boon, an imprint of HarperCollins*Publishers*
1 London Bridge Street, London, SE1 9GF

© 2017 Marie Rydzynski-Ferrarella

ISBN: 978-0-263-92354-4

23-1217

MIX
Paper from
responsible sources
FSC™ C007454

This book is produced from independently certified FSC™ paper to ensure responsible forest management.

For more information visit: www.harpercollins.co.uk/green

Printed and bound in Spain
by CPI, Barcelona

USA TODAY bestselling and RITA® Award–winning author **Marie Ferrarella** has written more than two hundred and seventy-five books for Mills & Boon, some under the name Marie Nicole. Her romances are beloved by fans worldwide. Visit her website, www.marieferrarella.com.

To
Melany,
The Best Daughter-in-Law
Anyone Could Ask For.
Welcome To The Family.

Prologue

"Is it true?"

Theresa Manetti looked up from the menu she was putting the final touches on to see who had just walked into her inner office. Most clients who wanted to avail themselves of her catering services either called or were brought in by one of her staff and announced.

As it turned out, this time Theresa found herself looking up at Jeannine Steele, an old friend she hadn't seen in at least six months. Not since she'd catered Jeannine's husband's funeral reception.

"Well, that's a new kind of greeting," Theresa commented, amused. "Most people usually say hello. Is *what* true?" she asked, nodding toward the chair on the other side of her desk, indicating that her friend should sit down.

Looking uncomfortable and nervous, Jeannine

lowered herself onto the chair, perching on its edge. "There's a rumor going around that in addition to your catering business, you're running some sort of a dating service on the side."

Theresa had known Jeannine since her own two children had been in elementary school with Jeannine's daughter, and in all that time, she couldn't recall the stately woman appearing anything but completely in control.

Always.

But not this time.

"Well, that's not exactly an accurate description," Theresa replied. "It's not really a 'dating service,' so much as a matchmaking service."

Confusion furrowed Jeannie's otherwise smooth, alabaster brow. "There's a difference?"

From her vantage point, Theresa could see the other woman twisting her long, slender fingers together. Theresa was experienced enough to know where this was heading, and did what she could to set her friend at ease.

"A big difference," she answered, pushing back her chair and rising to her feet. "Would you like something to drink, Jeannine?" she asked kindly. "I have everything from tea to soft drinks to something a little more 'bracing' if you'd rather have that."

Jeannine drew in a deep breath before answering. "I'll take tea," she replied. "Strong tea."

Theresa smiled as she went to the counter against the back wall, where she had a pot of hot water steaming. She had a preference for tea herself.

"So, it's been a while, Jeannine," she said in her customary easygoing manner. "How are you?"

"Concerned, frankly," the other woman admitted.

Recrossing the room, Theresa held out the cup of tea. "You're worried about Miranda, aren't you?"

Her friend nearly dropped the cup Theresa had handed her. Some hot liquid sloshed over the side. "How did you know?" she asked, surprised.

"To begin with, you asked me about my so-called 'sideline,'" Theresa answered, employing a whimsical term for the labor that had become near and dear not just to her heart, but to Maizie's and Celia's hearts, as well.

Theresa and the two women she had been best friends with since the third grade had weathered all of life's highs and lows together. The highs included marriage, children and the successful businesses all three had started in the second half of their lives and were currently running.

The lows included all three becoming widows. But she, Maizie and Celia had learned to push on past the pain. After all, they each had children to provide for. They were determined to lead productive, fulfilling lives. And above all else, they were always, always there for one another.

Their matchmaking had begun slowly, by finding matches for their own children. That was to be the end of it, but matching up the right two people brought such satisfaction with it, they'd decided to try their hand at it again.

And again.

With each successful match, their secondary vocation just seemed to take wings. They loved the businesses they had begun and nurtured individually, but there was something exceedingly fulfilling about bringing together two people who otherwise might never have found one another.

Two people who clearly belonged together.

It looked as if the adventure was about to begin again, Theresa thought.

"Tell me about Miranda," she coaxed, taking her seat once more. "How is she? Is she still as wonderfully generous and big-hearted as ever?"

Jeannine thought of her only daughter—her only living child—whose career path had been chosen at the age of ten. "Yes—and that's the problem. She's so busy giving of herself, working at the children's hospital, the women's shelter *and* the city's animal shelter, that she doesn't have any time to focus on herself. Don't get me wrong, Theresa. I'm prouder of Miranda than I can possibly say, but, well, I'm really afraid that if she keeps going like this, she's eventually going to wind up alone." Jeannine sighed. "I know that sounds like I'm being small-minded and meddling, but—"

Theresa cut her short. "Trust me, I know the feeling," she assured her. "We're mothers, Jeannine. It comes with the territory." With her business going full steam ahead the way it was these days, she could use a little diversion. "Tell me, do you have any idea what Miranda's dating life is like?"

"I have a very clear idea," Jeannine replied. "It's nonexistent these days."

"Really?"

"Really," she confirmed sadly. "The problem is that no man can compete with her full-time job, as well as all her volunteer work. Besides, what man wants to come in fourth?"

"Definitely not the kind of man we would want for your daughter," Theresa said with conviction.

Jeannine looked confused. "What are you saying?"

Theresa smiled as she began making plans. "I'm saying we need to change Miranda's focus a little."

"So you do think there's hope?" A glimmer of optimism entered the other woman's hazel eyes.

Theresa leaned over and patted her friend's hand. "Jeannine," she said confidently, "there is *always* hope."

Chapter One

"Ladies, we have work to do," Theresa announced the moment she entered Maizie Sommer's house.

She strode into Maizie's family room with the vigor of a woman half her age. Matchmaking projects always got her adrenaline going, creating a level of enthusiasm within her even greater than her usual line of work did—and it went without saying that she dearly loved her catering business.

"We certainly do," Cecilia Parnell agreed.

Already seated at the card table—their usual gathering place whenever they were discussing their newest undertaking in the matchmaking arena—Celia turned to look at her. "This one is going to be a real challenge for us."

"Oh, I don't know," Theresa protested, gracefully slipping into the chair that was set up between Celia and Maizie. "I don't think it'll be *that* hard finding someone suitable."

Taken aback, Celia looked quizzically at her old friend, who hadn't called ahead with any details about the person she felt should be their latest project. "Wait, how would you know?"

"How would I know?" Theresa repeated incredulously. "Because I've known Miranda Steele ever since she was a little girl. She has this incredibly huge heart and she's always trying to help everyone. Fix everyone," Theresa emphasized, which was why she had come to think of the young woman as "the fixer" in recent years.

"Miranda?" Celia echoed, decidedly more confused than she'd initially been. "Maizie and I were talking about Colin when you walked in."

It was Theresa's turn to be confused. "Who's Colin?" she asked, looking from Maizie to Celia.

"Police Officer Colin Kirby," Celia clarified, adding, "our latest matchmaking project. His aunt Lily is a friend of mine and she came to talk to me on the outside chance that maybe I—actually *we*—could find someone for him."

Without pausing, Celia launched into a brief version of the police officer's backstory. "Lily took him in when her sister, Vanessa, a single mother, died in a car accident. Colin was fourteen at the time. She said that he's a decent, hardworking young man who just shut down when he lost his mother. He enlisted in the Marines straight out of high school. When his tour of duty overseas ended, he was honorably discharged and immediately joined the police force in Los Angeles."

Maizie appeared a little dubious. "Los Angeles is a little out of our usual territory," she commented. "But I guess—"

"Oh no." Celia quickly cut in. "He's not in Los Angeles anymore, he's in Bedford now. Lily talked him into moving back down here. Her health isn't what it used to be and he's her only living relative, so he made the move for her, which, in my book, shows you what sort of a person he is.

"The problem is," Celia continued, "Lily says he's really closed off, especially after what he saw during his tour overseas and as a police officer in one of the roughest areas in Los Angeles. To put it in Lily's own words," she concluded, "Colin needs someone to 'fix him.'"

Smiling, Maizie shifted her gaze from Celia to Theresa. It was obvious that, in her estimation, they needed to look no further in either case. "You just said you have someone who likes to 'fix' people."

But Celia was more skeptical than her friend. She needed more to work with. "Fix how?"

Theresa gave them Miranda's background in a nutshell. "According to her mother, Miranda's a pediatric nurse at Bedford Children's Hospital who volunteers at a women's shelter in her free time. She also volunteers at the city's animal shelter and occasionally takes in strays until they can be placed in a permanent home."

Maizie's smile widened. "Ladies, maybe I'm getting ahead of myself, but this sounds to me like a match made in heaven. I'm assuming you both have a few more pertinent details that we can work with—like what these two look like and how old they are, for openers," said the woman whose decision to find her daughter a suitable match had initially gotten what turned out to be their "side business" rolling eight years ago.

"Miranda's thirty," Theresa told them, producing a photograph on her smartphone that Jeannie had sent her, and holding it up for the others to see.

"Colin's thirty-three," Celia said. "And I'll ask Lily to send me a picture."

So saying, she texted a message to the woman. In less than a minute, her cell phone buzzed, announcing that her request had been received and answered.

"Here we go," Celia declared. "Oh my," she murmured as she looked at the image that had materialized on her smartphone. Colin's aunt had sent her a photo of her nephew in his police uniform.

Maizie took Celia's hand and turned the phone around so she could look at it.

"Definitely 'oh my,'" she agreed wholeheartedly. Pushing the deck of cards aside, she gave up all pretense that they were going to engage in a game of poker this evening, even a single hand. Her gaze took in her two lifelong friends. "Ladies, let's get down to work. These two selfless servants of society need us. And from what I've heard, they also need each other," the successful Realtor added knowingly. "We'll require more information to bring about the perfect subtle 'meet' to get this particular ball rolling."

Filled with anticipation, the three old friends got busy.

Every year, the holiday season seemed to begin earlier and earlier, Miranda Steele thought.

Not that she was complaining. Christmas had always been her very favorite time of year. While others grumbled that the stores were putting up Christmas decorations way too soon, motivated by a desire to increase their already obscene profits, Miranda saw it as a way to stretch the spirit of Christmas a little further, thereby making the true meaning of the season last a little longer.

But sometimes, like now, the pace became a little too hectic even for her. She had just put in a ten-hour day at the hospital, coming in way before her shift actually began in order to help decorate the oncology ward, where she worked. She felt particularly driven because she knew that for some of the children there it would be their last Christmas.

As harsh and sad as that thought was to deal with, she chose to focus on the bright side: bringing the best possible Christmas she could to the children and their families.

At times, she felt like a lone cheerleader, tirelessly attempting to drum up enthusiasm and support from the other nurses, doctors and orderlies on the floor until she had everyone finally pitching in, even if they weren't all cheerful about it.

She didn't care if the rest of the staff was cheerful or not, as long as they helped out. And as was her habit, she worked harder than anyone to make sure that things were ultimately "just right."

If she were a normal person, about now she would be on her way home, having earned some serious bubble bath time.

But soaking in a hot tub was not on this afternoon's

agenda. She didn't have time for a bubble bath, as much as she longed for one. She had to get Lily's birthday party ready.

Lily Hayden was eight today. The little girl was one of the many children currently living with their moms at the Bedford Women's Home, a shelter where Miranda volunteered four days a week after work.

The other two or three days she spent at the city's no-kill animal shelter, where she worked with dogs and cats—and the occasional rabbit—that were rescued from a possible bleak demise on the street. Miranda had an affinity for all things homeless, be they four-footed or two-footed. In her opinion there never seemed to be enough hours in the day for her to help all these deserving creatures.

She had been working in all three areas for years now and felt she had barely been able to scratch the surface.

Agitated, Miranda looked at the clock on her dashboard. The minutes were flying by.

She was running the risk of being late.

"And if you don't get there with this cake, Lily is going to think you've forgotten all about her, just like her mom did," Miranda muttered to herself.

Lily's mother had left the little girl at the shelter when she'd gone to look for work. That was two days ago. No one had heard from the woman since. Miranda was beginning to worry that Gina Hayden, overwhelmed with her circumstances, had bailed out, using the excuse that the little girl was better off at the shelter, without her.

Stepping on the gas, Miranda made a sharp right

turn at the next corner, reaching out to hold the cake box on the passenger seat in place.

Focused on getting to the homeless shelter on time, Miranda wasn't aware of the dancing red and blue lights behind her until she heard the siren, high-pitched, demanding and shrill, slicing through the air. The sound drew her attention to the lights, simultaneously making her stomach drop with a jarring thud.

Oh damn, why today of all days? Miranda silently demanded as, resigned to her fate, she pulled her car over to the right. Even as she did so, something inside her wanted to push her foot down on the accelerator and just take off.

But considering that her newfound nemesis was riding a motorcycle and her car was a fifteen-year-old asthmatic vehicle way past its glory days, a clean getaway was simply not in the cards.

So she pulled over and waited for her inevitable ticket, fervently hoping the whole process was not going to take too long. She was already behind schedule. Miranda didn't want to disappoint Lily, who had already been disappointed far too often in her short life.

This wasn't his usual route. For some unknown reason, the desk sergeant had decided that today, he and Kaminski were going to trade routes.

Sergeant Bailey had made the switch, saying something about "mixing things up and keeping them fresh"—whatever that was supposed to mean, Colin thought, grumbling under his breath.

As far as he was concerned, one route was as good as

another. At least here in Bedford the only thing people shot at him were dirty looks, instead of bullets from the muzzles of illegally gotten handguns. He had to admit that patrolling the streets of Bedford was a far cry from patrolling the barrio in Los Angeles, or driving on the roads in Afghanistan. In those situations, a man had to develop eyes in the back of his head to stay alive.

Here in Bedford, those same eyes were in danger of shutting, but from boredom, not a fatal shot.

He supposed, after everything he had been through in the last ten years, a little boredom was welcome—at least for a while.

But he didn't exactly like the idea of hiding on the far side of the underpass, waiting to issue a ticket to some unsuspecting Bedford resident.

Yet those were the rules of the game here, and for now, he wasn't about to rock the boat.

First and foremost, he was here because of Aunt Lily. Because he owed her big-time. She had taken him in when no one else would, and to his discredit, he had repaid her by shutting her out and being surly. It wasn't her fault he had behaved that way; the blame was his.

In his defense—if he could call it that—he hadn't wanted to risk forming another attachment, only to have to endure the pain that came if and when he lost her. Lost her the way he'd lost everyone else in his life that ever mattered. His mother. Some of the men in his platoon. And Owens, his last partner in LA.

Colin's method of preventing that sort of pain was to cut himself off from everyone. That way, the pain had no chance of ever taking root, no chance of slicing him off at the knees.

At least that was what he told himself.

Still, he reasoned, playing his own devil's advocate, if there wasn't some part of him that cared, that was still capable of forming some sort of an attachment, however minor, would he have uprooted himself the way he had in order to be here because Aunt Lily had asked him to?

He didn't know.

Or maybe he did, and just didn't want to admit it to himself.

Either way, it wasn't something that was going to be resolved today. Today he needed to focus on the small stuff.

Right now he had a speeder to stop, he told himself, coming to life and increasing his own speed.

Because the woman in the old sedan was obviously not looking into her rearview mirror, Colin turned on his siren.

There, that got her attention. At least she wasn't one of those foolhardy birdbrains who thought they could outrace his motorcycle, Colin observed, as the car began to decrease its speed.

Watching the vehicle slow down and then come to a stop, Colin braced himself for what he knew was about to come. Either the driver was going to turn on the waterworks, attempting to cry her way out of a ticket by appealing to what she hoped was his chivalrous nature, or she was going to be belligerent, demanding to know if he had nothing better to do than to harass otherwise law-abiding citizens by issuing speeding tickets for offenses that were hardly noteworthy, instead of pursuing real criminals.

After parking his motorcycle behind her vehicle, he got off, then took his time walking up to the offending driver. Because the street was a busy one, with three lanes going in each direction, Colin made his way to the passenger side, to avoid getting hit by any passing motorist.

As he approached, he motioned for the driver to roll down her window.

She looked nervous. Well, the woman should have thought about this before she'd started speeding.

"Do you know why I pulled you over?" he asked gruffly.

Miranda took a breath before answering. "Because I was speeding."

A little surprised at the simplicity of her reply, Colin waited for more.

It didn't come.

The woman wasn't trying to talk her way out of the ticket she obviously knew was coming. He found that rather unusual. In his experience, people he pulled over in Bedford weren't normally this calm, or this seemingly polite.

Colin remained on his guard, anticipating a sudden turn on the driver's part.

"Right," he said, picking up on her answer. "You were speeding. Any particular reason why?"

He was aware that he was giving her the perfect opportunity to attempt to play on his sympathies, with some sort of a sob story. Such as she'd just gotten a call from the hospital saying her mother or father or some other important person in her life had just had a heart attack, and she was rushing to their side before they died.

He'd heard it all before. The excuses got pretty creative sometimes.

He had to admit that, for some reason, he was mildly curious to hear what this driver had to offer as *her* excuse.

"There's this little girl at the homeless shelter. It's her birthday today and I'm bringing the cake. The party starts in ten minutes and I got off my shift at the hospital later than I anticipated. I work at Children's Hospital and we had an emergency," she explained, inserting a sidebar.

"Where at Children's Hospital?" Colin asked, wondering just how far the woman was going to take this tale she was spinning.

"The oncology ward," she answered.

He should have seen that one coming. "Really?" he challenged.

Was he asking her for proof? That was simple enough, she thought. Because she'd been in such a rush, she was still wearing her uniform, and she had her hospital badge around her neck.

Holding up her ID, she showed it to him. "Yes, really, Officer," she answered politely. "Now if you'll please write out the ticket and give it to me so I can be on my way, I can still make the party on time. I don't want Lily to think I forgot about her, today of all days."

About to begin doing so, Colin looked up sharply. "Lily?" he questioned.

"That's her name," Miranda answered. "Lily."

Colin stared at the woman, a stoic expression on his face as he tried to make up his mind if she was actually serious, or trying to con him.

She couldn't possibly know about his aunt, he decided.

"My aunt's name is Lily," he told her, watching her face for some telltale sign that she was making all this up.

"It's a nice name," Miranda responded, waiting for him to begin writing.

Colin paused for a long moment, weighing the situation.

And then he did something he didn't ordinarily do. Actually, it was something he'd *never* done before. He closed his ticket book.

"All right, I'm letting you off with a warning," he told her. Then added an ominous "Watch yourself," before he turned on his heel and walked back to his motorcycle.

Chapter Two

Miranda's first impulse was to take off before the officer decided to change his mind about writing her that ticket. But as she thought about the fact that she had just dodged a bullet, an idea came to her. Rather than start her car and drive away under the police officer's watchful eye, Miranda opened her door and got out of her beloved vehicle.

"Officer?" she called, raising her voice.

Colin had already gotten on his motorcycle. Surprised, he looked in her direction. After a beat, he sighed and then slowly dismounted.

Now what? he silently demanded.

"Something on your mind, miss?" he asked, his voice low and far from friendly.

The officer sounded as if she was annoying him. But Miranda hadn't gotten where she was by giving in to the nervous quiver that occasionally popped up in her stomach—as it did now.

Raising her head so that her eyes met his—or where she assumed his eyes were, because he'd lowered the visor on his helmet, she stated, "I wanted to say thank you."

Colin grunted in response, because in his opinion, this wasn't the sort of situation where "you're welcome" suited the occasion. As far as he was concerned, she wasn't welcome. He'd just given in to an impulse that had come out of nowhere, and if he thought about it now, he was rather bewildered by his own actions.

"Do you have a card?" she asked him.

"A card?" Colin repeated, clearly perplexed by her question.

Miranda didn't think she was asking for anything out of the ordinary. "Yes, like a business card. The police department issues those to you, right?"

Instead of answering her question, or giving her one of the cards he carried in his pocket, Colin asked, "Why do you want it? You don't have anything to report me for," he pointed out gruffly.

It took Miranda a second to absorb what he was saying. Talk about being defensive. But then, maybe he had a reason. Some people were belligerent when dealing with the police.

"I don't want to report you," she assured him with feeling. "I just want to be able to call you."

So that was it, Colin thought. The woman was a groupie. He knew that there were people—mostly women—who were attracted to the uniform, some to the point of obsession. He had no patience when it came to groupies.

Colin got back on his motorcycle, ready to take off. "That's not a good idea," he told her in a voice that left no room for argument.

Or at least he thought it didn't.

"But the kids at the hospital would get such a big kick out of meeting a real live motorcycle cop," she said, hoping to change his mind.

She caught him completely off guard. He definitely hadn't been expecting that.

Now that he had transferred to Bedford, he didn't find himself interacting with any children. The ones back in the LA neighborhood he used to patrol saw police officers as the enemy, and either scattered whenever they saw him coming, or would throw things at him and *then* run.

"Look, I don't think—" Colin got no further than that.

Determined to convince him, Miranda attempted to submerge the police officer in a tidal wave of rhetoric. "A lot of the kids in that ward haven't been out of the hospital in months. I think meeting you would go a long way in cheering them up."

There had to be some sort of an ulterior motive at work here, Colin thought, and he wasn't about to fall for whatever trap she was trying to set for him.

"I really doubt that," he told her as he revved his motorcycle.

"I don't," Miranda countered cheerfully, refusing to be put off. "Why don't you come by the hospital and we'll see which one of us is right?" Mindful of procedure, she told him, "I'd have to clear it with my supervisor, but I don't see why she would say no."

"She might not, but I will." Then, just in case the woman still had any doubt about what he was telling her, Colin said, "No."

"But, Officer…" Rebounding quickly, Miranda tried again. "…it's Christmas."

Colin's eyes narrowed. "It's November," he corrected.

"*Almost* Christmas," she amended.

The woman just wouldn't give up, he thought, his irritation growing to astounding levels.

"Look, why don't you get back into your car and drive off before I decide to change my mind about issuing you that ticket?" Colin suggested tersely. "You said something about a birthday party for a little girl named Lily," he reminded her.

"Oh my goodness! Lily!" Miranda cried, genuinely upset. She'd gotten so caught up with her idea about having the police officer visit the children in the oncology ward that she'd forgotten the mission she was on right now. "The poor thing's going to really be upset if I don't turn up on time."

Whirling around, Miranda hurried back to her car and got in. She was starting the vehicle before she even closed the door.

Raising his voice, Colin called after her, "Remember the speed limit!"

There was next to no traffic at the moment.

Reining herself in, knowing that the officer would be

watching her pull away from the curb, Miranda gripped the steering wheel and drove off at a respectable speed, all the while wishing herself already at her destination.

Despite her hurry to get to the women's shelter, she made a mental note to track down the officer and get his name and number from his precinct the first chance she got. This wasn't over yet, she promised herself.

Miranda managed to catch all the lights and breeze through them, arriving at the women's shelter fifteen minutes later.

Rather than wasting time driving around and looking for a parking spot near the gray, two-story building's front door, she pulled into the first space she came to.

Grabbing the cake, she hurried into the building— and nearly collided with the blonde little girl who was anxiously waiting for her at the door.

"You came!" Lily cried happily, her furrowed brow smoothing out the second she saw Miranda.

"Of course I came," she said, pausing to kiss the top of Lily's head as she balanced the large cake box in her arms. "I told you I would. It's your birthday and I wouldn't miss that for the world."

Lily was all but dancing on her toes, eagerly looking at the rectangular box in Miranda's arms. "Is that a cake?"

"Aw, you guessed," Miranda said, pretending to be disappointed that her secret had been uncovered. "What gave it away?"

"The box," Lily answered solemnly, as if she'd been asked a legitimate question. And then she giggled as she added, "And I can smell cake."

"Well, since you guessed what it is, I guess you get to keep it," Miranda told her.

Lily was all but bursting with excitement. "Can I carry it to the dining room?" she asked.

That wouldn't be a good idea, Miranda thought. The box was large and would prove to be rather unwieldy for a little girl to carry.

"Well, it's kind of heavy," she told her. "So why don't I carry it there for you and you can open the box once I put it on the table?"

"Okay," Lily responded, obviously ready to agree to anything her idol suggested.

The little girl literally skipped to the dining area at Miranda's side. And she never took her eyes off the box, as if afraid it would suddenly disappear if she did.

"What kind of cake is it?" she asked.

"A birthday cake," Miranda replied solemnly.

Lily giggled and waved her hand at her friend. "I know that, silly," she told her. "I mean what kind of birthday cake?"

"A good one," Miranda said, still pretending that she didn't understand what Lily was asking her.

"Besides that," Lily pressed, giggling again.

"It's a lemon cake with vanilla frosting," Miranda told the bubbly little girl beside her as they reached the dining area.

Lily's eyes grew huge with obvious delight. "Lemon cake's my very favorite in the whole world."

"Well, how about that." Miranda pretended to marvel. "I didn't know that."

"Yes, you did," Lily said, a surprisingly knowing look on her small, thin face.

And then Miranda smiled affectionately at the girl. "I guess I did at that. Guess what else I've got," she said.

"Candles?" Lily asked in a hopeful whisper.

Miranda nodded. "Eight big ones. And one extra one for luck."

Instead of saying anything in response to the information, Lily threaded her small arm through one of her friend's and hugged it hard, her excitement all but palpable.

Miranda could feel her heart practically squeezing within her chest. This moment she was sharing with Lily was both humbling and sad. Other children her age would have asked for toys or expensive video games, and not shown half the excitement when they received them that Lily displayed over the fact that she was getting a birthday cake—with candles.

Drawn by the sound of Lily's squeals, Amelia Sellers, the tall, angular-looking woman who ran the shelter, made her way over to them. Her smile was warm and genuine—and perhaps slightly relieved, as well.

Amelia'd probably thought she wasn't going to make it. Most likely because she had a habit of being early, not running late like this.

"Lily's been looking forward to this all day," Amelia told her the moment she reached them.

"So have I," Miranda assured both the director and the little girl, who was looking up at her with nothing short of adoration in her eyes.

"I put out the plates," Amelia announced, gesturing at one of the dining tables. "So let's get started."

Miranda smiled down at Lily, who was obviously waiting for her to make the first move. She had to be the most well-mannered eager little girl she'd ever met.

"Let's," Miranda agreed.

Carefully taking the half sheet cake out of the box, Miranda moved the rectangular container aside and out of the way. She then put the candles on the cake, making sure she spaced them close enough together that Lily would be able to blow them all out at once when she made her wish.

The moment the birthday cake was placed on the table, children began coming over, clustering around the table, all hoping to get a piece.

Taking out the book of matches she had picked up when she'd purchased the candles, Miranda struck one and then carefully lit the eight plus one wicks.

Blowing out the match, she looked at all the eager faces around the table. "All right," she told the small gathering. "Everybody sing!"

And she led the pint-size group, along with the smattering of adults also gathered around the table, in a loud, if slightly off-key chorus of "Happy Birthday." All the while she kept one eye on Lily, who looked positively radiant.

When the children stopped singing, Miranda told the little girl, "Okay, Lily, make a wish and blow out the candles."

Nodding, Lily pressed her lips together, clearly giving her wish a great deal of thought. Then she looked up at Miranda and smiled.

Taking in a deep breath, Lily leaned over the cake and blew as hard as she could. The candles flickered and went out.

"You got them all," Miranda declared, applauding the little girl's accomplishment.

The children and adults around the table joined in, some loudly cheering, as well.

Miranda felt someone tugging on the bottom of her tunic. Glancing down, she found herself looking into the upturned face of an animated little boy named Paul.

"Now can we have some cake?" he asked.

"Absolutely," she replied. "Right after Lily gets the first piece."

Removing all nine candles, she set them on a napkin. Miranda proceeded to cut a piece of cake for Lily, making sure it was an extra-large one.

Out of the corner of her eye she saw Lily folding the napkin over the candles she'd just removed. The little girl covertly slipped the napkin into the pocket of her jeans, a souvenir of her special day.

"There you go," Miranda told her, sliding the plate to her.

"Thank you," Lily said.

To Miranda's surprise, rather than devour the cake as she expected, the little girl ate the slice slowly, as if savoring every morsel.

"This is the best cake I ever had," Lily declared when she finally finished it.

The other children had made short work of the cake

that was left, but Miranda had anticipated that. "You can have another piece," she told Lily. Not waiting for a response, she pushed her own plate in front of the little girl.

Lily looked tempted, but left the slice untouched.

"What's wrong?" Miranda asked.

"I can't eat that. That's your piece," she protested.

Miranda smiled at the girl. *One in a million*, she thought.

Out loud she stated, "And I saved it for you. I wanted you to have an extra piece and knew that the rest of the cake would probably be gobbled up fast. So don't argue with me, young lady. Take this piece. It's yours," she coaxed.

Lily still looked uncertain. "Really?"

"Really," Miranda assured her. "I'm the grown-up here. You have to listen."

Lily's face was all smiles as she happily dug into the second piece.

When she finished, Miranda cleared away the plates, stacking them on the side.

"That was the best cake ever!" Lily told her with enthusiasm, and then hugged her again.

"Glad to hear that," Miranda said, when the little girl loosened her hold. "By the way, I have something for you."

"For me?" Lily cried, clearly amazed. It was obvious that she felt the cake was her big prize. Anything else was above and beyond all expectation. "What is it?"

Miranda reached into the oversize purse she'd left

on the floor and pulled out the gift she had wrapped for Lily early this morning, before she'd left for the hospital.

Handing it over, she said, "Why don't you open it and see?"

Lily held the gift as if she couldn't decide whether to unwrap it or just gaze at it adoringly for a while. Her curiosity finally won out and she started peeling away the wrapping paper.

The moment she'd done so, her mouth dropped open. "You got me a puppy!" she cried.

"Well," Miranda amended, "I can't get you a *real* puppy because the shelter won't allow it, so for now, I want you to have this stuffed one. But someday, when you're in a home again, I'll come and bring you a real one," she promised.

Heaven knew she had access to enough homeless dogs at the animal shelter to pick just the right one for the little girl.

Lily threw her arms around her a third time and hugged her as hard as she could. "I wish you were my mom," she said breathlessly.

Touched though she was, Miranda knew she couldn't have the girl feeling like that. "Don't say that, honey. Your real mom's out there and she's probably trying to get back here to you right now."

But Lily shook her head. "I still wish you were my mom," she insisted, burying her face against Miranda as she clutched the stuffed dog. "Thank you for my cake and my candles and my puppy. Thank you for everything," she cried.

Miranda hugged the little girl, moved almost to tears

and wishing there was something she could do for her beyond giving her a gift and a cake.

And then it came to her. She knew what she had to do.

She needed to track down the police officer on the motorcycle. Not to bring to the hospital with her—that would come later—but to help her find out what had happened to Lily's mother. The man had resources at his disposal that she certainly didn't have.

All she needed to do, once she located him, Miranda thought, was to appeal to his sense of justice or humanity, or whatever it took to get him to agree to look for Lily's mother.

Smiling, she hugged Lily a little harder.

Chapter Three

Because she didn't want to risk possibly getting the motorcycle officer in any sort of trouble by going to the precinct and asking about him, Miranda spent the rest of that evening and part of the night reviewing her viable options.

By the next morning, Miranda decided that her best course of action was to literally track down the officer. That meant driving by the overpass where he'd been yesterday. She could only hope that he'd be there, waiting to ticket someone going over the speed limit.

But when she swung by the area that afternoon, after her shift was over, the police officer wasn't there.

Disappointed, Miranda had to concede that not finding him there stood to reason. If an officer frequented the same spot day after day, word would quickly spread and drivers would either avoid the area altogether or at the very least be extra cautious about observing the speed limit.

Still, as she drove slowly by the overpass, Miranda wondered how far away the police officer could be. Unless he had been relocated, there must be a certain radius he had to adhere to, so as not to cross into another cop's territory, right?

Giving herself a fifteen-minute time limit to find him, Miranda drove up one street and down another. She knew she was attempting to second-guess a man she knew absolutely nothing about, but at the moment she couldn't think of an alternative.

Fifteen minutes later Miranda sighed. The time was up and she still hadn't found the officer. She didn't want to be too late getting to the women's shelter. She knew that Lily's mother still hadn't shown up—she'd called Amelia to check—and the little girl would be devastated if she didn't come to see her as she'd promised.

She had to go, Miranda thought. Maybe she'd come across the traffic cop tomorrow.

Slowing down, Miranda did a three-point turn in order to head toward the street that would ultimately take her to the shelter.

As she approached the red light at an intersection, a fleeting glint from the left caught her attention. The setting sun was reflecting off some sort of metal.

Miranda turned her head in that direction, and found the sun was hitting the handlebars of a motorcycle.

A police motorcycle.

His motorcycle.

Although the officer was wearing a helmet, and virtually *all* police motorcycles in Bedford looked alike, something told her that this particular officer was the one who had pulled her over yesterday. Pulled her over and didn't give her a ticket. Miranda could feel it in her gut.

When the light turned green, instead of driving straight ahead, she deliberately eased her car to the left, into the next lane. Far enough to allow her to make a left-hand turn.

As she did so, she rolled down her window and honked her horn twice. Getting the officer's attention, she waved her hand at the man, indicating that she wanted him to make a U-turn and follow her. She then mentally crossed her fingers that she hadn't accidentally made a mistake, and that this *was* the same officer she'd interacted with yesterday.

Always alert when he was on the job, Colin tensed when he heard the driver honking. Seeing an arm come out of the driver's window, waving to get his attention, he bit off a curse. Was the woman taunting him? Or did she actually *want* to get a ticket?

And then, as he looked closer, he realized that it was the same car he'd pulled over yesterday. The one driven by that petite blonde with the really deep blue eyes.

The one who had that birthday cake on the passenger seat.

What was she doing here? Was she deliberately trying to press her luck? Because if she was, she was in for a surprise.

Her luck had just run out, he thought.

Biting off a few choice words under his breath, Colin made a U-turn and took off after her.

Less than thirty seconds later, he realized that she wasn't going anywhere. The woman with the soulful doe eyes had pulled over to the curb.

Something was definitely off, Colin thought as he brought his motorcycle to a halt behind her vehicle.

Training from his days on the force in Los Angeles had Colin approaching the car with caution. Every police officer knew that the first thirty seconds after a vehicle was pulled over were the most dangerous ones. If something bad was going to happen, it usually took place within that space of time.

Ninety-nine times out of a hundred, the pulled-over driver was harmless. It was that one other time that turned out to be fatal.

Although he had volunteered for this detail, choosing to patrol the city streets on a motorcycle over riding around in a squad car with a partner, he was not unaware of the risk that came with the job. A risk that always had his adrenaline flowing and his breath backing up in his lungs for that short time that it took for him to dismount and approach the offending driver's vehicle.

If he had a partner, there would be someone close by who had his back. However, Owens, his last partner, had been killed on the job, and although Colin never said anything to anyone about it, that had weighed really heavily on him, and still did. After that tragic incident, he operated alone. Patrolling alone meant he had to watch out only for himself. He liked it that way.

The second he peered into the passenger window

and saw the driver, he knew that he was facing another kind of danger entirely.

No one was going to die today, but it was still a risk.

Miranda rolled down the passenger window and leaned toward him. "Hi. I wasn't speeding this time," she said, greeting him with a cheerful smile and a chipper demeanor he found almost annoyingly suspicious.

He scowled at her. "No, you were just executing a very strange turn."

"I had to," Miranda explained. "If I went straight and turned at the next light, by the time I came back, I was afraid that you'd be gone."

Only if I'd been lucky, Colin thought.

Just what was this woman's game? "And that would have been a problem because…?"

She never missed a beat. "Because I had to talk to you."

The idea of just turning away and getting back on his motorcycle was exceedingly tempting, but for some reason he couldn't quite put his finger on, Colin decided to hear this overly upbeat woman out.

"You are persistent, aren't you?" he retorted.

"You say that like it's a bad thing." Miranda did her best to try to get the officer to lighten up a little and smile.

His stoic expression never changed. "It is from where I'm standing." He'd glimpsed her driver's license yesterday and tried to recall the name he'd seen on it. Maybe if he made this personal, he'd succeed in scaring her off. "What do you want, Miriam?"

"Miranda," she corrected, still sounding annoyingly

cheerful. "That's okay, a lot of people get my name wrong at first. It takes getting used to."

"I have no intention of getting used to it," he informed her. *Or you.*

As far as he was concerned, the woman was really pushing her luck.

"Look, I let you off with a warning yesterday," he reminded her. "Would you like me to rescind that warning and give you a ticket?"

Colin was fairly confident that the threat of a ticket would be enough to make her back off.

"No. That was very nice of you yesterday. That's the reason I came looking for you today."

She wasn't making any sense. And then he remembered what she'd said yesterday about asking him to pay a visit to some ward at the hospital.

That's what this was about, he decided. Something about sick children. Well, he was not about to get roped into anything. Who knew what this woman's ultimate game really was?

"Look, I already told you," he retorted. "I'm not the type to come see kids in a hospital. I don't like hospitals."

Rather than look disappointed as he'd expected her to, the woman nodded. "A lot of people don't," she agreed.

Okay, she was obviously stalking him, and this was over. "Well then, have a nice day," Colin told her curtly, and then turned to walk back to his motorcycle.

"I'm not here about the hospital," Miranda called

after him. "Although I'd like to revisit that subject at a later time."

Colin stopped walking. The woman had to be one of the pushiest people he'd ever encountered, not to mention she had a hell of a lot of nerve.

Against his better judgment, he found himself turning around again to face her. "And just what are you 'here' about?" he asked.

There was absolutely nothing friendly in his voice that invited her to talk. But she did anyway.

"That little girl I told you about?" Miranda began, feeling as if she was picking her way through a minefield that could blow up on her at any moment. "The one with your aunt's name," she reminded him, hoping that would get the officer to listen, and buy her a little more time.

"Lily," he repeated, all but growling the name. "What about her?" he asked grudgingly.

He wasn't a curious man by any stretch of the imagination, but there was something about this overly eager woman that had him wondering just where she was taking this.

"Lily's mother is missing," she told him, never taking her eyes off his face.

Rather than show some sort of reaction to what she'd just said, his expression never changed. He looked, Miranda thought, as if she'd just given him a bland weather report.

She began to wonder what had damaged the man to this extent.

"So go to the precinct and report it," Colin told her. "That's the standard procedure."

"The director at the shelter already did that," Miranda answered.

"All right, then it's taken care of." What more did she expect him to do? Colin wondered irritably as he began to walk away again.

"No, it isn't," Miranda insisted, stepping out of her car and moving quickly between him and his motorcycle. "The officer who took down the information said that maybe Lily's mother took off. He said a lot of women in her situation feel overwhelmed and just leave. He said that maybe she'd come to her senses in a few days and return for her daughter."

"Okay, you have your answer," Colin said, moving around this human roadblock.

Again Miranda shifted quickly so he couldn't get to his motorcycle. She ignored the dark look he gave her. She wasn't about to give up. This was important. Lily was depending on her to do everything she could to find her mother.

"But what if she doesn't?" Miranda asked. "What if she didn't take off? What if something's happened to Lily's mother and that's why she never came back to the shelter?"

He felt as if this doe-eyed blonde was boxing him in. "That's life," he said, exasperated.

"There's a little eight-year-old girl at the shelter waiting for her mommy to come back," Miranda told him with feeling. "I can't just tell her 'that's life.'"

Taking hold of Miranda's shoulders, he moved her

firmly out of his way and finally reached his motorcycle. "Tell her whatever you like."

Miranda raised her voice so that he could hear her above the sound of the cars going by. "I'd like to tell her that this nice police officer is trying to find her mommy."

Colin turned sharply on his heel and glared at this woman who refused to take a hint. "Look, lady—"

"Miranda," she prompted.

"Miranda," Colin echoed between gritted teeth. "You are a royal pain, you know that?"

Miranda had always tried to glean something positive out of every situation, no matter how bleak it might appear. "Does that mean you'll look for her?" she asked hopefully.

Colin blew out an angry breath. "That means you're a royal pain," he repeated.

With nothing to lose, Miranda climbed out on a limb. "Please? I can give you a description of Lily's mother." And then she thought of something even better. "And if you come with me, I can get you a picture of her that'll be useful."

He had a feeling that this woman wasn't going to give up unless he agreed to help her. Although it irritated him beyond description, there was a very small part of him that had to admit he admired her tenacity.

Still, he gave getting her to back off one more try. "What will be useful is if you get out of my way and let me do my job."

Miranda didn't budge. "Isn't part of your job finding people who have gone missing?"

"She's not missing if she left of her own accord and just decided to keep on going," he told the blonde, enunciating every word.

"But we don't know that she decided to keep on going. She did leave the shelter to go look for work," Miranda told him.

"That's what the woman said," Colin countered impatiently.

"No, that's what she *did*," Miranda stressed. "Gina Hayden has an eight-year-old daughter. She wouldn't just leave her like that."

"How do you *know* that?" Colin challenged. The woman lived in a cotton candy world. Didn't she realize that the real world wasn't like that? "Lots of people say one thing and do another. And lots of people with families just walk out on them and never come back."

Miranda watched him for a long moment. So long that he thought she'd finally given up trying to wear him down. And then she spoke and blew that theory to pieces.

"Who left you?" she asked quietly.

"You, I hope," he snapped, turning back to face his motorcycle.

He sighed as she sashayed in front of him yet again. This was beginning to feel like some never-ending dance.

"No, you're not talking about me," Miranda told him. "You're talking about someone else. I can see it in your eyes. Someone walked out on you, probably when you were a kid. So you know what that feels like," she stressed.

He needed this like he needed a hole in the head. "Look, lady—"

"Miranda," she corrected again.

He ignored that. "You can take your amateur psycho-babble, get back in your car and drive away before I haul you in for harassing a police officer."

Was that what he thought this was?

She had to get through to him. Something in her heart told her that he'd find Gina, She just needed him to take this seriously.

"I'm not harassing you—"

He almost laughed out loud. "You want to bet?"

Miranda pushed on. "I'm just asking you to go out of your way a little and maybe make a little girl very happy. If her mother doesn't turn up, Lily's going to be sent to social services and placed in a foster home. The only reason she hasn't been taken there already is that the director of the shelter agreed with me about waiting for her mom to come back. The director bought us a little time." And that time was running out, Miranda added silently.

"The kid can still be taken away," Colin pointed out. "Her mother abandoned her."

Why couldn't she get through to this officer? "Not if something happened to her and she's unable to get back."

Colin sighed. He knew he should just get on his motorcycle and ride away from this woman. For the life of him, he didn't know why he was allowing himself to get involved in this.

"Did you call all the hospitals?"

She nodded. "All of them. There's no record of any-one fitting Gina's description coming in on her own or being brought in."

So what more did this woman want him to do? "Well then—"

"But there could be other reasons she hasn't come back," she insisted. "Gina could have been abducted, or worse." Miranda looked at him with eyes that were pleading with him to do something.

Colin shook his head. "I should have given you that ticket yesterday," he told her gruffly.

He was weakening; she could just feel it. "But you didn't because you're a good man."

"No, because I should have had my head examined," he grumbled. "All right," he relented, taking out his ticket book and flipping to an empty page.

Miranda's eyes widened. "You're writing me a ticket?" she asked.

"No, I'm taking down this woman's description. You said you'd give it to me. Now, what is it?" Colin de-manded.

"What did you say your name was?" she asked.

"I didn't." He could feel her looking at him. Swal-lowing a couple choice words, he said, "Officer Colin Kirby."

"Thank you, Officer Colin Kirby."

Maybe he was losing his mind, but he could swear he could *feel* her smile.

"The description?" he demanded.

Miranda lost no time in giving it to him.

Chapter Four

"Okay," Colin said, closing his ticket book and putting it away. "I'll check with the other officer your director talked to. What's his name or badge number?" he asked.

Miranda shook her head. She hadn't thought to ask for that information when the director had given her an update. "I'm afraid Amelia didn't mention either one."

Colin looked at her. The name meant nothing to him. "Amelia?"

"Amelia Sellers," Miranda specified. "That's the shelter's director. She didn't give me the officer's name, but seemed pretty upset that he wasn't taking the situation seriously."

Colin read between the lines. He assumed that the officer the shelter director had talked to hadn't told her that he would get back to her. Not that he blamed the man.

"I take it this Amelia isn't as pushy as you," he commented.

Miranda wasn't exactly happy with his description, but the situation was far too important for her to get sidelined by something so petty.

"Actually, she can be very forceful. But the officer taking down the information really didn't seem to think that Gina was missing," Miranda said.

She was looking at him with the kind of hopeful eyes that made men seriously consider leaping tall buildings in a single bound and bending steel with their bare hands in an attempt to impress her.

If he was going to interact with this woman for any length of time, he was going to have to remember to avoid looking into her eyes, Colin told himself. They were far too distracting.

"I bet you were prom queen, weren't you?" he asked.

The question came out of the blue and caught her completely off guard. It took Miranda a moment to collect herself and answer, "Actually, I didn't go to the prom."

"No one asked you?" He found that rather hard to believe. She struck him as the epitome of a cheerleader. Was she pulling his leg?

Miranda didn't answer his question directly. She actually had been asked, just hadn't said yes.

"I had a scheduling problem," she said vaguely. "The prom interfered with my volunteer work."

"In high school?" Colin asked incredulously.

"You look surprised," she noted, then told him, "People in high school volunteer for things." At least, the people she'd kept company with had.

Shrugging, he said, "If you say so." He'd never concerned himself with social activities, even back then, nor did he involve himself with any kind of volunteer work. Most of his life he'd been a loner.

Securing the ticket book in his back pocket, he told her, "I'll see what I can find out."

"Don't you want the phone number at the shelter?"

He caught himself thinking fleetingly that he'd rather have her number. The next second he deliberately pushed the thought away. If he had her number, that might very well lead to complications, which was the very *last* thing he wanted. He supposed that obtaining the shelter's number was innocuous enough. Most likely if he used it he'd wind up speaking to the director.

"Right," Colin answered, doing his best to exercise patience. "So what is it?"

Miranda gave him the number to the shelter's landline, then waited for him to take out the ticket book again so he could jot it down.

Sensing what she wanted, he did just that. As he put the book away a second time he heard her asking, "Aren't you going to follow me to the shelter?"

It just didn't end with her, did it? he thought, exasperated. "Why would I want to do that?"

"To see Gina's picture," she reminded him. "I told you that there's one at the shelter. Lily has it."

He looked at her blankly for a split second until the information clicked into place. "Lily. Right, the little girl."

For a moment, he thought about telling her—again—that this wasn't something he did. His main sphere of expertise was keeping the flow of traffic going at a reasonable rate.

There were patrol officers who took this kind of information down, as well as detectives back at the precinct who specialized in missing persons. But he had no desire to get into all that with her. It would just lead to another prolonged debate.

Besides, it wasn't as if leaving the area was tantamount to abandoning a hub of vehicular infractions and crimes. And how long would following her to the shelter and getting that photograph of the runaway mother take, anyway?

Making no effort to suppress the sigh that escaped his lips, he said, "Okay, lead the way."

The officer's answer surprised her. She'd expected more resistance from him. Finally!

Her mouth curved. "So then, you are going to follow me?"

The woman had a magnetic, not to mention hypnotic, smile. He forced himself to look away.

"That's what 'lead the way' usually means," he answered shortly.

"I know that," she acknowledged. "It's just that I realize I'm asking you to go above and beyond the call of duty."

And yet here you are, asking me, he thought, irritated. Colin was beginning to think that the woman could just go on talking indefinitely. He, on the other hand, wanted to get this over with as soon as possible.

"Just get in your car and drive, Miranda," he instructed gruffly.

Her mouth quirked in another smile that made him think of the first ray of sunshine coming out after a storm. "You remembered."

"Yeah," Colin said shortly. He wasn't about to tell her that, like it or not—and he didn't—this fleeting contact with her had already left a definite imprint on his brain. "Well?" he prodded, when she continued standing there. "I don't have all day."

"Right."

The next moment she was hurrying back to her vehicle. Getting in, she started up the engine mindful of the fact that she had to be careful to observe *all* the rules. She had no doubt that if she exceeded the speed limit—and there seemed to be a different one posted on each long block—the officer behind her wouldn't hesitate to give her a ticket this time.

He'd probably see it as a reward for humoring her, Miranda thought.

But it didn't matter. She'd gotten him to agree, however grudgingly, to try to find Lily's mother, and that was all that *did* matter.

The shelter wasn't far away. Parking near the entrance, she got out of her car and stood beside it, waiting for the officer to pull into the parking lot.

When he did, he found a spot several rows away from her.

She watched him stride toward her. The dark-haired officer was at least six-one, maybe a little taller, and moved like one of those strong, silent heroes straight out of the Old West. She sincerely hoped that he would turn out to be Lily's hero.

"You've got ten minutes," Colin told her the moment he reached her.

He expected her to protest being issued a time limit. But she surprised him by saying, "Then I'd better make the most of it. Lily will probably be in the common area," she added. "That's where she watches for me to arrive."

"You come every day?" he questioned. Didn't this woman have a social life? He would have expected someone who looked the way she did to have a very busy one.

"I come here four, sometimes five days a week," she told him matter-of-factly. "Other days I work at the animal shelter, exercising the dogs."

Nobody did that much volunteering, he thought, opening the door and holding it for her. She had to be putting him on.

"What do you do when you're not earning your merit badges?" he asked sarcastically.

"Sleep," she answered, without missing a beat.

She sounded serious, but he still wasn't sure if he was buying this saint act. He was about to ask the woman if her halo was on too tight, cutting off the circulation to her brain, but he never got the chance. She'd turned away from him, her attention shifting to the little blonde girl who was charging toward her.

"There she is," Miranda declared, opening her arms just in time.

The next second she was closing them around the

pint-size dynamo, who appeared to be hugging her for all she was worth.

"Did you find her?" the little girl cried eagerly, her high-pitched voice partially muffled against Miranda's hip. "Did you find my mommy?"

"Not yet, darling," Miranda answered.

Slowly, she moved the little girl back just far enough to be able to see the man she'd brought with her. "But this nice officer—" she nodded toward Colin "—is going to help us find her."

Colin noted that the firebrand who had dragged him here hadn't used the word *try*. She'd gone straight to the word *help*, making it sound as if it would be just a matter of time before he located this missing mother who might or might not have taken off for parts unknown of her own free will.

He didn't like being tied to promises he had absolutely no control over, nor did he like deceiving people into thinking he could deliver on goods that he had no way of knowing he could even locate.

But when he began to say as much to the little girl, he found himself looking down into incredible blue eyes that were brimming with more hope than he recalled seeing in a long, long time.

How could this kid exist in a place like this and still have hope? he wondered.

"Are you going to find her?" Lily asked, all four feet of her practically vibrating with excitement and anticipation. "Are you going to find my mommy?"

"I'm—" He started to tell her that he would do what he could, because he wasn't in the habit of lying, not to anyone. Not even to children, who usually fell beneath his radar.

"Officer Kirby is going to need to see that picture you have of you and your mommy," Miranda said, cutting into what she was afraid the man was about to tell the little girl. "Can you go get it for me, Lily?"

The little girl bobbed her head up and down enthusiastically. "I'll be right back," she stated, and took off.

"I can't promise her I'll find her mother," Colin said in a no-nonsense voice.

"Maybe you could try," Miranda suggested. When she saw his expression darken, she tried to make him see it from Lily's side. "Everyone needs something to hang on to," she pointed out.

Colin looked totally unconvinced. "Hanging on to a lie doesn't help," he told her.

"It won't be a lie—if you find Gina," Miranda countered.

He couldn't believe she'd just said that. The woman obviously had her head in the clouds. "Does your plane ever land?" he asked.

"Occasionally," she allowed, and then, smiling, she added, "To refuel."

Colin was about to say something about the danger of crashing and burning if she wasn't careful, but just then Lily returned, burrowing in between them. The little girl was clutching a five-by-seven, cheaply framed photograph against her small chest.

Planting herself squarely in front of the police officer, she held out the picture for him to see. It was recent, by the looks of it, he judged. The little girl appeared the same in it and she was wearing the dress she had on now.

He caught himself wondering if it was her only dress, which surprised him. Thoughts like that didn't usually occur to him.

"That's us. Me and my mommy," Lily told him proudly. She held the framed photograph up higher so he could see it better. "Miranda says she's pretty," the little girl added. And then her smile faded as she asked, "You're not going to lose the picture, are you? It's the only one I've got."

Colin paused, looking at the small, worried face. "Tell you what," he said, pulling his cell phone out of his breast pocket. "Why don't I take a picture of your photo with my phone?" he suggested. "That way I'll have a copy to show around so I can find your mother, and you get to keep that picture for yourself."

He was rewarded with a huge smile that took up Lily's entire face. "That's a good idea," she told him. Her eyes were sparkling as she added, "You're really smart."

He was about to dismiss that assessment, flattering though it was, when he heard Miranda tell the little girl, "He's a police officer," as if the one automatically implied the other.

"Just seemed like a simple solution," Colin told the little girl evasively. "Now hold up the picture," he said to her, wanting to move on to another topic.

Lily did as he asked, holding the framed photograph as high as she could so that he had an unobstructed view. The moment he snapped the picture with the camera app on his phone and, after looking at the screen, pronounced it "Good," he suddenly felt small arms encircling his waist just below his belt and holstered weapon.

"Thank you!" Lily cried. "And thank you for looking for my mommy."

He was about to say that "looking" didn't necessarily mean finding, but before he did, something made him glance in Miranda's direction.

She was moving her head slowly from side to side, silently indicating that she knew exactly what he was about to say to the little girl, and imploring him not to do so.

Colin blew out his breath impatiently, then compromised and told the little girl, who still had her arms around him, "I'll do my best, Lily."

"You'll find her," she declared. "I know you will." Lily said it with the kind of unshakable belief that only the very young were blessed with.

"Lily, honey," Miranda prompted, "you need to let go of Officer Kirby so he can get started looking for your mommy."

"Oh."

He was surprised and maybe just a bit charmed, he discovered, to hear the little girl giggle.

"I'm sorry," she said, releasing him. "I just wanted to say thank you."

Again he wanted to tell her that just because he'd promised to *look* for her mother didn't mean that he was going to be able to *find* her.

Maybe it was because Miranda was standing so close

to him, or maybe it was all that hope he saw shining in the little girl's blue eyes, but the words he was about to say froze on his tongue, unable to exit. He couldn't bring himself to be the one to force Lily to face up to reality and all the ugliness that came with it.

So all he did was mumble, "Yeah," and then turn on his heel and begin striding toward the shelter's exit— and freedom.

It wasn't until he was way past the front door and standing outside, dragging in air to clear his head, that he realized the woman who had roped him into this was right behind him.

Now what?

Was she going to try to get him to pinkie-swear that he was going to come through on that half promise he'd been forced to make?

"Look, I'll do what I can," he said, before she could open her mouth to say a word.

To his surprise, the woman who was quickly becoming his main source of irritation nodded as she smiled at him. "I know. That's all anyone can ask."

No, Colin thought, as he mounted his motorcycle. The exasperating blonde was asking him for a hell of a lot more than that.

The thing that he *really* couldn't understand, he realized as he rode away, was that for some reason Miranda Steele was making him want to deliver on that vague nonpromise he'd just made to that little girl.

Chapter Five

He absolutely hated asking anyone for anything, even if it involved something in the line of duty. If he didn't ask, Colin felt that there was no chance of his being turned down. There was also the fact that if he didn't ask someone to do something for him, then he wouldn't owe anyone a favor in return.

Again he found himself wishing he had never pulled Miranda over to give her a ticket in the first place. If he hadn't done that, then he wouldn't be faced with the dilemma he was now looking at.

It was the end of his shift and Colin was tempted to just clock out and go home. But despite his desire to divorce himself from the situation, his mind kept conjuring up images of that little girl's small, sad face looking up at him as if he was the answer to all her prayers.

No one had ever looked at him like that before.

It was all that woman's fault, Colin thought grudgingly.

Miranda.

Who named their kid Miranda these days, anyway? he wondered irritably.

It was late, Colin thought as he walked into the locker room. Too late to really start anything today. To assuage his conscience, he decided to come in earlier tomorrow and maybe nose around, see if anyone had any information pertaining to a woman who matched this Gina Hayden's description.

After opening his locker, Colin took out his civilian clothes and began changing into them. He was tired and he'd be able to think more clearly tomorrow morning when he—

"The poor woman was lying there, slumped over by the Dumpster and hardly breathing. I thought she was dead. Really not the kind of thing you'd expect to see around here."

Colin stopped tucking his shirt into his jeans. The conversation that was coming from the row of lockers directly behind his caught his attention. He listened more closely.

"Lucky thing you found her when you did, Moran," a second, deeper voice commented. "Why did you go in that alley, anyway?"

Colin heard a locker door being closed before "Moran" answered the other officer. "I saw two kids running out of there. They looked pretty spooked."

"You think they were the ones who assaulted her?" the other patrol officer asked.

A second locker was closed. The officers sounded as if they were about to leave.

"There was no blood on either one of them," Moran was saying, "and frankly, they looked too scared to have beaten her that way. To be on the safe side, I snapped a picture of them as they took off. They ran into a building across the way. Shouldn't be all that hard locating them if I need to."

Colin closed his locker. What were the odds? he wondered.

At the very least, he needed to check this out.

Making his way to the next set of lockers, he was just in time to catch the two officers before they left the locker room.

"What happened to the woman?" Colin asked.

Officer Bob Moran looked up at him, surprised by the question. They knew one another vaguely by sight, but that was where it ended. They'd certainly never talked shop before.

"I called a bus for her," Moran answered. "The paramedics took her to Mercy General."

"Did you go with her?" Colin inquired.

Moran looked slightly uncomfortable. "No. It was the end of my shift and she was unconscious. I figured she'd be more up to giving me a statement tomorrow morning."

"What happened to her?" Colin pressed.

The fact that he was asking questions seemed to surprise the other two officers. Moran exchanged glances with Pete Morales, the second policeman, before answering. "Looked to me like someone stole her purse. I couldn't find any ID on her—or a wallet."

Colin took out his cell phone and flipped to the picture he'd taken of the photograph Lily had held up for him.

He turned his cell toward Moran. "This her?"

Bushy eyebrows rose high enough to almost meet a receding hairline. Moran appeared stunned. "Yeah, that's her, minus the swollen lip and the bruises." And then he looked at Colin. "You know her?"

He put his phone away. "No."

When he didn't volunteer anything further, curiosity had Moran asking, "Then why do you have her picture?"

Colin scowled. Granted, this wasn't exactly personal, but he still didn't like being put in the position where he had to elaborate. He preferred keeping to himself in general and answering questions only when he had no other choice.

But he didn't see a way out without arousing even more questions. Pausing for a moment, he finally said, "The woman was reported missing from a homeless shelter."

"That her little girl with her?" Morales asked, his demeanor softening as he looked at the child holding up the framed photograph.

"Yeah," Colin answered shortly. "Thanks for the information." Without any further exchange, he began walking away.

"You going to see her?" Moran called after him.

Colin didn't stop to turn around when he replied, "That was the idea."

"I can go with you," Moran volunteered, raising his voice.

Colin almost asked why, but supposed the other man's conscience had gotten the better of him. Or maybe Moran just wanted the credit. In either case, Colin didn't care.

"You've done enough. I'll take it from here." He kept on going, then slowed down long enough to throw the word *thanks* over his shoulder before he left the locker area.

He heard a somewhat confused "Don't mention it" in response.

Colin just kept on walking.

The last person in the world Miranda expected to see walking into the women's shelter that evening was the motorcycle officer she'd managed to talk into looking for Lily's missing mother.

Ordinarily, Miranda would have left by now, but she'd stayed at the shelter today to try to bolster Lily's spirits. Despite her normally upbeat, cheerful nature, it was obvious that the little girl was sincerely worried about her mother. The fact that several of the other children there had told her that her mother had "run away" and abandoned her didn't help any. Lily refused to listen to them.

"My mommy wouldn't leave me!" she'd cried. "She loves me!" The little girl was convinced that something had to have happened to her mom, preventing her from returning.

Miranda had stayed at the shelter until she'd finally managed to calm Lily down and get her to fall asleep.

She was just leaving when she saw the officer coming in.

One look at Colin's grim face had her thinking the worst—and fervently hoping she was wrong.

It was obvious that he didn't see her when he walked in. Miranda cut across the common area like a shot, placing herself in his path.

Trying to brace herself for whatever he had to say, she didn't bother with any small talk or preliminary chitchat. "You found her," she said breathlessly, willing him to say something positive.

Colin hadn't been sure Miranda would still be here, but she managed to surprise him by materializing out of nowhere.

"Yeah, I found her."

Miranda immediately felt her heart shoot up into her throat, making it almost impossible for her to breathe.

How was she going to tell Lily that her mother was dead?

Her mind scrambled, searching for words, for solutions. Maybe she could take Lily in as a foster parent, or maybe—

The woman standing in front of him almost turned white. That was *not* the sort of reaction he was expecting from her.

She also wasn't saying anything, another surprise, he thought.

"Don't you want to know where she is?" he finally asked.

The startlingly blue eyes widened more than he thought was humanly possible. "You mean she's alive?" Miranda cried.

"Well, yeah," he answered, surprised she was asking that. "If she was dead, I would have led with that."

"Dead? Somebody's dead?" an adolescent boy standing within earshot asked, instantly alert.

"Every single nerve in my body, for openers, Edward." Miranda blew out a shaky breath. "That's what I get for jumping to conclusions." She turned toward the police officer, who had just become her hero. Suddenly, tears were filling her eyes, spilling out and rolling down her cheeks. "You really found her," she whispered, clearly choked up.

"We've established that," Colin retorted. And then he looked at her more closely and realized what was going on. "Hey, are you crying?" he demanded, stunned.

Miranda pressed her lips together as she nodded. "Miracles make me do that," she told him hoarsely.

He wasn't sure if the miracle she was referring to was that he had found Lily's mother, or that he had bothered to look in the first place. Either way, he knew he wasn't about to ask her to elaborate. He was determined to keep communication between them to an absolute minimum—or as close to that as possible.

Digging into his back pocket, he pulled out a handkerchief and pushed it into her hand. "You're getting messy," he muttered.

Taking the handkerchief, Miranda smiled at him.

I see through you, Officer Kirby. You're not the big, bad wolf you pretend to be. You're a kind man under all that bluster.

Wiping her eyes, she asked, "What happened to her?"

He'd gone to the hospital to get as much information as he could before coming to the shelter. He knew there would be questions and he wasn't about to turn up unprepared.

Drawing her toward an alcove, he told Miranda, "From the looks of it, someone tried to rob her. When she held on to her purse, the thug decided to teach her a lesson. Doctor said she was pretty badly beaten. She was unconscious when they first brought her in," he added.

"But she's conscious now." It was half a question, half an assumption.

The woman had been just coming around when he'd gone to see her. "Yeah."

"Which hospital is she in?" Miranda asked.

"The paramedics took her to the one closest to where they found her," he answered. "Mercy General."

Miranda nodded, absorbing the information. Lily. She had to tell Lily.

She started to head toward the back, where some of the beds were located, when she stopped suddenly and whirled back around to face Colin again. Hurrying over, she caught him completely by surprise by throwing her arms around him.

Startled, Colin's ingrained training immediately had him protecting himself and pushing the person in his space away. But that turned out to be harder than he'd anticipated. For a rather willowy, dainty-looking woman, Miranda had a grip worthy of a world-class wrestling champion.

The second she'd thrown her arms around him, she'd felt Colin stiffening. She was making him uncomfortable.

Loosening her hold, Miranda took a half step back. "Thank you," she said.

He'd never heard more emotion stuffed into two words in his life.

Colin deflected the tidal wave of feelings as best he could. "I'm a cop. That's just supposed to be part of my job."

The smile on her lips was a knowing one, as if she had his number—which was impossible, because they were practically strangers. Still, he couldn't shake the feeling that his protest was falling on deaf ears.

"The key words being 'supposed to,'" she told him. "I didn't think you were going to look for her," Miranda admitted.

That made no sense. "Then why did you ask me to?" he asked.

Her face seemed to light up as she answered, "A girl can always hope." And then she grabbed his hand and said, "Come with me."

But Colin remained rooted to the spot, an immovable object. "Come with you where?"

"To tell Lily that you found her mother," she answered, tugging on his hand again.

But Colin still wouldn't budge an inch. "You can tell her."

Miranda was nothing if not stubborn. He had done the work and he deserved to get the credit, which in this case involved Lily's gratitude. "You found her. Lily is going to want to hear it from you. And then after you tell her, you can take us to the hospital to see Gina."

She had this all mapped out, didn't she? He didn't like being told what to do. "You're assuming a hell of a lot, aren't you?"

Miranda gazed up at him with what had to be the most innocent look he had ever seen. "So far, I've been right, haven't I?"

"Well, guess what? Your lucky streak is over," he informed her.

But just as he was about to break free and walk away, Colin heard a high-pitched squeal coming from the far side of the room. Looking in that direction, he saw a small figure with a flurry of blond hair charging toward him.

Obviously, someone had woken the little girl and told her he was here. She must have put the rest together on her own.

"You did it!" Lily cried. The next moment, she had wrapped herself around him like a human bungee cord. "You found her! You found my mommy, didn't you?" Tilting back her head so that she could look up at him, Lily gushed, "Thank you, thank you, thank you!"

Utterly stunned, Colin looked at the woman standing behind Lily. "How—?"

"It's not just the walls that have ears here," she told

him, beaming just as hard as Lily. She nodded toward the cluster of children who had been steadily gathering around them as if that should answer his question.

"Can we go see her now?" Lily pleaded. She looked from her hero to Miranda and then back again. "Please, can we? *Can* we?" she asked, giving every indication that she intended to go on pleading until her request was granted.

Looking at the officer's expression, Miranda made a judgment call. The man looked far from eager to go with them and he had done enough.

"Officer Kirby has to go home now, Lily. But I'll take you," Miranda said, putting her hand on the little girl's shoulder.

"And I'll drive," Amelia told them, approaching from yet another side.

The director had been drawn by the sounds of the growing commotion and just possibly by her own pint-size informant. In any case, the woman appeared relieved and thrilled at the news.

"Officer Kirby found my mommy," Lily told the director excitedly.

"So I heard," Amelia replied. Nodding at Colin, she smiled her thanks. "All of us here at the shelter—especially Lily—really appreciate everything you've done, Officer Kirby," she told him.

Colin wanted to protest that he really hadn't done anything. He certainly hadn't gone out of his way to find Lily's mother. The information had literally fallen into his lap and all he had really done was follow up on it.

But something told him that the more he protested, the more gratitude he would wind up garnering. His protests would be interpreted as being modest rather than just the simple truth.

So he left it alone, saying nothing further on the subject.

Instead, he decided that going home could wait a while longer.

Turning toward the director, he addressed her and the little girl who was jumping up and down at his side. "I'll lead the way to the hospital, since I know what floor Lily's mother is on."

He deliberately avoided looking at Miranda, sensing that if he did glance her way, he'd somehow wind up being roped into something else, and his quota for good deeds was filled for the month.

Possibly the year.

Chapter Six

"Wait!"

The order came from the head nurse sitting at the second floor nurse's station.

When the three adults and child continued walking down the corridor, she hurried around her desk and into the hall to physically block their path.

Surprised, Miranda told the woman, "We're going to see Gina Hayden. We won't be long," she promised.

"Clearly," the nurse snapped, crossing her arms over her ample chest. "Visiting hours are done," she informed them in a voice that would have made a drill sergeant proud. "You can come back tomorrow."

Lily looked stricken. "But she's my mommy and we just found her," the little girl protested in distress.

"She'll still be here tomorrow," the woman told her,

sounding detached. It was obvious she wanted them off the floor and wasn't about to budge.

Lily's lower lip trembled. "But—"

"Rules are rules, little girl," the nurse maintained stiffly.

Colin felt Lily tugging on his sleeve, mutely appealing to him for help. He made the mistake of looking down into her worried face.

Swallowing an oath, he took out his badge and held it up in front of the nurse so she couldn't miss seeing it. "But they can be bent this one time, can't they?" It wasn't a question.

The head nurse looked no friendlier than she had a moment ago, but she inclined her head and backed off—temporarily.

"Ten minutes, no longer. Ten minutes or I'll call security," she warned.

"No need," Miranda promised the woman. A small victory was better than none. Taking Lily's hand, she urged the little girl, "Let's hurry."

"She's in room 221," Colin told them gruffly.

They moved quickly. He followed at his own pace.

There were four beds in the room, two on either side. Lily's head practically whirled around as she scanned the room looking for her mother. Seeing her lying in the bed next to the window, she sprinted over.

"Mommy!" she cried happily, and then skidded to a stop as she took a closer look at the woman in the hospital bed.

Her mouth dropped open in surprise. Her mother

was hooked up to two monitors as well as an IV. The monitors were making beeping noises.

The scene was clearly upsetting to the little girl, as were the bruises she saw along her mother's arms and face.

Inching closer, Lily asked in a hushed voice, "Did you fall down, Mommy?"

Gina turned her head and saw her daughter for the first time. Light came into the woman's eyes and she tried to open her arms so she could hug the little girl, but she was impeded by the various tubes attached to her.

"Oh, Lily-pad, I did. I tripped and fell down," Gina told her daughter.

Miranda squeezed the woman's hand lightly, letting Gina know that she understood she was lying for Lily's sake.

"We were all worried about you," she told her. "But Lily never gave up hope that we'd find you."

The expression on Gina's face reflected confusion and embarrassment. "I don't remember what happened," she admitted.

"That doesn't matter right now, darling," Amelia said in a soothing, comforting voice. "All that matters is that you're here and you're being taken care of."

"Officer Kirby found you for me," Lily told her mother excitedly. Taking Colin's hand, Lily pulled on it to bring him closer. "This is Officer Kirby, Mommy," she explained, showing off her brand-new champion to her mother.

Eyes that were the same shade of blue as Lily's

looked up at him. They glinted with sheer appreciation. "Thank you."

"No thanks needed," Colin told her, then explained, "It's complicated."

Miranda suppressed a sigh. The man just couldn't accept gratitude, she thought. She wanted to call him out on it, but this definitely wasn't the moment for that.

"We're out of time," she told Lily, as well as Amelia and Colin. And then she explained to Gina, "We promised the nurse on duty to only stay for ten minutes because it's after hours."

"We'll come back tomorrow, Mommy," Lily promised her solemnly.

Miranda bit her bottom lip. She wouldn't be able to come by with Lily until after her shift at the hospital. She looked at the director, a mute request in her eyes.

Picking up the silent message, Amelia nodded obligingly. "See you then," she told Gina, then patted the young mother's hand. "Feel better, dear."

Colin waited for the three females to file out of the room before he started to leave himself. He almost didn't hear Gina say, "Thank you, Officer Kirby."

Again, he wanted to tell the woman that he hadn't been the one who had located her. But that would take time and the nurse at the station had given every indication that she would come swooping in the second their ten minutes were up. He didn't trust himself not to snap at the nurse, which would undoubtedly upset the little girl, and in his estimation, she had been through enough.

So he merely nodded in response to the woman's thanks and left the room.

"Mommy has to be more careful," Lily said authoritatively as she and the three adults with her headed toward the elevator.

Miranda looked at the little girl as they got on. It wasn't entirely clear to her if Lily actually believed what she was saying, or if she was saying it so as not to let the adults with her know that *she* knew something bad had happened to her mother.

In some ways, she felt that Lily was an innocent girl; in other ways, she seemed older than her years. Only children were often a mixture of both.

"That was a very nice thing you did," Miranda told Colin once they reached the ground floor and got off the elevator. When he stared at her blankly, she elaborated. "Getting the nurse to allow us to see Gina."

The officer said nothing. There was no indication that he had even heard her, except for his careless shrug.

The man was a very tough nut to crack. And she intended to crack him—but in a good way. Miranda smiled to herself. Whether Officer Kirby knew it or not, he had just become her next project.

They split up when they reached the hospital parking lot, with Miranda and Lily going back with Amelia, while Colin headed for his vehicle, a vintage two-door sport car that was a couple years older than he was.

"Goodbye, Officer Kirby!" Lily called after him. When he glanced over his shoulder in response to her parting words, Lily waved at him as hard as she could. It looked as if she was close to taking off the ground.

Colin nodded once, climbed into his car and drove off.

Lily insisted on standing there until she couldn't see him any longer.

"He's a hero," she told the two women when she finally turned around and got into the director's car.

"Yes, he is," Miranda agreed.

A very reluctant hero, she added silently.

"Hey, Kirby, there's someone here who's been waiting to see you for some time now," the desk sergeant told Colin when he came into the precinct and walked by the man's desk.

It was past the end of his shift and Colin was more than tired. It had been two days since he'd led that little safari of females into the hospital and he'd assumed—hoped, really—that Miranda was now a thing of the past.

But the moment the desk sergeant said there was someone waiting to see him, he knew in his gut that it had to be *her*. Granted, it could have easily been anyone else; Bedford wasn't exactly a minuscule city and it felt as if the population was growing every day. But somehow he just *knew* it had to be the woman he had made the fatal mistake of pulling over that day.

The annoyingly perky, pushy woman he just couldn't seem to get rid of. She was like a burr he couldn't shake loose.

"Where?" Colin growled.

"Need your eyes checked, Kirby?" the desk sergeant asked. "She's sitting right over there." He pointed to the bench situated against the wall fifteen feet away.

Reluctantly, Colin sighed and looked in the direction the desk sergeant was pointing.

Damn it, he thought.

It *was* her—and she was looking right at him. It was too late to make an escape.

He might as well find out what she wanted.

Striding over to the bench, he saw her rise to her feet. The woman appeared ready to pounce on him.

Now what?

Bracing himself for the worst, he skipped right over any kind of a formal greeting and asked, "Something else you want me to do?"

Just as sunny as ever, Miranda thought, more convinced than before that he needed her to turn him around. "No, actually, I brought something for you," she told him, hoping that would get rid of the scowl on his face.

It didn't.

He needed to stop her right there, Colin thought, instantly on guard. "I can't accept any gifts," he told her. "The department frowns on its officers taking any sort of gratuities in exchange for services rendered, either past, present or in the future."

He sounded so incredibly uptight, Miranda thought. They'd crossed paths not a moment too soon.

"This isn't a gratuity," she assured him, trying to put his fears to rest.

He wasn't about to stand here exchanging words with her. For one thing, she was far better equipped for a verbal battle than he was. For another, he didn't have time for this.

"Whatever you want to call it—gratuity, gift or bribe—I can't accept it." He concluded in a no-nonsense voice, thinking that would be the end of it.

He should have known better. The woman had shown him that, right or wrong, she wasn't one to back off.

And she was clearly not listening to him but was reaching into the large zippered bag she'd picked up from the bench. Extracting something from inside it, she held up what appeared to be an eleven-by-fourteen poster board for him to look at.

It was a drawing.

"Lily drew this just for you," Miranda told him. She pointed to the blue figure in the center of the page. It was twice as large as the four other figures present. "In case you don't recognize him, that's you."

And then she proceeded to point out the other people in the drawing. "That's Lily, her mother in the hospital bed, Amelia, and that's me." Miranda indicated the figure in the corner, who was almost offstage, appearing to look on.

Colin couldn't help staring at the central figure. "I'm a giant," he commented, surprised that the little girl would portray him that way.

As if reading his mind, Miranda explained, "That's how she sees you. You are a giant in her eyes. Heroes usually are," she added.

The term made him uncomfortable. "I'm not a hero," he retorted.

"I hate to break this to you, but you are to Lily," she told him.

Colin continued looking at the drawing, still not taking it from her. His attention was drawn to the stick figure the little girl had drawn of Miranda.

"You could stand to gain some weight," he observed, still not cracking a smile.

"That's good," she responded, as if they were having an actual serious conversation. "That means I get to indulge in my craving for mint chip ice cream."

He glanced at her rather than the drawing, his eyes slowly running over her, taking in every curve, every detail.

"You don't look as if you indulge in anything that's nonessential," he told her.

She laughed. It was a melodic sound he tried not to notice.

"You'd be surprised," she told him. When she saw him look at her quizzically—most likely because she *was* thin—Miranda explained, "I do a lot of running around—at the hospital, at the women's shelter and especially at the animal shelter." They had her exercising the dogs, which meant that *she* was exercising, as well.

"Don't you take any time off for yourself?" Colin asked, positive that she was putting him on.

Miranda smiled. The man just didn't get it, did he? "The women's shelter and animal shelter *are* my 'time off' for myself," she stressed. "I like feeling that I'm helping out and doing something productive. It makes me feel good about myself," she explained.

He still wasn't completely convinced. "Did you ever hear the saying 'Too good to be true'?"

She tried to suppress the grin that rose to her lips. "Are you saying that you think I'm good?"

"You're missing the point of the rest of the saying," he pointed out. Taking a breath, he decided that this meeting was over. "Anything else?" he asked her, impatience pulsing in his voice.

"Well, since you asked—have you thought any more about visiting my kids at the hospital?"

She called them 'her' kids, not just 'the' kids. Did she feel as if they were hers? he wondered incredulously.

He should never have asked if there was anything else. "No, I haven't," he answered, upbraiding himself.

Not about to be put off, Miranda asked, "Well, would you think about it? Please?" she added. "Christmas is getting closer."

Why should that make a difference? Christmas had ceased to have meaning for him when he'd lost his mother.

"Happens every year at this time," he answered.

Miranda gave it another try. "Well, like I told you, I think it would do them a lot of good. Their lives are really hard and they don't have all that much to look forward to."

"And my visiting would give them something to look forward to?" he asked sarcastically.

She never wavered. "Yes, it would."

The woman just wasn't going to give up. He didn't like being made to feel guilty.

"I'll think about it," he said, only because he felt it was the one way to get her to cease and desist. And then he looked at his watch. "Don't you have to be someplace, volunteering?"

"Actually, I do," she said, slipping the straps of her

bag over her shoulder. "I promised I'd come by the ani-mal shelter. There's this German shepherd that needs a foster home until she can be placed."

The woman was a relentless do-gooder. "Right up your alley," he cracked.

Miranda smiled at him. He saw the corners of her eyes crinkling. "Actually, it is."

"Then you'd better get to it."

"I will. Oh, don't forget your picture," she prompted. Picking up the poster board drawing, she forced it into his hands.

"Right," he muttered, less than pleased.

He was still standing there, looking down at the drawing, as she hurried out the door.

Chapter Seven

Colin frowned. He needed to have his head examined. He obviously wasn't thinking clearly.

Or maybe at all.

Why else would he be out here, parked across the street from Bedford's no-kill animal shelter, waiting for that overachieving do-gooder to come out?

As far as he knew, he was free and clear, which meant that he could go on with his life without being subjected to any more taxing, annoying requests.

So why the hell was he here, *willingly* putting himself in that woman's path again? Why would he be setting himself up like this?

It wasn't as if he didn't know what Miranda was like. He'd learned that she was the kind of person who, if given an inch, wanted not just a mile but to turn it into an entire freeway.

Colin sighed. Knowing that, what was he doing out here?

Satisfying his own curiosity, he supposed.

A curiosity, he reminded himself, he hadn't even been aware of possessing a short while ago—not until life had thrown that woman into his path and she'd come charging at him like some kind of undersized, stampeding unicorn.

Damn it, go home, Kirby, he ordered himself, straightening up beside his vehicle. *Go home before anyone mistakes you for some kind of stalker and calls someone from the department on you.*

He'd talked himself out of being here and was just about to open his car door when he heard the sound of metal scraping on concrete across the street. A second later, he realized that the gates in front of the animal shelter were being opened.

Someone was coming out.

Colin's suspicions were confirmed a heartbeat later when he heard someone calling his name.

"Officer Kirby, is that you?"

He froze.

You should have been faster, he upbraided himself. Better yet, he shouldn't have been here to begin with.

Caught, he turned around, to see Miranda hurrying across the street toward him.

She wasn't alone.

She had a lumbering, overly excited German shepherd running with her. Miranda appeared to be hanging on to the leash for dear life. At first glance, it was difficult to say exactly who had who in tow.

Both woman and dog reached him before he had a chance to finish his thought.

Her four-footed companion suddenly reared up on its hind legs and came within an inch of planting a pair of powerful-looking front paws against his chest.

"You sure you can handle him?" Colin asked, far from pleased and moving back just in time to escape the encounter.

"Her," Miranda corrected, tugging harder on the leash. "It's a her."

That, in his opinion, was not the point. Whether the animal was too much for her was.

"Whatever." He never took his eyes off the dog. "You look like you've met your match," he told her as he took another step back.

"Down, Lola," Miranda ordered in an authoritative voice. The mountain of a dog immediately dropped to all four legs, resuming her initial position. "Good girl," Miranda praised, petting the German shepherd's head while continuing to maintain a firm hold on the leash with her other hand. Her attention shifted to Colin. "You're not afraid of a frisky puppy, are you, Officer?"

Colin continued eyeing the animal cautiously. "That all depends on whether or not that 'puppy' is bigger than I am."

"Don't let Lola scare you," Miranda told him. "She was just excited to see you." She petted the dog again. Lola seemed to curl into her hand. "I think she sees everyone as a potential master."

"Uh-huh." He wasn't all that sure he was buying this. Colin continued to regard the dog warily.

"Heel, Lola," she ordered, when the dog started to move in Colin's direction again. When Lola obeyed, Miranda looked at the police officer, wondering what he was doing here. This was not his usual patrolling area, and he was out of uniform. "Were you waiting for me, Officer Kirby?" she asked.

The expression on her face was nothing short of amused. A week ago, seeing an expression like that, seemingly at his expense, would have been enough for him to take offense, but for some reason now, he didn't.

Instead, he let it ride. Reaching into the back seat of his car, he took out the drawing she'd given him the other day at the precinct. "I came by to give you this."

Lola's ears perked up and the animal looked as if she was debating whether or not the drawing he was holding was something to eat.

Miranda pulled a little on the leash, drawing the dog back.

"That's not for you, Lola," she informed the eager German shepherd. Her eyes shifted back to the police officer. "Why are you giving it to me?" she asked. "Lily drew it for you. She wanted you to have it. It was her way of saying thank you."

Colin shrugged. "Yeah, well, I don't have anyplace to put it," he told her, still holding out the drawing.

He kept one eye on the German shepherd to make sure Lola didn't grab a chunk out of the poster board. He didn't want it, but there was no reason to let it be destroyed.

Holding the dog's leash tightly, Miranda made no effort to take the drawing from him. Instead, she looked at the tall, imposing police officer. The solemn expression in his eyes convinced her more than ever that the man needed fixing.

"You don't have any closets?"

"Of course I have closets," he retorted. What kind of question was that? Did she think he lived in a public park?

"Well, you could put the drawing in one of your closets," she suggested helpfully. "That is, if you don't want to hang it on your refrigerator."

Still not taking it from him, she glanced at the drawing. Thinking back, Miranda could remember producing something like that herself when she was younger than Lily. Hers had been of her parents and herself—and Daisy, her father's beloved Doberman. That had stayed on display on the fridge for almost a year.

"Most people put artwork like that on their refrigerator," she added, smiling encouragingly. This was all undoubtedly alien to him. "You must be new at this."

Colin furrowed his brow in concentration as he wondered what made this woman tick—and why she seemed to have singled him out like this. "I guess I'm new at a lot of things," he observed.

Her smile turned almost dazzling. "Hey, even God had a first day."

He thought of the last few days since he'd run into this sorceress. She made him behave in a manner that was completely foreign to his normal mode of operation. Exactly what was this secret power she seemed to have that caused him to act so out of character?

"Not like this," he murmured under his breath.

He heard Miranda laugh in response. The sound was light, breezy, reminding him of the spring wind that was still three months away.

For some reason, an image of bluebells in his mother's garden flashed through his mind, catching him completely by surprise. He hadn't thought of his mom's garden for more than twenty-two years.

He shook his head, as if to free himself of the memory and the wave of emotion that came with it. Colin felt as if he was getting all turned around.

"Is something wrong, Officer?" Miranda asked, concerned.

"You mean other than the fact that I should be home nursing a beer, instead of standing out here trying to make you take back this drawing?" Colin asked, exasperated.

"It's not my drawing to take," Miranda reminded him. "Lily wanted you to have it." And then she abruptly switched subjects. "Seriously? A beer?" she asked. "What about dinner?"

Colin stared at her. "Is this mothering-smothering thing of yours just something that spills out without warning, or do you have to summon it?" he asked.

She ignored his question. Instead, she made a quick judgment call.

"Tell you what," she said. "I owe you a dinner. Why don't you come on over to my place and I'll make it?"

"What?" he cried, dumbfounded. There was no way he could have heard her correctly.

"I'd offer to come over to your place and make dinner there—you know, familiar surroundings and all that to keep you from getting skittish—but I've got a feeling the only things in your refrigerator, now that we've established the fact that you have one, are probably half-empty cartons of ten-day-old Chinese takeout. Maybe eleven days."

He continued to stare at her, as close to being overwhelmed as he had ever been.

When she finally stopped talking for a moment, he jumped in and took advantage of it. "You done yet?"

"That depends," she answered, lifting her chin as if getting ready for a fight. "Are you coming?"

"No," he said flatly.

"Then I'm not done." Glancing at the dog by her side, she added, "I have a very persuasive companion right here who could help me make my argument. All things considered, I'd suggest that you avoid her attempts to convince you to see things my way and just agree to come along to my place."

Damn it, this was insane. But he could actually feel himself weakening. He really *did* need to have his head examined.

Colin put on the most solemn expression he had at his disposal. "You know, there're laws against kidnapping police officers."

Rather than back away, Miranda leaned forward, her eyes sparkling with humor. "Not if, ultimately, that police officer decides to come along willingly."

Then, as if on cue, Colin's stomach began to rumble and growl. Audibly.

Miranda smiled broadly. "I think your stomach is siding with Lola and me," she told him.

Colin scowled in response. She continued to hold her ground. He had to be crazy, but he found himself actually admiring her tenacity. If he had an iota of sense, he'd jump in his car and get the hell out of here.

But he didn't.

"That dog couldn't care less one way or another," he told her, thinking that might blow apart her argument and finally get her to back off.

She studied him for a long moment. Lola tugged on her leash, leaning forward as far as she could, but Miranda continued regarding the man before her, and seemed practically oblivious to the German shepherd. She was mulling over his response.

"You never had a pet when you were growing up, did you?" she asked Colin.

"Why would you say that?"

Miranda smiled. She had her answer. He hadn't told her she was wrong—which told her she was right.

"Because of what you just said," she murmured. "If you'd ever had one, you'd know that pets, especially dogs, *do* care about their humans."

He had her there, he thought. "I'm not her human," Colin pointed out.

"No, but at least for now, I am, and I care about you," she told him. "Lola picked up on that."

That was all so wrong, he didn't even know where to start.

"First of all, you said you were probably going to take a German shepherd home to give him—*her*—" he corrected, "a foster home. That means you're taking this dog home for the first time. She doesn't know a thing about you and she's not really your dog yet," he stressed. "And second of all—or maybe this should be first—" he said pointedly, "why the hell should you care if I have anything in my house to eat or not?"

Miranda never blinked once during what he considered to be his well-constructed argument. Instead, she looked at him, totally unfazed, and when he was done she asked, "Why shouldn't I?"

"Because we're *strangers*, damn it," he muttered in exasperation. "You don't *know* me," he added for good measure. Why didn't this woman *get* that?

In a calm voice, she went on to quietly refute his argument.

"You pulled me over to give me a ticket, then didn't after I explained why I went over the speed limit and where I was going." She paused for a moment, then told him what she felt in her heart had been his crowning achievement. "And then when I told you that Lily's mother was missing, you found her."

He felt like he was hitting his head against a brick wall. No matter what he said, she kept turning it into something positive.

"That wasn't my doing," he told her, repeating what he'd said the other day. "That all happened by accident."

Despite the fact that he had raised his voice, the woman just didn't seem to hear his protest. Or if she did, she wasn't listening. Instead, she went on to make her point.

"You came to the shelter to tell Lily her mother was at the hospital—when you didn't have to—and then you went out of your way to go with us to the hospital—when you didn't have to."

"Damn it, you're twisting things," he shouted.

At the sound of his raised voice, Lola pulled forward, as if to protect her.

"Stay!" Miranda ordered, stilling the anxious dog. And then she looked at Colin. "Why are you so afraid of having people think of you as a good guy?"

"Because I'm *not*," he insisted.

She inclined her head. "I guess we'll just have to agree to disagree on that point," she told him philosophically.

"*We* don't have to do anything," he retorted impatiently.

She smiled at him knowingly. "I think that you might see things differently on a full stomach. Here's my address," she told him, pausing to take a card out of her shoulder bag and handing it to him. "You might find it easier to just follow me," she suggested.

"I might find it easier to just go home," he contradicted.

About to cross back to her vehicle, Miranda stopped and sent him a smile that seemed to corkscrew right through his gut.

"No, you won't." She said it with such certainty, she stunned him. And then his stomach rumbled again. "See?" she said. "Your stomach agrees with me. Just get in your car and follow me. And after dinner, you're free to go home. I promise."

Heaven help him, she made it sound appealing. And he *was* hungry. Involved in a car chase this afternoon, he'd wound up skipping lunch, and his stomach was protesting being ignored for so long.

He shifted gears, going on the attack. "You know, it's dangerous to hand out your address like that," he told her.

Miranda smiled again, running her hand over Lola's head and petting the dog. "I'm not worried," she answered. "I have protection."

Colin decided to keep his peace and made no comment in response. He'd already lost enough arguments today.

Besides, he *was* hungry.

Chapter Eight

Colin nearly turned his car around.

Twice.

However, each time, he wound up curbing his impulse and talking himself into continuing to follow Miranda. He knew that if he didn't show up at her place for that dinner she seemed so bent on making for him, she would show up at his precinct tomorrow just as sure as day followed night. Probably with some sort of picnic lunch or something like that.

That was the last thing he wanted or needed.

Colin muttered a few choice words under his breath and kept going.

He might as well get this over with, and then maybe the book would finally be closed: he had done a good deed in her eyes and she paid him back with a dinner she'd made for him—hopefully not poisoning him in the process.

Caught up in his thoughts, Colin missed the last right turn Miranda took.

Watching his rearview mirror, he backed his vehicle up slowly, then turned right. When he did, he saw that her car was halfway up the block in front of him. Idling.

Miranda was obviously waiting for him to catch up.

Once he came up behind her, she started driving again.

His gut told him that he'd been right. There was absolutely no way this woman would have allowed him to skip having this payback dinner with her.

Her house turned out to be two residential blocks farther on. It was a small, tidy-looking one-story structure that seemed to almost exude warmth.

He caught himself thinking that it suited her.

Miranda parked her vehicle in the driveway. He parked his at the curb. It allowed for a faster getaway if it wound up coming to that, he thought.

She got out of the car, then opened the passenger door for the dog she'd brought home. Lola jumped down onto the driveway and they both stood at the side of her vehicle, waiting for him to come up the front walk.

"Don't trust me?" Colin asked, just the slightest bit amused, when he reached her.

"We just wanted to welcome you, that's all," she told him, nodding toward the German shepherd, which had somehow become part of this impromptu dinner.

Leading the way, Miranda went up to her front door

and unlocked it, then walked inside, still holding on to Lola's leash.

She threw a switch that was right next to the door. Light flooded the living room.

"Welcome back to your home, Lola," she cheerfully told the dog. After bending to remove the leash, she dropped it on the small table that was just a few feet beyond the entrance.

"She's been here before?" Colin asked. From what she'd said earlier, he thought Miranda was bringing the dog home with her for the first time.

"A couple of times," Miranda answered. "It was kind of a dry run to see how she fared in my house."

"And how did she?" he asked, shrugging out of his jacket as he walked into the house.

Miranda smiled. "Well. She fared well."

Colin was about to make a flippant comment in response, but he'd just glanced around and his attention had been completely absorbed by what he saw.

There was a Christmas tree in the center of the room. Not just a run-of-the-mill Christmas tree but one that looked to be at least ten feet tall. Overwhelming, the tree appeared to only be half-decorated.

The rest of the Christmas ornaments were scattered all over the room—in and out of their respective boxes—waiting to be hung up.

"It looks like a Christmas store exploded in here," he commented, scanning the room in total disbelief.

"I haven't had a chance to finish," Miranda explained. "I don't have much time left over every night to hang up decorations," she tossed over her shoulder as she made her way to the kitchen. "I'm usually pretty beat by that time."

Miranda was back in less than a minute with a dog bowl filled with fresh water and set it down in a corner by the coffee table.

"There you go, Lola, drink up," she told the animal. "Dinner will be coming soon."

Despite himself, Colin was surprised. "You've got a dog dish."

She paused for a moment to pet the dog's head. She viewed it as positive reinforcement. "Like I said, this isn't her first time here. And I believe in being prepared."

Obviously, he thought. Colin looked back down at the decorations that covered three-quarters of the living room floor space.

"Are these all your decorations?" he questioned incredulously. He'd seen Christmas trees in shopping centers with less ornaments on them than were scattered here.

"Well, if I'd stolen the decorations, it'd be pretty stupid of me to bring a police officer into my house to see them, wouldn't it?" she asked. Not waiting for a response, she told him, "Half these ornaments belonged to my parents. I've just been adding to the collection over the years."

"And the ten-foot tree?" Colin asked, nodding toward the towering tree. Most people opted for a smaller tree, if they had one at all. He couldn't remember the last time he'd put up a tree for the holidays.

"That was theirs, too. I inherited it. My mother decided that she needed to scale back and get a smaller tree. I couldn't see throwing away a perfectly good tree," she told him. Since he was asking about the tree, she said, "You can help me hang up a few of the ornaments after dinner if you like." Seeing the wary look on his face, she added, "But you don't have to."

The next moment, she turned back toward the kitchen.

"If I'm going to make that dinner I promised you, I'd better get started," Miranda announced. And then she caught him off guard by asking, "Would you like to keep me company?"

Thinking that she might ask him again to hang up ornaments if he chose to remain in the living room, he said, "Yeah, sure, why not?"

Miranda grinned. "That's the spirit. How are you at chopping vegetables?" she asked, moving toward the refrigerator.

"Depends on how you want them chopped," he answered drolly.

"Into smaller vegetables," she answered, her eyes sparkling with amusement. "I just want to be able to cook them faster."

Placing a cutting board and large knife on the counter in front of the police officer, she took three kinds of vegetables out of the refrigerator and deposited those in a large bowl. She put the bowl next to the cutting board.

"Have at it," she told him.

Colin regarded the items on the counter. "You didn't mention that I'd have to make my own dinner," he said.

"Not entirely," Miranda corrected. "It's just a little

prep work," she explained. "I figured you'd want to join in."

Cooking was something he usually avoided. Takeout and microwaving things was more his style.

"And exactly what made you 'figure' that?" he asked.

"Easy," she answered. "You don't strike me as the kind of person who likes standing around, doing nothing while he's waiting."

"I wasn't planning on standing, I was planning on sitting," he told her.

"You'll be sitting soon enough," Miranda promised cheerfully—in his opinion, *nobody* was this damn cheerful. What was wrong with her?

Turning away from the counter, she opened the pantry on the side and took out a medium-sized can from the bottom shelf. He assumed that whatever was in the can was going to be part of dinner. He watched her placing the can under a mounted can opener. Once the can was opened, he was surprised to see her emptying the can's contents into a bowl that was beside Lola's water dish.

She was feeding the dog.

"I take it that wasn't part of our dinner," he quipped drily.

Picking up the large knife, he made short work of the carrots he found in the large bowl.

She grinned at him. He deliberately looked away. "Not unless you have an insatiable fondness for ground up turkey liver."

"I'll pass," he told her.

"Hopefully, Lola doesn't share your lack of enthusi-

MARIE FERRARELLA 99

asm," she said, glancing over her shoulder toward the
dog. The dog was eating as if she hadn't been fed for
days, a fact that Miranda knew wasn't the case. She
smiled as she watched. "Looks like she doesn't."

Lola was making short work of the liver that had
been deposited in her bowl. Within seconds, the liver
was almost completely gone.

A moment later, licking her lips, Lola looked up at
her. She made no noise, but it was obvious what the
dog wanted.

"Sorry, that's it for now, Lola," Miranda told her,
walking away. "Play your cards right and you might get
something later after we have our own dinner."

"If I were you," Colin commented as he went on
chopping vegetables, "I'd consider myself lucky if she
didn't destroy half those ornaments you have strewn
all over the floor."

Miranda looked unfazed. "Lola's a good dog. She
doesn't destroy things. Her philosophy is live-and-let-
live," she told the policeman, taking out a large package of boneless chicken breasts from the top shelf in
the refrigerator.

"How do you know that?" he challenged.

"I can just tell," Miranda answered, sounding a great
deal more confident than he would have been, Colin
thought.

Opening the package, Miranda proceeded to cut each
of the individual breasts into tiny pieces with the shears
she'd taken out of the utensil drawer. The pieces fell
into a big pot that she'd put on the larger of the two
front burners.

Watching her, Colin came disturbingly close to cutting one of his fingers with the knife that he was wielding. Sustaining a nick, he pulled back his finger just in time and then, swallowing a curse, he asked, "What are you doing?"

"Getting dinner ready," she answered simply, turning up the burner beneath the pot. Turning, she saw the tiny drop of blood. She took a napkin and attempted to dab at it, but he was not about to cooperate. "Do you want a Band-Aid?"

"No. I'll live." Taking the napkin from her, he wrapped a small piece of it around his finger only to keep the blood from mingling with the vegetables. "What *is* dinner?" he asked.

"Stir-fry chicken and vegetables over rice—unless you'd rather have something else," she offered, dubiously watching his injured finger.

The chicken pieces were already beginning to sizzle in the pot. "Seems a little late for that now," he told her.

Undaunted, Miranda shook her head. "It's never too late."

Colin got the distinct impression that the woman actually believed that—and that she applied it to life.

"Stir-fry chicken is fine," he told her. He was not about to have her start something from scratch. Who knew how long *that* would take?

His response was rewarded with a smile that reminded him more and more of sunshine each time he saw it.

The fact that it did bothered him to no end because he wasn't used to having thoughts like that. His was a dark world and he had gotten accustomed to that. This new element that had been introduced into his world disturbed the general balance of things and he wasn't sure what he was going to do about it if it persisted.

"Good," Miranda responded, stirring the chicken so as to make sure that both sides were browned. "Because that means that we're more than halfway to getting dinner on the table."

There was that word again.

"We."

He wasn't in the habit of thinking of himself as part of a "we."

Granted that he was part of the police department, but he was a motorcycle cop, which meant by definition that he operated alone. He was a loner and didn't worry about having anyone's back. "We" brought a whole different set of ground rules with it and he wasn't comfortable with those rules.

Coming here had been a bad idea, Colin thought. And yet, he wasn't abruptly terminating his association with this living embodiment of Pollyanna, wasn't walking out of her kitchen and her house. He was still standing here, in that kitchen, chopping vegetables like some misguided cooking show contestant.

Something was definitely wrong with him, Colin thought, exasperated.

"Perfect!" Miranda declared.

Taking the large bowl filled with the vegetables he'd just chopped, she deposited the entire contents into the pot. She stirred everything together, then poured in a can of chicken broth, followed by several tablespoons of flour.

Stirring that together, Miranda proceeded to drizzle a large handful of shredded mozzarella cheese into the mixture and added a quarter cup of ground up Parmesan cheese.

Watching her, Colin frowned. "That isn't stir-fry chicken."

"That's *my* version of stir-fry chicken," she clarified and then told him, "Give it a try before you condemn it."

"I'm not condemning it," he retorted. "I'm just saying that it's…different."

"And that's what makes the world go around," she told him with a smile.

Stirring the pot's contents again, she lowered the heat under the pot and turned her attention to making the last additive: the rice.

Measuring out two cups of water and pouring them into a small pot, she told Colin, "I do have a can of beer in the refrigerator. You're welcome to it and you can retreat into the living room if you like."

He glanced toward the living room and saw the German shepherd she'd brought from the shelter. As if on cue, Lola raised her head. He felt as if the dog was eyeing him, waiting for him to step into the room.

To what end?

He wasn't afraid of the dog, but why borrow trouble?

The next moment his mind came to a skidding halt. *Why borrow trouble?* That was a phrase he remembered his aunt used to like to say. He felt something pricking his conscience. He hadn't been to see his aunt for several months. He supposed he should stop by and pay the woman a visit. After all, it was getting close to Christmas and Aunt Lily *was* the reason he'd moved back to this city in the first place.

His aunt would probably approve of all this, he realized.

She'd approve of the decorations lying all over the living room, of the animal shelter dog hovering over the empty dog dish—and most of all, she'd probably *really* approve of this do-gooder-on-steroids who was fluttering around the kitchen, preparing some strange concoction that very possibly might just wind up being his last meal.

"Colin?" Miranda asked when he made no response to her suggestion.

Aware that he had just drifted off, he blinked and focused his attention on Miranda. "What?"

"Would you like that beer?" she asked again, nodding toward the refrigerator.

He glanced over his shoulder toward the living room again. The German shepherd was still looking straight at him. Colin shrugged indifferently.

"No," he answered. "I can wait until dinner's ready."

"Well, guess what?" she said, looking very pleased. "Your wait is over. Dinner is ready and about to be served."

Good, he thought, blowing out a breath. The sooner it was served, the sooner he could leave.

Chapter Nine

Miranda waited for what she felt was a decent interval but the silence continued to stretch out as she and Colin sat opposite one another at the small dining room table.

It was giving every indication that it would go on indefinitely. Even Lola remained quiet, sitting under the table close to her feet.

Finally, feeling the need to initiate some sort of a conversation between them, Miranda looked at her incredibly quiet guest and said a single word.

"Well?"

Colin glanced up at her and then back down at the meal he was presently eating. He assumed she wanted him to make some sort of a comment about the dinner she had served.

"Not bad," he told her.

"Coming from you, that's heady praise," Miranda

commented, amused. "But I wasn't asking if you liked the dinner."

"Seemed like it," he answered. And then Colin put down his fork and gave her his full attention. For a supposedly easygoing woman, she certainly didn't make things easy, he thought. "Then what *were* you asking?"

"I wasn't asking about anything specially. I was just asking for *something*—anything you might want to talk about. You know, most people make conversation when they eat."

He had no interest in what "most" people did. "I usually eat alone," he told her.

"It shows," she answered.

Okay, this had gone far enough. He'd let her feel as if she'd paid him back for the debt she'd mistakenly thought she owed him. But now this was over. It was time for him to go.

Putting the napkin on the table, he began getting up to leave. "Look, I—"

Miranda cut into whatever he was about to say and gave in to her curiosity by asking him, "Why'd you become a police officer?"

The question came out of the blue and caught him off guard.

He stared at her for a long moment, trying to make heads or tails of what was happening here. Was she actually asking him that or was there some kind of other motivation at work here?

"Is this an interview?" he asked sarcastically.

"I'm just curious, that's all," Miranda answered. "Being a police officer is all about 'protecting and serving,'" she said, referring to the popular credo. "You don't look all that happy about protecting and you just don't seem like the type who wants to serve."

He would have said the same thing, but life had a strange way of taking twists and turns. "What I am is someone who doesn't want to be analyzed," he told her curtly.

"I'm sorry, I didn't mean to sound like I'm invading your space, I'm just trying to understand you."

Her answer made no sense to him. "Why?" he challenged suspiciously.

"Because I'd like to be friends and friends understand each other."

"Friends?" Colin echoed, stunned as he stared at her. "We're not friends."

"Not yet," Miranda pointed out in her easygoing manner.

"Not ever," Colin corrected sharply.

He was resisting. Well, she hadn't thought this was going to be easy. "Everyone needs a friend," she told him.

He didn't appreciate the fact that she thought she had his number. She didn't. And if she believed that she did, she was way out of her depth.

"I don't," he snapped. Storming to the front door, he yanked it open.

"Yes, you do," she persisted softly.

If he stayed here a second longer, he was going to wind up saying things that he'd regret saying once he calmed down.

So he bit off, "Thanks for dinner," and left, letting the door slam behind him in his wake.

Miranda stood there, looking at the door for a long, long moment.

Maybe she'd pushed too hard. He was a man who needed to be eased into new situations, into accepting that being alone wasn't the answer.

About to turn away from the door, it occurred to her that she hadn't heard the sound of a car starting up—or pulling away, for that matter.

Curious, she opened the door and found herself looking up into the face of a man who was struggling to come to terms with the fact that maybe he had allowed his temper to flare and then spin out of control much too quickly.

Frowning, Colin mumbled, "I forgot to finish my beer."

"I didn't clear the table," she told him, then asked, "Would you like to come back inside?"

He inclined his head and rather than say "yes" he just followed her back into the house.

Still not ready to apologize or say that he shouldn't have just stormed out the way he had, Colin just asked, "Anyone ever tell you you're too pushy?"

Miranda pretended to consider his question as she walked back into the dining room.

"No," she answered. "Not that I know of."

He snorted shortly. "Then you're either not listening, or you're dealing with people who don't want to hurt your feelings."

"But you don't have that problem," she guessed, a smile quirking her lips.

Colin scowled. "My only problem seems to be you."

"I'll work on that," Miranda promised. And then she nodded toward his empty dish. "Would you like some more?" she asked.

"No, just the beer," Colin responded, sitting down again.

But Miranda wasn't finished being his hostess. "I have some ice cream in the freezer if you'd like to have dessert," she offered.

"Just the beer," he repeated.

"Just the beer," Miranda echoed, backing off for the moment. She smiled at him as she sat down again opposite him.

Colin shook his head. He'd just yelled at the woman and she was smiling at him. He just didn't get it. Blowing out an annoyed breath, he sat back and regarded her in silence for a long moment.

Then, still frowning, Colin forced himself to apologize.

"I'm sorry I lost my temper and yelled at you." This was a first for him. He wasn't used to apologizing.

"It's in the past," Miranda told him cheerfully.

He stared at her, trying to make sense out of what she'd just said. "Yeah. Five minutes in the past." Which meant, as far as he was concerned, that it wasn't in the past at all.

But he realized that wasn't the way Miranda obviously looked at things because she said, "Still the past.

And I'm sorry if you felt that I was invading your space. That wasn't my intention."

"Right. I know. You want to be friends," Colin responded, unable to fully cover up the exasperated edge in his voice. It frustrated him that he couldn't figure her out, couldn't get a handle on the woman.

Who talked like that? Or thought like that? Just what was her angle? There was no way all of this was genuine.

"Would that be so bad?" she was asking him. "Being friends?"

He felt like he was trying to get a sticky substance off his hands—and failing miserably no matter how hard he tried.

He tried one more time to make her understand. "Look, lady, we don't have a thing in common," Colin pointed out. "Not a single thing. You seem to see the world as this wonderful, shining place and I see it the way it really is."

"And how's that?" she asked him, wanting to hear what his answer was.

He never hesitated. "A dark place where everyone's out for themselves."

"I'm not," she told him.

He frowned. He had a feeling that she would say that. "Well, maybe you're the exception."

She'd expected him to say that and she was ready with a response. "And maybe there are more exceptions."

"Pretty sure you're the only one."

"What about your Aunt Lily?" she asked Colin pointedly. "Wouldn't you say that she's one?"

He eyed her sharply. "How do you know what my aunt's like?"

"Easy," Miranda answered. "When you asked me why I was speeding and I told you about being late for Lily's birthday, you said that you had an aunt by that name. One look on your face immediately told me you cared a great deal about that aunt."

"So now you're into face reading," Colin said mockingly.

"Not exactly," she corrected him. "You might say that I'm more into reading people."

Colin drained the last of his beer from the can and set it down on the table. He knew if he lingered, he was going to regret it. The woman was getting to him—and nothing good could come of that.

"I've got to get going," he told her, standing up.

Miranda rose to her feet, as well. Following her lead, Lola came to attention.

"Sure I can't talk you into hanging up a few ornaments with me?" Miranda asked. She was fairly certain that she knew his answer, but she wanted to ask just the same.

"Sorry. I'm totally out of practice," he told her as he started walking out of the dining room for a second time that evening. "I'd probably just wind up breaking them."

The way he said it had her drawing conclusions. "You don't have a Christmas tree?" Miranda asked.

"Not for a long, long time," he answered. "Thanks for dinner—and the beer."

She smiled as she walked him to the door. "My pleasure."

He shook his head. By all rights, she should be relieved he was leaving. He hadn't exactly been the kind of guest that a hostess kept asking to come back—and yet she was acting as if she'd enjoyed his company.

"You are incredible," he murmured.

Miranda's smile widened. "If I was incredible, I'd be able to talk you into coming to the hospital ward to visit my kids."

"You just don't give up, do you?" he asked in disbelief.

"What's the point of that?" she said. "If you give up, nothing happens. This way, there's always a chance that it might."

He made no comment on that. Instead, Colin merely shook his head. "There's such a thing as spreading yourself too thin, you know," he told her, trying to get her to be realistic.

There was that smile again, he noted. The one that told him she knew something that he didn't—and was pleased by it.

"Hasn't happened yet," she told him.

"Doesn't mean it's not going to." It was his parting shot.

He had every intention of going straight home. Heaven knew he'd earned it. Spending time with that chipper do-gooder had really tired him out. Hell, it had all but wiped him out, actually.

But it had also started him thinking. Not about Miranda and what was starting to sound like her endless tally of good deeds. What it had gotten him thinking about was the fact that he hadn't been to see his aunt since…well, he wasn't all that sure when the last time had been, exactly.

So rather than going home and having that beer that was waiting for him in his own refrigerator—a beer that would still be waiting when he finally did get home, he reminded himself—Colin rerouted his path and drove over to his aunt's house.

Of course, his aunt might be out, he told himself as he made his way there. But it was the middle of the week and Aunt Lily wasn't exactly the carousing type.

Colin pulled up in her driveway. If it turned out that she wasn't here, well, he'd tried, and according to that Pollyanna who had insisted on making him dinner tonight, trying was what counted.

After parking his car, he got out and walked up to the front door. It could use some paint. Maybe he'd come by and paint it for her over the holidays. He had a lot of time accrued because he usually didn't take any days off. There wasn't anyplace he wanted to go as far as vacations went, and staying home just meant he'd be alone with his thoughts, which was why he'd rather be working.

Colin rang the doorbell and waited.

He'd give it a total of ten minutes, and if Aunt Lily didn't come to the door by then, well, at least he'd—

"Colin?" The small, genteel woman standing in the doorway was looking at him in utter surprise. "Colin, is anything wrong?"

"No. Why would you think something was wrong?"

"Because it's Wednesday," she said. "I mean, because it's the middle of the week and you never come by in the middle of the week."

"Yeah, well, I don't really come by much at all," Colin admitted, feeling somewhat guilty about that. Especially since Aunt Lily never complained that she didn't see him.

"I know," she responded. Then, obviously realizing how that had to sound, she amended by saying, "I mean…" Reaching up, she touched his face lovingly. "You're sure nothing's wrong?"

"I'm sure." He laughed, shaking his head. "The only thing that's wrong is that I haven't been by much to see you."

"I understand, sweetheart. You've been busy," Lily told him. Wielding guilt had never been her way. Tucking her arm through his, she gave in to the sheer pleasure of seeing him. "Come in, come in. Have you eaten?" Not waiting for an answer, she offered, "Can I fix you something?"

"I already had dinner, Aunt Lily," he told her.

She closed the door behind him and then turned to look at her nephew.

"Today? You had something to eat today?" she questioned, then went on to say, "You look so thin."

"The department doesn't like to see fat motorcycle cops, Aunt Lily. It's hard on the bikes."

Lily shook her head. "It's a wonder they can see you at all. Are you *sure* I can't get you something to eat?"

In her own way, his aunt was as persistent as that

do-gooder was. "How about coffee?" he said. "I'll take some coffee."

"How about some banana cream pie?" Lily offered, preceding him to the kitchen. "You used to love banana cream pie when you were a little boy," she recalled.

He knew she wouldn't stop until he agreed to have something, and obviously coffee wasn't going to cut it. "Okay, I'll have a piece of pie. But I really just came by to see how you were."

Lily smiled. "I'm wonderful now that my favorite nephew's stopped by."

"I'm your only nephew, Aunt Lily," he reminded her, amused.

"That makes this that much more special.," She gave him one final penetrating look. "You're absolutely certain nothing's wrong?"

"Absolutely," he assured her.

"All right, then come to the kitchen and let's have some of that pie," she told him, hooking her arm through his again. Smiling up at his face, she said, "I've been dying for an excuse to have some—and this is certainly it."

"Glad to help," Colin told her.

Lily merely smiled.

Chapter Ten

Colin realized that he was more on edge and alert than usual. That was because he kept looking around for Miranda to pop up. He told himself that he *didn't* want to run into her. If he saw her coming, he could avoid her.

So he remained vigilant, expecting the woman to materialize somewhere along his usual route, the way she had the day she'd waylaid him about that little girl's missing mother.

He didn't drop his guard when he walked into the precinct, since she'd turned up there, as well.

But she didn't turn up there, nor did she track him down along his route. Not that day, nor the next day. Nor the day after that.

When the third day passed, he told himself he should feel relieved. That maybe "the curse" had been lifted.

But he didn't feel relieved. Instead, he had this uneasy, growing feeling of impending doom. He sensed that the second he let his guard down, Miranda would strike again.

The odd thing was that he felt edgier when she wasn't around than when she was and he was interacting with her.

So after the third Pollyanna-free day came and went, he began to think that something was wrong. Rather than leave well enough alone, he found himself needing answers in order to gain some sort of peace of mind— or a reasonable facsimile thereof.

Maybe she hadn't been around because Lily's mother had taken a turn for the worse. Or possibly that German shepherd Miranda had brought home with her—Lulu or Lola or something like that—had turned on her. It had been known to happen.

Not all German shepherds took after Rin Tin Tin, although Colin was still annoyed with himself for not just being grateful that she wasn't around, but actually seeking her out.

He refused to examine what he was doing, because if he had, he would have labeled himself as certifiably insane. What else would you call willingly leaping out of the frying pan into the fire?

As if in self-defense, he jabbed the doorbell before he could think better of it, get into his car and drive away as if the very devil was after him.

Run, you idiot! Get out of here before it's too late!
But he didn't.

He heard barking in the background the second he pressed the doorbell. Either that canine Miranda had brought home had turned into a guard dog, or she was trying to get his attention because something had happened to her mistress.

Damn it, what the hell was wrong with him? Colin wondered. He didn't *think* this way.

Calling himself a few choice names, he turned on his heel and began to walk away.

"Colin?"

Miranda had the same surprised note in her voice that he'd heard in his aunt Lily's when he'd showed up at her place.

Apparently nobody expected him just to drop in. So why was he doing it?

"Yeah." Colin answered almost grudgingly, half turning toward her. "I just wanted to make sure everything was all right—with Lily's mother," he added belatedly, not wanting Miranda to think that he was here checking up on her.

Knowing the perverse way the woman's mind worked, he'd never hear the end of it if she thought that.

Miranda's surprise gave way to a welcoming smile. "She's doing fine, thanks to you," she told him. She opened the door farther. "Why don't you come on in? Lola would love to see you," she added, glancing over her shoulder to the German shepherd, who was fairly leaping from paw to paw.

As if she knew that she had temporarily taken center stage, the dog barked at him.

Miranda laughed, then told her visitor, "And I've got some more beer in the refrigerator."

When he still made no move to come in, she took

hold of his arm and coaxingly pulled him across the threshold.

He should have made his getaway when he had a chance, Colin thought, allowing himself to be drawn in.

And then he thought of her offer. "Do you even drink beer?" he asked.

"No."

Okay, like everything else that had to do with her, that made no sense. "Then why do you have it in your refrigerator?"

That was easy to explain. She released him. "A few of the women I work with at the hospital and the animal shelter stop by on occasion. I keep the beer on hand for them."

Again Colin told himself he'd made a mistake in coming here. "I can't stay—" he began.

Miranda felt that maybe he needed to be coaxed a little more. "Well, you came all the way over here, so surely you can stay for one beer."

"It's not that far from your place to mine," he protested. His point was that he hadn't gone out of his way all that much—but he realized his mistake the moment the words were out of his mouth. He'd inadvertently given her too much information.

Her next words confirmed it.

"So you do live in Bedford." Not all members of the police department did. "What neighborhood?"

He was not about to compound his mistake. "There are stalking laws on the books, you know."

There was a knowing, amused smile on her lips.

"You're the one who showed up on my doorstep, and at the animal shelter before that," she pointed out.

He was immediately defensive. "Are you saying you think I'm the stalker?"

"I'm just saying it's only fair that I know where you live, since you know where I live." With a wink, she added, "Not everything has a hidden agenda. Sit," she told him. "I'll go get that beer."

When she walked back in, she saw that he was still on his feet and was looking at the Christmas tree.

"Haven't gotten very far decorating it, have you?" he commented.

Miranda handed him the cold can of beer. "Like I said, I only get to hang up a few ornaments every night. I can't seem to convince Lola to hang up any while I'm out." When his eyes narrowed and he looked at her, puzzled, she told him, "That's a joke."

"I never know with you," he admitted drolly.

She would have loved to just sit down beside him and talk, but she had a feeling he might think she was crowding him. It would seem more natural to him if she worked on the tree, so she asked, "Would you mind if I put up some decorations while you're here?"

Colin waved a careless hand. "Don't let me keep you." As Miranda got back to hanging up the ornaments, he took a long pull from the can. Lola had plopped herself next to his feet and looked up at him. The scene was far too domestic for him.

And yet...

"You decided to keep the dog?" he asked, assuming that was why the animal was still here.

"Well, at least until after Christmas," Miranda answered. Arming herself with several decorations, she moved around the tree, seeking out empty spaces. "Everyone who comes to the shelter at this time of year is looking for a cute little dog to give to their kids." She glanced over at the German shepherd and said fondly, "Lola's cute, but she definitely isn't little."

He laughed drily. "That's an understatement." He studied the animal. "She's got to be the biggest female German shepherd I've ever seen. I thought they were supposed to be a little smaller than this."

"Obviously Lola hasn't read the German shepherd handbook," Miranda quipped, stretching to hang up a long silver bell. "But what she lacks in daintiness she makes up for with friendliness. I've been working at the animal shelter for a couple of years now and she's got to be the most docile dog I've ever encountered." Picking up a few more ornaments, she searched for more empty spaces she could reach. "Most dogs freak out when they see a vacuum cleaner, much less when they hear one being operated. Lola, bless her, is completely indifferent to it. I could probably vacuum Lola and it wouldn't faze her in the slightest."

The dog wasn't all that easygoing, he thought. "I heard her barking when I rang the doorbell."

"That's because when she thinks someone is trying to come in, she instantly gets into her protective mode. She's being protective of me," Miranda explained, her voice coming from behind the tree. "Once she sees that I'm okay with you, she's fine."

Colin remained on the sofa, sipping his beer and absently petting the dog as he watched Miranda circling the Christmas tree, hanging up ornaments whenever she found a space.

"Damn," he heard her murmur under her breath. She'd worked her way back to the point where she'd started.

"What's the matter?"

She sighed. "I'm going to have to bring out a ladder from the garage to hang up any more of the ornaments tonight. The tree's beginning to look kind of bottom heavy and I can't reach the higher branches," she explained.

She was doing it again, he thought. Roping him into helping. If he had half a brain, he'd just ignore her.

Sighing, Colin stood up. Leaving his beer on the coffee table, he crossed to her. "Where do you want to hang that?" he asked, nodding at the decoration in her hand.

"Higher than I can reach," she answered.

Taking the decoration from her, he reached up to the branch that she'd obviously targeted and easily hung the ornament on it.

"That looks very nice," she told him, somewhat surprised that he had willingly volunteered to help.

"I wasn't exactly performing brain surgery."

"No," she agreed. "You were performing a service." And then she grinned as she held out another ornament. "You up for another one?"

"Yeah, sure. Why not," he said carelessly, taking the decoration from her and hanging it on the next branch over. Turning to face her, he saw the huge smile on

Miranda's face. "You're grinning like a little kid," he pointed out.

"Why shouldn't I?" she asked. "I've just witnessed a Christmas miracle."

Colin snorted. "Let's not get carried away here."

Her smile only grew; he didn't think that was possible, but it obviously was.

"Getting carried away is fun," she told him. "You should try it sometime."

The thought of doing just that—of getting carried away—popped into his head out of nowhere. It had nothing to do with hanging up decorations or anything even remotely along those lines. In his case getting carried away involved the sudden desire to find out what those smiling lips tasted like.

The thought zipped through his brain like a lightning bolt, daring him to follow through.

Okay, time to go, Colin thought sternly. He didn't know where that thought had come from, but he wasn't about to stick around and risk acting on it.

Turning his back on the tree and the miscellaneous ornaments that still needed to be hung up, he said, "Thanks for the beer—again."

Miranda looked at him in surprise. "You're leaving?"

"Yeah, I shouldn't have stayed this long," he told her. "I just wanted to find out how the kid's mother was doing."

They both knew that was just an excuse, but Miranda nodded as if she wholeheartedly believed what he was saying.

"Thanks for coming by," she said, walking alongside him to the door.

Colin stopped in his tracks. He didn't need an escort. Putting space between himself and the woman was the whole point of his leaving.

"I know my way out," he protested.

"I know that," Miranda answered.

Her tone of voice was friendly but firm, as if to let him know that she *wanted* to walk him to the door and wasn't about to be talked out of it.

As they approached the front door, Miranda began to broach another subject. "Since you're being in such a generous mood…"

Instantly on his guard, Colin looked at her warily. The woman seemed to know just how to get to him. He *knew* coming here had been a mistake on his part.

"Yeah?"

"The kids at the hospital would still love to see you," she told him.

"You just never give up, do you?"

Rather than be insulted or put off by his sharp tone and his question, she smiled as if she'd thought over what he'd asked. "What's the fun in that?"

He scowled. Maybe she thought of this as fun, but he certainly didn't.

He answered her seriously—and hopefully, once and for all. "I can't come to the hospital. We work the same hours."

"That's okay, I'll wait," she answered breezily. "Just tell me what time you can get there."

"Not until my shift is over," he snapped. "By then

you're on your way to one or the other of those two shelters where you volunteer." And that was that.

The next moment, he realized that he really should have known better.

"You know, the good thing about volunteering," Miranda told him cheerfully, "is that it's extremely flexible. There are no hard-and-fast hours for me to maintain."

Colin read between the lines. "I can't get out of this easily, can I?"

"You can." She certainly couldn't force him to come to the hospital. If nothing else, the man was a lot bigger than she was. "But between you and me, I don't think you really want to."

"So you've added mind reading to your list of talents, is that it?" he asked.

"No, no mind reading," she answered. "But as I said before, I can read people pretty well, and despite your bluster and your 'Big Bad Wolf' attitude, I think you're a good guy under all that."

Colin laughed wryly. "I guess it's a good thing you're not trying to earn your money as a mind reader. You'd wind up starving to death."

Her eyes met his—and then she gave him that soul-melting smile of hers. "So then it's a yes?" she asked innocently.

Every fiber of his being was geared up to shout "no" at her, that he wasn't about to be corralled or bullied into agreeing to turn up at a hospital ward like some sort of living, breathing show-and-tell object. He had absolutely nothing to say to one kid, much less an entire ward full of them.

But she was looking up at him with those eyes of hers, those eyes that despite all his attempts to shut them out seemed to get past all his safeguards and burrow right into him, giving him no peace.

"We'll see," he finally growled.

Miranda caught her lower lip between her teeth as if debating what to say next. "So that's a yes?" she asked again.

"No," Colin corrected, holding his ground. "That's a 'we'll see.'"

"Almost as good," she told him with more enthusiasm than he felt the phrase merited. The woman was incredible. She found optimism where absolutely none existed.

The next moment, she joyfully told him, "Thank you!"

With one hand on his arm to steady herself, Miranda rose up on her toes to kiss his cheek in gratitude.

That was the exact moment he turned his head to tell her that he hadn't done anything yet and most likely would not.

He never got the chance to say it, because when he turned his head, her lips made direct contact with *his*.

And just like that, an unexpected, harmless kiss on the cheek turned into something else.

It turned into an actual kiss, and what had started out as fleeting evolved into a great deal more.

Surprised, Miranda began to pull back, but then

paused as their contact blossomed into something far more intense than just a kiss between friends.

Before she knew it, Miranda had her arms around his neck and he had his wrapped around her waist, drawing her closer as the kiss deepened.

He was making her breathless, which in turn was making her head spin.

What was going on here?

And how did she get it to continue?

Chapter Eleven

Colin had no idea what came over him. He had never been one of those men who would size up a woman, biding his time until he could seduce her. It wasn't that he was immune to attractive women. He just felt maintaining any sort of a relationship with one was too complicated, and one-night stands could prove to be troublesome.

He found it easier just to steer clear.

But there was something incredibly compelling about this particular woman that just reeled him in. There was no other explanation as to why he'd sought her out tonight when he didn't have to.

And why else was he even considering showing up at that hospital ward of hers? He'd never thought of himself as someone to take up causes or go that extra mile. Yes, he'd been in the Marines, and yes, he'd become a police officer, but neither had come about out of some compulsive need to help his fellow man. He'd joined the Marines and later the police force because it just seemed like the thing to do at the time. The situations suited him; it was as simple as that.

But although Miranda Steele presented herself as straightforward, there was nothing simple about this woman. And right now, he had an uneasy feeling he was in way over his head. Though he wasn't someone who was ruled by desire, Colin had a feeling there would be no turning back for him if he stayed here a minute longer. And he wasn't all that certain that the road ahead was one he should be venturing onto.

The sound of Lola barking in the background was what finally broke apart the moment—and forced him back to his senses.

Taking a step away from her, he looked at Miranda. Her lipstick was blurred from the imprint of his lips and she looked as dazed as he felt.

He was shaken up inside and it was a struggle not to show it. "Did you do that so that I'd come down to your children's ward?"

That hurt, Miranda thought. Did he really believe she was that kind of person? The kind who physically manipulated people?

"No," she answered, her voice low as she tried to collect herself. "I was just trying to kiss your cheek. *You* were the one who turned his head."

His expression remained stoic and unyielding. "So you're not trying to seduce me into seeing things your way?"

"No, I'm not," Miranda cried, stunned. The moment had shattered and what had seemed so wonderful a second ago no longer was. "Forget I asked you," she told him stiffly.

Damn it, those were tears filling her eyes. He hadn't meant for any of that to happen. He wasn't accustomed to dealing with a woman who didn't have some ulterior motive—except for his aunt.

Hell, he wasn't really used to dealing with women at all, Colin thought, feeling helpless and annoyed at the same time.

Unable to find the right words to express his regret for having hurt her, he marched to the front door, opened it and stepped outside.

He heard the door close behind him. Heard the lock being flipped into place. For just a split second, he considered turning around and knocking on the panel, to apologize.

But words didn't come to him now any more than they had before.

If he tried to say anything, he'd only make things worse, he knew. Communication was not his forte, so instead he walked away.

Numb, confused, Miranda wiped away the tears sliding down her cheeks with the back of her hand. She wasn't all that sure what had just happened here. All she knew was that Colin had taken off like a man who had been ambushed and then suddenly given the chance for a clean getaway.

She heard a car starting up and then taking off.

His car.

She didn't understand. He had given off mixed signals. Why had he bothered coming over in the first place?

Turning away from the door, she sighed. "I really do wish I was a mind reader, Colin. Then maybe I could understand what's going on here."

She realized that she was absently running her fingertips along her lips. She could almost swear she could still feel his lips against hers.

Taste his lips against hers.

She closed her eyes for a moment, trying to focus her brain. She'd never been the type to let a guy throw her, or mess with her mind. But she'd never *felt* what she had felt this evening when he'd kissed her.

"C'mon, Miranda, this isn't like you. Get a grip." Opening her eyes, she saw that Lola was looking at her as if she understood what was going on here.

"You're right, Lola. I don't have time to waste like this. We have a tree to decorate and we don't need anybody's help, right, girl?"

Lola yipped, making her laugh.

"Of course right. So let's get started. I'll hang, you supervise. Deal?"

Lola barked again.

"Deal," Miranda agreed, grinning.

With that, she went to the garage to get the ladder she was going to need in order to reach the higher branches.

Colin did his best to talk himself out of it and he succeeded.

For a day.

But the following day, he did something he had never done before. He called in and told his sergeant that he was taking half of one of his many accumulated vacation days.

The man sounded rather surprised. "Just a half day?"

"That's all," Colin answered.

If he took the whole day, he knew he'd wind up getting roped into spending the entire time visiting sick kids—kids who didn't have the odds in their favor. He didn't like admitting that he wasn't strong enough to face something like that for more than a short amount of time.

It was obvious that Miranda was made of stronger stuff than he was, which was why he was going to the oncology ward as she'd wanted him to. He owed her an apology for the way he'd behaved the other night, and this was the only way he knew how to apologize.

He was probably going to regret this, Colin thought, not for the first time. But if nothing else, he was a man who always paid his debts. It was part of his code.

Miranda peered into one of the few private rooms that were located on the floor. Jason Greeley still appeared to be asleep. His mom had been here with the little boy all night. But the single mother had to go to work, so had left an hour ago. Since then Miranda had been checking on the five-year-old every few minutes. She didn't want him waking up by himself.

Moving closer to the boy, she adjusted his covers. "You usually don't sleep this long after a treatment, Jason," she said, deliberately sounding cheerful. Cheer begot cheer, in her opinion. "Don't turn lazy on me now. Your mama was here all night. She hates leaving you, but she had to go to work. But don't worry, she'll be back soon. And I'll be here all day until she gets here," Miranda promised.

The boy stirred a little, but didn't open his eyes. His even breathing told her that he was still sleeping.

Miranda went on talking as if he could hear every word she said. "I've got cherry Jell-O waiting for you the second you open your eyes. You told me that was your favorite, so I made sure there's plenty. All you have to do to get some is open your eyes. C'mon, baby, it's not that hard."

When he didn't, Miranda sighed. "Okay, play hard to get. But you're going to have to open them sometime. No sense in letting all that cherry Jell-O go to waste, you know."

"How do you do it? How do you deal with this without falling apart?"

Startled, pressing one hand against her chest to contain the heart that had all but leaped out, nearly cracking her rib cage, she swung around to see Colin, all 6'2" and broad-shouldered, standing just inside the room. He was wearing his police uniform.

It took her a second to find her voice. "What are you doing here?"

"I was in the neighborhood and thought I'd drop by," he quipped. And then his voice lowered. "Besides, I figured after the other evening, I kind of owed it to you."

She wasn't sure if he was referring to the kiss they'd shared or his walking out on her, but felt it best not to pursue the question. He was here, and right now, that was all that mattered.

"You don't owe me anything," she told him. "But these kids will get a big kick out of seeing a real police officer." And then she glanced at her watch. It was early. "Speaking of which, aren't you supposed to be out there, handing out tickets right now?"

"I took half a vacation day." He expected her to ask him why he hadn't taken a full day, followed by a whole bunch of other questions. Instead she just smiled at him, looking pleased.

"That's great," she enthused. "But if you're only here for a little while, we'll have to make the most of it."

He wasn't sure exactly what she had in mind, but he'd come to expect the unexpected with Miranda. "And exactly how are we going to do that?"

Her mind was already racing. "We've got a big recreation room where the kids play games and where we hold their birthday parties. Right now, it's where we put up the ward's Christmas tree."

"But all the kids aren't—"

She knew what he was going to say—that there were more holidays than just Christmas this season. She answered his question before he had a chance to voice it. "That's all right. All kids like bright lights and presents. It helps to cheer them up a little."

"And feel normal?" he guessed. That had to be what she was shooting for.

"They *are* normal," Miranda told him calmly. She had to make him understand. "They just have more than their share of health issues, but you'd be surprised how they bear up to that. It makes me ashamed when I let everyday, mundane problems overwhelm me."

"You? Overwhelmed?" he asked, teasing her. "I don't believe it. Joan of Arc would probably see you as a role model."

That was his idea of a joke, she realized. Her smile widened.

"Mama?" Jason opened his eyes and looked around the room, disoriented, obviously expecting to see his mother there instead of his nurse and a strange policeman.

"Hey, I didn't mean to wake him up." Colin looked contrite as he addressed Miranda. "I'm sorry," he murmured.

She put her hand on his arm to keep him from leaving. "No, this is a good thing," she assured him. "We were waiting for him to wake up." She turned her attention back to the boy. "Jason, guess what? Remember that police officer I told you about?"

"The one who wouldn't give you a ticket," Jason answered. "I remember."

"That's right, he didn't give me a ticket," she repeated, raising her eyes to Colin's for a moment before shifting them back to the boy. Colin looked surprised. "Well, this is him—and he's here to visit," Miranda announced.

"Cool," the little boy said, with as much enthusiasm as he was able to muster, given that he was still trying to come around. Shifting in his bed, he looked to Miranda for help. "I want to sit up."

Colin was about to press a button on the remote con-

trol attached to the guardrail on the boy's bed when he
saw Miranda slowly shake her head at him.

"You remember what to do, Jason," she prompted.
"We practiced."

"Oh yeah." Small fingers pulled the remote a little
closer and then pushed one of the arrows. The back of
his bed began to rise. He beamed, looking very proud
of himself. "I got it right."

"Of course you did." She tousled his hair affectionately. "That's because you're such a smart boy."

Jason's chocolate brown eyes shifted to look at the
policeman who had come to visit him. "Is that a real
badge?" he asked, pointing toward Colin's chest.

He glanced down and nodded. "It sure is."

Jason looked at him hopefully. "Is it okay if I touch
it?"

Colin came closer and leaned over the boy's bed.
"Go ahead."

Small fingers reached out and very slowly and rev-
erently traced the outline of the badge.

"Wow," Jason murmured. "When I grow up, I'm
gonna be a police officer just like you."

No one had ever said anything like that to him
before—since he didn't interact with children—
and Colin found himself truly moved, more than he
thought possible. Especially since the boy was talking
so positively about a future he might not live to see.

"And you'll be a really great police officer. Maybe
even a police detective, if you study very hard," Miranda told the little boy. She could see that Colin had
been affected. It wasn't that she wasn't as moved as

Colin. She had just learned to handle her own onslaught of emotions so they wouldn't get in the way of her being the best possible nurse she could be for the sake of the children.

"I'll study *real* hard," Jason promised. He sounded sleepy. And then he yawned. "I'm tired, Miranda."

"Well, then I suggest you'd better get some sleep," she coaxed.

It was obvious that he was trying not to let his eyes close. "But then I'll miss seeing Officer Colin," the boy protested.

"Tell you what," Colin said. "I'll come by again and see you before I leave."

"And will you be back tomorrow, too?" the little boy asked. It was clear that he was losing his battle to keep his eyes open.

"Not tomorrow," Colin answered honestly. "But I'll come back soon."

"Promise?" Jason asked sleepily.

"I promise," Colin told him, saying the words as solemnly as if he were talking to an adult.

But the boy was already asleep again.

Miranda moved the covers up higher on Jason's small body. "That was very nice of you," she told Colin with genuine warmth.

He shrugged. "I didn't do anything out of the ordinary."

"Jason might argue with you about that—if he could argue," she added, looking at the boy with affection. She glanced at her watch. "C'mon, we need to spread that charm of yours around before your coach turns into a pumpkin."

Colin shook his head, mystified. "I never understand half of what you're talking about."

Miranda laughed. "You might just be better off that way."

He inclined his head in agreement. "I was thinking the same thing."

But Miranda didn't hear him. She was on her smartphone, busy summoning the other nurses.

Chapter Twelve

In less than three minutes after Miranda finished making her call, the hallway outside Jason's room was alive with activity.

As Colin looked on in amazement, nurses and orderlies pushed children in wheelchairs and patiently guided others who were using walkers, crutches or braving the way to the recreational room on their own under the watchful eye of an aide or a parent.

To Colin, it looked as if an organized mass evacuation was having a dry run. The whole thing seemed incredible to him, given the average age of the children. However, rather than leaving the building, everyone was going to the large recreation room that currently held the Christmas tree.

Glancing back, Miranda realized that the "guest of honor" directly responsible for this mass migration was still standing just outside Jason's doorway. Determined to change that, she took Colin's hand in hers.

"C'mon," she coaxed.

The expression on his face was rather uncertain as he took in the masses. "That's an awful lot of kids," he told her.

She gently tugged on his hand. "They don't bite," she said cheerfully. "And having them all together in one place means you won't have to repeat yourself. You can say things just once."

The uncertain expression deepened. "What things?"

Miranda had nothing specific to offer, but she was confident that issue would be resolved naturally.

"It'll come to you," she promised. "And the kids'll probably drown you in questions once they get started. C'mon," she coaxed again, drawing him down the hall-way. "You're not afraid of a bunch of little kids."

She said it as if she believed it, Colin thought. And it wasn't the kids he was afraid of; he was afraid of in-advertently saying something that might wind up hurt-ing one of them.

But now that she had started this parade of hospi-talized children, like some sort of modern-day Pied Piper, he couldn't very well hang back and watch from the sidelines. The sidelines had virtually disappeared in any case, as Colin found himself surrounded on all sides by children streaming into the rec room.

"Kids," Miranda said in a slightly louder voice, when the commotion had died down and the children had all settled in. "This is my friend Officer Kirby. When I told him that some of you had never met a policeman or seen one up close before, he insisted on coming by to say hello." Turning to look at Colin over her shoulder, she grinned at him and said, "Say hello, Officer Kirby."

On the spot and feeling decidedly awkward, Colin murmured, "Hello."

The moment he did, a cacophony of "Hellos," mostly out of sync, echoed back at him.

Pattie, a little girl with curly red hair seated in a wheelchair in the front row, was the first to speak up. "Are you really a policeman?" she asked.

"Yes." And then, doing his best not to sound so wooden, Colin added, "I am."

The two extra words seemed to open up the floodgates. Suddenly he heard questions coming at him from all directions.

"Do you have a gun?" one boy in the back asked.

"Do you shoot people?" a boy beside him added.

"How many bad guys have you caught?" a little blonde girl ventured, while a smaller girl with almost violet eyes shyly asked him if he was "a good cop."

Taking pity on him, Miranda spoke up, hoping that the piece of information she told them would somehow help the children to get a better image of the kind of police work he did. "Officer Kirby rides a motorcycle."

A dark-haired boy with crutches beside his chair cried, "Cool!"

A little girl to Colin's left asked, "Can you do a wheelie?"

"Did you ever fall off your motorcycle?" one little boy wearing a brace asked. "I fell off my bicycle once and broke my neck bone."

"Your collarbone," Miranda corrected gently.

"Oh yeah, my collarbone," he amended. He was still waiting for an answer. "Did you ever fall off?" he asked again.

"No," Colin answered. "I never have."

"Did it take you a long time to learn how to ride your motorcycle?" a little girl sitting near the Christmas tree asked.

As he began fielding the questions a little more comfortably, more and more came his way. Before he knew it, Colin found himself immersed in a give-and-take dialogue with approximately twenty-five children of varying ages, confined to the hospital ward for a number of different reasons.

He was surprised, given the relative seriousness of their conditions, how eager the children all seemed to hear about his job and what he did on his patrols.

Some asked run-of-the-mill questions, like how long it had taken him to become a police officer. Others wanted to know what he thought about while he was out on patrol. Still others asked totally unrelated questions.

The queries came one after another, some voiced eagerly, others shyly, but there were no awkward silences. Everyone had questions, usually more than one. Or two.

Pleased, Miranda stood back, happy to see the children so caught up in their visitor. She kept a watchful eye on Colin, as well, ready to step in if it got to be too much for him. But as the minutes went by, she was fairly certain that he was doing fine. He didn't need her to bail him out.

When the motorcycle officer answered a little girl

named Shelly's question if he'd ever had a pet hamster—
he hadn't—Miranda finally decided he'd had enough
for one day and stepped in.

"I'm afraid Officer Kirby is going to have to be
going," she told the children. The news was met with
youthful voices melding in a mournful "Oh," tinged
with surprise as well as disappointment.

"Can he come back?" the girl with the curly red hair,
Pattie, asked. Then, not waiting for Miranda to reply,
she took her question straight to the horse's mouth. "Can
you, Officer Kirby?"

"If I get the chance," Colin answered diplomatically.

Progress, Miranda thought. She'd expected him to
make an excuse outright. The fact that he hadn't, that
he'd said something half hopeful in response, made her
feel that he was beginning to come around and see the
light.

He was starting to see the children as people.

"When?" A persistent little boy wearing a wool cap
over his bare head looked at his new hero hopefully.

"When his sergeant can spare him again," Miranda
told the child, grasping at the first handy excuse that
came to her. The look in Colin's eyes when their glances
met assured her she'd come up with a good one. "Now,
everybody, say goodbye to Officer Kirby."

A swell of voices, more enthusiastic since the kids
had gotten to spend some time with him, chorused
loudly, "Goodbye, Officer Kirby," while others added,
"Come back soon!"

Putting her hand on Colin's elbow, Miranda took
control of the situation. She gently guided him out of

the room. They swung by Jason's room and he spent a little time there.

After that, Miranda walked him to the elevators.

"Well, you survived," she observed happily, offering him a pleased smile.

"I guess I did, didn't I?" There was no missing the relief, as well as the surprise, in his voice. Colin paused, looking back over his shoulder in the general direction of the rec room. "Are all those kids…you know…?"

Somehow, even though he'd spent more than an hour talking with them, Colin couldn't get himself to say the word. Saying it made it that much more of an evil reality.

Miranda seemed to know exactly what he was trying to ask her. If the children were terminal.

"Treatments have greatly improved over the last five years. A lot of those kids have more of a fighting chance to beat the odds and get well, or at least have their diseases go into remission. Meanwhile, every day they have is special to them, and we all have to make the most of it.

"They really enjoyed having you come," Miranda went on. "Thank you for letting me bully you into coming to the hospital to talk to them."

"Is that what you call it?" he asked, amusement curving his mouth. "Bullying?"

"No," she admitted honestly, raising her eyes to his. "I don't. But that's what I figure you'd call it, so I thought I'd put it into terms that you could relate to more easily."

Her eyes were at it again, he thought. Doing that funny little laughing, twinkly thing that captivated him.

The elevator arrived and he put his hand against one of the doors to keep it from closing. He searched for words to answer her and finally said, "Maybe I'll let you bully me into it again soon."

There was no other way to describe it but to say that he saw joy leap into her face. "Just say the word," she told him.

Doing his best not to stare, Colin nodded. "Maybe I will," he said.

Stepping inside the elevator, he dropped his hand. Her smile was the last thing he saw before the doors shut.

During the remainder of the day, after he returned to the precinct and went on duty, Colin tried to tell himself that the heat he was experiencing radiating through his chest and his gut was nothing more than a case of heartburn. But he had a strong suspicion that even if he consumed an entire bottle of antacid tablets, that wouldn't have any effect on the warmth that was pervading him.

He should have been annoyed. That pushy woman had invaded his world and messed with his routine. She'd completely messed up the natural order of things.

But somehow, try as he might, he couldn't drum up the slightest bit of irritation. To make matters worse, he caught himself thinking about her.

A lot.

Thinking about her and wondering if he wasn't inadvertently sealing his own doom if he just happened to stop by her place and see her again sometime in the near future.

Like tonight.

Telling himself that it was the holiday season and that everyone was guilty of experiencing some sort of generosity of spirit—why try to be different?—he didn't go home after his shift was over. Instead, he hung around the precinct for a while, killing time by catching up on the paperwork that was the bane of every police officer's existence.

And when he was finished and he'd made sure to file all the reports before leaving, Colin decided to play the odds. For this to work out, Miranda needed to be home instead of one of the two places she volunteered.

He had less than a fifty-fifty chance of finding her there, but he went and picked up a pizza anyway.

With the tantalizing aroma from the pizza box filling the interior of his vehicle, Colin made one more quick stop, at a pet store that was along the way, and then drove on to his final destination, Miranda's house.

He wasn't aware of holding his breath that last half mile until he found himself releasing it.

Her car was parked in the driveway.

Apparently, Miranda was done doing good deeds for the day, Colin thought happily as he parked his vehicle at the curb and got out.

When he passed her car on the way to her front door, he felt heat coming from her engine.

She must have gotten home just minutes ago, he thought with a faint smile.

Juggling the extra-large pizza, Colin rang the doorbell. Inside, Lola instantly began barking. The familiar sound was oddly comforting, though he couldn't begin to explain why. He was afraid that if he thought about it too much, he'd turn right around and go home. Coming here like this carried many implications, and he wasn't sure he was ready to face them.

The best way to deal with those implications at the moment was just to ignore them. Ignore them and focus on the hungry feeling in the pit of his stomach. The one that involved not having eaten.

When Miranda opened the door she was obviously more than a little surprised to see him.

"Hi, what's up?"

"Um, I thought that since you made me dinner that other time, I should reciprocate." Rather than continue—because he felt himself about to trip over his tongue—he held up the cardboard box. "Pizza," he added needlessly, since the aroma—as well as the shape and the label—clearly gave away what he had brought.

"You made me a pizza?" Miranda asked, amused.

Her question threw him for a second. "What? No. I picked this up on the way over here. I guarantee you wouldn't want to eat any pizza that I made," he told her with a self-deprecating laugh.

"Oh, it couldn't be all that bad," she stated, ushering Colin in and then closing the door behind him.

Lola came bounding over the moment he walked in. The animal's attention was totally focused on him and, more specifically, the aromatic box he was carrying.

Miranda caught the dog's collar to keep the German shepherd from knocking Colin over. "She's happy to see you."

Colin harbored no such illusions. "She smells the pizza," he said.

"And you," Miranda added. "Dogs have incredibly keen senses of smell—and they can separate one thing from another. The pizza's the draw," she agreed. "But Lola clearly *likes* you."

Colin made no acknowledgment of that statement one way or the other. Instead, he took a small paper bag out of his jacket pocket. The sack had the insignia of a local pet store chain embossed on it. Thinking ahead, he had stopped to pick up several doggie treats before coming by. At the very least, he'd wanted to be able to distract the dog for a few minutes so that he and Miranda could have their pizza in peace.

"I brought these for her," he announced, passing the bag of treats to Miranda.

Opening it, she looked inside and then smiled broadly at him.

"I think that before the evening is over, Lola is going to be madly in love with you."

Lola had begun to nudge the paper bag with her nose before Miranda finished her sentence.

"I was just hoping to distract her long enough for us to eat the pizza," Colin explained.

Miranda laughed. "In that case, you should have bought out the entire pet shop. Have you ever watched a dog eat? It's like watching a furry vacuum cleaner. The treats'll be gone before we have a chance to sit down.

"But that's okay," she assured Colin. "I've been

working with her and she's getting to be a little more well behaved than she was." Her grin widened as she added, "We might even get to eat an entire slice apiece before she starts begging for a bite—or ten. The trick," Miranda told him with a wink, "is not to give in."

Easier said than done, Colin thought. The dog was already looking up at her with soulful eyes.

Chapter Thirteen

"I see you finished decorating your Christmas tree," Colin commented as he followed her into the kitchen.

Miranda nodded cheerfully. "Yes, finally. All those boxes and ornaments were starting to make the living room a real obstacle course, not to mention pretty messy. So I made up my mind that I wasn't going to go to bed until I had hung the last ornament on the tree.

"The next day I happily put all the boxes away." She looked down at the dog, who was eyeing the pizza box as if expecting to see slices come leaping out. "This way Lola has a little more room to move around, don't you, girl?"

"She doesn't strike me as the type to be put off by a bunch of boxes," he observed. "I can see her plowing through them."

"She kind of does plow through things when she wants to get somewhere," Miranda agreed.

He set down the pizza box and watched her take a couple plates from the cupboard. She placed them on either side of the box. "I thought you said she was becoming more obedient."

"I said we were *working* on it," she corrected. "Right now," Miranda told him, patting the German shepherd's head, "she's a work in progress."

There was no missing the affection in the woman's voice. "You seem kind of attached to her," Colin observed.

"It's hard not to be." Taking out a bottle of beer, she set it next to Colin's plate. "She's very affectionate and lovable." She saw the confused way Colin was looking at the beer. "I just replaced the can you drank the other day," she explained.

"Uh-huh," he responded, taking her explanation at face value. He waited for her to sit down opposite him. "What are you going to do when someone adopts her?" he asked.

"Be happy for her," she answered.

Her response sounded rather automatic to him. Miranda probably meant that on some level, because she was a selfless person. But on another level, he had a feeling she would miss the German shepherd a great deal if the dog was placed in another home. "Why don't you adopt her?"

Taking a large slice of pizza, she bit into it. And then laughed softly. "If I adopted every dog I fostered, I'd wind up being cited by the police for having way too many dogs in my house. This area isn't zoned for kennels," she reminded him.

He shrugged. After all, she probably knew what was best for her. It was just that there seemed to be a bond between her and the dog she was fostering. But then, he hadn't known Miranda all that long and most likely she was like this with all the dogs she took care of—just like she was with all the children she looked after at the hospital.

"This is really good pizza," she commented. Looking at the box, she read the name written across the top. "Rizzoli's." She shook her head. It didn't ring a bell. I don't think I'm familiar with that chain."

"That's because it's not a chain," he told her. He was finishing up his second slice and then slid a third one onto his plate in between washing them down with beer. "It's this little hole-in-the-wall of a place in the next town. Easy to miss," he told her. "It's been there for about twenty years. I discovered it when I moved back to Bedford."

"The next town?" Miranda repeated. "That's a long way to travel for something that's available in practically every shopping center in Bedford."

Colin shrugged and then his eyes met hers. "Sometimes quality is worth going the extra mile or so."

Miranda grinned. Leaning over, she took her napkin and wiped away a dab of sauce from the corner of his mouth. Maybe it was her imagination, but she could have sworn a spark of electricity zapped through her. "I'm glad you think so."

What was she up to? he wondered, and why was he

so captivated by her? Why wasn't he just walking out instead of sitting here across from this do-gooder?

"Why do I feel like I'm being set up for something?" he asked Miranda.

"Because you're a cop and you're naturally suspicious," she replied with a warm laugh. "You're not being set up for anything," she told him, and heaven help him, he believed her. "Besides, setting you up would be an awful way to pay you back for bringing over this really great pizza."

Lola had been whimpering since they'd started eating. Her whimper was growing louder by increments. Obviously antsy, the German shepherd had moved from Miranda's right side to her left and then back again, watching her with big brown eyes that seemed to grow larger each time she moved.

Upping her game, Lola dipped her head and slipped it under Miranda's arm, nudging it.

Miranda laughed. "Okay, okay, I surrender." Tearing off a piece from her slice, she held it out to the dog. Less than half a second later, the piece was gone, disappearing between Lola's teeth.

"Hey, you could lose a finger that way," Colin warned, instantly alert.

"No, she's very careful," she assured him. "For a dog with such big teeth, Lola's incredibly gentle when she takes food from my hand."

He knew that in Miranda's place, he would have flinched, hearing those teeth click shut. But she had remained completely unfazed. "I take it this isn't the first time she's eaten out of your hand."

"No, it's not," she confirmed. "Lola likes to kibitz when I'm having dinner."

"You're spoiling her," he told her. There was disapproval in his voice.

It was Miranda's turn to shrug. "Lola's been through so much, I figure she's entitled to a little spoiling." As he watched, Miranda's expression darkened. "Her last owner chained her up in the backyard, then beat her and starved her. He didn't give her any water, either."

"How did Lola wind up at the shelter?" Colin asked her.

"A neighbor heard her whimpering and looked over this guy's fence. Lola was half-dead. Horrified, he called the police. They arrived just in time. Another couple of days and Lola would have died," she told him fiercely. "Needless to say, they took her away."

Colin had set his beer down when she started telling him about Lola's background. "What happened to the owner?" he asked.

Every time she thought about the incident, Miranda was filled with anger.

"He got off with a fine. If it were up to me, I would have had him drawn and quartered in the town square and made an example of." She saw Colin looking at her incredulously. She wondered if she'd set off some alarms in his head since, after all, the man was a police officer. "What?"

"I've just never seen you angry before. I didn't think you were capable of it," he confessed.

"Oh, I'm capable of it all right," Miranda assured him. "Cruelty of any kind gets me very angry—especially when it comes to children or animals." She saw his reaction. "Why are you grinning?"

For once his poker face failed him. "You look kind of…I don't know…*cute* when you get angry like that. You don't exactly fit the part of an avenging angel, that's all."

Miranda pressed her lips together, but her anger was abating. Her eyes did narrow a little, though. "You're making fun of me," she accused.

"No, not really." He polished off yet another pizza slice. "It's just nice to know that you have this darker side to you. Up until now," he admitted, "I wasn't sure you were human."

"I'm all too human," Miranda told him. She pushed away her plate. "I'm also stuffed."

Colin doubted it. "You only had two and a half slices," he pointed out.

"And I'm stuffed," Miranda repeated.

"How?" he asked. He nodded at the dog, who was still circling the table. "Lola could probably eat more than you just did."

"Undoubtedly," Miranda agreed with a laugh. She watched the dog for a moment "She burns it all up running around in the backyard."

Colin snorted. "And you, of course, just lie around like a slug."

Tickled, Miranda grinned at his assessment. "I don't need much fuel."

He nodded at her empty plate. "Obviously."

Her attention shifted toward the open pizza box. There were several slices still in it. "Speaking of which, why don't you take what's left home with you when you go? You can do it more justice than I would. And if you leave it here, I'll only wind up giving it to Lola when she starts begging."

He sighed, shaking his head. "You're going to have to learn how to say no."

Amusement curved her mouth as she raised her eyes to his. "I'm working on it."

For just a moment, he wondered if Miranda was putting him on some kind of notice—and if she felt she needed to. Which in turn led him to wonder why. Was she afraid that he thought bringing over pizza entitled him to make a move on her?

Where the hell had that come from? Colin silently demanded. He was here because he was paying her back for the dinner she'd made him, nothing more. He certainly wasn't thinking of her in any sort of a romantic light. Just because they'd accidentally kissed didn't mean he wanted to capitalize on it—even if it *had* been a memorable kiss.

Damn it, he upbraided himself, he was overthinking the whole thing. Maybe he *should* go home now.

As he wrestled with his thoughts, Miranda rose and took her plate to the sink.

He still had part of a slice—his fifth one—on his plate. Making a decision, Colin picked up what was left of it and lowered his hand to Lola's level.

On cue, the German shepherd quickly rounded the table to his side. Colin hardly saw her open her mouth. Just like that, the pizza was gone.

"Now who's spoiling her?" Miranda asked with a knowing laugh.

Colin's shoulders rose and fell in a careless shrug. "I don't like seeing food go to waste," he told her.

"Neither do I," she replied. "Of course, if I keep this up with Lola, she is definitely going to wind up being a blimp."

He looked at the dog, who seemed to know that no more slices were coming her way tonight. With a satisfied yawn, she stretched out at his feet.

This was far too domestic a scene, Colin thought uneasily. He really should be on his way home.

But somehow, he remained sitting where he was. "I don't think there's much chance of that," he told Miranda. "She looks pretty lean to me."

"Hear that, Lola?" Miranda asked. She finished drying her hands and left the towel hanging on the hook next to the refrigerator. "The nice police officer just paid you a compliment."

Hearing her name, Lola barked in response.

Miranda's eyes crinkled as she suppressed a laugh. "She says thank you," she told Colin.

"You didn't tell me you can communicate with dogs." But to be honest, it wouldn't have surprised him if she said she did.

"You don't have to speak the language to be able to communicate," Miranda answered. Rather than sit down at the table again, she paused and glanced toward the rear of the house. "Oh, by the way, I have something for you."

"What do you mean by 'something'?" he asked warily, on his guard.

"Don't look so worried. It's not a bribe," Miranda teased. "It's harmless. Wait right here." With that, she hurried out of the kitchen. "I got it on my lunch break," she called, raising her voice so that it carried back to him.

Minutes later, Miranda returned to the kitchen, carrying a two-foot potted fir tree. The tree was decorated with a string of lights and tiny silver and blue Christmas balls.

"This is for you," she told him, setting the tree on the table. "I took a chance that you still hadn't gotten a Christmas tree."

"I didn't," he answered.

Colin was about to add that he had no plans to get one and that he *never* got a tree at Christmas time. The last time there'd been a Christmas tree in his house, he was living at his aunt's and the tree in question had been hers, not his.

But something stopped him from telling Miranda any of that, at least for now.

"I was going to get a bigger tree, but I didn't think you'd want it, so I settled for this small, live one," she explained.

He didn't want one at all, but since she'd gone to the trouble of going out and buying it for him, he bit his tongue and refrained from saying that.

Instead, curious, he asked her, "Did the tree come with decorations?"

"Not exactly," she confessed. "But to be honest, I

didn't think you'd decorate it if I handed you a naked tree, so I did it for you. It was kind of fun, being able to deck out a Christmas tree in half an hour." Her momentum picked up as she added, "And when the season's over, you can plant it in your backyard."

"Just one problem with that," Colin told her. He broke off a small piece from one of the remaining pizza slices. Out of the corner of his eye, he saw Lola come to attention again. "I don't have a backyard."

Miranda never missed a beat. "Or you can transplant it into a larger pot as it starts to get bigger." Second-guessing Colin's objection to that suggestion, she offered, "I could do that for you if you're too busy."

"Because you have so much time on your hands," he said with a touch of sarcasm. He felt his conscience taking him to task. Miranda was only trying to be nice, he reminded himself. "Sorry, I didn't mean that the way it came out."

"No offense taken," she told him. "Besides, haven't you ever heard the old saying 'If you want something done, ask a busy person to do it'?"

"No, I haven't. But I'll take your word for it." He looked at the tree with its dainty ornaments and the bright red foil wrapped around its base. "Thanks. It's a nice-looking tree." He left it standing on the table for now. "But you really didn't have to get me one," Colin stressed.

"Let's just say it makes me happy doing so," she told him. "I couldn't stand the idea of you not having at least a little tree—so I got you one."

It was little, but he would have preferred an even smaller one—or better yet, none at all.

Colin pinned her with a piercing look. "But why would that bother you?" he couldn't help asking. "Not having a tree doesn't bother me."

"I know, but it does me." She could see they could go on dancing endlessly around the same point, so she tried something else. "It's a reminder of goodwill toward one another."

It took a lot to suppress the laugh that rose to his lips, but somehow, he managed. "Maybe if everyone thought the way you do, there'd be no need to be reminded. It would just be a given," Colin mused.

"That's the nicest thing anyone ever said to me," she told him, her eyes misting.

"If it's so nice, why are you crying?" he asked. If he lived to be a hundred and fifty, he would never understand women.

Miranda shrugged. "I guess I'm one of those people who cries when she's happy."

Colin shook his head. "Talk about mixed signals," he murmured.

He needed to leave.

He could feel barriers weakening within him, walls being breached and beliefs he'd held as hard and fast truths dissolving like cotton candy left out in the rain.

This woman was turning him inside out without lifting a finger, he thought grudgingly. If he didn't leave now, he didn't know what sort of mental condition he'd be in by the time he *did* leave.

"Okay," he said, rising. "I'd better be going." Belatedly, he remembered the little Christmas tree on the table. "Thanks for the tree."

"Thank *you* for dinner and for coming to the hospital today," she told him. "The kids just couldn't stop talking about you after you left. You were definitely the highlight of their week."

He had no idea how to respond to that. Being on the receiving end of gratitude was totally new to him. "Yeah, no problem."

"Oh, I think it was a problem for you, which was why having you come was so special—for everyone," she added meaningfully.

"You included?"

Now why the hell had he just said that? Was he *asking* for trouble? Colin silently demanded.

Miranda took a breath before answering. "Me most of all."

Chapter Fourteen

The moment, wrapped in silence, stretched out for a long time. He didn't know how to respond to what she'd just said.

Me most of all.

Finally, he stumbled through an awkward answer. "Oh, um, good to know."

Miranda felt sorry for him. Colin looked completely out of his element. Deftly, she changed the direction of the conversation.

"I'll walk you to your car," she offered.

"No," he said, perhaps a little too forcefully. All he wanted to do now was to get into his vehicle—quickly— and drive away. "You don't have to," he added.

She nodded at the things still on the table. "You can't carry the Christmas tree and the pizza box at the same time."

The German shepherd presented herself right next to him, a plaintive look on her face. He read between the lines.

"Um, I think that Lola would probably prefer if I left the pizza here."

Miranda pushed the pizza along the table so it was closer to him.

"Which is exactly why you're taking it with you. Too much people food isn't good for her and you've already seen what a pushover I am around Lola."

He wasn't accustomed to women who owned their shortcomings. He found himself smiling at Miranda in acknowledgment. "That's something you're going to have to overcome when you have kids."

He'd just said *when*, not *if*, Miranda noted. Was that just a careless slip of the tongue on his part, or did Colin really see her as a mother?

She rather liked the idea that he did. Of course, that would have to mean she'd have to slow down long enough to actually *have* a child.

Miranda took the pizza box, leaving the Christmas tree for him to carry. When he picked it up, they began to walk to the front door.

"Disciplining is something that I think I'll delegate to my husband," she told him, adding, "He'll probably be the strong and masterful type."

Colin's laugh was dry as he thought over her comment. "He would have to be."

Miranda cocked her head, trying to decide how he meant that. "Was that a compliment or a criticism?" she asked, curious.

He was talking too much, Colin decided. That had never been a problem for him before he'd met this woman.

"Take it any way you want," he answered, thinking that being vague was the safest way to go right now.

Miranda felt Lola trying to crowd her, attempting to push her way outside.

"No, girl, you have to stay in. I'll be right back," she promised.

Tucking the pizza box under her arm, she cringed slightly as she both heard and felt the remaining slices sliding together.

With her free hand, she gently steered the dog back into the house. Then, trying not to drop the box, she pulled the door closed behind her.

Looking on, Colin said with approval, "You're making progress."

"Well, I had to," Miranda told him. "You were watching me."

"So if I wasn't here…?" He left the end of the sentence up in the air and waited for her to finish it.

She did, but not as he expected. "…I wouldn't have pizza to keep away from her in the first place."

Colin shook his head, impressed despite himself. "I've got to say, you really do know how to dance around a subject."

"I've learned from the best," she said, grinning. She watched his brow furrow as he looked at her over his shoulder, perplexed.

Miranda hadn't meant for it to sound cryptic. Following him to his vehicle, she explained, "Kids. They can spin tales that'll make you dizzy."

Stopping beside his car, Colin looked at her pointedly. "I know the feeling."

He took his keys out of his pocket. Unlocking the doors, he put the potted Christmas tree on the floor in the rear. Taking the pizza, he placed the box on the passenger seat, then turned to face her.

"Well, thanks for your help with the pizza. And thanks for the tree," he added belatedly.

He watched as a smile filled her eyes. "Don't mention it. It's the least I can do after all that joy you brought my kids."

Her thanks made him feel awkward again. "I just showed up," he insisted again, not wanting to make any more out of it than that. But with Miranda he should have known better.

"You did a lot more than that," she insisted. "You brightened up their day. Their parents come as often as they can—and that's a good thing," she assured him. "But having you come to their ward was something out of the ordinary. Something special," she said with feeling.

He opened his mouth and then shut it again. When he saw the curious look on her face, he told her, "Well, I'm not going to argue with you, because I'm beginning to get the feeling that no one stands a chance of winning an argument with you."

"Sure they do," she declared, although, offhand, she couldn't think of a single example to cite.

"Uh-huh." His response as he started to go reeked of skepticism.

"Oh, and Colin?" Miranda called after him, raising her voice.

Colin was about to round the hood to get into his side of the vehicle, but stopped. "Yes?"

"Promise you won't forget and leave the tree in the car. It's a hardy little thing, but if you leave it in the car indefinitely, it'll wilt and lose all its needles."

Indulging her, he promised, "I won't forget."

"Oh, and drive carefully," she called after him.

Colin paused again. He should feel annoyed or insulted that, given the nature of his work, she still felt the need to say something like that to him. And yet this whole scene just made him smile. He had no idea why.

Waiting, he turned around. "Anything else?"

Miranda knew that she was pushing her luck to the absolute limit, but then nothing ventured, nothing gained, right?

Taking a breath, she forged ahead. "Well, there's a Christmas Eve party, if you'd like to come."

He hadn't expected her to say that; he'd just assumed she'd have more trivial slogans to send his way. "At the hospital?"

He'd done his part at the hospital and she was now focusing on the other two places where she volunteered her time.

"Well, yes, there, too," she allowed. "But I was thinking of the shelter."

She still wasn't narrowing it down, he realized. "Homeless or animal?"

"Homeless. Although, now that I think about it, we are having a party at the animal shelter, too," she told him. "It's an adoption party. There's one every month, but there's an extra push to find the animals a home just before Christmas."

"Of course there is." Listening to her, he shook his head. It was a wonder the woman didn't just fall over and collapse. "When do you have time for *you*?" he asked.

"All of this is for me," she responded. Seeing the doubtful look on his face, she insisted, "I derive pleasure out of seeing the animals find new homes and the kids getting better and going back to their families. And the women at the shelter taking stock of their situation and finding a way to create new lives for themselves and their children."

Saints have less to do, he thought. Colin shook his head again, but the corners of his mouth had curved ever so slightly.

"All of this is for you, huh?" He watched as she nodded with feeling. "I don't think I've ever met anyone like you before, Miranda Steele," he told her in all sincerity.

"Is that a good thing?" she asked.

"I'm thinking on it," he answered, remaining deliberately vague.

She couldn't read his expression, and her curiosity was getting the better of her even though she knew it shouldn't. "Let me know what you come up with."

"I have a feeling you'll be the first to know."

Colin suddenly found himself fighting the urge to pull her into his arms. If he didn't leave now, he might wind up doing something stupid, and as unique as this woman was, he didn't need any complications in his life.

He'd already gotten too involved with her as it was.

He needed distance, not closeness, Colin insisted silently.

So why wasn't he getting into his car and leaving? Why was he turning around and crossing back toward the woman?

Miranda was standing at the curb, ready to wave at him as he pulled away.

When instead of leaving, he approached, she looked at him uncertainly, slightly confused even while she felt her heart climbing up into her throat.

Her breath was backing up in her chest. "Did you forget something?"

"Yeah," he muttered. "My sanity."

Her confusion mounted. "I don't know what that means."

Colin didn't respond. At least not verbally. Instead, he took her into his arms just the way he'd told himself not to, and kissed her the way he *knew* he shouldn't.

The way every fiber of his being felt that he just *had* to.

Confusion ran rampant all through Miranda. One moment she was standing at the curb, getting ready to watch Colin drive down the street and disappear; the next moment she found herself smack in the middle of an old-fashioned twister, being sucked up into its very core and whirling around so hard she couldn't breathe. She certainly couldn't think or get her bearings.

But then, bearings were highly overrated, she decided.

Standing up on her toes, Miranda dug her fingertips into his shoulders in a desperate attempt to anchor herself to something solid before she was swept so completely away she would never be able to find her way back again.

This *wasn't* a kiss. She'd been kissed before, kissed by faceless, unremarkable men who faded from her memory before they had a chance to even walk out the door.

But this—*this* was an experience. A mind-blowing, incredible experience that she would remember to her dying day even if she lived to be a hundred and ten.

Colin fought the urge to deepen this kiss and take it to its natural conclusion. Fought the urge to sweep her up into his arms and carry her back inside her house so that he could make love with her. Make love with her until they were both too exhausted to even breathe.

He came within a hair's breadth of giving in to that urge, that desire.

And then a last sliver of sanity rose up, stopping him.

He couldn't do this, he silently insisted, couldn't make love with her. Because if he did, he would be willfully bringing his darkness into her world.

She was a bright, shining ray of light, bent on bringing happiness to everyone and everything. If he took this to its natural conclusion, he would be guilty of if not extinguishing that light, then at the very least dimming it considerably.

He couldn't be responsible for that, couldn't do that to her and all the other lives that Miranda would wind up touching.

Although every fiber of his being fought it, trying to keep him from following through, he separated himself from Miranda. He removed her arms, which she'd wound around his neck, and pushed them down against her sides, held them there for a long moment—until he could collect himself.

"I've got to go," he told her hoarsely.

Then, without another word, Colin got into his car and turned on the ignition. He pulled away from the curb without a single backward glance.

Then, unable to help himself, he looked in the rearview mirror.

Miranda was still standing there at the curb where he had left her.

A pang of regret seized his very being.

Colin struggled with the impulse to turn the car around and head back to her. Instead, he pushed down hard on the accelerator, determined to put more and more distance between them.

"Count yourself lucky," he said, addressing the figure that was growing progressively smaller and smaller in his rearview mirror. "You don't need someone like me in your life."

He had a very strong feeling that if he had given in to himself tonight, if he had weakened and made love to Miranda, he wouldn't have been able to walk away from her, short of being sandblasted away.

That would be a very bad thing.

For her.

Miranda had a sinking feeling as she watched Colin drive off that he could very well be gone from her life for good.

There'd been something about the set of his shoulders, about the foreboding expression on his face as he had removed her arms from around his neck and stepped away, that made her think of an iron gate coming down, separating the two of them.

Cutting her off from him.

But even so, she kept watching for him every time she looked up, every time her attention was drawn to something—a noise, a flash of light out of the corner of her eye.

Every time she raised her eyes, she was looking for Colin.

And every time she did, he wasn't there.

He wasn't leaning in the doorway of any of the hospital rooms belonging to the small patients she attended, wasn't standing across the street from the animal shelter, waiting for her to come out. He wasn't walking into the women's shelter, wasn't ringing her doorbell and standing on the front step until she opened the door.

He wasn't anywhere in her life—except in her mind, and there he had set up housekeeping, big-time.

If she was going to function properly, she was either going to have to purge him from her mind and forget all about him, or else beard the lion in his den, Miranda thought in a moment of madness.

Get hold of yourself, she silently lectured.

She was far too busy for this, far too busy to mentally dwell on a man who—a man who...

In the middle of her rounds, Miranda abruptly came to a dead stop. She'd initially been drawn to the tall, dark, silent police officer not because he could kiss like nobody's business and set her soul on fire. She'd been drawn to him because of the sadness she saw in his eyes. She remembered thinking that Colin needed someone to brighten his world, to help him find hope and hang on to it.

He needed *her*, and somehow, she had lost sight of that.

But not anymore, she vowed. She was back on track and determined to strip that sadness, that darkness out of him until Officer Colin Kirby found a reason to smile of his own accord.

He could keep those lips to himself. That wasn't what was important here. What she wanted was his happiness.

And she was determined to help him find it if it was the last thing she did.

Chapter Fifteen

Despite his resolve, he couldn't seem to get Miranda out of his head. Not that day, nor the next. The harder he tried, the less success he had. His thoughts turned to the bubbly nurse over a dozen times a day. More, if he was being honest with himself.

For the first time in his adult life, Colin's laser-like focus completely failed him.

He couldn't get himself to concentrate exclusively on his work. Images of Miranda's face kept materializing in his mind's eye at the worst possible times, impeding him at every turn.

Colin had never been one to throw in the towel. He struggled to regain control over himself and his thoughts. He'd triumphed over the racking pain of losing his parents—especially his mother, who he'd been so close to—and managed to keep going during his tour overseas when more than half his platoon had been wiped out all around him.

And though they hadn't been close, guilt had skewered him when he'd lost his partner, Andrew Owens, while on the job.

But he'd managed to rise above all that, erasing it from his mind and functioning as if his insides hadn't been smashed into a thousand pieces. He did it to survive, to continue putting one foot in front of the other and moving on the path he found himself on.

But this—this was completely different. For some mysterious reason, he'd lost his ability to isolate himself, to strip all distracting thoughts from his mind.

He'd lost the ability to continue, and he knew he had to resolve this if he had any hopes of functioning and moving on with his life.

He just had to figure out how.

How had this happened? It felt as if Thanksgiving had been only yesterday, then somehow she'd blinked, and now Christmas was a week away and Miranda had more than enough to keep not just herself but half a dozen people busy.

To paraphrase Dickens, it was both the best time of the year and the worst time of the year, mainly because of all the things that were associated with the season. The shelters as well as the hospital needed her more than ever, and there was enough for her to do thirty-six hours a day if she could somehow find a way to create that many hours out of thin air.

But even with everything she had to handle, she

couldn't stop thinking about Colin. Worrying about Colin. It was interfering not just with her ability to devote herself to her work as a nurse, but also as a volunteer—in both areas that used her services.

She needed to talk to Colin, she decided, and she needed to do it face-to-face, not over the phone. Any other means would be far too impersonal.

Because of the hectic pace this time of year generated, taking time off from the hospital was not an option. The only thing she could do was try to shave a little time from her volunteer work. The pace there was hectic, as well, and there were a great many demands on her time whenever she had any to spare. But she *had* to do this. Because not talking to Colin was unthinkable.

The problem was, since she still didn't know where the man lived, the only place she could hope to find him was along the route he patrolled or at the precinct before he went off duty.

However, both conflicted with her shift at the hospital.

Still, maybe if she played the odds and really hurried—and hopefully he was getting off late—she might be able to catch Colin before he left work for the day.

Miranda felt stressed because even if she was lucky enough to catch him, she'd have to talk fast because the women's shelter's Christmas party, the one she'd helped organize for the children, was scheduled to begin the minute she walked through the door.

She was exhausted already.

As Miranda dashed to her car, all set to take off for the precinct, her cell phone rang.

Please let it be a wrong number, she prayed as she took it out of her purse and then quickly put in her password.

The caller ID that came up belonged to the homeless shelter. Specifically, to Amelia.

Maybe the director was just checking in with her, Miranda thought, mentally crossing her fingers as she answered.

"Hi, Amelia." She used her free hand to buckle her seat belt. "What's up?"

"We've got an emergency," the woman said, without even bothering to return the greeting. "I just hung up with Santa Claus. He called to say he's stuck in traffic in LA and he's not going to be able to get here in time."

Miranda knew the director was referring to the man she had hired to play Santa for the kids at the shelter. Thinking of the children's disappointment, she felt her heart sink.

The words came out before she could stop them. "But the kids are expecting to see Santa Claus."

"I know. I know," the director answered. "The toys are here, but they're going to feel really let down that Santa Claus couldn't make it to hand them out."

Her mind going in all directions, Miranda searched for a solution. And then she thought of something. "Do you still have that old Santa suit from last year?"

"I think so," Amelia answered. "The last time I saw it, it was in the storage room, shoved behind some cans of paint. Why?"

"Find it," she told her. "I'll be at the shelter as soon as I can get there," Miranda promised, terminating the call.

So much for waylaying Colin today, she thought, dropping her phone into her purse.

"Looks like you've gotten a reprieve, Officer Kirby," Miranda murmured under her breath, starting up her vehicle and then peeling out of the hospital's parking lot.

She was going to need padding. Lots and lots of padding if she had a prayer of pulling this off. She'd have to have Amelia round up a whole bunch of pillows.

Miranda was still trying to figure out exactly what she would do as she pulled into the women's shelter's parking lot. If she hadn't been so lost in thought, she would have seen him.

As it was, she didn't.

Not until after she'd jumped out of her car and run smack-dab into him, so hard she all but fell backward. Only Colin grabbing her by the arm kept her from meeting the concrete skull-first.

Stunned, for a split second Miranda thought she was hallucinating—until her brain assured her that she really wasn't conjuring Colin up.

He felt much too real for that.

"Colin?" she cried, shaken. "What are you doing here?" Miranda still wasn't a hundred percent sure that she wasn't just imagining him, putting his face on another man's body.

The police officer released her slowly, watching her intently to make sure she was all right.

"I guess I'm not as noble as I thought," he answered with a self-depreciating shrug.

Maybe she *had* hit her head, Miranda thought,

blinking. She didn't understand what he was telling her. "Why?"

"Because," he confessed, "I was going to stay away from you."

Miranda continued staring at him. He still wasn't making any sense to her.

"Why is staying away 'noble'?" she asked.

He might have known she'd want an explanation. This wasn't easy for him to say. "Because I would only bring you down, and you don't need that."

Miranda thought of the kids in the shelter. She was still in a hurry, but the emergency would have to wait, at least for a couple minutes. This needed to be cleared up, and it needed to be cleared up *now*.

"First of all," she told him, "I do have free will and a mind of my own. I'm not just some ink blotter that indiscriminately absorbs whatever happens to be spilled on it—"

"I'm not saying that you're an ink blotter!" Colin protested.

"I'm not finished," she informed him crisply. "And second of all, I can make up my own mind whom I want or don't want in my life. That's only up to you if you don't want to be in my life because you can't abide being around me."

Colin stared at her in astonishment. How could she even *think* that, much less *say* it?

"You know that's not the case." Angry at how the situation was devolving, he had to rein himself in to keep from shouting the words at Miranda.

"Well, then there's no problem, is there?" she concluded. Turning on her heel, she started to walk toward the building.

Before he could think better of it, Colin caught her by the arm to keep her from leaving. "Oh, there's a problem, all right."

Her desire to resolve this warred with her sense of responsibility. She was going to be cutting it very close, Miranda thought. For all she knew, Amelia might not have located the Santa suit yet.

"Walk with me," she requested. When Colin fell into step beside her, she asked him to elaborate on what he'd just said. "Do you want to tell me just what *is* the problem?"

Colin tried to smother his frustration. He felt as if he was talking to a moving target, but then, that was part and parcel of who this unique creature was.

He thought of waving away her question, or just telling her flatly, "no." But he had started this and had to be man enough to own up to it.

Colin forced himself to say, "I can't get you out of my head."

Miranda's eyes were shining. She spared him a smile as they came up to the shelter's double doors. "Still not seeing the problem."

"But you will," Colin predicted.

She highly doubted that. "Then we'll put a pin in this now and talk about it later. Right now, I have an emergency to deal with," she told him as she reached for the door's brass handle.

So she wasn't just running from him, Colin thought.

Taking charge, he nudged her hand away and opened the door for her. "What sort of an emergency?"

She glanced at her watch. "The Christmas party starts in less than half an hour and Santa Claus is still in LA, stuck in traffic."

Okay, this was convoluted, even for her. "You want to run that by me again? And this time, try to speak slower than the speed of light."

Miranda took a breath. "Amelia hired this professional Santa Claus for the party, and now he can't get here in time because he's stuck in traffic. These kids have been disappointed an awful lot in their lives. I'll be damned if I'm going to let it happen again if I can do something about it."

"Just what is it you have in mind?"

"Amelia said there's an old Santa suit here at the shelter. If we can find it, I'm going to play Santa Claus."

Colin looked at her for a long moment. And then he laughed. Hard. It occurred to Miranda that she had never heard him laugh out loud like that before, but now wasn't the time she wanted to hear it. "You got a better idea?"

It took him a second to collect himself and stop laughing. "Sorry, Miranda, I don't mean to laugh at you, but you just don't look like *anyone's* idea of Santa Claus." He paused again, thinking. And then he nodded. "And yes, I've got a better idea."

She thought she knew what he was going to say and she shook her head, shooting down his idea.

"Just handing out the gifts to the kids isn't going to be enough. These children want Santa Claus giving them those gifts. They want to be normal and see Santa Claus, like every other kid this time of year. They've got a right to that," she insisted passionately.

Just seeing her like this nearly undid Colin. "That wasn't the idea I had," he told her. "Let's go see if we can find that Santa suit. I've got a better chance of pulling this off than you do."

It didn't happen very often, but Miranda found herself practically speechless. When she did recover, she cried, in astonishment, "Really?"

Colin nodded. "Really."

Miranda continued staring at him, waiting for some sort of a punch line. When none came, she had to ask, "You're going to willingly play Santa Claus without having me twist your arm?"

He really did like surprising her.

"Without bending any of my body parts," he assured her. "Now are we going to go on standing here talking about it or are you going to take me to wherever you think that Santa suit is stashed so we can get this show on the road?"

Her response to his question sounded incredibly like a squeal. The next second, Miranda had grabbed his hand and was dragging him through the shelter's main room.

Before they had crossed it, Amelia approached them.

"Did you find it?" Miranda asked breathlessly. "The Santa suit?"

"It's in my office." The director seemed a little surprised by the man Miranda had in tow. "Officer Kirby, it's so nice to see you again. Are you going to be joining the party?"

Before he could answer, Miranda cried, "Definitely!"

Turning on her short, stacked heel, Amelia followed Miranda and the policeman to her office.

Still somewhat bewildered, the woman sounded uncertain as she asked Colin, "You're not going to be playing Santa Claus for the children, are you, Officer Kirby?"

Glancing her way, Miranda answered the question for him. "It's a real Christmas miracle, isn't it?"

The dignified director was smiling so hard she was practically beaming. "It most certainly is. The suit's going to be a little big on you," she warned Colin. "So I found some pillows." She gestured to some stacked on the battered, secondhand easy chair that stood in the corner of her small office.

Colin briefly glanced at them. "They'll work," he told her.

Looking pleased, Amelia said, "Well, I'll give you some privacy…" And she eased herself out of her office.

"And I'll go get the sack of toys ready so you can hand them out," Miranda volunteered. "I'll meet you back here in Amelia's office. If you finish dressing before I return, wait for me. You don't want to go into the main hall empty-handed."

No matter how much Miranda had built up the importance of Santa Claus making an appearance, he knew that the toys were the main attraction. "Not a chance," he assured her.

But as he turned to look at her, he found that he was talking to himself. Miranda had already hurried off.

"That woman's got way too much energy," he murmured as he began to change.

Chapter Sixteen

Miranda turned around when she heard the office door behind her opening. About to tell Colin that she'd gotten the bulging sack of toys for him to hand out while he'd been changing into his costume, she instead wound up saying, "Wow."

"Does it fit all right?" He glanced down at himself critically.

"You look just like Santa Claus," Miranda declared. "I wouldn't have known it was you if I hadn't handed you the costume." She circled him, then nodded with approval. "Laugh."

He eyed her warily. "What?"

"Santa's jolly, remember? You're going to have to go 'ho, ho, ho' at least a few times, so let's hear it."

"Ho, ho, ho," Colin said.

"You're frowning under that beard, aren't you?" she

guessed. "Never mind," she told him when he started to answer. "The beard covers it. But put some gusto into it. And here's your bag of presents." She indicated the sack next to her.

Taking hold of it, he began to swing it over his shoulder. Then his eyes widened. "You carried this here?"

"Dragged, actually," she admitted. "It's kind of heavy."

"That's an understatement," Colin muttered under his breath. "Okay, let's get this over with."

"A little more 'ho, ho, ho' spirit," she advised.

"I'm saving myself," he responded, following her back to the main room.

"Hey, look, everybody! Look who's here," Miranda called out to the children the moment Colin walked into the common area.

The space was filled with kids of all sizes who had been anxiously waiting for the legendary elf to make his appearance. As they turned almost in unison in his direction, their faces lit up with delight, Colin saw.

"It's Santa!"

"Santa's here!"

"Santa!"

A chorus of excited voices called out, creating a cacophony of eagerness and joy blended with disbelief that Santa had actually come to the shelter—and he'd made it ahead of Christmas Eve, as well.

The next second, Colin found himself surrounded as children eagerly rushed up to him.

Miranda took control. Raising her voice, she told the children, "Okay, give him a little space. We don't want to overwhelm Santa. He's still got a lot of places to visit before the holidays are here." Waving the little ones over to her side, she instructed, "Line up, kids. You'll all get your turn, I promise."

As Colin watched in surprise, the children obediently lined up as ordered and patiently awaited their turn.

His eyes shifted in Miranda's direction. This was definitely a new side to her, he thought in admiration.

"That's your cue to get started," she prompted.

"Oh, right." Colin set down his sack and opened it.

To his relief, Miranda stayed by his side the entire time and helped him hand out the gifts. As each child came up to him, she very subtly fed him his or her name to personalize the experience for the child.

Any doubts or uncertainty he'd harbored about volunteering to play Santa vanished within the first few minutes. The excitement, gratitude and awe he saw shining in the eyes of the children who surrounded him managed to create nothing short of an epiphany for Colin.

He began to understand why Miranda did what she did. Being there for these children brought about an incredibly warm feeling that he'd been unacquainted with prior to today.

He really got into the part.

Colin continued digging into the sack and handing out gifts until the very last child in line cried, "Thank you, Santa!" and hurried away, clutching her present against her.

It took him a second to process the fact that there

was no one left in line. Turning toward Miranda, he asked, "Is that it?"

"Yup. You saw every last kid in the place," she told him happily.

The sack sagged as he released it, and it fell to the floor. "Good, because there's only a couple of gifts left. I would have hated to run out of presents before you ran out of kids," he told her. He saw the wide grin on her face. "What?"

"Look at you," she said proudly. "All full of Christmas spirit."

He didn't want her making a big deal of it. "There's a difference between being full of Christmas spirit and not behaving like Scrooge."

"Not in my book," Miranda responded. Leaning into him, she whispered, "Lighten up, Santa, and take the compliment."

Colin glanced down at the suit he was wearing. She saw the look in his eyes and took an educated guess as to what he was thinking. "Itchy, huh?"

He lowered his voice. "You have no idea."

"You held up your end very well," she told him. "Let's get you back to Amelia's office so you can get out of that suit." Miranda looked around at the children, all of whom were happily playing with their toys from Santa. Some were still regarding their gifts in awe. "C'mon, the coast is clear," she whispered. "Let's go."

Following her lead, Colin slipped out of the room. When he didn't hear any of the children calling after him, he breathed a sigh of relief and quickly went down the hall to the small office at the rear of the building.

He went in and was surprised when Miranda followed.

"I'll leave in a minute," she promised, "so you can get out of that costume. I just wanted to indulge a fantasy."

"A fantasy?" he questioned, surprised. She struck him as being so squeaky clean, so grounded, and not the type to have fantasies. His curiosity was aroused. "What kind of a fantasy?"

Mischief danced in her eyes. "I've always wanted to know what it was like to kiss Santa Claus," she told him. "Do you mind?"

Was she kidding? He could feel the whiskers in his fake beard spreading as he grinned. "Not at all."

Miranda wasn't certain just what had possessed her to behave like this. Maybe it was the fact that Colin had volunteered—of his own accord—to help, and by doing so, had literally managed to save the day, which in turn had created a really warm feeling within her.

Or maybe it was because the memory of that last kiss was still lingering on her mind, making her long for a replay. Besides, there was something safe about kissing "Santa Claus" here in the director's office, with a building full of people nearby.

Whatever excuse she gave herself didn't really matter. What did matter was that a moment after she'd asked, she found herself being kissed by "Santa."

Or more specifically, by Colin.

And she discovered that the third time around was even better.

This time, her knees turned to mush right along with the rest of her, and she really did have to hold on for dear life as Colin/Santa deepened the kiss by soul-melting degrees until her mind slipped into a black hole.

Only the sudden awkward noise in the doorway kept the kiss from totally engulfing not just her but both of them.

"Oh, I'm sorry, I—I didn't mean to interrupt," Amelia stuttered, obviously embarrassed about having walked in on them like this. Averting her eyes and addressing the nearby wall, she said, "I just wanted to thank you, Officer Kirby. You really made all those kids extremely happy."

The director turned her head slowly, as if to make sure it was safe to look at them. She breathed a sigh of relief to see that neither was annoyed with her for the accidental intrusion.

"Well, I've said my piece," she added, "so I'll leave you two alone. Thank you again, Officer Kirby."

"Um, yeah. Don't mention it. I got a kick out of it," Colin confessed.

"I'll wait for you out here," Miranda told him, quickly slipping out of the room right behind Amelia. She closed the door in her wake.

When he came out less than five minutes later, the director was nowhere in sight. However, true to her word, Miranda was standing out in the hall close by, waiting for him.

"I'm leaving the suit on the chair in the office," Colin said, nodding toward the room.

"That's perfect," Miranda assured him. "Amelia'll put it away until next year."

He'd already forgotten about the costume. His mind

was on something more important. He searched for the right words.

"Are you going home?" he asked.

Miranda nodded. "Lola's waiting for her dinner. She's probably right in front of the door."

"So she's still with you." It wasn't really a question. He'd just assumed that the dog had become more or less of a fixture at Miranda's house, even though she'd called the situation temporary.

Miranda smiled as she nodded. "Still with me. And I have to say that I'm really getting used to having her around."

"Then why not keep her?"

"It wouldn't be fair," she told him. "Lola needs kids to play with."

He didn't understand why she thought that. "What that dog needs more is love, and you seem to have that covered."

His comment surprised her. It wasn't like him. "I think that Santa suit transformed you."

Colin waved away her assessment. "I don't know what you're talking about. I just say it like it is. Speaking of which…" He let his voice trail off as he framed his next sentence. He didn't want her getting the wrong idea, but didn't want to be so low-key that she turned him down.

When he paused, Miranda cocked her head, waiting for him to finish. "Yes?"

"Would you mind if I came home with you? Just for a while," he qualified a little too quickly. "I feel like I need to wind down a bit after this whole Santa thing."

She laughed. "Too much adulation to handle?" she guessed, amused. This had to be all new to him.

He shrugged carelessly. "Something like that. Is it all right?" he asked, still waiting for her to tell him whether or not he could come over.

"Sure," Miranda replied, wondering why Colin would think that it wouldn't be. "Lola would love to see you."

He laughed drily. Miranda made it sound as if he had some sort of a relationship with the German shepherd. "I'm not so sure about that."

"I am," she said, hooking her arm through his. Thinking he might like to leave with a minimum of fuss, she suggested, "We can take the side door if you want to avoid walking through the main room and running into the kids."

"No, that's all right," he told her. "We can go out the front."

He really had changed, she marveled. And she definitely liked this new, improved Colin. "Maybe you should have put on that Santa suit earlier."

He shrugged. It wasn't the suit; it was what had prompted him to put it on: Miranda.

"Maybe I should have," he allowed casually. "By the way, how was it?"

He'd lost her. "How was what?"

"Back in the director's office, you said you wanted to see what it felt like, kissing Santa Claus," he reminded her. He knew he was leaving himself wide-open, but he was curious about what Miranda would say. "So how was it?"

She smiled up at him and said, "Magical."

He had no idea if she was kidding or not, but they had just entered the common room. Most of the kids were still there and he didn't want to say anything that could draw attention to them, so made no comment on her response.

As they crossed the floor to the front door, he saw the director looking their way. Colin nodded at the woman and she mouthed, *"Thank you."* He smiled in response but kept walking.

"I've got a question for you," Miranda said once they were out the door and in the parking area.

Colin braced himself. "Go ahead."

It was already cold and the wind had picked up. Miranda pulled her jacket more tightly around herself. "How did it feel to save the day? Or is that something you've pretty much gotten used to, being a police officer and all?"

Colin laughed to himself, shaking his head. She was serious, he realized. "Miranda, I'm a motorcycle cop, remember? I usually ruin people's day, not save it."

"You know, it doesn't have to be that way."

"Oh? And what is it that you suggest?" he asked, humoring her.

"Well, did you ever think about switching departments?" Miranda asked.

Colin grew solemn. "I *was* in a different department when I worked in LA."

"What happened?"

His expression grew grim as he remembered. "My partner got killed. On the job," he added. Confronted with that information, she would surely drop the subject. But he'd obviously forgotten who he was dealing with.

"All right," she said slowly, processing what he'd just told her and extrapolating. "Bedford's got a canine unit. You could ask to be transferred there," she told him. She thought of the way he interacted with Lola. "You'd be really good at it."

"We'll see," Colin answered, just to get her to stop taking about it.

But Miranda was on to the way he operated. "Just something to think about," she told him. For now, she tabled the subject. Pointing to her vehicle, which was farther down the lot, she said, "I'm parked over there. Do you want to follow me home?"

"I do know where you live, Miranda," Colin reminded her.

Miranda's smile widened as she inclined her head. "Then I'll see you there. I'll make dinner," she added.

He didn't want her to feel obligated. "You don't have to—"

"I've got to eat," she told him. "And I've seen you eat, so I know that you do, too." She gave him a knowing look. "You don't have to turn everything into a debate, Colin."

He supposed he was guilty of that—at least part of the time. "You do have a way with words."

She grinned. "As long as you know that, everything'll be fine."

He wasn't sure about that, Colin thought, as he walked over to his car. Ever since he'd met Miranda, he'd been doing things completely out of character.

Getting into his vehicle, he started it up and pulled out of the parking lot.

His simple routine of eat, sleep, work, repeat, had gone completely out the window. Ever since he'd moved back to Bedford, he hadn't socialized, even remotely. But since he'd crossed paths with Miranda, he found himself entertaining strange thoughts. He *wanted* to socialize. How else could he explain what he had done today?

Never in his wildest dreams would he have thought that he'd put on a Santa suit, much less wear it for more than two hours the way he'd done, while handing out toys to a whole bunch of kids. Even letting those kids crawl onto his lap, and not just putting up with having some of them hug him, but actually, deep down in his soul, *liking* it.

It felt as if he'd lost sight of all the rules he'd always adhered to. Not just lost sight of them but willfully abandoned them.

If he wasn't careful, he would never be the same again.

What "if"? he silently jeered. There was no "if" about it. He wasn't the same now—and did he even want to be?

All these years, he'd been sleepwalking, moving like a shadow figure through his own life—and that wasn't living at all, he silently insisted.

For weeks now he'd kept thinking that if he hadn't crossed paths with Miranda, his life wouldn't have been turned upside down. As if that was a bad thing.

But maybe it wasn't. Maybe it—and she—had actually been his salvation.

And maybe, he told himself as he approached Miranda's house, he'd be better off if he just stopped thinking altogether.

Chapter Seventeen

Colin never got a chance to ring Miranda's doorbell. The front door flew open the minute he walked up to it.

Seeing the surprised look on his face, Miranda explained, "Lola heard your car pulling up and she barked to let me know you were here. I looked out the window and saw she was right."

Walking in, Colin paused to pet the German shepherd's head. He didn't really have much of a choice since she was blocking his path into the house.

"She let you know it was me," he repeated incredulously.

Moving around them, Miranda smiled as she closed the door. "She has a different bark when a stranger comes."

"I'm flattered, Lola." In response, the dog jumped up, placing her paws against his chest. He had a feeling he knew what she was after. "I'm sorry, girl, I don't have anything for you this time. I came straight here from the shelter."

"Don't worry," Miranda said. "I'm always prepared." To his surprise, she reached around the dog and slipped something into the front pocket of his jeans. "I'm not getting fresh," she told him. "I'm just giving you a couple of treats to give her. What?" she asked, when she saw the amused expression on his face.

"I don't think I've ever heard that phrase—getting fresh—outside of an old movie from the sixties, maybe earlier. No offense," he added quickly. "I think it's kind of cute."

"None taken—now that you've redeemed yourself," she added cheerfully. "C'mon, dinner's on the table."

Colin stared at the back of her head, stunned, as he followed her to the dining room. "How did you manage to get anything ready so fast? You couldn't have gotten here more than five minutes ago."

"Ten," she corrected. "I know a shortcut. And I really didn't have to cook. Those are leftovers from yesterday." She gestured at the covered tureen in the center of the table. "Nothing fancy. Just some chicken Alfredo over angel-hair spaghetti."

"Leftovers," Colin repeated, nodding. "That makes more sense. I didn't think even you were *that* fast."

She dished out the spaghetti, then the chicken Alfredo, first on one plate, then the other.

"Am I being challenged?" she asked him, the corners of her mouth curving.

"I didn't mean it that way," he said, then qualified, "Unless you wanted me to."

All she wanted right now was to sit down to a peaceful dinner with him.

"Eat," she prompted. "Dinner's getting cold. And, you," she said, looking down at Lola, who had presented herself at the table. "Let the man eat in peace, girl. He already gave you a bribe."

He was amused by the dog's antics. "I think she's expecting more."

Miranda sighed. "You were right. I have been spoiling her. But her new owner is going to do a better job of making her toe the line," she said.

Surprised, Colin lowered his fork. "New owner? Lola's been adopted?"

Miranda nodded, looking oddly calm to him. He would have expected her to be more upset. "Her papers were all put through and her fee was paid."

"Fee?" he questioned. He had no idea how pet adoption was conducted.

"Every dog and cat that the shelter takes in gets all their shots and they're neutered or spayed, depending on the animal's gender. When they're adopted, the new owner is charged a nominal fee for those services. It's to ensure that the next homeless animal can be taken care of."

Something didn't make sense to him. "If Lola's been adopted, why is she still here?" he asked.

The surge of disappointment he was experiencing over the news of the adoption really caught him off guard. He realized with a pang that he was going to miss Lola once her owner picked her up.

"That's rather a funny story," Miranda answered. "I'll tell it to you once we finish eating."

Colin filled in the blanks: they were going to be taking Lola to her new owner right after dinner. That was why Miranda was holding off telling him the story until later.

He honestly didn't know if he wanted to go with her. Watching the German shepherd being handed over to someone else wasn't something he wanted to witness.

But then it occurred to him that maybe Miranda was asking him to come along because *she* was going to need some moral support for this. He knew that she had gotten close to the animal. She'd said as much herself. What surprised him was that he had, too.

Picking up his fork again, Colin continued to eat, but he was no longer tasting anything and twice had to rouse himself because he'd missed what Miranda was saying.

"You're awfully quiet," she noted, finishing her dinner.

"I'm just thinking," Colin told her without elaborating.

"Okay," she announced, rising from the table. "Let's do this."

He looked at the empty plates on the table. She was leaving them where they were. "You're not going to do the dishes first?"

"They can wait," she told him loftily. "I'll do them later."

That wasn't like her. Giving up Lola and taking her to her new owner was undoubtedly hard on Miranda, he thought. He wanted to shield her from this, but had no idea how.

"Okay, let's get it over with," he told her.

Responding, Miranda took his hand and led him into the living room.

"Aren't you forgetting something?" he asked, nodding at Lola. Miranda hadn't stopped to put a leash on the dog. In fact, she'd left her in the dining room, gnawing on a bone that she had given her.

"I don't think so," Miranda answered innocently.

Instead of walking to the front door, she stopped in front of the Christmas tree. Bending down, she picked up a flat, rectangular box sporting shiny blue wrapping paper and held it out to him.

"Merry Christmas," Miranda declared. "A little early."

"What is it?" he asked, perplexed.

When he didn't take it from her, she gently shoved the box into his hands. "You could open it and see."

She was being very mysterious about this, Colin thought. Still not opening it, he told her uncomfortably, "I didn't get you anything."

"You've given me more than you think—and you were Santa Claus for all those kids," she added. "Now, are you going to open that? Or are you going to just keep looking at it?"

He would have preferred going with the latter, but knew that wouldn't be fair to her, especially after she had gone through all the trouble of not just getting him something but wrapping it, as well.

Colin made his decision. "I'll open it."

"Good choice," she told him with approval. Watching him do so, she could only marvel. "You tear off wrapping paper slower than anyone I've ever seen." Finally, he finished removing the wrapping paper to reveal a decorative gift box beneath. "Now take the top off the box and see what's in it," she coaxed.

When he did, Colin found paperwork. Specifically, paperwork that belonged to Lola, saying that she'd received her rabies vaccination as well as a number of other vaccinations. There was also confirmation of a license registration with the city of Bedford that was good for one year. The certificate stated that her name was Lola Kirby and that she belonged to—

Colin's head jerked up. "Me?" he asked, stunned. "I'm Lola's owner?"

Nodding, Miranda told him, "I didn't know what to get you for Christmas and then it came to me. You needed to have a friendly face to come home to, and Lola needed a home. It seemed like the perfect solution."

"But I can't take care of her," he protested. "I'm never home."

"Sure, you can take care of her. And when you need to take a break, you can leave her with me. I'll dog-sit Lola for you," she volunteered cheerfully.

He was as close to being speechless as he had ever been in his life. Shaking his head, Colin muttered, "I don't know what to say—you're crazy, you know that?"

"I would have accepted 'Thank you, Miranda. It's just what I wanted,'" she responded. Then, growing serious, she told him, "I saw it in your eyes, you know. The way you felt about Lola."

Moved, he came closer to her. So close there was hardly any space for even a breath between them. His gaze met hers. "What else did you see in my eyes?"

Lola was still in the dining room, working away at her soup bone. Except for the sound of teeth meeting bone, there was nothing but silence in the house.

Silence and heat.

"What else was I supposed to see in your eyes?" Miranda asked, her voice dropping to barely a whisper. Her mouth suddenly felt extremely dry, even as she felt her pulse accelerating, going double time.

"You, Miranda," he replied softly. "You were supposed to see you."

She could hardly breathe. "I thought that was just wishful thinking on my part," she confessed.

"You're trembling," he said.

She couldn't seem to stop. Grasping at straws, she said the first thing that came to mind. "It's cold in here."

"Then I guess I'll have to warm you up," Colin told her, his voice low and seductive as he took her into his arms.

The next thing she knew, Colin had lowered his mouth to hers.

And then the whole world slipped into an inky, endless abyss. There was nothing left except the two of them.

This time, there was no hesitation, no second thoughts.

For the first time since he'd met her, he felt no need to put on the brakes, or to tell himself that being with her like this was a mistake.

He wanted her.

Wanted her more than he wanted to breathe.

Because he had come to understand that this woman was what made his existence worthwhile. Just by being herself, she had brought happiness into his life. She'd taken his dark existence and illuminated it, bringing color into his world.

Color and warmth and desire in such proportions they completely overwhelmed him.

And humbled him.

He kissed Miranda over and over again, each kiss more soul-stirring than the one that had come before it. And then, just as she was about to utterly succumb to the passion that was making her head spin, he drew back for a moment.

Miranda felt confusion taking hold.

Oh Lord, he wasn't stopping again, was he? She didn't think she could bear it if he stopped.

Colin drew in a shaky breath. He needed to make his intention clear to her. He didn't want Miranda to look back on this later and feel that he had somehow used the madness of the moment to take advantage of her.

He wanted to be sure—and most of all, he wanted *her* to be sure.

"Miranda, I want to make love with you."

A laugh escaped her lips, a laugh of relief. "It's about time."

And then suddenly, just like that, everything felt right.

He kissed her with more eagerness than he thought he could possibly possess. His lips never left hers as desire surged through him, guiding him.

Controlling him.

He didn't remember undressing her, but he remembered every smooth, tempting curve of her body once her clothing had been stripped away. Remembered the thrill of passing his hands slowly over her silky skin. Remembered the rush he felt as he mentally cataloged every part of her, making it his.

Passion grew to incredible proportions, demanding an appeasement that couldn't be reached, because each time he drew closer to the peak, it moved that much further out of reach, tempting him to kept going, to keep taking refuge in all parts of her, in everything she had to offer.

The sound of her breathing, growing shorter and more audible, drove him wild.

He wanted to take her now, this moment. Wanted to bury himself in her. But with iron control, he reined himself in.

For her.

He wanted Miranda to remember this night, to remember him, and for that to happen, he needed to slow down. To make this all about her—and that, in turn, would make it about them, which had become so very important to him.

Sweeping her up in his arms, he carried her to her bedroom. He closed the door with his back, automatically creating their own private little world. Carrying her over to her bed, Colin placed her down on it gently.

His heart was hammering in his chest and echoing in his head as he lay down beside her. Demands collided within him, making it increasingly difficult to hold himself in check, to not give in to the ever-mounting desire just to take her.

Somehow, he managed to pace himself, but it was the hardest thing he had ever done.

Trailing his lips along Miranda's body, he anointed every part of her, thrilling to the sight and to the feel of her growing more and more excited. She was twisting and turning beneath him as if trying to absorb every sensation that he was creating for her.

With her.

When she ran her hands up and down his torso, when she turned the tables and mirrored all his movements, spiking his desire to unbelievable heights, Colin came exceedingly close to losing total control. But again, at the last moment, he caught himself, vowing to go one more round before he surrendered and made them into one joined being.

He feasted on her lips, the hollow of her throat, working his way down to her belly and farther. Her unbridled gasp when he brought her to her first climax reverberated within his chest, exciting him so much that he tottered on the very edge of restraint.

And then, fearing he couldn't hold on for even another heartbeat, Colin worked his way back up along her damp body, with Miranda rising and twisting against him as he went.

Suddenly, he was over her, his eyes meeting hers, his fingers entwining with hers.

Her legs parted beneath him, issuing a silent invitation he welcomed with every fiber of his aching being. When he entered her, they instantly moved together as if this was the way it was always meant to be. The tempo increased, the rhythm grew to demanding proportions that neither of them was capable of resisting.

Passion wrapped heated wings around them as they raced to the very top of the summit. To the very end of their journey.

When the explosion finally came, fireworks of majestic dimensions showered over them.

And Colin clung to her as if she was his very salvation.

Because she was.

Chapter Eighteen

A myriad of feelings vied for space within Colin as the heated, comforting glow of euphoria he'd been experiencing slowly began to recede. Feelings he wasn't able to completely sort out just yet.

Feelings that had been missing from his life for more than a decade.

As fierce passions settled down, he drew Miranda to him, happy just to have her here next to him on the bed. Contentment, something he was unfamiliar with up until now, washed over him.

He felt like a different person.

Colin wondered if there was a way he could remain here like this indefinitely, her breath mingling with his, the scent of the light, flowery body wash she used filling his senses.

He came close to drifting off when a noise caught his attention.

Moving his head to hear better, Colin couldn't quite place the sound. "You hear something?" he asked Miranda.

She turned her face toward him, managing to rub her cheek against his chest. He could literally feel her smile on his skin.

Raising her head just a little, she looked at him. "You can't tell what that is?"

"So then you *do* hear something." He was beginning to think that he was imagining it.

"Sure. That's Lola scratching against the door," she murmured. "I guess she finished gnawing on that bone and decided to track you down."

"Me?" he questioned. "Why me?" It didn't make any sense to him.

"My guess is that she wants your attention." He could feel heat beginning to travel through his body again as every inch of Miranda seemed to be smiling at him. "Why don't you open the door and let her in?"

"In here?" he asked, surprised.

Miranda didn't see why he would hesitate. "Why not? She's got the run of the place already."

"But we just, um…" Colin seemed to trip over his tongue.

She hadn't thought that he could be this incredibly sweet, so delicate that he didn't know how to go about saying that they'd just made love. She came to his rescue and glossed right over his meaning.

"Which is why she probably tracked you down," Miranda told him. "Lola knows that you're the alpha male and she wants to be the alpha female."

Colin stared at the woman in his arms, stunned as well as confused. "This is getting way out of hand. I don't understand any of it."

Miranda laughed. "Don't worry," she said, patting his chest. "I'm here to talk you through this if you need help. Just think of Lola as a fuzzy child. She needs discipline, a firm hand and lots of love—just like any child."

Colin sat up, looking at the door. The scratching continued.

He dragged a hand through his hair, trying to think, and feeling totally out of his element. "Taking care of a dog is a lot of responsibility."

"Yes, but it has a lot of compensation, too. Like boundless love."

He still looked uncertain. "I don't think I'm ready for this."

Since he wasn't getting up, Miranda did, wrapping the sheet around her.

"Not ready for being on the receiving end of boundless love? Sure you are," she exclaimed, making it sound as if she knew him better than he knew himself.

But he was thinking of the responsibility part. "No, if I'm going to be her new owner, I'm definitely going to need help," he said, looking at Miranda pointedly.

Meanwhile, she had opened the door and Lola came flying in. In two steps the German shepherd went from standing out in the hallway to standing on the bed. She came close to knocking Colin off the mattress in her enthusiasm and then started licking his face.

"Lots and lots of help," Colin declared, doing his best to sit up again and gain some semblance of the upper hand over the dog.

Miranda laughed as, still wearing the sheet like a Roman toga, she climbed back into bed. Lola was between them and was acting as if this was some sort of new game. Her head practically spun as she looked from one of them to the other, as if to say that she didn't know the rules to this game yet, but was more than willing to play.

Watching her, Miranda stated, "I think she wants you to pet her."

Stroking the animal, he looked over Lola's head at Miranda. "Now you see, I'm going to need that sort of insight to help me navigate through this pet ownership thing."

She was certainly on board with that, Miranda thought. "Like I said, you can give me a call anytime you need help."

"I appreciate that," he told her. "But then you'd have to find the time to come over, or I'd have to come over to you and bring the dog. That would consume an awful lot of downtime and we're both pretty busy as it is."

She knew she'd taken a chance when she'd decided to make him Lola's owner, but she'd thought he would last longer than a few hours.

Miranda took a breath, resigning herself to the inevitable. "You're saying you don't want the dog." She gave it one more shot, taking Lola's muzzle in her hands and turning the dog's head in his direction. "How can you say no to this face?"

"I'm not saying no," Colin told her. "I'm saying we need a different solution."

She took the only guess open to her. "You're saying you want her to stay with me."

But Colin shook his head. Stroking the dog's back—Lola had settled down and was now lying in the bed, content to have one of them on either side—he said, "That's not it, either."

At a loss now, she asked, "All right then, so what is it?"

Nerves all but got the better of him. This was brand-new territory for him and he didn't know how she would receive what he was about to say. "If you stop making guesses and just listen, I'll tell you." The moment the words were out of his mouth, he knew he'd sounded short with her.

"Okay." Miranda crossed her arms, waiting for him to go on.

The sheet slipped down just enough to give him a tantalizing glimpse of what he'd availed himself of earlier. Thinking about that, Colin found he had to struggle to keep his mind on what he was trying to say.

"So talk," she prompted, when he remained silent.

Here went nothing, Colin decided.

"I thought that we could move in together," he told her.

He was surprised that the words came out as easily as they did.

Miranda's mouth dropped open. But not a single sound emerged.

She was speechless, he realized, and he didn't know if that was a good thing or a bad one. Was she trying to find the words to turn him down gently, or was she so shocked that she'd lost the ability to talk?

"Move in together," she said, repeating his words.

"Yes," he confirmed, then went on to elaborate. "You could move in with me. But my place is small. It's an apartment and it might be kind of crowded for you, especially with Lola. Or I could move in here," he said, watching Miranda's face intently for her reaction.

"Move in together," she repeated again. "For the sake of the dog." The last words were uttered in semi-disbelief.

"Well, yes," he agreed. Something was off and he felt like a man trying to walk across a lake on very thin ice. He could feel the ice cracking beneath his feet with every step he took, yet he had no choice but to forge on. "You were the one who gave her to me, so I figured you'd want to do what was best for her."

"You want to move in together because of the dog," she said, as if trying to wrap her mind around what he was telling her.

"Well, that's one reason," he agreed. He was having a devil of a time getting the words out.

"Oh, so there's another reason?" she asked innocently.

Feeling awkward and totally inarticulate, not to mention afraid of being turned down once he told her the real reason behind his suggestion, Colin seriously thought about throwing up his hands and just abandoning the whole idea, lock, stock and barrel.

But then something egged him on.

It was all or nothing.

If he didn't say anything, he'd already lost, so there was nothing to lose by speaking up.

Frustrated, he shouted at her, "Of course there's another reason."

Lola instantly sat up, a canine barrier intent on protecting whichever one of them needed protecting.

"It's okay, Lola," Miranda said soothingly, rubbing the tip of the animal's ear, a trick she'd learned to calm a dog down. "It's okay. Lie down, girl."

After a moment, the dog obeyed.

"Okay," Miranda said, turning her attention back to him. "You were saying there was another reason…" She trailed off, waiting for him to pick up the conversation.

"You know there's another reason," he told her. When she continued silently looking at him, waiting, he blew out a breath. "You're going to make me say this, aren't you?"

"I'm afraid so." The corners of her mouth curved ever so slightly. "I need clarification, Colin. What's the other reason you want us to move in together?"

Exasperated, he raised his voice again. "Because I love you, damn it."

She struggled not to laugh. "Is that one word?"

"Miranda…" He sounded very close to the end of his rope.

Once again she came to his rescue. "I love you, too, damn it," Miranda said, mimicking his exact intonation. And then she asked, "Are you sure about this?" She would hate for him to look back with regret because it had all come about in the heat of the moment.

"Sure that I love you?" he questioned. "Yes, I'm sure. I just didn't want to have to say it. Putting myself out there is hard for me," he told her. "It's not something I do."

Reaching over the dog, who appeared to be close to falling asleep, she touched Colin's face and smiled. "I was talking about moving in together, but what you just said was very nice."

"Just 'very nice'?" he asked in surprise, mimicking *her* intonation.

There was humor in Miranda's eyes as she told him honestly, "I'm afraid if I say any more, I'll scare you off."

"After everything I've just been through, that is *not* going to happen," he stated.

"Since words are so difficult for you—" Miranda rose up on her knees, allowing the sheet to fall away and pool around her thighs "—why don't I just show you how I feel about what you said?"

She was about to lean into him when Colin put a finger to her lips, stopping her. "Hold that thought."

The next moment, he got off the bed, coaxing the dog to do the same. Holding on to Lola's collar, he guided the animal to the bedroom's threshold.

"C'mon, girl," he told her, "you need to go back into the other room for a few minutes."

"Just a few minutes?" Miranda pretended to question him.

"Maybe an hour—or two," he amended.

After taking Lola out, Colin was gone for a couple minutes. Returning, he made sure to close the door behind him.

Miranda cocked her head, listening for a moment for scratching noises.

Or whining.

She heard neither.

"Nothing," she said. "You really are good at disciplining." She wove her arms around his neck as he joined her.

Rather than say anything in response to her compliment, Colin murmured, "I hope you didn't have any plans for that other soup bone in the refrigerator."

So that was why the dog was so quiet. Miranda could only laugh. "You're as bad as I am."

"I really hope so," he told her.

And with that, there was no more talk. About anything. He had far better things to do than talk, and was more than eager to get started.

Epilogue

"Ladies, I think that it's pretty safe to say this is quite possibly the most unique wedding venue we have ever attended," Maizie told her two friends as she sat on the white folding chair between Theresa and Celia.

There was row after row of folding chairs in the hospital rec room, in the same area of the children's ward that just a few months ago had housed the giant Christmas tree.

The large room was all but filled to capacity with small patients from the ward, a great many women and children from the shelter, and several volunteers who worked with Miranda at the animal shelter.

"Thank goodness Miranda's mother and Colin's aunt were here early to make sure the altar was set up before it got so crowded in here," Theresa commented.

She and her catering team had arrived early, as well.

Working quickly, they had prepared everything for the reception that was to follow immediately after the ceremony.

"If they knew there was going to be this many people attending, why didn't they just opt for someplace bigger?" Celia asked.

"That's simple enough to answer," Theresa told her. "Miranda didn't want the children here missing the wedding. A lot of them aren't able or well enough to leave the hospital—and all of them are very attached to her. Miranda wouldn't dream of leaving any of them out."

Maizie nodded, pleased. "You ask me, Colin's getting a hell of a girl," she said to her friends. "There aren't many young women who are that thoughtful."

Theresa was beaming as she kept her eyes peeled for any sign that the bride was about to enter. "I really think that we outdid ourselves with this particular match, girls."

"Well, none of this would have happened if Maizie hadn't charmed that desk sergeant into rescheduling Colin's regular route so that he'd be right there when Miranda whizzed by," Celia commented. She turned toward Maizie. "How *did* you know that Miranda would be driving too fast?"

"And how did you really get that sergeant to change Colin's schedule with the other police officer's?" Theresa asked.

Maizie merely smiled, remaining tight-lipped, at least for now. "A girl's got to have some secrets, ladies," she told them with a wink.

"Not at this stage she doesn't," Celia told her life-long friend.

"Shh, they're starting to play the wedding march. You don't want to miss any of this," Maizie said.

Those who could rose to their feet. The rest of the attendees remained seated, anxiously anticipating the entrance of the bride.

Miranda was standing just outside the recreation room's closed doors, holding on to her bouquet of pink and white carnations and willing the sudden burst of butterflies in her stomach to go away.

"Nervous, darling?" Jeannine asked her daughter.

"A little. Mostly just afraid of tripping before I reach the altar," Miranda answered, a small smile curving her lips.

"You won't," Jeannine said confidently. "You're the steadiest person I ever knew."

Miranda took a breath, pressing one hand against her stomach as if that would get the butterflies to settle down.

"I wish your father was here," Jeannine said in a soft whisper. "He would have loved to see you in your bridal gown."

"He's here, Mom. I can feel it." The music swelled. Miranda took a breath. "That's our cue."

"I love you, Miranda," Jeannine told her.

"And I love you." She looked at her mother. The woman's cheeks were wet. "Please don't cry, Mom. You'll get your contacts all foggy."

Jeannine laughed, brushing the tears away. "Don't worry, I'll get you there. I promise."

The doors parted, drawn open by two of the orderlies. Miranda saw a sea of faces turning in her direction, but they all blended together before her eyes. Looking out at them, she could make out only one face in that enormous crowd.

The only face that mattered to her right at this moment.

Colin's face.

He was standing at the altar, looking incredibly handsome in his black tuxedo and dark gray shirt. She had half expected him to come in his police uniform. She wouldn't have cared what he wore, as long as he came.

"Ready, darling?" Jeannine asked.

Her eyes not leaving the man she had never expected to come into her life, Miranda answered, "More than ready, Mom."

They made their way up the makeshift aisle until they reached the minister, who was standing in front of the altar, waiting to say the words that would join her to Colin.

"Who gives this woman?" the man asked when she came before him.

"I do," Jeannine replied, her voice trembling. And then she withdrew so that the ceremony could begin.

"You look beautiful," Colin whispered to Miranda.

"You do, too," she told him.

He nearly laughed. It was a good feeling, he couldn't help thinking. Miranda had brought laughter into his life and into his heart.

More than a few of the children giggled as they

watched Lola trot up the aisle next, the wedding rings tied around her neck with a navy blue bow.

"We can begin," the minister announced.

Colin never thought he would ever be this lucky. When he looked at Miranda, just before they began to exchange their vows and their rings, he realized that she was thinking the same thing.

He could see it in her eyes.

They really were meant for one another, he thought. And he for one would always be eternally grateful for that.

* * * * *

For even more Christmas cheer from
Marie Ferrarella, make sure to check out
A BABY FOR CHRISTMAS
Available now from Cherish!

Don't miss previous titles in the
MATCHMAKING MAMAS *series:*

A SECOND CHANCE FOR THE SINGLE DAD
MEANT TO BE MINE

Available now from Mills & Boon Cherish.

And keep an eye out for
AN ENGAGEMENT FOR TWO,
the next book in this heartwarming series,
releasing in February 2018!

The Men Who Make Christmas

Meet the Hammond brothers—will they find their own happiness under the mistletoe?

For James and Justin Hammond, Christmas should be the most joyful time of year. It's Hammond's Toy Stores' most profitable time of the year, and their Christmas window displays are legendary. Yet it reminds them of the most heartbreaking event in their family history.

But when they meet two delightful women for whom the festive season means everything, the Hammond brothers can't help but be captivated by their infectious Christmas spirit! This year, can they make Christmas the most magical time of all?

Don't miss this sparkling Christmas duet!

Christmas with Her Millionaire Boss
by Barbara Wallace
November 2017

Snowed in with the Reluctant Tycoon
by Nina Singh
December 2017

SNOWED IN WITH
THE RELUCTANT
TYCOON

BY
NINA SINGH

First Published in Great Britain 2017
By Mills & Boon, an imprint of HarperCollins*Publishers*
1 London Bridge Street, London, SE1 9GF

© 2017 Nilay Nina Singh

ISBN: 978-0-263-92354-4

23-1217

MIX
Paper from
responsible sources
FSC™ C007454

This book is produced from independently certified FSC™ paper to ensure responsible forest management.

For more information visit: www.harpercollins.co.uk/green

Printed and bound in Spain
by CPI, Barcelona

Nina Singh lives just outside of Boston, USA, with her husband, children and a very rambunctious Yorkie. After several years in the corporate world she finally followed the advice of family and friends to 'give the writing a go, already'. She's oh-so-happy she did. When not at her keyboard she likes to spend time on the tennis court or golf course. Or immersed in a good read.

To my mother and father. For all their faith.

CHAPTER ONE

THE HOUSE WAS COLD.

Carli Tynan wasn't surprised. In fact, she'd never once entered this mansion and ever felt warm. Regardless of the season. And, despite the myriad of Christmas decorations currently adorning the foyer, nothing about the home felt particularly festive. Or even like a home. No, the Hammond estate felt more like a staid museum.

The eleven-foot-tall pine Christmas tree that nearly touched the ceiling notwithstanding.

Shaking the thin layer of snow off her wool coat, she peeled off her faux leather gloves, the bound portfolio tucked under her right arm. The darn portfolio was the only reason she was here, the reason her usual morning routine had been so handily disrupted. Carli was not a fan of disruptions. She'd already had to deal with way too many in her twenty-six years.

Her boss, Jackson Hammond, had asked her just this morning to drop off the file on her way in to work. Right after she'd gotten back from her early-morning run. It had barely given her time to shower, let alone to put herself together as well as she normally liked. As a result, her unruly curls were now a mess of tangles hastily secured in a haphazard bun on top of her head. She hadn't even had a chance to iron her remaining clean suit. The only other option was a stretch pencil dress that had recently shrunk after she'd accidentally thrown it in the dryer. Comfortable, it was not.

But she had a day full of meetings in the office, and this was the best she could do. Not at all the way she would have preferred to start off her morning. Or any morning for that matter.

All because the prodigal son was returning home.

Justin Hammond, Jackson's second-born, had been the one to request the portfolio. And apparently, he needed it before he could make it into the office. Carli had to accommodate him. Why was he suddenly heading back into town anyway? Justin hadn't had anything to do with Hammond's Toys since she'd been employed there. Now, suddenly, he was interested. Carli stepped farther into the foyer and couldn't resist the urge to roll her eyes. No doubt Justin's sudden interest was due to his older brother James's recent distractions, so to speak. James had apparently met someone and was now taking a well-deserved break from the day-to-day business. Little brother must have concluded that this was an ideal time to strike.

Never mind that Carli should be the one next in line to take over any of the duties James may be ready to relinquish. She couldn't help but feel a little insulted.

And hurt. Well, she'd just have to get over it. Then she'd have to work even harder to ensure she got the position she deserved.

She walked up to the foot of the stairs and yelled up toward the second floor. "Mr. Hammond, I'm dropping off the file."

No answer.

Jackson's hearing wasn't what it used to be. She shrugged

off her coat and dropped it on the nearby black leather settee, then walked halfway up the grand spiral stairway.

"Mr. Hammond, where would you like the files?"

Again, nothing. Carli let out a huff of frustration. She
certainly didn't want to risk having come out here only to
have the portfolio overlooked because the Hammond men
couldn't find it. She would have texted Jackson, but he was
notorious for wanting to have nothing to do with technology. He probably didn't even look at his phone every day.
Hence the request for a paper file. As for Justin Hammond, she barely knew a thing about him, let alone his
cell phone number.

She walked all the way up to the hallway and toward
Mr. Hammond's suite. The shower was running. Great.
She would have to yell through the door at the top of her
lungs, or he would never hear her.

Could this morning get any worse? She didn't think so.

Stepping into the master suite, she walked over to Mr.
Hammond's antique mahogany desk and dropped the portfolio atop it. Then yelled as loud as she dared across the
room toward the closed master bathroom door. "The portfolio is on your desk, Mr. Hammond."

A muffled acknowledgment sounded from the other
side, and Carli breathed a sigh of relief. Now she could
get out of here and finally start her day.

But the day had other plans. When she was midway
down the stairs, the front door opened and a shadowy,
tall figure stepped into the foyer. He dropped his suit-
case to the floor and seemed to hesitate before entering
any farther. Carli's step nearly faltered as she took in the
sight of him. Tall and dark with a firm square jaw and jet-
black hair. There was no mistaking who he was—Justin,
the other Hammond heir. All three men shared the same

rugged features, but the one standing before her had a different vibe altogether. An aura she would be hard-pressed to describe.

Regaining her balance, she managed to finally make her way down the stairs.

Justin finally looked up as she reached the foyer. He seemed to do a double take. Most men did when they first got a look at her. A fact she was quite aware of. And quite uncomfortable with.

"I'm sorry," he began, though he looked anything but. "I didn't realize anyone was here." He looked downright annoyed.

She tried to summon a polite smile, but her facial muscles seemed useless. Justin Hammond had eyes that a sorcerer would envy. The lightest shade of hazel littered with gold specks. What was wrong with her? She so wasn't the type to notice men's eyes, for heaven's sake.

"Um, your father's in the shower. I'm sure he'll be right out." In an awkward attempt to introduce herself, she extended her right hand. "I'm Car—"

But he stopped her midsentence. "Look, that's hardly necessary."

Carli blinked. Okay. No time for a quick introduction? Maybe he was just jet-lagged and tired from travel. Or perhaps he was just plain rude.

She cleared her throat. "Oh, I guess—" She looked to the side, unable to bear his gaze much longer given the awkwardness. "I guess I'll be on my way then."

He merely nodded, then stepped aside.

Carli tried not to flinch. She'd just effectively been shown the door! By the man who threatened the job she'd been working so hard for, no less.

Straightening to her full height, Carli stepped around

him and went to grab her coat from the settee. Then did the only thing she could. She left.

Her words about the morning not getting any worse mocked her.

Justin watched as the woman walked out and firmly shut the door behind her. Perhaps he'd been on the slim side of rude just now, but he so hadn't been expecting a stunning bombshell to come down the stairs as he entered his boyhood home. Not that he'd really been expecting anything in particular after having been gone over two decades.

Looked like his father's womanizing ways hadn't changed.

He glanced out the side palladium window as the woman walked down the driveway toward the parked car outside. *Ravishing.* It was the only word that came to mind. She had curves that would stop a monk in his tracks. The dress she wore hugged those curves in all the right ways. His father apparently liked them much younger these days; she had to be barely in her late twenties.

Well, it was no business of his. He was only here for a few days to analyze some numbers his father wanted him to look at. Though why the old man suddenly requested his younger son's help after all these years was a mystery, one Justin had no interest in investigating. He'd been ready to turn down the request and tell his father where he could go, but his mother had insisted he do Jackson Hammond's bidding. The old man still held the purse strings after all. And his mother had always been all about the Hammond purse strings.

Even after she'd fled this house and his father all those years ago, taking their younger son, him, along with her. He'd been the lucky one to get whisked away in the middle of the night once his mother finally decided she'd had enough.

He hadn't been back since. Until today.

Justin tried to get his bearings as he examined the foyer he hadn't walked through since he'd been a small child. Everything appeared smaller. The traditional Christmas decorations were as spectacular as he remembered. The tall pine by the stairs glittered with gold and silver ornaments. Sparkling lights adorned the stairs and banisters, a line of poinsettias graced the walls. So festive. In a nauseating and annoying way. All that was missing was a background track of loud Christmas music.

Bah, humbug.

What was he doing here? He should have refused his parents' requests and the hell with the consequences. Who did they think he was? Who did his father think *he* was? This was the same man who had ignored him until his older and rightful heir had decided last month that he'd needed some time off to go do…whatever he was doing. Justin had no idea, but it probably involved a woman. Maybe his brother had fallen in love.

Yeah, right, Justin thought as he made his way toward the living room. He sincerely doubted it. The Hammond genes weren't really conducive to such things. Love wasn't in their DNA.

More Christmas decorations greeted him in the living room, which had been updated with new furniture in addition to a slightly less dark shade of green painted on the walls. Or perhaps that had been the same color all along. He'd been gone from home a long time. Not that it ever really felt like a home to begin with.

Overall, reentering his childhood house so far felt somewhat surreal. Like he'd stepped into a previous life.

The sound of footsteps coming down the stairs pulled

him out of his musings. Steeling himself against the anger barely contained under the surface, Justin turned to face Jackson Hammond—the man who had watched a young Justin being yanked out that front door all those years ago without lifting a finger to stop it.

Past history, Justin thought as he turned to greet his father. Or more accurately, the man who had sired him.

To his surprise, Jackson hadn't changed all that much. The graying at his temples had spread through to most of his thick, wavy hair. A few more wrinkles framed the area around his mouth. Other than that, Justin felt as if he could be looking at the same face he had last seen all those years ago.

"Thank you for coming, son," his father said, and extended a hand. It was the most awkward handshake Justin had ever performed.

"You're welcome."

"I know what a busy man you are, so I really appreciate it."

Justin merely nodded. No need for Jackson to know that if it weren't for his mother's insistence, Justin would still be on the other side of the country.

"Given your global reputation as a management consultant, I figured it was about time you did a full assessment of the company you're part heir to," his father added, then shook his head as if in disbelief. "Something I should have requested long ago."

"I suppose that makes sense," Justin offered.

"You've accomplished quite a lot for such a young age," Jackson added. "That consulting firm of yours is known all over the world." Was that a look of pride on his face? If so, it was too little, and much too late.

"Business has been good."

"So I've read. As well as reading about your fast rise in the industry."

Justin processed his father's words. Words that would have meant the world to him when he was a teenager, or even a college student. How many school events or sporting events had he desperately searched the audience on some small glimmer of hope that Jackson might have shown up? How many times had the phone rang on his birthday with none of the calls being from his father?

No. Justin had long ago stopped pining for any acknowledgment from the man standing before him. "Why don't I get started then?" he prompted, changing the subject.

What had Jackson expected? If his father had any notion that this visit was to be a touching reunion between long-lost father and son, he was in for a disappointment.

Carli found herself becoming more and more annoyed as she drove away from the Hammond mansion. Of all the nerve! She'd never been dismissed by anyone in such a fashion—and she'd grown up in a houseful of siblings. Undivided attention wasn't exactly something she was used to. But the way Justin Hammond had just practically ejected her had been downright insulting. To make matters worse, she'd done nothing but stood there like a stunned doe. How pathetic.

She took the curve around the next bend a little too fast and realized she was letting her anger get the best of her. Deep breaths. So what if her new boss was a rude, insensitive clod? She could handle it.

He would not get to her. She'd worked too hard and overcome too much to get to where she was in her career. Her job with Hammond's Toys meant everything. And she was good at it, damn it!

Why did Justin Hammond have to show up and put all

of it in jeopardy? But there was an even bigger question, she had to admit. Why hadn't she stood up for herself? It was like she'd looked into his eyes and gone totally mute. Recalling his gaze just now had her drawing in a deep breath. Heavens, those caramel-hued eyes were the devil's tool for distraction. And there was something behind them, a distant, haunted look if she'd ever seen one.

She hmmphed. Now she was just getting fanciful. He was just her new boss. And she had to deal with him, that's all.

The honk of a horn behind her startled her out of her thoughts. She'd stopped at a red light and hadn't even noticed it had turned. Time to get a grip.

Justin Hammond had already taken way too much of her time, and she had things to do.

That reminder became all too evident when she made her way into her office. Her assistant was already there at the desk, with a file of papers waiting for Carli's signature or attention. The latest cost-cutting initiative was becoming quite the project—one she'd been given the primary responsibility for. Until Justin was called in, that was.

"Hey, Jocelyn. Sorry I'm late."

The petite brunette gave her a friendly smile. "Don't sweat it. You're not that late."

"Well, it's late for me."

"Please tell me it's because you had a hot, steamy date last night that turned into a wild night. And that he wouldn't let you get up out of bed this morning."

"Last night was a Tuesday."

Jocelyn gave her a blank look. "What's your point?"

Why did she bother? "Never mind. Are those the latest data points?"

Her assistant nodded and handed her the thick pile of

folders. "I printed them like you requested. The electronic file is in your inbox."

"Thanks. You know where I'll be for most of the morning. These numbers are going to take a while to get through. And I'm already behind." *Due to an unexpected project I was just given this morning*, she added to herself. A project for the sole purpose of getting Justin Hammond up to speed on the latest business figures.

"Well, you can't be working on them all morning."

Carli lifted an eyebrow. "Why's that?"

"Mr. Hammond just called and asked me to schedule yet one more meeting. We have an unexpected guest coming in."

Oh, no. Carli could venture to guess who it might be. "Please tell me it's not Justin Hammond."

Jocelyn gave her a curious smile. "I could do that. But I'd be lying to you."

Great. Just great. Was the man sent here just to vex her at every turn? Apparently, she was supposed to jump whenever Justin Hammond needed anything.

Jocelyn studied her, the amused smile still on her face. "Something wrong?"

Carli tried to shake off the frustration. "I just have a lot to do. And he happens to be the reason I'm late to begin with."

"Aha! So I was right."

"Right about what?"

"You were indeed late because of a sexy man."

Jocelyn just didn't know when to let up. "Only because I had to prepare a report for him at the last minute and then deliver it before I got in today."

Her assistant waved her hand in dismissal. "Details."

"Honestly, Jocelyn. I barely met the man for a few scant moments."

"So tell me. Is he as handsome as he appears in all the photos?"

"I didn't notice."

That earned her a disbelieving look. "See. This is why I worry about you. Justin Hammond is one of the most eligible bachelors on the planet. He's on the celebrity sites weekly. Wealthy, successful and handsome. And you didn't even notice his looks?"

"Not really, no." She could fib quite well when she had to.

Jocelyn slammed her hands on her hips. "That's just disappointing. Most of the female staff around here are breathless with anticipation at his arrival. And you act like it's an ordinary day. You gotta give me something. Some small detail I can throw to them."

"That's just silly. He's just the other Hammond heir."

"Right. A mere handsome millionaire who not only has claim to half the largest retail toy company in North America but also made gobs of money on his own."

She did have a point there. Justin's life story so far was a bit on the exceptional side. She was about to begrudgingly admit to that when a small commotion outside her door drew both their attention. Looked like Jocelyn was about to find out firsthand what she was so curious about. Justin had arrived. And he was causing quite a stir, no doubt with most of the female staff. Carli heard "can I get you anything, Mr. Hammond" more than once.

Jocelyn jumped to the door. "Ooh, he's here." She gasped. "And he's heading right to your office."

A strange sensation spread through Carli's chest. Despite seeing several photos of him throughout the years, she had to admit he wasn't what she'd been expecting. All the pictures hadn't really done him justice. They hadn't captured the soft, tawny hue of his eyes. Or the way his hair fell sloppily over his forehead. She hadn't realized she'd noticed so much of him during those brief moments in the Hammond foyer earlier.

A quick knock on the door, and then Justin stepped into her office. He blinked in surprise when he saw her. "You?"

What was that supposed to mean? Did he want her out already? Genuine surprise registered on his face. Was he here to lay claim to her office, having expected her to vacate it for him already?

Too stunned to speak, Carli was relieved when Jocelyn stepped up to him. "Mr. Hammond, I'm Jocelyn Sumner. We weren't expecting you so early. The meeting isn't until nine thirty."

He hadn't taken his eyes off Carli. She resisted the urge to look away from the intense stare.

"I figured I'd get started," he answered Jocelyn. "I'm looking for the person who put this together." He held up the file of papers Carli dropped off less than an hour ago. "I was told this is their office."

Carli finally found her tongue. "It is."

He blinked at her. "Can you tell me where to find him now?"

Him. "You have," she answered, deliberately omitting further clarification. Let him hang in the wind a bit.

He lifted an eyebrow.

"I'm the one who put it together. I was dropping it off this morning when we…met." She added some emphasis on the last word.

Justin's eyes grew wide as understanding clearly dawned. Jocelyn stood between them, her gaze switching back and forth as if she were watching an exciting tennis game.

Justin cleared his throat. "You did this?" he asked, indicating the file in his hand. "It's, uh, very thorough. Very impressive."

Carli tried not to bristle at his surprised tone. How very insulting. This man didn't know a thing about her. But he'd made his initial judgment already. She wasn't surprised. Men like Justin always came to the most obvious conclusion when it came to her.

How disappointing that he was so typical.

CHAPTER TWO

GREAT, JUSTIN THOUGHT as the woman across the room shot daggers at him. He hadn't realized this morning that she worked for the company. He'd managed to offend one of Hammond's employees on his first day back in town. No, make that his first *hour* back.

She crossed her arms in front of her chest. "Well, you needn't look so surprised. I'm a project manager at Hammond. I can put together a business report."

"That's not what I meant." But what was she doing coming down from his father's suite at that hour? He couldn't be blamed for having jumped to the most obvious conclusion. And he still wasn't sure he was totally wrong. But clearly there was more to the circumstances. "I'm just surprised to see you here, that's all."

"This is my office. Of course, I'm here."

"Not here, in this room. Here at the company."

She merely quirked an eyebrow. A gesture that seemed to add a haughty quality to her features. Her almond-shaped eyes were a deep chocolate brown. Several tendrils of hair escaped her tight bun and framed an olive-shaped face.

Not classically beautiful, but she was striking in an unusual and rare way.

And her figure—he didn't even want to go there.

"Never mind," she declared, and stepped around her desk. "My name is Carli Tynan. I'm regional project manager for Hammond Retail. James hired me, but I work more closely with Jackson."

He reached his hand out to shake hers just as she said, "You, of course, need no introduction."

Her tone suggested she didn't mean that in a complimentary way. "Nice to meet you."

She pointed to the file he still held. "Is there anything you'd like to go over?" This woman was all business. Regardless of what she'd been doing at the mansion earlier, he had no doubt she was an efficient employee who clearly had things under control.

"I made a few notes, things that I wouldn't mind some further clarification on."

She indicated the chair in front of her desk. "Have a seat. We have some time before the meeting."

Justin hesitated. He wasn't used to being ordered around; the feeling made him uncomfortable. As did the incessant echo of Christmas music playing in the lobby.

"Would you mind if we closed the door?" he asked her, already walking to it.

"Any particular reason?"

"I can't focus with the cursed Christmas tunes playing in the background."

He shut the door and turned back to find her studying him with curious eyes. "You have something against Christmas music?"

"Christmas is one day. But for some reason the whole world is burdened with listening to those blasted tunes for weeks on end. That doesn't happen with any other holiday, now does it?"

"Christmas is hardly like any other holiday."

"Only because the whole world insists on dragging it

out. It's one day, yet we insist on calling it the holiday season."

"Some would argue it's at least twelve days," she countered.

Clever, she'd referenced another Christmas carol. "Don't tell me you're one of those types. The ones who make their shopping list in October. You pull out the tree and decorations as soon as the Thanksgiving turkey is consumed. Am I close?"

"And what would be so wrong about it if I was?"

He shrugged. He wasn't going to try to explain it. Christmastime around his house as a young boy had usually meant the start of weeks of arguments followed by loud, drunken fights. With his father working long hours and his mother growing more and more resentful at his absence. Of course, there were problems throughout the year, but the holiday season seemed to bring out the worst in his parents. An excuse to purge their anger and throw everything in the open. By the time Christmas morning rolled around, he and his brother were more than ready to have it all over with. Even the toys weren't enough to make up for the turmoil and chaos.

How had they even gotten into this conversation anyway? Justin wondered. All he'd asked was to shut the door so he didn't have to hear the music from the lobby. He didn't need to explain himself to a woman he'd just met.

Carli was still staring at him expectedly. She'd asked him a question that he'd left hanging. "Nothing. Never mind. Forget I said anything."

"Okay. But I feel I have to say just one more thing."

Why was he not surprised? "Go ahead."

"That you have to realize how—" she paused and glanced at the ceiling, as if scrambling for the correct word "—curious your perspective about Christmas is. Given who you are."

Of course he realized that. He was heir to one of the most successful retail toy operations in the Northern Hemisphere. A business that earned most of its profits in the weeks between Thanksgiving and Christmas Eve. Sure, it was true that as an adult he'd made his own way and had become a successful businessman in his own right. But he'd been granted worldly advantages at birth that most people could only dream of. He should be thanking his lucky stars for the gift of Christmas and the commercialism that surrounded it.

And to anyone on the outside, he probably sounded like an ungrateful, cranky Scrooge who didn't appreciate all the blessings he'd been granted.

Judging by Carli's expression, that's exactly what she was thinking.

Carli watched as Justin walked out of her office half an hour later, relieved to finally have some time to herself. What a strange morning it had been. It had taken all she had to remain cool and professional once he'd walked in here. She'd pulled it off, but barely. The whole while she was speaking with Justin regarding the business, her insides had felt like jelly. Thank heavens she hadn't eaten anything this morning. It probably wouldn't have stayed down.

The problem was, she wasn't sure what was causing all the turmoil. Sure, it had been upsetting when he'd so casually dismissed her as she was trying to introduce herself. And she'd known he was judging her by her appearance. But none of that was anything new for her.

People always underestimated her at first. She just made sure to prove herself, had been doing so her whole life.

Not to mention, she'd had to find ways to somehow differentiate herself from her four siblings. Right smack in the middle, she was oh-so-easy to overlook. Tammy was the wise oldest sister, happily married with a lovely little boy. Janie, the beautiful one. People in their town actually called her JB, short for Janie Beautiful. Janie had the sort of looks that made men stammer when they spoke to her. While Carli was curvy and voluptuous, her next older sister was gorgeous in an angelic and soft way that Carli could never compete with. She certainly hadn't been able to last year…

Don't even start with that.

And the twins…well, they were twins. That fact alone made them stand out.

Carli was just the middle sister. Nothing special there. Barely noticeable in the crowd. So she made sure to work harder than any of them. Years of study and long hours, first at business school and then at the office, she hadn't taken anything for granted.

And now the arrival of the other Hammond son might be threatening all of that. No wonder she felt so out of sorts when Justin was near. She had to do something to fix that, but what exactly?

Jocelyn tapped lightly on her door before she could answer her own question.

"Come in."

"Hey, how did it go? Were you even able to focus?"

Carli shrugged as she opened her email inbox. "Of course," she said, though it was a fib. "Why in the world wouldn't I?"

"I'm sure I wouldn't have been able to. Not with those deep dreamy eyes focused on me."

Carli resisted the urge to grunt. "Not this again." No way was she going to admit, not even to herself, that there might be a kernel of truth to Jocelyn's words, that in fact it *had* been pretty distracting every time she'd looked up and found herself under the intense focus of Justin's gaze.

"Jocelyn, you need a date."

Her assistant groaned with frustration. "Don't I know it."

"Are you bringing anyone to the party tonight?"

She answered with a sad shake of her head. "I'm really looking forward to it, still. You're very sweet to host one every year."

Being sweet really had nothing to do with it. Carli loved throwing that regular yearly party. She'd been planning and shopping for it since October.

"Well, in any case, you need to stop focusing on Justin Hammond's looks or his appeal," she admonished the younger woman, though part of her was addressing herself. "For all intents and purposes, the man is our boss."

Jocelyn pulled out the chair across from Carli's desk and plopped into it. "I know, I know. I'm just admiring him from afar. I wouldn't dream of going after the man who owns part of the company I work for."

"Good, I'm glad to hear it."

A mischievous smile formed on Jocelyn's lips. "Besides, he hardly glanced in my direction when he was here. He was much more focused on someone else."

Carli didn't like where she was going with this. "I want no part in where you're trying to take this conversation."

Jocelyn leaned forward in the chair, gave her a smile that could only be described as wicked. "Oh, come on! You had to notice."

"Notice what?"

"The way he was looking at you. Or more accurately, how he couldn't look away."

"All I noticed was how to make sure I gave him all

the information he needed to get himself situated. He just needed more info about how the company operates."

Jocelyn looked skeptical. "Right. Just admit it."

"I don't see the point." The last thing she wanted to talk about, in her office no less, was the way men looked at her. The way Justin had looked at her. Recalling the way his eyes had roamed over her sent a shiver down her spine even now.

"Does there have to be a point to everything?"

Carli couldn't help but smile. Had she ever been that lighthearted? She couldn't remember a time. Not even as a child. There was always too much to do. Always a mess to clean up or a sibling to look after.

"I'd just like to figure out why he's really here. After all these years," she said, trying to change the subject back to business.

Jocelyn shrugged slightly. "I thought it was just because James is going to be away for a while. And that Mr. Hammond, as both their father and CEO, decided it would be a good time to bring him on board with his older brother otherwise occupied."

Carli knew that's how things looked on the surface. But it still didn't explain Justin's sudden appearance. She was more than capable of holding down the fort while James Hammond was away. That wasn't self-aggrandizing or conceit. The eldest Mr. Hammond had expressed the notion in countless ways over the years.

"I'm glad he is here!" Jocelyn exclaimed. "Things were getting way too droll around this place. We needed some excitement."

"You just like looking at him."

"No doubt!" Jocelyn actually giggled. "I mean, what's not to like? He's downright dreamy. I've been watching him for years in all the tabloids. With one exotic model after another. Or that actress, what's her name. She was in that romantic comedy last year. I hear he's single now though."

"Uh-huh."

"Personally, I'm of the opinion that he should try to find someone with more substance. I mean, what are the chances he would ever fall for an everyday, average woman though, right? Men like that never do. He's way too glamourous and worldly for that. Wouldn't you agree?"

Carli's request to finally terminate this conversation died on her lips when she noticed someone had arrived at her open door. The blood left her brain when she realized who it was. Justin.

How long had he been standing there? And how much had he heard?

If the floorboards opened up and swallowed her whole, it wouldn't be enough to lessen her mortification.

This was just fabulous. On top of everything else, now he was going to see her as nothing but an office gossip.

His reputation preceded him yet again, Justin thought as he hesitated outside Carli's office door. He'd caught just enough of the women's conversation to realize it was absolutely about him. Also that it was mostly one-sided. Carli had barely spoken a word. In fact, she appeared ready to give her assistant a hard shake.

The other woman's back was turned to where he stood, but Carli had clearly seen him.

Damn.

This was awkward. Unable to come up with anything appropriate to say, he simply cleared his throat. Jocelyn, the assistant, actually jumped in her chair.

Carli didn't take her disapproving eyes off her when

she spoke. "Justin, something else I can do for you? Joc-elyn was just leaving."

"Yes, yes, I was." Jocelyn bolted up and ran out of the room, making sure not to look Justin in the eye.

Carli motioned to the newly abandoned chair in front of her desk. "Please, have a seat." She glanced at her watch. "Though we don't have a lot of time before the staff meeting."

Her cheeks were flushed, and she wouldn't meet his eyes either. Still awkward.

"It's okay," he began, then sat. "This won't take long."

"What can I do for you?"

Justin swore under his breath. This was going to be even more uncomfortable after he'd walked in on the previous conversation. But it was too late to back out now. Besides, he owed her an apology. He took a deep breath. "Listen, I know we got off on the wrong foot. I mean this morning. At my father's house."

She quirked an eyebrow in surprise.

"I'm not usually so…"

"Rude?" she supplied as he trailed off.

"That's probably an accurate description. In my defense, I'd been traveling all night. Not that it's any kind of excuse."

"I agree. It's not any kind of excuse."

Wow. She was a tough one. He didn't need this; he was only trying to apologize. Albeit doing a terrible job at it. But instead of being annoyed by her directness, he found it somewhat intriguing. Refreshing in a way. Most people didn't bother to challenge him under any circumstances. Carli Tynan was clearly not like most people. Her gaze pinned him where he sat. He hadn't noticed before just how her eyes appeared to go from deep chocolate to hazel when the light hit her face a certain way. Or the fullness of her lips, even as tightly pursed as they were at the moment.

"You're right. I just wasn't expecting to see anyone in my father's house that early. Especially someone like you, coming down the stairs at that hour. My mistake."

Her eyes grew wide, and the color in her cheeks heightened to a deep shade of red. Her grip on the pen she held grew so tight that her knuckles turned pale. This did not bode well, he thought.

"What are you saying exactly, Mr. Hammond?" she asked through gritted teeth. Uh-oh. He'd just gone from being Justin to Mr. Hammond in the span of a few moments.

"Nothing. I mean, I'm simply trying to clear the air. To explain my reaction upon seeing you."

"Maybe you should do that. Explain exactly what your reaction was when you first saw me this morning."

She threw it out like a challenge. One he wasn't foolish enough to even attempt to accept. He'd begun this apology all wrong. But the conversation he'd overheard between Carli and her assistant had thrown him off. Heck, Carli herself kept throwing him off. It was like he didn't even know how to behave around her.

Where was it coming from?

"Never mind. It's not important," he said, hoping she would drop the whole matter.

Apparently, that was too much to hope for. He should have known better. She immediately shook her head. "No, please clarify. I'm very interested in what exactly it is you're trying to say."

The woman was relentless. "Look, it's not important. I simply wanted to offer an apology."

She studied him in a way that made him feel like a lab specimen under a microscope. Perhaps some sort of insect. If he wasn't so damn uncomfortable, he would have almost laughed at her scorn at him.

"Which you still haven't done," she said.

"What?"

"I've yet to hear an apology. Or a valid explanation, for that matter."

His mouth grew dry. Damn it, he was a successful executive, known for his cut-throat business style and ruthless negotiation skills. How was this woman cutting him off at the knees? And why was he almost enjoying it?

"Um? Explanation?"

She gave him a smirk of a smile, like he'd been caught. He supposed he had. "For why you behaved as you did. I was simply delivering a file at your father's request. And instead of introducing yourself, you dismissed me and practically shooed me out of the house."

Justin cringed at her description. He couldn't believe he'd been such a boor to her. Nor could he believe the way he was botching this apology now. Not only had be managed to insult a valuable Hammond employee, he couldn't even apologize for it in a sufficient manner. True to form, when it came to anything Hammond related, Justin was woefully lacking. He may have started his own wildly successful consulting firm and grown it from a one-man operation to a major international business. But when it came to being a Hammond, all he'd ever managed was failure. More proof that he didn't belong here back in Boston. Or at Hammond's Toys for that matter.

He had to pull himself together. Find a way to explain himself. But how? It's not like he could come out and admit to jumping to the worst conclusion—suspecting Carli to be his father's mistress. Though it was obvious she'd figured it out. If looks could kill and all that.

Nothing to do now but be completely straight. And

hope the damage could be repaired somehow. He and Carli would be working together for the next several days. She was clearly a major asset to this corporation, and he had managed to insult her in a major way. He had to fix this.

"The truth is there is no excuse or explanation for the way I behaved. Please believe that it had nothing to do with you personally and everything to do with my father."

She remained silent, not ready to give an inch.

"I can only say I'm sorry," he added. "And that I will somehow find a way to make it up to you."

She shrugged with derision, and though she didn't say the words, her response was clear: *as if you could.*

Maybe she was being petty, but Carli wasn't going to give him the benefit of a response. Justin Hammond had made a horribly insulting assumption about her and the older man she worked for. That's something she would not readily forget.

Still, she couldn't help but feel more than a little touched at his genuine apology. Even given how badly he'd botched it up. He really did seem to feel remorseful. If the circumstances were different, if he weren't the boss's son and instead they were somehow new friends, she might have explained to him that she'd been dealing with such impressions all her life.

But he *was* a Hammond. And they definitely were not friends.

She would do her best to help him while he was here and hope that his tenure at Hammond's Toys was a short one. The events of this morning proved that Justin was walking in blind. He'd had no clue who she was or just how much she was in charge of. She didn't have time to babysit the prodigal son on a long-term basis.

She stood up from her chair and walked around her

desk. "Well, I guess the prudent thing to do would be to move on and try our best to work together as productively as possible."

Justin stood, as well. He looked notably relieved. "I agree. And I appreciate it."

"We can start with this staff meeting. I asked Jocelyn earlier to forward you a copy of the agenda."

He nodded. "I got that. Thanks."

He followed her down the corridor to the meeting room where several employees had already gathered. After a brief round of introductions, Carli began the meeting with the first item on the agenda.

The first time she stammered, she chalked it up to feeling exhausted and due to the mishaps of the morning. By the third mistake, however, she had to admit that she was off her game. She also had to admit that it had everything to do with the new face sitting at the table.

Justin leaned forward, listening attentively and frequently jotting down note after note. He preferred old-fashioned paper and pen, which surprised her. Most of the executives she dealt with couldn't wait to purchase and show off the latest technology e-tablet or the sleekest new laptop.

Aside from an occasional question or request for clarification, he was mostly quiet. Still, his presence was jarring.

She wasn't the only one who seemed to think so. Several furtive glances were cast in Justin's direction. One of the younger new recruits from sales smiled at him demurely, not even pretending to pay attention to Carli's updates. Though annoyed, she could hardly blame the other women. Justin had a presence. Add to that the mystery surrounding his arrival, and people were having trouble feigning indifference.

Herself included.

At the conclusion of the meeting an hour later, she was more than ready to be done and to get out of there. A cup of coffee would be heaven right about now. She hadn't been able to get her usual cup due to her detour, and a dull ache was beginning to throb behind her eyes. No doubt the caffeine withdrawal had been at least partly responsible for her less than stellar performance.

"Well, if that's everything, I think we can wrap up."

Everyone stood except for a few stragglers who stuck around to discuss their next to-do or to make small talk. Eventually, even they slowly filed out of the room.

In fact, when she looked up, Carli found that everyone had left except for one lone holdout. Justin remained seated. He studied her with avid interest. He clearly had something to say.

Carli set her jaw. Looked like her caffeine hit was going to have to wait. "Was there something else, Justin?"

"Yes, as a matter of fact. If you have a few moments, I think there are some things we should probably discuss. Sooner rather than later."

Something in his tone made her stomach twist. She sat back down.

"Go on."

"I've been going over the numbers, and Hammond's profit margins are mostly impressive. But there are areas that are lagging."

"I'm aware of that."

"Then you also realize that a handful of the retail stores have seen steadily declining sales."

"I'm aware of that too. There are several ideas in the pipeline to address this. As I just mentioned."

He glanced down at the notes in his leather-bound notebook. "Yes, I heard. All well-thought-out ideas involving online expansion. The modifications to the website are particularly impressive."

"But?"

"My concern is that there's a need to remove some of the more sluggish units, so to speak. Hammond's should be making some cuts."

"What sort of cuts?" she asked, though she knew exactly where this was headed. The twist in her stomach turned a bit tighter.

"With your background and experience, I'm sure you've concluded which brick-and-mortar stores are just not pulling their weight. In fact, their only real profits register during the holidays."

"It's a very seasonal business."

"Nevertheless. Some of these stores just don't get enough foot traffic during the year to justify keeping them open." He glanced down at the file she had handed him just hours ago. "There's one in particular we need to seriously consider the future of. It hasn't seen any kind of significant sales for the past half decade."

Carli bit down on her lip. She knew exactly which store he was referring to. The one she'd started out in as a lowly retail clerk trying to save enough money for college. The same store that currently employed several people she'd grown up knowing and caring for. The one situated at the heart of Westerson, MA—a quaint, touristy spot along the inland coast of Cape Cod in Massachusetts. The same town she'd grown up in.

And Justin wanted to shut it down.

CHAPTER THREE

HER PARTY GUESTS were going to be here within the hour, and Carli was just now stepping out of the shower. So far, this day had been nothing but one big race against the clock. She should have started prepping as soon as she got home. Instead, she'd taken the time to go over the sales figures.

Not that there was any use, and Carli had known it. But she'd hoped for some small miracle that had somehow been missed. Something, anything she could use as leverage to argue that Justin should nix the idea of closing the doors of the Cape store for good.

Of all the retail stores in the Hammond chain, why did that have to be the one performing the worst? She'd practically grown up in that store. Mr. Freider, the manager going on twenty years, had always welcomed her with open arms. As a child, she'd go into that store by herself, just to pass the time in peace when things were just too noisy at home. During her teenage years, she'd spent countless hours in the Book Nook, the corner of the store dedicated to latest in children's and young adult books. She'd devoured a world of stories in that small area, Mr. Freider never complaining about her lack of purchases—purchases she couldn't afford. In fact, he'd been kind enough to bring hot chocolate on cold days and sweet lemon iced tea during summer.

That same kind man would very well lose his job if it were up to Justin.

There had to be something she could do. Perhaps she could go straight to Jackson. Plead her case. The only problem was, she didn't really have a professionally sound one. Essentially, that would amount to asking for a favor, as his protégé. As steep as the stakes were, she couldn't bring herself to do that. She'd never once approached Jackson Hammond as anything less than a professional and wouldn't start now. Not even under these circumstances.

Carli blinked away the thoughts. She had to get going already; no doubt some of the invitees would be straggling in early, ready to party on this cold December Boston evening without much else to do. She hadn't even towel dried her hair yet.

What had possessed her to plan a Christmas party on a Wednesday night anyway? And just her luck, it had happened to fall on the same day that Justin Hammond had blown into town and thrown her whole world into a spiral.

Now she was running late and dripping wet just as most of her colleagues were about to descend on her apartment for some yuletide Christmas cheer. A timer went off in the kitchen, a reminder to take the crab cakes out of the oven. Thank goodness she'd put out all the decorations weeks ago, the day after Thanksgiving. A tradition from her childhood. Exactly as Justin had guessed. The Tynan family may not have had much in the way of material things, but they made sure to celebrate their ceremonial traditions. Ceremonies that often got downright unruly and chaotic. She supposed that was to be expected in a family of five children.

By some Christmas miracle, she was ready when the

first guests arrived: Jocelyn and some of the account reps along with a couple of regional managers. Carli didn't even recognize two of the arrivals. That's what happened when you posted an open invite. She didn't mind. These people were her second family now, Hammond's Toys was her second home. She was lucky to have such an opportunity with such a wonderful company. Current situation with the boss's son notwithstanding.

In fact, an hour later when the party was in full swing and several champagne bottles had been corked, she found herself blessedly distracted and finally able to enjoy herself. Until one of the elderly secretaries walked in. She wasn't alone.

"I hope you don't mind," Miranda Sumpter said, her gray hair framing her maternal face. "I brought someone with me."

Carli tried to hide her surprise. Justin, to his credit, looked less than pleased to be there.

Miranda was staring at her expectedly. "I mean, it said open invitation on the company wide email. And Justin's definitely part of the company. You don't mind, do you?"

"Yes! No! I mean. Of course he's welcome." Now Justin just looked bemused. Carli gripped her glass flute in her hand tight enough that her fingers ached. Then she took a large swig.

Justin stepped toward her. "I didn't realize you'd be the host, Carli."

Well, how was she supposed to respond to that? Was the implication that he wouldn't have come if he'd known?

Miranda stood staring at the two of them as an awkward silence settled. Carli cleared her throat. "So, how do you two know each other?" she finally managed to ask.

Miranda gave Justin's arm an affectionate squeeze. "Oh, he and I go way back. I used to babysit this little hurricane when he was no more than a mischievous toddler. When I first started out in the Hammond secretarial pool and needed some extra cash."

She turned to Carli. "They were always looking for a sitter for this one. Couldn't handle him without a little help. He was constantly getting into trouble."

He still was, Carli thought. If the tabloids were to be believed.

"I just about fell over when I saw him in the hallway this afternoon," Miranda continued. "Almost didn't recognize him."

Justin gave her a playful wink. "I've changed just a bit, huh?"

"You still look plenty mischievous." The older woman laughed. "You should have seen some of the disasters he used to get himself into," Miranda said Carli. "Always in trouble. His parents were at their wits' end most days."

The tone was lighthearted, Miranda laughing merrily. But Carli couldn't help but notice Justin fidgeted as she spoke. He turned the watch on his wrist and pulled on the band. He was clearly uncomfortable. Probably regretted having come here now that he realized this was her party.

"I've since matured a bit," he offered.

"I would certainly hope so." Miranda laughed again. "You were quite the hellion."

"Yes, I recall my parents not being able to wait to rush out of the house as soon as you showed up."

Carli detected an undercurrent in his tone, a hardness. As the middle daughter in a family with five girls, she could certainly relate to growing up in a chaotic, messy household. But she couldn't remember her parents ever trying to "rush out" to get away from any of them. Lord knew, they'd given both Mom and Dad plenty of reasons to want to.

"At least I got to leave at the end of the night. Your parents were stuck with you, weren't they?" Miranda gave him a playful pinch on the cheek.

"I'm surprised you kept coming back."

"There were plenty of times I was tempted not to."

For such a playful conversation, Carli couldn't help but feel slightly uncomfortable. All she really knew about the Hammonds was that the parents had split while the boys were ten and twelve respectively. And for some unfathomable reason, one parent stayed with one son while the other took off with the other to live on the West Coast. She knew for a fact James hadn't seen his mother more than once or twice since the divorce. And she suspected the same of Justin and his father.

It was an incredibly sad scenario if one really thought about it. For all the turmoil and hassles of growing up with four siblings, Carli couldn't imagine years going by without seeing any one of them. Even after what had happened last year between her and her sister Janie.

She winced at that memory before realizing that Justin had just said something to her. Also, Miranda had excused herself and walked away.

"I'm sorry, I missed what you said."

"I was commenting on how festive your apartment is. You've obviously put a lot of effort into decorating for the holidays."

It was clearly an attempt to change the subject, but she couldn't help but feel a little flattered at the compliment.

She was about to give him a warm smile and answer that this decorative effect had taken weeks to achieve. But then she remembered what he wanted to do with the Cape Cod store.

"Thank you," she said with a curt nod. "Now, if you'll excuse me, I have other guests I should attend to."

* * *

Justin watched Carli walk away and grabbed a glass of wine off one of the trays sitting in the corner. It was hard not to appreciate the view as she made her way across the room. The woman was shaped like sin.

Looked like his apology hadn't quite cut it as it was clear she was still unhappy with him. He wasn't sure why that bothered him so much. It really shouldn't have. He'd only just met the woman this morning. They wouldn't even be working together for that long. He'd do what was asked of him by his father and return to the West Coast in a few days. Really, the opinion of some midlevel executive at Hammond's Toys should be the last thing on his mind.

Still, he had to admit he was vexed. His transgression toward her this morning wasn't that bad. Was it?

He bit out a silent curse as he thought about it. Yeah, he was fooling himself. It was bad. To assume she was his father's mistress. Simply based on the hour of the day and the way she looked. He couldn't blame her for still being upset.

Doubtful his older brother, James, would have ever been careless enough to make such a mistake. No, James probably always displayed the utmost professionalism and leadership. Usually, Justin wouldn't hesitate to describe himself the same way. Apparently not when he was here, however. In Boston and around Hammond Enterprises, Justin was out of his element to the point of near incompetence.

Clearly, Justin was a Hammond in name only.

The question was, what was he going to do about it as far as Carli was concerned?

Someone tapped on his shoulder as he tried to find Carli from the crowd of people in her apartment. He turned to find a petite, dark-haired woman smiling at him. It took him a minute to recognize her. Jocelyn, Carli's assistant.

She looked different without the professional ponytail she'd been wearing this morning.

"Well, hello," Jocelyn said, loud enough and with enough enthusiasm that two people turned to see who had spoken.

"Hello."

"I didn't expect to see you here."

He spread his arms and bowed slightly. "Here I am."

"Fantastic. We were sort of sad that James was going to miss it this year. And here you are in his place."

Justin tried not to snort with irony. As if there was any way he would ever be able to take his brother's place in any way, shape, or form. Not as far as Hammond's was concerned. And certainly not in his father's eyes.

He gave Jocelyn a neutral smile. "Glad I could make it."

"I'm glad Carli saw to it that you came," Jocelyn said, and took a sip of her ruby red wine.

He had no intention nor desire to correct her. Actually, he had no intention of staying around much longer. There was no feasible reason he hadn't left as soon as Carli walked away.

Other than some silly desire to see her again this evening. Funny how he'd never been a glutton for punishment until this very day. Carli didn't want anything to do with him.

He spotted her coming out of the kitchen with more drinks. Several people stopped her along the way; she gave one woman an affectionate air kiss. Several men approached her as well, one taking part of the load off her hands. They seemed friendly but not overly familiar. These men were all clearly just colleagues.

Not that it was any of his business. For all he knew she already had a steady boyfriend or partner. Women who looked like Carli and who had as much going for them weren't single for long.

Jocelyn waved a hand in front of his face. "Hello? Where'd you just drift off to?"

He smiled apologetically. "Sorry, I was just admiring all the Christmas decorations. Carli's got quite a talent for it."

"Really? Is that what you were admiring?"

Uh-oh. He had to be careful here. He couldn't be caught ogling his father's project manager. "What else?"

She gave him a knowing look but luckily dropped the matter. "Anyway, I'm glad two Hammond men will be at Carli's party after all."

Justin turned his full attention to her. "Excuse me?"

"You and your father. He never misses one of Carli's soirees."

Damn. The last thing Justin needed was to run into his father right now. Their brief meeting this morning had been awkward enough.

"I don't see him yet though," Jocelyn added. "He always seems to arrive much later. Likes to make an entrance."

That definitely sounded like the attention-craving father Justin remembered from his childhood. And from everything he'd been told or had read about the man.

He still had the chance to make his getaway before Jackson arrived. All the more reason to leave right now. So, what was stopping him?

He should have never come in the first place. He knew it had been a mistake. He never even went to these events at his own company. But seeing Miranda again after all these years, remembering how she'd always been so kind to him. Even as he'd been making her life miserable with one childish antic after another.

Still, he had every intention of gently turning Miranda down. But the woman had not taken no for an answer.

Someone turned up the volume on the sound system and "Holly Jolly Christmas" started pounding through the room. Great. Now he was going to have to put up with the damn Christmas carols again.

Jocelyn squealed as the song came on. He'd almost forgotten she was standing in front of him. Again. "I love this song!" she exclaimed. "Let's dance!"

Before he had a chance to protest, she pulled him into the center of the room where two other couples were already bouncing along to the tune. This wasn't the traditional version of the song he was used to. It was a bouncy, bassy remake of some sort. With a bit of urban rap lyrics thrown in between verses. As if the original song wasn't annoying enough. He was supposed to dance to this?

Pretty much a version of hell. Still, he knew what to do. Several years of mandated dance lessons thanks to his society-norm-conscious mother came in handy during moments like this. He matched Jocelyn's steps and earned a girly giggle when he dipped her.

By the time the song ended, Jocelyn was smiling from ear to ear. "You are quite a dancer, Mr. Justin Hammond."

"I am a man of many talents."

"Well, I don't want to hog you all to myself," she said, and before he knew it, she had somehow managed to steer them toward where Carli stood talking to a middle-aged man with a bad comb-over.

"You are the host of this party. You should be dancing too," Jocelyn admonished as she pulled Justin in front of her. "Justin is a terrific dancer. And he needs a partner." She turned to comb-over guy. "Tom, may I have the honor of this dance?"

Justin watched with both bemusement and dismay as Jocelyn and Tom walked onto the middle of the floor and started dancing.

"My assistant is not subtle," Carli said. "Obviously."

"Does that mean you're not interested in dancing with me?"

She tilted her head. "I'd never dream of making you dance. To a Christmas song, no less. I know how much you dislike them."

With that flippant comment, she tried to walk away. But he wasn't going to let her. It was about time they hashed out some stuff, he figured. Otherwise, he was just going to keep letting her get under his skin. That would not bode well for either of them. Even if he was only going to be around her for a few days.

"On the contrary, I'd love a dance," he said as he gently took her by the arm and led her to the makeshift dance floor.

The protest died on her lips as he spun her around toward him and started swaying with her to the music. He was close enough to sniff a hint of her perfume, a flowery subtle scent. Jasmine perhaps. It suited her.

As did the cocktail dress she wore, a silky, drippy number that hung on her curves in a tasteful, flattering way. He noticed she had whimsical snowman earrings dangling from her dainty lobes.

"See, I can dance to anything. Even annoying versions of Christmas songs."

She gave an exasperated huff. "How can you not like Christmas carols? There's got to be one that you're fond of."

He shook his head. "Can't think of one."

"Not even 'Jingle Bells'?"

"I find that one particularly grating."

The look she gave him was one mixed with both sympathy and bewilderment.

Justin sighed. She must think him the biggest Scrooge. "Christmas wasn't quite the jolly and wonderful time in the Hammond household as it was for most people," he admitted.

He twirled her around playfully as he said it.

"Makes no sense, I know," he added. "Given how we make our livelihood. In some ways it just made things worse."

"How so?"

"Well, for one thing, my father became even more obsessed with sales figures and profit projections. He'd go into the office early and come home late. Even more so than usual. His increased hours gave my parents yet one more excuse to argue."

He almost laughed at that. *Argue* was hardly an adequate word for the knockdown, soul-crushing fights his parents used to have.

"It made for less than a peaceful holiday," he added. Why was he telling her these things? This wasn't something he particularly liked to talk about with anyone. Let alone a woman he'd just met a few hours ago. A woman who'd made it painfully clear that she didn't seem to like him very much.

"That's so very sad. I can't imagine Christmas being a time of turmoil for a young child."

Well, now she felt sorry for him. "I wasn't looking for sympathy," he said, with a little more force in his voice than he'd intended. "Besides, it's not like I helped the situation. I was a bit of a frustrating child. As Miranda just pointed out."

"You were just a child."

"A rambunctious, unruly, very disobedient child."

She shook her head. "But still a child."

The look in her eyes was intense, he had the disquieting feeling she was looking deep into his soul in the most intimate way. What a silly notion that was. They were in the middle of an office holiday party, surrounded by people.

Before he could respond, the music changed. The upbeat, bouncy rhythm of "All I Want for Christmas" transitioned to the slow, rhythmic melody of "Baby, It's Cold Outside."

Carli immediately stopped. But he wasn't ready for this to end just yet. Whatever *this* was. Before he could give it too much thought and before she could turn to go, he stepped closer to her and took her by her waist. She felt warm and soft under the silky material of her dress. After a gentle nudge, she began to move with him to the slower tempo of the song.

Justin pulled her closer, until they were mere inches apart. Her eyes grew wide with shock but she didn't make any kind of move to pull away.

Good thing, he thought. Because he wasn't sure he'd be able to let her go.

CHAPTER FOUR

WHAT IN THE world was she doing?

Carli knew she should excuse herself and slip out of Justin's arms. Instead, she just stayed there, lulling herself into the cocoon of his embrace. Not even the fact that her guests were starting to stare could seem to make her pull away. And they weren't merely guests, she reminded herself. These were her colleagues. She'd never been anything less than professional and straitlaced in front of every single one of them. But for the life of her, she couldn't bring herself to end the dance.

Justin was indeed an ideal dance partner. He moved with fluid grace and coordination. It was hard not to enjoy being with him this way.

More than that, she couldn't stop thinking about the things he'd just confessed to her about his childhood. She'd heard rumors about the Hammonds' failed marriage, of course. Hammond's Toys was no different than any other company when it came to office gossip. But she'd never given the matter much thought. And certainly neither James nor Jackson had ever broached the topic.

She'd had no idea things had been that bad before the marriage ended.

"Let's talk about something else," Justin said quietly in

her ear. His proximity sent a shiver down her spine. "I'm bordering on party-pooper status here."

He'd just given her the perfect opportunity to bring up the disturbing topic that had been looming in her mind. The Cape Cod store. She could try to make a case for giving it another chance. The numbers weren't that bad, and surely they could be turned around. But she couldn't bring herself to answer with such a daunting subject. Not right now.

After all, was this really the time or place?

"What would you like to talk about?" she asked instead. She'd find some way to bring up the matter at some point. When the time was right.

And that decision had nothing to do with the way he was holding her right now.

"How about you? Tell me what your Christmases were like. You obviously have fonder memories related to the holiday than I do."

"What makes you say that?"

He laughed softly at the question. "It's rather obvious. One big clue is the sheer amount of decorations in here. You'd give the Hammond's Manhattan store a run for its money in comparison. The garland alone is impressively lavish."

"I have a confession to make," she admitted.

"What's that?"

"These are my regular Christmas decorations. Not just for the party."

His laughed once more, and Carli found herself smiling in return.

"This is what your place looks like under normal circumstances?"

"Only at Christmastime."

"And you did it all yourself?"

"Who else?"

He shrugged. "We always hired professional services to do our holiday decorating and to hang our lights. First at the house and then the various apartments my mom had us living in over the years."

Carli tried to imagine watching as strangers handled her delicate ornaments, or the tiny figurines that made up her Christmas village. She treasured every one of those items. Some she'd paid for with her own hard-earned funds, and others had been cherished gifts from friends or relatives. Every piece was a part of her in a tiny yet significant way. Each time she set one out, it triggered a special memory. Some of them even made her homesick. The idea of strangers handling such sentimental trophies made her shudder.

It occurred to her that Justin had most likely never experienced anything like that.

"I can't imagine having someone else do it."

"And I can't imagine even knowing where to put anything."

She could show him, was her first thought. An unbidden image flashed in her mind of the two of them standing in front of a brick fireplace with a roaring fire as they hung stockings above the mantel. She blinked it away. How utterly ridiculous of her.

She really had to get a grip. This man was the boss's son. Which essentially made him her boss. There was a chance he was going to usurp her duties while he was here. And there was an even greater chance that he was going to shut down the store that had meant the world to her growing up. She had zero business dreaming up idyllic, romantic fantasies of the two of them.

And anyway, he was absolutely not her type. Not that she even knew what her type was anymore. Not after the fiasco with Warren and his utter betrayal. In fact, she decided then and there that she no longer had a type. She'd sworn off men entirely. At least until she was fully established in her career.

Justin was invoking sensations she'd held dormant for too long, and this was not the way she wanted to reawaken them. With a man who was so outrageously out of her league in every single way.

Blessedly, the song ended and she moved to step away from his embrace.

But a commotion of noise and boisterous cheers distracted them both before she could excuse herself.

Jackson Hammond had just arrived.

Justin knew the exact moment his father walked in. He didn't have to see Jackson to know he was here. Even if other guests hadn't been calling out Jackson's name in greeting, Justin would have sensed his presence. The air changed whenever someone like his father entered a room.

The magic of dancing with Carli seemed to dissipate as the real world returned along with his father's arrival. He sighed slowly and let her go. Served him right. He'd forgotten for a brief moment that he wasn't one of those men who could dance carefree with a beautiful woman in her quaint, charming apartment full of holiday cheer.

Damn it. He should have left when he'd had the chance. What had he been thinking? Allowing himself to be distracted by Carli and her notions of perfect Christmases with happy memories. Now he had to make nice with the father he'd barely seen in several years who for some sudden, inexplicable reason had needed his expert financial advice.

He wasn't even curious as to why. He honestly didn't care. He just wanted to do what was asked of him and return to his life. There was nothing in Boston that endeared it to him. Though he couldn't help but glance at Carli as that thought flitted through his head. If only he'd met her in a different time, under different circumstances.

And if only he'd been a completely different man.

"Looks like dear old Dad is here," he remarked.

Jackson made a beeline right to where they stood as soon as he spotted them. Smiling, he placed a firm grip on Justin's shoulder. "I didn't expect to see you here, son."

Justin winced inwardly at the last word. "Miranda can be quite persuasive."

"She always did have a soft spot for you." He turned to Carli and gave her a nod. "I see you've met the host of this lovely get-together. She's also better known as my right hand."

"Justin and I have gotten to know each other a bit over the past few hours," Carli offered.

If his father had any kind of untoward feelings for his young, beautiful project manager, he was doing an excellent job at hiding it. Maybe Jackson had indeed changed and was no longer the notorious philanderer his mother had frequently accused him of being. More likely, Carli was the type of professional who would not abide that type of attention from a man she worked for.

Justin hadn't known her for long, but he realized now what a huge error in judgment it had been to even entertain the notion that Carli would be the type of employee who would date her elderly boss.

"Yes, she's been very helpful. The report she prepared and delivered held a wealth of useful information. Enough that I was able to make some quick initial judgments."

Jackson studied him. Was that appreciation he detected in the old man's eyes? Probably more for his protégé and the file she'd prepared, Justin figured.

"Well, I don't like to get into business discussions at these events," Jackson said. "Let's go over everything tomorrow, the three of us, and you can tell me what you've concluded."

Justin was ready to agree when Carli surprised him by holding her hand up. "Wait. I'd like to say something about all this."

Both men turned to look at her. She appeared downright apprehensive. "Carli, do you have an issue with meeting tomorrow?" Jackson asked. "Is your schedule full?"

She shook her head, a tight firm line to her lips. "No, my schedule isn't the issue, Mr. Hammond."

"Then what is it?"

She turned to Justin. "I know what your first recommendation is going to be, Justin. And I'd urge you to reconsider."

"Reconsider?"

She swallowed. "Yes, I know you're going to argue that Hammond's should close the Cape store. And I realize you're the expert. But I think that would be a big mistake."

"I don't understand."

She inhaled on a deep breath. "If that's indeed your recommendation, I'm afraid I'll be fighting your decision."

Jackson at that point stepped slightly between them. "All right. Clearly we have some things to discuss. But I think we should save it for the office. This is not the time or place."

Carli looked ready to argue but then abruptly closed her mouth and looked away. "You're right, Mr. Hammond."

Justin nodded his agreement as an awkward silence descended. Finally, Justin excused himself and went to grab his coat hanging from the rack by the front door. He'd give his regrets to Miranda later about having left without saying goodbye. Right now, he had other things on his mind.

Looked like he and Carli Tynan were about to butt heads on yet another matter.

CHAPTER FIVE

SHE WAS EARLY; it had been impossible to sleep. Carli adjusted the collar of her business jacket and took a sip of her coffee. Jackson and Justin would be here in a few minutes. She was more than prepared to try to make her case, but the enormity of the task was not lost on her. The facts were definitely not on her side. How in the world was she supposed to convince a hard-nosed, by-the-numbers businessman that he should keep open a store that was seeing declining profits?

He'd appeared somewhat shocked last night at the party. She hadn't meant to blurt it out. But there was no way she could have kept quiet knowing where it was all leading.

Jackson's idea was that they sit together first thing this morning and hammer it all out.

Pulling out a chair at the long mahogany conference table, Carli took a deep breath and sat down. The whole floor was eerily quiet. No one else had come in yet. Traffic outside on Boylston Street had yet to pick up. The sun just now starting to burn through the crisp winter air.

The dinging of the elevator signaled the arrival of someone else. She glanced at her watch. Still another twenty minutes. So she was surprised when Justin appeared in the doorway. Dressed in a white shirt and silk navy tie, he looked every bit the successful tycoon.

Such a different image than the one he had projected last night at her party. Then he'd been casual, lighthearted. He'd danced with her, confided in her. He'd been friendly and open. Until the whole matter of the store.

He gave her a tight nod before entering the room. "Carli. Good morning."

"Justin."

"I see we're both early."

There was no hint of the genteel man who had swayed with her to hip-hop Christmas carols last night. The thought tugged at her heart. How she wished they could just sit down and discuss all this as just two friends who happened to work for the same company.

But Justin gave no indication that he was feeling at all friendly. The man was solidly in back-to-business mode. So be it. There was really only one objective here.

He glanced at his watch. They were both thinking the same thing: the sooner Jackson got here, the sooner they could get this all over with.

"There's coffee in the break room," she offered. For lack of anything else to say. The awkward silence was starting to rankle her.

"I've already had three cups this morning," he said dismissively.

"Oh."

"Thanks though," he said, his tone softer this time.

It was Carli's turn to check the time. She glanced at the classic wall clock behind Justin. Only five minutes had passed. What were the chances Jackson would be early for once in his life? Slim to none, she figured.

Clearing her throat, she made one more attempt at light conversation. "So, did you have fun last night? At the party?"

He looked up from his cell phone, his eyebrows lifted.

"Yes, I was having a great time." At his words, she real-ized how much fun she'd been having too. The way Jus-tin had held her, how warm his arms had felt around her waist as they danced.

"Even with all the annoying Christmas music playing?"

He smiled at her. "Yes, even so."

Her mind automatically recalled the way it had felt to slow dance in his arms. The hammering of her pulse at the way he'd held her, pulled her closer to him on the dance floor. She'd felt his heartbeat against her chest, and it had served to accelerate her own.

It had been months since she'd even been out on a date, let alone been touched by a man. And to have that man be Justin Hammond of all people. She'd been thinking about it all night, when she wasn't fretting about this meeting.

Like a silly girl with a crush.

"I'm glad you came last night," she admitted, surpris-ing herself. "I probably should not have brought up the matter of the store. It was really not the time nor place."

He merely shrugged.

"You're probably not used to being second-guessed. And I understand why that would make you frustrated," she began, and then cringed as the words left her mouth. The phrase was straight out of a management training handbook or seminar on dealing with difficult colleagues. She could tell by his expression that the same thought had occurred to him.

Carli hated this. This wasn't her. She was usually the articulate, straightforward professional who knew exactly what to say to get her point across. With Justin she just seemed to keep stumbling.

"That's not quite the word I would use."

She was trying to come up with an answer to that when he suddenly stood. "Perhaps I will go get a cup of coffee," he said, and moved to the door. "Would you mind texting me when Jackson comes in?"

He left the room before she could say yes.

Justin paced the hallway outside the break room and felt his phone vibrate with Carli's text. He'd had no intention of getting any coffee; the last thing he needed was more caffeine. He'd just had to get out of that conference room.

Carli Tynan affected him like no other woman he'd ever known. What had all that been about last night? He'd been about to give his father an overview of his observations on the retail operations when she'd cut him off like he was an errant child. Then she'd made some cryptic remark about how he was wrong on one major point, and she wanted a chance to explain.

Jackson had stepped in then and suggested they all meet this morning to get to the bottom of it all. Not that it would prove useful. Justin could guess what was happening. Carli must feel unsettled that he was here now. She'd been the one running the show alongside his brother and father. No doubt she felt threatened because of his presence.

He didn't even really blame her.

Well, now that his father was here, they could finally get to the bottom of it, once and for all.

He found Jackson at the head of the conference table when he arrived back in the meeting room. He nodded in greeting. Carli remained where she had been seated.

"Now, what's this all about, you two?" Jackson wasted no time.

Justin paused. Damned if he knew. He waited for Carli's answer.

She cleared her throat. "As you know, I prepared some figures and analysis for Justin like you requested."

"Thank you for getting that done so quickly," Jackson told her.

"You're welcome. It was just a matter of pulling together all the info."

"It was all very useful information," Justin added.

"So what's the problem, Carli?" his father asked.

She appeared visibly nervous. "I know Justin has come to some conclusions based on the information."

"That's correct," Justin jumped in. "Several issues can be addressed to increase profit margins. Some major, some minor."

"It's one of the more major ones that I have an issue with," Carli said. "Something Justin mentioned yesterday that he is considering."

Both men waited for her to continue.

"Justin is thinking of closing one of our stores. The one on the Cape. I have to stress that I think that would be a big mistake."

That's what this was all about? The closing of a store that was bleeding cash? If he recalled correctly, that particular location hadn't been in the red for about five years.

"I see," Jackson said, rubbing his chin.

Justin looked from one of them to the other. "I'm afraid I don't. The store is nothing but a drain. Frankly, I'm surprised no one's suggested shutting its doors before this."

"I'm very familiar with that store, Justin. I grew up in Westerson. Even worked there as a teen. It's how I ultimately came to work for Hammond's Toys corporate office. I'm personally aware of all it's potential."

Ah, so this was all about the human factor, even if Carli didn't want to admit it. Perhaps not even to herself. But as a businessman, every part of his being told him that something had to be done. The store just wasn't viable as a business unit.

"The fact of the matter is, that location cannot continue to run as a viable retail store. It's just not performing. That's my professional opinion."

Carli set down her pen. "But perhaps if we could just give it a chance to turn things around. I know the head manager. He's very hardworking. And flexible. He's been ill the past few years. But now that he's back on his feet, I think he'll be able to make the store profitable again now that he can devote all his time."

"I don't see how," Justin countered.

"There are several ways. For one, logistically the bulk of the town's children are getting older, so we'll need to invest more in things like video games and high end technology toys like drone flyers. Like I said, the store manager just hasn't been able to spend as much time on following the trends. But he's fine now."

"And if he gets sick again?" Justin knew it sounded like a cold and heartless question. The way she sucked in her breath and shot a surprised look at him said she thought so too. Something shifted in his chest at the thought that he'd disappointed her. He squelched it down.

He felt for Carli. He really did. But he'd been asked his professional opinion. He would have to be honest giving it. "I was asked to come here and offer my analysis based on experience. And to make suggestions. I'm only stating the facts. The brick-and-mortar stores are not where the sales are. Their expenses continue to grow as their sales slide more and more every year. This particular store is probably just the start."

Jackson raised a hand; he'd been surprisingly silent up until now. "I believe there's really only one way to approach this," he began.

Carli and Justin both looked at him expectedly. When he spoke again, it was with clear authority. "I'm going to have both of you go to the Cape for a few days. Look at the store, make some observations. See if there are indeed any opportunities to turn things around."

Carli's jaw dropped. Justin was taken a bit aback himself. What was there to see at the physical location that the file hadn't already told him?

"But Mr. Hammond—" Carli began before Jackson stood and stopped her with a curt nod.

"That's my final say." He pushed his chair in. "I'd like you both to spend at least a week. This is the ideal time to go. Right before Christmas. Go to the Cape. Make the decision together. We'll regroup once you get back."

A whole week? This was a disaster in the making. How was she supposed to spend a whole week with Justin? In her hometown, no less?

Carli shut her office door and leaned back against it. She had to somehow get her mind around this new development. All she'd wanted to do was make a case this morning to give the Cape store some more time to turn things around. Not in her wildest imaginings would she have guessed this would be the result.

This was so not the way she'd imagined returning home after everything that had happened last year. The truth was, she wasn't even sure if she was ready to go back. It was all too fresh. Sure, her family had come to visit her in Boston, even Janie. But she hadn't been able to make her way back to town. Not yet.

Now she was going to have to do it with Justin Hammond in tow.

A knock on her door startled her. She opened it to find Justin on the other side.

"I suppose we better discuss some of the logistics," he

said as she showed him in. She motioned for him to take a seat.

"We should probably leave within a day or so," she said with a sigh. "It's about a three-hour drive. Depending on traffic."

"I didn't bother to rent a car. I'll have to do that."

"Don't be ridiculous. I can drive you. It's my hometown." Not like she had a real choice. It would have been rude and unprofessional to not offer him a ride. Though no doubt it would be the longest ride of her life. "I'll pick you up from the house tomorrow morning."

"Can you recommend a place to stay?" he asked.

Carli nodded. "I'll have Jocelyn arrange it. There's a nice B and B near the beach. Within walking distance of the store."

"What about you?"

She shrugged. "I can stay with my parents. My childhood room is still empty, believe it or not."

"Won't that be a burden? On your mom and dad on such short notice?"

She blinked at him. A burden? On her own parents? The thought would never have occurred to her. Or her parents, for that matter. In fact, she was certain her parents would absolutely be thrilled that she was finally making her way back. "No. My parents are used to constant visitors at their house. I have a large family."

"How large?"

"I'm the middle child of five kids. All girls."

His eyes grew wide. "Wow."

"All my sisters still live in town. The younger ones are still in high school so still at home. My parents will hardly be fazed by another adult child visiting for a few days." They'd been gently pressuring her to do so for months. She didn't add that last part out loud.

He seemed to consider that like it was some sort of novel idea. Of course, he'd grown up with a single mom. Most likely in penthouses and palatial summer estates. Wait till he got a load of the small colonial house and rinky-dink town she'd grown up in.

"Maybe I'll get a chance to meet them all," Justin said, shocking her. She groaned inwardly. Introducing her worldly, sophisticated boss to the messy chaos that was her family was going to be another treat to this whole experience.

"I have no doubt," she told him. The Tynan clan wouldn't have it any other way. Once they found out she was in town with the other Hammond brother, all hell would break loose. Not just with her family either; the Westerson gossip mill would go into full swing.

"I'm sure my mom will want to feed you at some point. She's famous for her homemade lasagna."

He smiled at that. "That would be nice. I haven't had a home-cooked meal in I can't remember how long."

She couldn't tell if he was just being polite or if he really meant that. Probably the former, she decided. This man was used to dining in the finest restaurants all over the world, after all.

"Speaking of which, I should probably call her and let her know we're coming." She picked up her cell phone, already anticipating her mother's pleased excitement that she'd be returning after close to a year. Even if it was for business purposes.

Justin took the hint and stood to go. "Until tomorrow morning then."

CHAPTER SIX

BY THE TIME Carli arrived to pick him up the next morning, Justin was ruing his decision to ever come back to Boston in the first place. He should have never listened to his mother. He should have put his foot down and told them both, her and his father, that he wanted nothing to do with Hammond's Toys. When all this was over, he was going to return to the West Coast and try never to set foot in this state again.

This trip to the Cape was futile. It wasn't going to warrant any more information. In the end, he would have to be firm and reiterate the decision he'd already made. And upset Carli further. His final opinion wasn't going to be any different; he would just have to break Carli's heart.

He refused to let himself feel guilty about that. This was simply business. She had to understand that. He would expect no less if the shoe were on the other foot.

How many times had he been turned down by venture capitalists when trying to launch various projects? He'd been immensely disappointed too every time it had happened. But he'd moved on, found another way.

The Westerson store and its employees could do the same. And besides, the final decision wasn't his. He was merely there as an outside consultant. He had no intention of fabricating an untruth simply to tell people what they wanted to hear.

He just hated that he'd be the one delivering the lesson.

That was a completely new experience for him. Never before had he second-guessed himself about delivering a recommendation. But now, for some inexplicable reason, he hated that he'd be the messenger of bad news. It had everything to do with Carli.

She pulled up in front of the driveway and popped her trunk open. After tossing his bag in, he slid into the passenger seat.

"Thanks for the ride."

"You're welcome. We should be there way before after noon sometime. I can take you to the inn, and then we can talk about where to start. Mr. Freider is expecting us."

Justin recalled the name as the store's manager. "Sounds good."

"And I hope you haven't made any plans for dinner," she told him.

He laughed to himself. What kind of plans would he possibly have? He didn't know a single person in the town he was about to visit. He barely knew a soul in all of New England. Except for Carli.

"None whatsoever. Why?"

"I was right about my mom. She insists we have dinner with them this evening. Won't take no for an answer."

"That's very nice of her."

She signaled and looked over her shoulder as they merged onto the highway. A double-wide semi blew past them, barely slowing down. He'd only been here a few days and had already found Boston drivers deserved their nasty reputation.

"You may not think so once you get there," Carli warned. He couldn't even tell if she was serious.

"Come again?"

"It won't be a quiet affair. Dinner at my parents' house never is. All four of my sisters will be there. One of them with her husband. Along with my nephew. Who may actually bring a friend."

Justin pulled down the visor against the harsh morning glare. How many people were going to be at this dinner? "That does sound rather, um, busy."

"You mean chaotic, don't you?" Carli asked, not taking her eyes off the road. "Like I said, they don't take no for an answer. I tend to pick my battles when it comes to my parents."

The way she said the last few words held a wealth of emotion. He had to wonder what the story was there. Then he had to wonder what made him so damn curious about this woman. It was really none of his business why her voice grew wistful sometimes as it had just now. Just like it had the last time she'd spoken of her family.

"Sounds like you're all very close." That much at least was clear.

"Sometimes I think we may all be way too close."

He waited for her to elaborate, but she didn't expand on the comment. This was going to be a very long ride if he couldn't figure out a way to move the conversation forward. The last thing he wanted to do was bring up the closing of the store. That would just make the air too thick with tension. And how was he supposed to say anything relatable to her about her large family? He had only one sibling, and he'd rarely seen James over the years.

"You mentioned you have a young nephew?"

The tight line of her lips spread into a wide grin. "Yes, he's four. Quite a little dynamo." Her voice held genuine affection. Even a hint of awe.

"I have zero experience with children."

She gave him a quick side-eye. "Yeah, you don't really strike me as the babysitting type."

He chuckled. "Believe me, I'm not. I can't even keep a cactus plant alive."

"Well, don't let little Ray be a nuisance. He can be quite chatty. Just tell him to run along if he starts to bother you at dinner."

"How bad of a nuisance can he be?"

Carli's laugh was so deep and so sharp that he twisted in his seat to face her. "What?"

"You really haven't been around children, have you? And definitely not around four-year-olds."

"Never," he admitted.

"Well, you are in for a novel experience."

"I'm guessing you don't mean that in a good way?"

Her answer was another laugh.

"I'm starting to worry a bit," he admitted, only partially joking.

"Don't get me wrong. My nephew, Ray, is absolutely a little love. One of the biggest joys in my life. But he can resemble a tiny destructive tornado at times." She adjusted the heat setting on the dashboard, then continued, "It takes his two parents, all his aunties, a set of grandparents and practically most of the town to handle him. We take turns finding ways to channel all his considerable energy."

"It takes a village?"

"For Ray it certainly does." Despite her words, the love and affection she felt for her nephew were clear in the tone of her voice and the set of her jaw as she spoke about him.

Justin couldn't help but summon his own childhood memories. Carli was describing her nephew the same way he might have been characterized as a child. All he'd had were his mom and dad and slightly older brother. James was just a child, barely older than him. His father was gone most of the day. Various nannies and babysitters eventually just threw their hands up in utter defeat.

His mother was too busy trying to defeat her own demons to pay him any mind. The isolation had only grown worse when she'd finally left Jackson and James, taking only her younger son with her. They'd moved from one city to another, and she'd dated a string of men, never finding one who quite fit her needs.

His only paternal figures had been nannies who changed every time they moved. By the time he was a middle schooler, he'd known better than to develop any kind of affection for any of them.

Unlike Carli's nephew, Justin hadn't had anything resembling a village in his corner.

They were making good time until about halfway through the ride. Traffic suddenly slowed and then, much to Carli's dismay, became an annoying pattern of stop and go.

"Is there some sort of accident?" Justin asked.

Carli sighed and shook her head. "No. I'm afraid it's just impossible to time Cape traffic. You never know if you're going to hit a bottleneck."

"Sounds like California traffic," Justin commented.

"It's especially tricky this time of year, with the outlet mall along the way. Christmas shoppers looking for bargains."

"Another mark against the season."

Carli turned to look at him. How could he be such a downright Grinch? She gave her head an exasperated shake.

"What?"

"Nothing," Carli uttered as a mini-hatchback swerved and cut her off. "It's just that the irony of it all is almost too much. The second heir of Hammond's Toys, the biggest toy retailer in the Northern Hemisphere wants nothing to do with Christmas."

"Well, like I said at your party, we didn't celebrate like normal people. For us, it was mostly about the business. And things always got even more heated between my parents."

Carli felt a deep surge of sadness at his statement. He really had no clue what he'd missed out on. Or maybe he did. She couldn't decide which would be sadder.

"You don't have any good memories of that time of year? Not at all?"

"Not many." He seemed to hesitate. "There was maybe a…"

"What?"

"Nothing really. Just one time when I was about six. We were driving back from some store event, it was early evening. There was this drive-around with multiple light displays. The sign said Christmas Wonderland. I don't even remember what town it was."

He looked out the passenger side window. "Much to James's and my surprise, my father actually had the chauffeur drive through it. The displays and lights were magical. I thought so as a child anyway."

Carli felt a smile touch her lips. So he *was* human.

But then he added, "It was the first and last time we ever did anything like that."

How incredibly sad that as a child he hadn't been exposed to more such experiences during the holidays.

Then she realized what was up ahead, just off the next exit. It was almost too perfect. And since they were just sitting here stuck in traffic anyway.

"You happen to be in luck," she told him.

"Yeah? How so?"

"We happen to be very close to just such a setup. It's

not exactly a wonderland, so to speak. Just a town park to walk through. But every year they put up various Christmas displays and panoramas. Of course the lights won't be on this time of day, but we can go check out the decorations and everything else. I think we should stop in."

He laughed at the suggestion before turning to study her. "You're serious."

"Of course, I'm serious. It's just off the next exit. We can spend the time there waiting for the road to clear rather than sitting in stop-and-go traffic for an hour. It's not exactly as spectacular during the day, but it's better than watching rear taillights."

"Carli. It's really not necessary. It was just a useless childhood memory in answer to your question."

Useless. Why was he so stubborn? Did he ever allow himself to do anything just for fun or kicks? "Then do it for me. I could use the time to stretch my legs on a little walk. Not to mention, they have a stand that serves the tastiest hot spiced cider. And I'm feeling a little thirsty."

He sighed in defeat. "Then far be it from me to keep you from quenching your sudden thirst. Or depriving you of a good leg stretch."

"Thank you. It's the least you can do for your long-suffering driver."

"My empathy knows no bounds."

That made her laugh, and she was still chuckling several moments later as she turned her blinker on and got off the expressway at the next exit. Moments later they pulled into the parking lot of the town recreation area, which was now set up as a holiday bazaar. A large sign at the gate read Santa's Village in big bright letters. Several children ran past it shrieking and laughing as three harried moms followed close behind.

"This is it," she declared as they both got out of the car.

"Why exactly are we doing this again?" Justin asked. Judging by the hint of a smile on his face, he couldn't be too put out about it.

She ignored the question. "Let's start with the cider."

"Whatever you say."

"Follow me."

He did so but paused as they approached the barn where several children were feeding the livestock. "Are those reindeer?" His disbelief was audible.

"They are indeed."

She took him by the arm and continued their walk. "I don't recommend petting them before we get the cider."

"I had no intention of petting them at all."

In her haste and distraction, Carli didn't notice the patch of ice before planting her foot square in the center. Her leg slid out from under her, and then the other leg followed and gave way. Carli braced herself for the fall and prepared for the impact of falling hard on her bottom.

Until a strong arm suddenly grabbed her by the waist and pulled her up. Instead of on the ground, she found herself braced against Justin's hard length. Her heart did a jump in her chest.

"Nice reflexes." Her voice caught as she said it. There was that spicy, sandalwood scent again. She fought the urge to lean in closer to get a better whiff.

"Careful," Justin admonished. "I'd hate to present you to your family with any broken bones." He made no attempt to let her go, and heaven help her she didn't try at all to pull away. Her gaze dropped to his chin. He'd nipped himself slightly with the razor, the smallest of cuts near his ear. That observation led to an unbidden image of him shaving in the morning, shirtless.

Carli sucked in a breath and tried to regain some focus. What had he just said? Oh, yeah, something about her breaking a bone. "Thank you for saving me from such a terrible fate. That would certainly put a damper on the holidays."

He smiled at her, and she had to remind herself to breathe. Reluctantly, she pulled herself out of his grasp. "For that, the cider is on me." On wobbly legs, she resumed walking, making sure to watch where she was going this time. She didn't need Justin to have to catch her in his arms a second time. Though it was more tempting than she wanted to admit.

That thought made her visibly shudder.

Justin must have misread her reaction as a response to the temperature. He removed his scarf and held it out to her. "Here. You appear to be cold."

She wasn't about to explain what her shiver had really been about. "I can't take your scarf."

He ignored that and stopped her with a hand on her arm. "The only reason you're out here in the cold is because I foolishly revealed some long-lost memory that you're kind enough to help me try to relive. The least I can do is give you my scarf." Turning her to him, he wrapped the featherlight material around her neck.

It smelled of him. Carli sank into the sensation of the soft material against her skin as this time she allowed herself to breathe in Justin's scent.

Carli cast a furtive glance in his direction as they continued walking. Once again, she had to remind herself he was her boss. And there was way too much at stake for her to entertain any romantic illusions where he was concerned. Regardless of how handsome she found him. The last thing she needed at this point in her career was any gossip that she'd gotten ahead professionally by pursuing the boss's second son. She'd had enough of gossip to last her an entire lifetime after her last relationship. According to her oldest sister, the hometown folks were still talking about the details of her breakup a year later. Even if most of it was concern on her behalf, it wasn't the kind of attention she needed nor wanted. Something like that would be all the worse if it was happening to her in a professional capacity.

Not to mention, she had no intention of getting her heart broken again. The wounds were still too fresh. Justin had just told her to be careful. He had no idea how hard she was trying. But it was becoming more and more tempting to throw caution to the wind with each passing moment she spent in his company.

The scent of spice and cinnamon grew stronger the farther they walked. Along the way, they passed display after display of Christmas scenes with moving figurines and colorful backgrounds. Justin found himself actually laughing at some of the funnier ones—including one of a large mechanical dog scarfing down the plate of cookies that had been left out for Santa.

Finally, they approached a small shed with a small line in front. The spot was without a doubt where the delicious aroma had been coming from.

Carli ordered for both of them and handed him a steaming hot cup.

"Be careful," she warned him just as he took it from her. "It's even hotter than it looks."

She waited with expectation as he took a sip. "Well?" she asked. "Was it worth the stop?"

It was good. But Justin didn't say what he was thinking. He didn't tell her that the stop had been worth it simply because of the way she'd looked at him earlier when he'd caught her before she fell. And for the way her bright chocolate eyes were studying him with anticipation right at this moment, simply to gauge his reaction to tasting the cider.

Instead of trying to find the words, he lifted the cup toward his temple in a mock salute.

Carli gave a whoop. "I knew you'd like it!"

The enthusiasm this woman displayed, the sheer enjoyment of the simple pleasantries around her was an utterly new experience for him. She definitely worked hard; what he'd witnessed back in Boston and the level of her success left zero doubt about that. But clearly also appreciated the blessing she'd been given in life. To witness it was like a magnetic pull for someone like him.

Outside of his employees or clients, when had anyone ever really cared what his opinion was? Or if he was enjoying something as simple as a glass of juice outside on a cold December day?

When had anyone bothered to do anything like try to find a way for him to relive a silly childhood memory?

"It's like drinking an apple pie," he told her.

"That's exactly the way it is." She looked around at the various displays surrounding them. "We used to come here every year when we were young children. We don't so much anymore. But it used to be tradition."

He took another sip of his cider and studied her over the rim of the foam cup. "You and your family seem to have had a lot of those."

"Doesn't everyone?"

He shrugged. "I guess I wouldn't know. We didn't really. Unless you count lots of yelling and broken glass."

She reached out and placed a gentle hand on his arm. "You'll just have to start new ones then."

He hmmphed out an ironic laugh. Like what? All he ever wanted to do every Christmas Eve was watch an old baseball game on the DVR and enjoy a peaceful dinner alone. That was traditional enough for him. A picture popped into his head of someone with a startling resemblance to Carli Tynan sitting there at the table with him. He promptly shoved it out of his mind.

"What? It's never too late," she said softly next to him.

Justin didn't reply, just downed the rest of his beverage then tossed the cup into the trash can behind him. Carli hesitated for a moment before turning around. "Come on. Let's go say hello to Santa."

Surprisingly, an hour and half had gone by when they finally made it back to the car. Somehow, Carli had even persuaded him to pet the reindeer after all.

He studied her as they pulled back onto the expressway.

A little of the color had returned to her cheeks now that the car heater was fully on and blowing at them. Many of her wayward curls had escaped the tight band at the top of her head, and several dark tendrils framed her face. Why did she even bother putting her hair up? She'd been licking her lips and biting them after drinking the spiced cider. The abuse from her teeth turned them a pinkish red hue. He had an absurd urge to reach over and rub his fingers over her mouth to soothe them.

Damned if she hadn't been right. The little excursion had been a welcome respite from everything; he would even call it fun. That was the problem. It was way too easy to forget the world and just have fun with Carli Tynan.

He thought about what she'd said back there in the park. Her statement about starting new traditions. She was giving him way too much credit. He wouldn't even know where to start.

Her optimistic words just drove the truth home. They were too different. Trips to parks decorated with Christmas displays were all too common for someone like her. She had the kind of love and affection in her life that fully embodied everything that was good about Christmas. For him, Christmas was just another reminder of all he'd never had and never would.

CHAPTER SEVEN

"THIS IS IT," Carli said, and parked the car behind several others already in the driveway of a double structure colonial complete with a front porch and white picket fence. "Brace yourself," she warned. "Looks like everyone else is here too."

"Uh. Who would that be exactly?"

"Well, my two younger sisters live here. They're just teenagers. Marnie and Perri. Twins actually." She motioned with her chin to the white minivan. "Then there's my oldest sister, Tammy. That's her vehicle right there. Which means my nephew and brother-in-law must be here, as well. And that mini-coupe belongs to my other sister, Janie. She's about two years older than me. And I'm guessing her boyfriend came with her." The last statement held just a hint of tightness, lacking the soft quality he'd heard in her voice when referring to the other members of her family. He knew he hadn't imagined it. Something had happened between Carli and her next older sister.

Carli opened her door and stepped out of the vehicle. "And of course there's my mother and father."

He tried to count in his head all the names she'd just mentioned. How in the world was he going to keep track of all these people? Also, how did they all fit in that small structure?

"Come on. I'll make all the introductions inside," she told him, leaning back into the vehicle. "And you can get cleaned up. It's been a long ride, I know."

It had taken hours to get here. But Justin had to admit, it hadn't felt that way. In fact, he had to admit he was somewhat disappointed that his time alone with Carli in the car had come to an end. They'd decided to come straight to her home, as the delay of traffic made them even later. As much as he would have appreciated the time to stop by his room at the inn, he didn't want to risk being late and rude. Not an ideal first impression.

Though why he was so deeply concerned about Carli's family's perception of him was something of a mystery. He didn't plan on seeing any of these people again once this week was over.

Carli used her key and opened the front door. "Hello? We're here."

They stepped into a small but tidy living room. A large red sofa sat against the wall, covered with thick, plush cushions. A patterned throw rug sat atop the hardwood floor. Several toy trucks lay scattered throughout the area and down the hall. A Christmas tree without the lights turned on decorated the corner by the fireplace. It had to be the coziest looking room he'd ever stepped into.

"In the kitchen," someone called in response. Carli shook off her coat and indicated for him to do the same. She hung up both in a closet adjacent to the front door. He followed her farther inside. The aroma of rich seasonings and an appetizing mix of spices hung pleasantly in the air. He realized he was famished.

"Carli! You're here." A small woman with a broad smile approached them. Her apron had a cartoon picture of a large, red lobster wearing a Santa hat. It said Santa Claws in bold letters across the top.

Justin immediately saw the resemblance. Carli's mother had the same subtle features, the same deep brown colored eyes. She embraced her daughter in a tight hug.

"I'm so glad to have you home," the older woman said. Were those tears glistening in her eyes?

Carli cleared her throat and motion toward him. "Mom. This is Justin Hammond. He's uh...my boss."

Justin extended a hand. "Nice to meet you, Mrs. Tynan."

She ignored his outstretched hand and gave him a tight hug also. "Oh, you must call me Louise."

Justin awkwardly wrapped his arms around her shoulders. He tried to remember the last time he'd been bear-hugged by a middle-aged woman in a long apron, and couldn't recall a single time.

"Thank you for having me, Louise. Your home is lovely." In hindsight, he realized he should have brought some sort of house gift. How embarrassingly uncouth of him. He would have to pick something up in town. But visiting an employee's family in small-town Massachusetts was not his regular MO. He was a bit off his game here.

"Where are the others?" Carli asked, plucking a thick bread stick from a glass plate on the center of the table. She bit off the end and started chewing. Justin found himself momentarily distracted by the motion of her lips. He blinked and forced his attention back to her mother.

"Your father is out getting some groceries. Everyone else went for a quick walk," Louise answered. "Trying to wear out little Ray a bit. He wouldn't even take a nap this afternoon."

Carli smiled. "That sounds like our little Ray."

"He's very excited about his aunt Carli visiting. So it's partly your fault."

Carli laughed. "As if Ray needs an excuse to be over-excited."

"No, no, he doesn't." Louise turned to Justin. "Do you have any nieces or nephews?"

"No, ma'am. It's just me and my brother." Best to answer with a short and general response. No need to get into how Justin barely knew his own brother. Someone like Louise, with the family she had, would never understand the way he and James had grown up. On different sides of the coast. Hardly seeing each other, even on holidays or birthdays. It was the polar opposite of what Carli had grown up with.

"I've heard quite a bit from Carli about hers, though," he added, to turn the conversation spotlight elsewhere. "Can't wait to meet the little guy."

Though what he would say to a small child was beyond him.

Carli couldn't contain her laugh. As Justin's words left his mouth, a small blur in a puffy coat barreled through the kitchen and hurled itself into her.

"Aunt Carli! Aunt Carli! You're here. You're finally here!"

She kneeled down to Ray's height and wrapped her arms around her nephew. A swell of love and affection moved through her core. It never ceased to amaze her how much sheer emotion this child could invoke in her. Simply by the way he reacted whenever he saw her.

"Hey, little man." She tousled his hair. "I've missed you."

"I missed you too!" he said loudly.

Ray had no concept of an inside voice. Despite repeated attempts by all his elders to check him on it.

"You've grown," she observed and earned a huge smile.

"Momma says I'm a weed."

"You're growing like a weed. Let's see if I can even still

pick you up." She gave an exaggerated show of false effort as she lifted him. "Oh, you're so heavy! This is probably the last time I'll be able to lift you."

"Prolly," her nephew agreed.

With Ray still in her arms, she turned to Justin. "I'd like you to meet a friend of mine."

Justin appeared confused. He lifted his hand before dropping it right back down to his side. Then he lifted his other hand and gave a small wave. He was trying to determine the right protocol when it came to meeting a kid. Carli had to hide her amusement at the thought. Why was he always so serious?

"Who is dis?" Ray asked, his dark eyebrows lifted in his small face.

"Don't be rude, Ray," Carli admonished. "This is Justin Hammond. You should call him Mr. Hammond."

"Mr. Hammond," Ray repeated. Only his pronunciation and his missing teeth made it sound like ham bone. Carli couldn't decide whether to laugh or groan at that.

Justin stepped closer to the two of them. "Actually, I'd prefer it if you called me Justin. May I call you Ray?"

The child giggled. "Of course you can! It's my name!" he said with pride. Then to her horror, he added, "And your name is funny sounding."

"Ray…" Carli began but stopped when Justin laughed in response.

"My name is funny?"

Ray nodded. "Yup."

"What do you mean?" he asked with a curious smile.

Carli heard the other adults slowly make their way into the house as Ray wiggled in her arms.

"It's funny cause your last name has ham in it."

Justin lifted an eyebrow, seemingly deep in thought. "Hmm, that hadn't occurred to me. I suppose you're right."

Ray grinned. "Your first name is funny too."

Oh, sheesh. Now he was pushing it, Carli thought. Justin had zero experience with kids. He couldn't be expected to patiently listen to the silly ramblings of a four-year-old regarding the qualities of his name.

But he seemed to be playing along. "My first name too? How so?" he asked Ray.

"'Cause it sounds like something my mom says to me all the time."

"It does?"

"Yeah. Like she says 'Ray, it might be cold out. Put your coat on. Just in case.'"

Justin laughed out loud, and Carli couldn't help the humor that bubbled up from her throat either.

"Or she says 'There's your father. Just in time.'"

"Oh, Ray," Carli admonished, unable to keep the amusement out of her voice. "It isn't nice to make fun of people's names."

Ray turned to Justin. "I sowwy," he said, turning big chocolate-brown puppy dog eyes on him. Though he looked anything but. In fact, he looked plenty pleased with himself at the reaction he was getting.

To his credit, Justin turned serious in a very fake way. "Well, you've certainly given me something to think about," he said.

The others strolled into the kitchen just then. Carli made the proper introductions after receiving a welcoming hug from her oldest sister, Tammy.

Janie, on the other hand, seemed hesitant to approach her. As was she hesitant to approach Janie. Carli hated this. She hated the distance that now seemed so insurmountable between them. Up until a year ago, they'd grown up as close as two peas in a pod. The expression on her mother's face said she was displeased too.

She dared a glance at Justin. He'd noticed the tension in the air between her and her older sister. That much was clear.

And then Warren entered. Carli's chest tightened, and her pulse pounded in her veins. She gave Janie's current boyfriend as polite a smile as she could muster.

"Carli, nice to see you again," Warren said, then went to stand next to Janie. Seeing the two of them so close together still didn't feel right, and she had to look away.

But she was over it all, Carli reminded herself. She had to be.

"Warren. Hello."

She motioned to Justin. "I'd like you to meet Justin."

The two men shook hands just as Ray shouted out, "I think that's Aunt Carli's boyfriend!"

Carli tried not to gasp in shock and horror as she set her nephew down. She didn't dare look in Justin's direction.

"Oh, my God!" Tammy exclaimed, then addressed Justin. "I apologize for my son's behavior. We are working on manners."

"No need for apologies," Justin assured her. Then surprised her by saying, "He's actually quite entertaining."

Carli took a deep breath. "No, that's not right." She corrected the boy. "I just work with Justin."

Ray simply shrugged. "Okay. Wanna see my new truck?"

The innocence of the question immediately ebbed Carli's annoyance. "Sure," she said, and tousled his hair once more.

Ray turned to Justin. "You come too," he ordered with a mischievous smile. Carli was just about to remind him to say please when he impishly added, "Just in case you like trucks too!"

Carli certainly wasn't kidding when she said dinner at her parents' place would be chaotic. Everyone talked over each other; multiple hands reached for various dishes. As the guest, he was offered each dish first. After that, it seemed to be a free-for-all.

Everyone participated in the rapidly changing conversation, even little Ray to the extent that he could. No one shushed the child, no one told him he was a messy nuisance when he dropped half his salad on the floor. In fact, they all actually laughed at the mess he'd created at the base of his chair. One of the twin sisters simply cleaned it up, gave him a peck on his chubby cheek, then sat back down to her dinner.

It was the loudest dinner Justin had ever sat through. It was also the most enjoyable. So different from the silent meals he'd had to endure as a child. If his mother even deigned to join him, that was. And this certainly beat the stuffy business dinners he regularly had to sit through.

Whereas this one had to be the loudest meal he'd ever sat through, if anyone had asked him about that prospect a week ago, he would have said it sounded like a nightmare. So why in the world was he enjoying it so much?

"Justin, would you like another piece of lasagna?" Carli's mother asked.

He shook his head. "That would make it my third piece."

"So what's your point?" Carli's brother-in-law cracked from the other side of the table.

Her oldest sister poked the man in the ribs. "He's just saying that 'cause his average is about four servings each time Mom makes it."

Before Justin could answer, the twins started a mini tug-of-war in front of him with the last bread stick. It finally snapped in two, and for some reason they both thought that was the funniest thing and broke out in a peal of laughter.

Their little nephew joined in. Justin, in turn, couldn't help his own laughter. Apparently, a preschooler's giggles were highly contagious. Pretty soon, the whole table had broken out into laughter.

So this was what family meals normally looked like. A far cry from the silent dinners he and his brother shared around the television while their mom was up in her room wallowing in self-pity and their dad was still at the office. Back then, at least he hadn't been eating alone.

He hadn't even had that much after his mom had taken him away.

Carli watched as Justin laughed at something her brother-in-law told him by the hearth as they both sipped their after dinner coffee. Why was she not surprised that he had somehow fit so well in with her loud and boisterous family?

Sure, the Tynans had a way of making people feel welcome in their midst. But it was as if they'd all known him for years rather than having just met him. She'd daresay Justin seemed like he actually *belonged*.

She sighed. Probably just her imagination. Despite the circumstances, and despite the imminent danger he posed to the existence of her beloved store, Carli had to admit, deep down, he wasn't so bad. In fact, she might actually be growing quite fond of him.

Ray approached him right then and gave a tug on his pant leg. Justin immediately put down his cup and kneeled to hear what the boy had to say. The whole picture tugged at something within her chest, a longing she didn't want to examine in any way.

Carli made herself look away. What in the world was wrong with her? The man had simply had dinner with them. That's all that was happening here.

And a week from now, he'd be go back to being nothing more than a name on the company letterhead.

She turned to go back into the kitchen. As far as she could get from Justin and the picture he made in her family's living room.

Justin waited for Carli the next morning in the lobby of the Sailor's Inn Bed and Breakfast so that they could head over to the toy store. Overall the inn was a quaint, charming establishment unlike anything he would have encountered on the West Coast. The décor screamed New England, complete with a boat anchor hanging above a large hearth fireplace as well as the requisite ship in a glass bottle displayed in the center of the lobby.

Unbelievably, he was hungry. He didn't think he'd be able to eat for another week after the way Carli's parents had fed them last night. Louise had prepared enough food for an entire football team. Not that the numbers weren't damn near comparable. Carli had a large family.

As if reading his thoughts, or perhaps she'd heard his stomach grumbling, a matronly rotund woman appeared from the back holding a tray of steaming muffins.

"You weren't trying to sneak out without eating something first?" she asked.

She then smiled and set the tray next to a silver carafe on a side table against the wall. "I'm Betty Mills. My husband would have checked you in last night."

Justin shook her hand and introduced himself.

"Help yourself," she said, pointing to the tray from which drifted a delicious aroma of sweet sugary dough. "I've made vanilla almond and raspberry chocolate chip this morning. Plus, there's always the standard corn ones."

Justin's mouth actually watered. This certainly beat the dry granola bars he hastily grabbed on his way into work most mornings.

Betty laughed. "Or you can have one of each," she offered, clearly reading his mind once again.

The front door swung open behind them, and Carli walked through, bringing with her a gust of cold New England air.

Betty greeted her with a familiar smile. "Carli Tynan. So nice to see you back in town."

"Good morning, Betty. Justin." She glanced at the muffin tray. "I see you're taking good care of my friend here."

"I'd offer you some too, but I'm guessing Louise has handled that already?"

Carli patted her stomach and rolled her eyes. "She's been feeding me nonstop since I got here."

Justin couldn't take any more talk of food. He reached over and plucked one of the vanilla almond muffins, taking a big bite. A small burst of heaven exploded in his mouth.

He looked up to catch Carli watching him with a knowing smile.

"You're lucky to be here on vanilla almond day. Those are Betty's particular specialty. Though the cranberry comes in a close second."

"They go real well with a cup of coffee," Betty said, pouring him some of the chicory-colored brew. "How do you take it?"

"Black, please," Justin answered and took the beverage from her. The heat from the ceramic mug warmed his hands. He liked his Seattle brew just fine, but the smell of this coffee sparked his senses.

"And what brings Mr. Hammond into town?" Betty asked.

Justin looked to Carli, unsure how to answer. How much was she willing to share with the town about the trouble that had brought the two of them here? He'd been in Westerson less than twenty-four hours and could already tell what a tight, close-knit community it was. Hearing about the potential closing of one of their businesses would probably not sit well.

And it certainly wasn't how he wanted to introduce himself.

To his relief, Carli answered for him. "Justin is here to visit his family's store." She offered no further details.

Luckily, Betty didn't push.

Moments later, they were out on the street among scores of other pedestrians all bundled up against the harsh December air.

"Betty's quite the baker," Justin offered by way of conversation.

"Yes, quite." Carli seemed preoccupied. She had to be thinking about what he would say when after visiting the store. And how much credence his father would give it. He wished he could reassure her, he really did. But he'd been asked his professional opinion. He had an obligation to give it. Honestly and factually.

Even if it meant disappointing the woman next to him. Admittedly, that bothered him more than he cared for. Which made no sense. He had just met her a few days ago. This sense of familiarity and closeness that was developing within him had no basis in any kind of reality. Even so, he wanted badly to believe that it wasn't one-sided.

Several people waved and stopped them along the way to chat. Carli introduced him to everyone. At this rate, they would never get to Hammond's. She seemed to know every other person who walked by. Westerson wasn't the type of town where one could rush anywhere. Small talk and friendly conversation were a developed talent around here. A talent Carli had clearly perfected. She had kind words and a warm smile for everyone who approached.

Until one man in particular turned the corner. Carli's

step actually faltered at the sight of him. Justin immediately recognized who it was. He'd met him last night at dinner. Warren, her sister Janie's boyfriend.

All night, Justin had sensed a strange coldness between the two of them. As if they were both going out of their way to avoid each other. The sister seemed just as uncomfortable when she looked at them.

If he thought he was imagining it, the look on Carli's face right now reaffirmed any suspicion. Justin had no doubt that if it hadn't been so blatantly obvious that they'd spotted him, Carli would have ignored Warren and continued walking.

It was a strange dynamic for a family that otherwise seemed so devoted and close. Had Carli expressed some sort of objection to her sister's boyfriend?

Warren approached from the other direction. He offered a small wave. Carli merely nodded in his direction. To Justin's surprise they all kept right on walking. He'd been fully expecting to stop and say *something*, just as they had with so many others along the way so far. The whole thing made him wonder. Warren had seemed friendly enough last night. He was clearly good to the sister.

But there was no doubt. Whatever issues Carli had with the boyfriend, they seemed to run deep.

Carli had been enjoying the walk to the store. She really had. She'd missed this town. And strolling through the center of Westerson this time of year had always served to lift her spirits. It was doing so now.

Like every other year, the town council had spared no effort or expense with the decorations. Festive wreaths hung on each lamppost. The winterized bushes had been wrapped up like big presents or otherwise adorned with silvery tinsel and bright colorful ornaments. Her fellow townspeople knew how to do Christmas right, and she was glad to that was on display for Justin to see.

But her mood went south when Warren Mathews turned the corner and made a beeline right to them. It had been uncomfortable enough to have him there at dinner last night. For a split second, Carli thought about pretending she hadn't seen him. But he was directly in their line of sight. She had to acknowledge him in some way. So she did, just barely.

"It's just a bit farther, past this corner," she told Justin, more so to break the awkward silence than to give him an ETA update.

Justin remained wisely silent about the nonexchange with Warren just now. She gave him a side-eye glance. His hair was dotted with a slight layer of snow, his strong neck wrapped in a different cashmere scarf. The coat he wore fit him perfectly. Every inch of him looked the competent, successful tycoon that he was.

It was impossible not to notice the double takes that every woman who walked by gave them.

He definitely stuck out in this small town.

At that thought, Carli gave herself a mental kick. This was so not where her focus needed to be right now. Not when they were on their way to the store so that Justin could make observations about the way it was run. About its very existence.

A nervous flutter spun in her gut about what his reaction might be. Last night he'd been warm and friendly, fitting in with her family easily. But his reputation as a no-nonsense, numbers-oriented businessman preceded him. She couldn't let herself forget why they were even here in the first place.

It would be a mistake to take anything for granted when it came to Justin Hammond.

He held the door open for her when they arrived at the store. The heat hadn't quite kicked in yet for the day; a slight chill still hung to the air. It was still early. Yet the shelves were neat, and the displays were cheery and festive.

A tooting whistle sounded overhead. Carli looked up just as a model toy train went past above her head on a hanging track. That was new. Justin looked up too, but he didn't seem impressed. Probably making a mental note of how much constructing it must have cost the company.

"So this is it, huh?" Justin asked.

"Yes. Everything's organized by age group." She explained the layout as they walked. "The toddler toys line the aisles up front. As you move back, you start to get into the board games and such for the older children. Followed by video games."

"Makes sense."

"There's a corner that houses all the reading materials, the Book Nook. And a café that serves coffee, juice and some basic pastries. Shall we start there?"

"Sure."

"Mr. Freider is probably setting up in the café," she informed Justin. "It's in the back." She motioned for him to follow.

The aroma of hot chocolate and freshly baked croissants greeted them as they approached the café counter. Several customers were already in line for a quick breakfast. A young lady she didn't recognize waited on them with a cheery smile. Carli breathed a sigh of relief that Justin was witnessing the early-morning traffic in the store.

She turned to him. "I'd just like to point out that despite the early hour, the store has drawn several customers already."

"You'd like to point that out, huh?"

"Yes."

"The problem is we don't know yet how many of them will actually purchase an item before they leave. Notice there's no one at the registers."

She waved her hand in dismissal at that suggestion. "It's still early. Besides, a lot of people come to look around and help make their child's wish list to Santa."

"Which they may very well go purchase elsewhere. Most notably, online."

She was about to object to that comment when Mr. Freider stepped out of the kitchen area carrying a pitcher of creamer.

"Carli! I've been expecting you." He brightened when he saw them.

He set his load down and offered a hand to Justin. "Mr. Hammond."

"Call me Justin, please."

Carli realized she was holding her breath. Goodness, she was so nervous on Mr. Freider's behalf. The poor man had no idea of the reason behind their impromptu visit into town.

He took Carli gently by the arm. "I'm so glad you've decided to visit again, dear. It's been way too long."

"You sound like my parents, Mr. Freider," she teased.

"I'm just glad you're here. I was worried that scoundrel was going to keep you away for good."

Carli could feel the blood drain out of her face. Justin gave her a curious look. The last thing she wanted to talk about right now was Warren Mathews.

She frantically scrambled around in her brain for a way to head off the topic immediately. But Mr. Freider wasn't having it. He was old school and had no qualms whatsoever about speaking his mind.

"I don't care what anyone says about how these things

are meant to be." He shook his head with indignation and outrage on her behalf. "It's a disgrace the way Warren treated you."

Justin sat down next to Carli in the corner of the store she'd called the Book Nook. It was like being in a small book closet. The three surrounding walls were nothing but shelves of books. They were going through the several binders Mr. Freider had provided them about the store's numbers and operations. Dear heavens, the man hadn't even bothered to computerize any of the tracking data. How did he keep it all organized?

They'd started out in Freider's office, but there were just too many binders to go through and spread out. As a result, Justin felt ridiculous as all the chairs out here were clearly made for small children. Not to mention, customers were constantly stepping around them to peruse the books.

Still, Carli seemed to prefer being out here. And so far, they were both doing a remarkable job of conveniently ignoring Mr. Freider's cryptic comment earlier. It didn't mean Justin had stopped thinking about it, though.

A flash of anger surged through his chest. From what he knew of her so far, Carli was kind and soft hearted. Generous to boot. The thought of someone treating her badly or taking advantage of her made him want to crush something. Or to find the offender and personally make him answer for the transgression.

He gave his head a shake. How caveman of him. Again, none of this was really any of his business. His visit to Westerson would be a short one. He was only here to do a job.

To Carli's credit, she'd been right about the flow of traffic into the store. And he had to concede that people were actually purchasing items at a fairly steady rate at the registers. Maybe there was hope for the location after all. Or maybe he was just trying to come up with ways not to disappoint the lady sitting next to him.

"Well, isn't this a déjà vu!" Mr. Freider approached them, carrying a tray of scones and hot coffee. "Carli Tynan, sitting at the Book Nook. It's like all these years haven't gone by at all."

He set the tray amid the pile of files and binders. "Thought you both might like some refreshments."

"Thanks," both she and Justin said in unison as they both reached for the same scone. He could have sworn an electric current shot through his arm clear to his chest at the contact. Carli looked up at him in surprise. Had she felt it too?

"Please, go ahead." Justin nodded toward the tray, but he continued to let his fingers linger on hers. Heaven help him, she made no attempt to remove her hand either.

Mr. Freider hadn't moved. He stood staring at the two of them, a curious look on his face. "There's plenty more where that came from." He finally turned. "I'll let you two get back to work then."

Justin watched the older man walk away. "What did he mean exactly? About the whole déjà vu thing?"

Carli ducked her head slightly, didn't look up at him. "I spent a lot of time here as a kid. Guess I should admit that. Most of that time was spent right here in this very corner."

"I'm not surprised you were a big reader."

She turned to another page, her gaze still downward. "You have no idea. Sometimes it was the only escape."

He paused, wondering if he was being pushy. What exactly was the protocol under such circumstances? His curiosity won out. "How so?"

She gave a small shrug. "You've seen how loud and

busy living in that house can be. It's always been that way. Sometimes I just needed to be away from it all."

Justin thought about that. He hadn't known anything but solitude. And here she was telling him she'd actually sought that out.

"It's not like it was really noticed when I was gone," she added, shocking him. "As long as I returned home at a reasonable hour."

He waited in silence, giving her a chance to continue or stop. Though he was itching to know the truth behind that statement. He almost breathed a sigh of relief when she started speaking again.

"As you know, I was the middle child," she said, and highlighted an item on the page she was studying. "Sometimes, often, actually, that might be why I was easy to overlook."

"So you sought refuge here."

She nodded. "Books always gave me a whole other world to call my own. And even during the busy months, I always found it peaceful here." She finally looked up at him then. His breath caught at the depth of feeling shining in her eyes. "My sisters always had something that needed tending to. Tammy being the oldest was always on the brink of something new. The twins were so small, and they were double the work. And Janie...well, you've seen Janie." She blinked as if pushing away a thought. "My parents were always busy with one or all of them at once. I thought it best to just try to stay out of the way."

He didn't quite get her last point about her next older sister but didn't dare interrupt her.

"Me, I had my books at Hammond's Toys," she added.

Justin wanted to kick himself. He hadn't fully grasped her connection to this place. No wonder she was so invested in the success of the store. Still, he'd never, ever made a business decision based on anything but hard-core facts and data.

Logically, there was no reason to start doing anything differently now.

So why did he feel like such a lowly heel?

CHAPTER EIGHT

A CHILLY GUST of wind met Carli and Justin as they stepped outside later that afternoon. The light, barely noticeable flurries of earlier had turned into a steady snowfall.

Justin had tried really hard to focus on the plans for the store Mr. Freider had been discussing with them and on the figures he'd presented. But his usual sharp focus had failed him. He couldn't stop thinking about what the store manager had said to Carli. That Warren had some-how done Carli wrong. And then all the things Carli had revealed to him as they sat over the binders.

"Aunt Carli! Mr. Justin!" A child's voice rang out. Across the street, in what looked to be the town square, stood a short squat figure in a thick coat and a bright red hat. Ray. His mom sat reading on a bench a few feet away.

Justin felt an automatic and genuine smile. Carli imme-diately started walking to them, and he followed.

"Hey, little man," she said when she reached her nephew. "What are you up to?"

His mother stood and gave them a warm greeting.

"We got some hot chocolate and a doughnut. And then I wanted to build a snowman. There it is." He pointed to a bowling-ball-size pile of snow in the center of the square. "I just started."

"He wanted to enter the snowman contest. But he was

told he'd have to wait a few more years before being eligible," Tammy offered.

Ray's lip quivered. "It's not fair. Both Aunt Marnie and Aunt Perri are doin' it."

"They're quite a bit older than you." Carli looked up at her sister. "They've entered again, huh? Those two can't resist finding ways to compete with each other."

"Don't I know it."

Carli addressed Justin. "It never goes well. We'll just have to pray that neither one finals if the other doesn't."

Justin lifted an eyebrow in question. "Or?"

"Or you'll see fireworks in the middle of December."

Before he could comment, he felt a tug on his pant leg. "Wanna help me build a snowman, Mr. Justin?"

The question took Justin aback. He'd never actually built a snowman. Or a snow anything for that matter. Not even as a child. But how hard could it be? You just had to make three big balls of snow, then stack them.

He shrugged. "Sure, why not?"

Carli was staring at him with something akin to surprise on her face. "What?" he asked her. "Do you now doubt my snowman-making ability the same way you doubted my mechanical skills?" He wiggled his eyebrows at her in mock offense. That earned him a giggle from all three of his companions.

"Maybe we should hold our own little competition then?" he challenged.

"Yeah!" Ray chimed in, excitement ringing in his voice. "It'll be Aunt Carli and Mom against me and Mr. Justin. Boys against girls!"

"And who's going to judge?" Carli asked.

Ray looked over to the toy store. Mr. Freider stood by the window working on a Yuletide display. He gave them a friendly wave. "Mr. Freider will!"

Justin held his hands up. "Wait a minute. We need some kind of wager, or it's hardly worth it."

"Losers have to shovel Mom's walkway after the nor'easter," Tammy offered.

"Agreed." Justin gave Ray a fist bump. "Let's get started."

About thirty minutes later, he was definitely regretting his decision. The women had a medium-height structure that they'd clothed with Carli's scarf and decorated with various items from Tammy's handbag. It sported a trendy pair of sunglasses and a bright hair bow.

He and Ray had barely managed to form two balls of snow, and the one they tried to put above the other kept rolling off. Ray looked to be on the verge of tears. But to his credit, he was trying to keep it together.

Justin knelt to his height. "Don't worry. I have an idea. Trust me, okay?"

Ray gave him a brave nod.

They called Mr. Freider out to commence with the judging. He took one look at the males' creation and crossed his arms in front of his chest. "Is your snowman laying down?"

"That's a snow turtle!" Ray informed him.

Mr. Freider bent closer to look at the two uneven balls of snow that Ray and Justin had pushed together. Two black pebbles sat atop the smaller one.

"Those are his eyes," Justin added, trying very hard to keep a straight face.

"I see." Mr. Freider rubbed his chin, deeply considering. He turned to the ladies' snowman, then back to their "turtle."

Ray actually looked nervous. The poor kid was probably holding his breath, Justin thought.

"I have a decision," Mr. Freider declared. "Anyone can make a snowman. But a Christmas turtle? Now that's something special. The boys win!" he said with a dramatic bow in their direction. Ray squealed in delight and ran over to give him a high five.

Tammy and Carli protested with outrage. But Mr. Freider stood firm. "I have made my decision." He shook Ray's hand and then Justin's to congratulate their victory.

It was right then that Justin felt something cold and wet hit the back of his neck. Someone had just fired off a snowball! The culprit was no mystery. Carli had a distinctively smug look on her face. With no hint of guilt whatsoever.

Well, two could play at that game. He picked up a handful of snow and formed it into a tight ball, threw it right at her midsection. But she was too fast for him. She ducked to the side just in time. Then managed to pelt him with another snowball she'd prepared and had at the ready.

In moments, all five of them were ducking and launching snow at each other. Mr. Freider even joined in. Justin was marveling at the older man's accurate aim when Carli smacked him with yet another one. It landed on the side of his head that time. She clearly thought that was hilarious. Her laughter filled the air. Laughter at his expense!

That was it. Justin gave chase. He caught up to her by the side of the large gazebo that stood in the center of the square.

Grabbing her by the waist, he pulled her into his grasp from behind. She giggled and squirmed in his arms.

"You are not getting away. Sore loser."

"Let me go," she demanded, still laughing.

But then he turned her to face him. They stood nose to nose, his arms still wrapped around her middle. Her cheeks were rosy, eyes lit up with merriment. Her curly dark hair was in complete disarray, falling out of her wool knit cap.

She was the most stunning woman he'd ever laid eyes on.

He knew he should let her go. Knew they were in the

middle of a very public square. But even under her thick coat, he could feel the warmth of her skin. The faint scent of her fruity shampoo tickled his nose.

He was too far gone; there was no way he would be able to stop himself from kissing her.

So he didn't even try to resist.

Carli's laughter died on her lips as Justin leaned in. Before she knew it, somehow his lips were on hers. Her breath caught in her throat at the contact. A heady shiver ran down her spine, clear to her toes. His lips were firm and warm against mouth. Just as she'd imagined. And she had imagined it.

And now here he was, holding her. Kissing her.

This was insanity, complete foolishness. She was standing in the middle of Westerson town square in Justin Hammond's arms as they kissed. The taste of his mouth on hers felt like paradise. Every single cell along her skin tingled with desire. She'd been trying to fight it, but now there was no denying. She was attracted to him like she'd never been to any other man.

It scared her silly.

Justin was merely in New England for a business project. He had his own life, and his own business back on the West Coast. Oh, and there was also the small matter of him being heir to the company she worked for. She had to regain some sense.

With a sigh of regret, she made herself pull out of his grasp. Forcing herself to meet his eyes, she realized Justin looked just as shaken as she was.

A small hand tugged at the hem of her coat. "Hey. I thought you said he wasn't your boyfriend. Why you kissing him then?" Ray demanded.

Heavens, how in the world was she supposed to respond to the child? Not like she had any kind of real answer.

She looked away, desperate to come up with something she could say. Only to find her sister staring at her, eyes wide with shock. Great, just great. There was no way this little event wouldn't be shared with every member of her family.

Mr. Freider muttered something about having to return to the store and walked away. She was certain she'd seen a hint of a smile on the his face.

Correction, Carli thought. The bit of news about Carli kissing her boss would be shared with every member of the town, not just her immediate family. How could she have been so reckless?

She took a deep breath, fighting to regain some composure.

Thankfully, her sister saved her from having to answer Ray when she walked up and lifted the boy into her arms. "Hey, you're looking pretty wet. Let's get you home and cleaned up."

Carli mouthed a silent *thank you*. The look her sister returned left no question that they would be discussing the matter in due time. Carli suppressed a groan at that prospect. Nevertheless, Tammy had just saved her from what would have no doubt been a cringe-inducing conversation with her nephew. Now, if only someone would save her from what was sure to follow with Justin.

Justin looked down out his window at Main Street Westerson. The late-afternoon sun shone glaringly on the thin blanket of snow that covered the town. And word was there was more snow expected. The forecast predicted a powerful nor'easter that really just sounded to him like an overblown snowstorm. If he'd experienced any during his childhood, he couldn't recall. Not that he would. He'd perfected the art of burying his childhood memories over the years.

He was way more focused on the storm that had been brewing inside him. He'd managed to get in a few hours of work, but it had been like swimming against the current. The events of the morning kept playing through his head.

The walk with Carli when she'd reacted so strangely to Warren as they'd encountered him. Mr. Freider's words about whatever had happened between the two of them.

The snowball fight. And what it had somehow inexplicably led to. The way Carli had responded when he'd kissed her.

Justin rammed a frustrated hand through his hair. This was useless. He wasn't going to get anything done when his mind was a jumble of thoughts about Carli.

The digital clock on his nightstand read close to five o'clock. A bit earlier than he normally liked to eat but getting dinner would at least give him something mundane to do. He'd noticed a charming mom-and-pop pizza joint this morning on the way to the store. And the walk would do him good. Grabbing his coat, he took the stairs to the first floor.

Almost everyone he ran into on his way either offered a friendly nod or a smile. Several said a simple hello. This was so not Seattle. Or any other city he'd visited over the years. The townspeople of Westerson were beyond friendly straight to outgoing. It explained Carli's personality somewhat. She was a product of this town.

Maybe it was just the approach of Christmas that had all of them behaving in such a manner. This atmosphere couldn't be a permanent characteristic, could it? He wasn't going to be here long enough to find out.

Either way, he was enjoying it now, but he wasn't the

type who could really fit into a town like this. Everyone knew each other. He preferred the anonymity of the big city.

He made it to the pizza parlor where an early crowd of hungry customers had already gathered. The rich aroma of tangy tomato sauce and yeasty dough made his stomach growl. He'd intended to get a slice or two but decided a whole pie might be in order.

Someone tapped him on the back as he stood in line.

One of Carli's younger twin sisters. "I thought that was you," Perri told him with a smile.

"Fancy meeting you here."

Her eyes narrowed on him with confusion. What a fuddy-duddy thing to say to a teenager. "It must be pizza Sunday in Westerson, huh?" he asked, motioning to the growing crowd.

"Nah, it's always this packed at Diammatta's. Plus there's a hockey game on tonight. Pizza and hockey go great together."

"I suppose they do."

"You don't watch hockey?"

"No, not really. I'm more of a baseball fan."

She shrugged. "Anyway, I hope this doesn't take too long."

"You have plans?" What was there for a teen to do in a town this small?

"I wanna go work on my snowman. For the competition over at the tree farm next week. They decide the winner on Wednesday."

"I heard about that. You and your sister both entered"

Perri rolled her eyes. "Don't know why she bothers. As if she could beat me." There was no animosity or spite in the way she said it. Just a healthy dose of youthful confidence.

"Pretty sure you'll win, huh?" he asked, then thought about his pathetic attempt earlier with Ray. That only had him remembering the kiss he'd shared with Carli.

Damn.

The pizza line was barely moving despite several people taking orders behind the counter. Not that he was in a rush; the only thing waiting for him was an empty hotel room and a bottle of beer from the mini fridge.

"Marnie doesn't stand a chance," Perri declared. "She's been talking smack about it all week. I'll show her. Wait till you see my creation."

"I wasn't really planning on attending, actually."

She looked him up and down. "Well, why not?"

Justin shrugged. "I wasn't really invited."

"Well, consider yourself invited as of this very moment. By the likely contest winner, no less. Oh, and you should join us for dinner tonight too."

It struck Justin how poised this young lady was, how composed and confident. She'd met him two days ago. Yet she felt certain he would be accepted and welcome at her house for dinner, without having to run it by anyone else. Whatever Louise and her husband had done in raising their girls, they'd instilled in them a strong sense of self-worth. A rare thing these days.

The real question was, would Carli feel the same way about Perri's invitation? He had to admit, he really wanted to see her.

"Come on," Perri insisted. "Have pizza at our house."

He did owe the Tynan family a meal. They'd so graciously cooked for him his first night here. The least he could do was reciprocate with pizza tonight.

"I'd love to. On one condition."

"What's that?"

"The pizza is my treat."

She grinned. "I can't think of a reason to turn that down."

Maybe not. But Carli probably might. Would she be angry that Justin had found a way to see her? It was a chance he was willing to take.

It took close to an hour, but they were finally out the door with several steaming boxes of thick crusty pizza with various toppings. Perri made them rush back to the Tynan house to keep them as hot as possible. Between the steam from the boxes and the near run, Justin was in a sweat by the time they reached the front porch.

Carli was the one who answered the door. The shock on her face at seeing him on the other side had him questioning the spontaneous decision to come.

"Look who I found at Diammatta's!" Perri exclaimed as they made their way in. "He's treating us."

Carli's mom and dad were already in the kitchen, pulling out plates and cups. "How nice," both parents said in unison.

He noticed Carli didn't make eye contact as he moved past her to put down the pizzas. A whiff of her shampoo wafted to his nostrils, and his thoughts immediately went once again to the kiss they'd shared. It hadn't been his wisest move, but he'd hardly been thinking straight when he'd kissed her. Hell, he could barely think straight now with her just standing in the same room. He'd thought about that kiss all afternoon, had barely been able to focus on a conference call with his office assistant back home. The way she'd tasted, the way she'd felt in his arms. The way she'd responded.

He knew those things would haunt him for a good long while once he returned to Seattle. He was hardly likely to meet anyone else like Carli Tynan. That's why it made no sense that he was so damn attracted to her. Carli was nothing like the women he normally ran into. Most of the women he'd dated were practically carbon copies of each other. Wealthy, socialite types who could barely be bothered with much more than shopping for the next gala on their calendar.

He and Carli were from two different worlds. She had family, friends and a career she loved. Her Christmas party back in Boston showed she had the affection and respect of her colleagues.

Above all, she worked for his father, a man Justin wanted nothing to do with once this little project was over.

Yes, kissing her had been nothing less than foolish.

Finally, once slices were plated and drinks poured, Carli deigned to acknowledge him with a tight smile, albeit one that didn't quite reach her eyes. "You didn't have to spring for the pizza, Justin," she told him in a clipped voice.

"It was the least I could do after your family's been so gracious."

"It was really not necessary."

The exchange earned a shocked look from both her parents.

"That's just rude," Marnie admonished her, not holding back, like the younger sister that she was. "What she means to say is thank you."

Justin studied Carli's stern facial expression and the tight set of her jaw. Judging by her reaction since he'd first walked in, and the rigid set of her spine right now, she was far from thankful that he was here. In fact, she looked more than ready to toss him out on his behind.

Normally, Carli loved pizza from Diammatta's. Their pies were the best this side of the state. Tonight however, she could hardly taste any flavor. In fact, she may as well have been eating cardboard. No fault could be placed on the cook. It had nothing to do with the food but had everything to do with the man sitting across from her at her parent's kitchen table. She'd almost dropped in shock when she'd opened the door to find Perri standing there with him.

Her behavior bordered on being rude, she was well aware, barely having said more than a few words to him since he'd walked in. Luckily for her, both her younger sisters and parents were seasoned conversationalists.

But what was there for her to say? She could hardly make small talk, pretending that what had happened between them earlier today wasn't foremost in her mind. Justin was thinking about it too. She could tell by the way she caught him looking at her, how his gaze lingered on her lips whenever she took a bite. How in the world was she supposed to try to eat?

When all she could think about was if she would ever be kissed that way again.

Forget the fact that she worked for the company Justin was heir to. Men like him didn't fall for women like her. He was only in New England for a short-term project, one aspect of which she was desperately trying to get him to change his mind about. After that, he would be gone for good.

If she hadn't been able to maintain a relationship with someone she'd known for years and who had grown up in the same town, how could she dare hope to interest someone as worldly as Justin Hammond?

Blessedly, an hour later the dishes were finally cleared and the table wiped down. Carli was more than ready to show Justin the door. But then her father did the unthinkable. He invited Justin to stay to watch the hockey game.

Leaving her with no choice but to join them.

It would look suspicious to her parents to try to get out of it. She never missed watching a game with her father while in town. Her dad already had a roaring fire started in the fireplace when they all made it into sitting room. Normally, she would have grabbed one of the sofa cushions and plopped herself down in front of the flames as they cheered and shouted at the TV. But there was no way she was going to enjoy either the fire or any of the ice action tonight.

If any of her family members sensed her discomfort, they didn't show it.

At the end of the second period, she was more than ready to come up with an excuse and call it a night. But her father caught Justin staring at one of the framed sketches hanging on the wall.

Oh, no.

"Those make us proud of our girl's talent," her father boasted.

Justin raised an eyebrow in surprise. "One of your daughters drew that?"

Her father lifted his chin in a show of pride. "Sure did. That one sitting right there. The one who works for you."

Carli tried not to groan out loud. She did not want to talk about her portrait sketches with Justin Hammond. Especially not tonight. Then her father made it even worse when he added, "It's second-period intermission, Carli. Why don't you show him the others that are hanging around the house?"

Justin turned to her expectedly. She had no choice but to stand up. He followed her down the corridor.

"This one is of my two younger sisters," she said, pointing to a frame hanging near the kitchen hallway. It was a profile picture of Perri and Marnie about four years ago when they were thirteen or so.

She tried to move on, farther down the hallway where a

portrait she'd drawn of her mother hung. But Justin stopped her with a hand on her arm.

"Carli, wait."

She stopped in her tracks, but couldn't look him in the eye.

"First of all, these are amazing," he stated, motioning to the sketch on the wall. "I'm no expert but even to a novice it's clear you have a real talent."

She inhaled a deep breath, oddly touched by the compliment. It wasn't anything she hadn't heard before, but somehow coming from him... It just felt *more*.

"Thank you. It was just a hobby I had a while back."

"You had?"

She shrugged. "I haven't drawn in a while. I have my reasons." Reasons she had no intention of getting into with him of all people.

As far as she was concerned, the last sketch she'd started would be her last one. The only one she'd ever torn to shreds.

Justin looked as if he was ready to question her further but apparently changed his mind. Must have been her closed expression.

"Second," he began, "I know I should I apologize for what happened this morning. In the town square." He took a deep breath before continuing. "But I'd be lying if I said I was sorry."

Well, that was certainly a straightforward and honest statement. She had no idea what to make of it, however. What exactly did he mean? That mistakes happened? Did he even consider it a mistake?

"I think we should just move past it," she blurted out, too tired and too frazzled to analyze any of it further. The truth was, she would welcome his kiss even now. As ridiculous as it was, part of her wished he would take her in his arms right here in the hallway.

"Move past it?"

She nodded with emphasis, though not entirely certain exactly what she was arguing for. "It was a fluke, right? We were both having fun and then things just took an unexpected turn. Nothing more."

Justin stepped closer, so close she could see the hint of shadow that had appeared on his chin since this morning. The scent of his aftershave wafted to her nose, and she had to resist the urge to lean into him and take a deeper sniff.

"So you'd like to just forget it happened."

Carli's answer was interrupted when the front door swung open and Tammy walked in with Ray in tow.

"Aunt Carli. Mr. Justin," Ray squealed when he saw them and made a beeline to where they both stood.

"Aunt Marnie texted that there was pizza. I love pizza!"

Carli took the interruption as a chance to catch her breath, thankful for her clueless nephew's disruption. Things with Justin were getting just a tad too intense. She didn't think she'd be able to give him the same nonchalant response if he asked her about the kiss again.

"Did you guys save me any?" Ray asked with a hint of panic in his voice, as if it just occurred to him that there might not be any pizza left.

"Of course we did," Carli reassured him. "Your favorite, extra cheese. Let's go get you some."

She reached for her nephew's hand and started to lead him to the kitchen.

Justin cleared his throat. "I guess I should get going. I haven't answered any emails all day, and it's already eight o'clock."

Ray stopped in his tracks and turned to him, clear disappointment etched in his small face. "Do you really have to go, Mr. Justin?"

Carli felt a little taken aback. Ray was clearly developing a fondness for him. In the span of two short days, Justin had already made an impression on the little boy. Her heart sank. It was no wonder. Besides Carli's father and his own dad, Ray was surrounded mostly by women. Another man around was probably a real novelty for him. He was going to be heartbroken when Justin left. Add that to the list of casualties when Justin walked out of their lives for good in less than a week.

Justin leaned over to Ray's height. "I'm afraid so."

"Can you come over tomorrow? Aunt Carli and I are baking cookies."

Carli groaned inwardly. She'd promised Ray on the phone they would make a batch of Christmas cookies, then spend part of the day decorating them.

Why did her family keep inviting Justin to events? First Perri, now Ray.

She couldn't exactly rescind the invitation. Even if had just come from a four-year-old.

"I would," Justin answered, "but I'm not much of a cook."

"That's okay. I can show you what to do. Please?" He gave Justin a big, toothless grin. "Me and Aunt Carli could teach you how."

Justin looked up and met her eyes above her nephew's head. "I'd like that," he said. "I'd like that a lot."

CHAPTER NINE

CARLI TOSSED AND TURNED. Her bedside clock said it was 12:30 a.m. This was the same bed she'd slept in as a teenager. Right in this very room. She was never uncomfortable here. Not even during all those years of dramatic teenage anguish. But tonight was a different story. She couldn't find a comfortable position. And she couldn't seem to fall asleep.

Her thoughts kept returning to the man about three blocks away at the Sailor's Inn Bed and Breakfast. Was he fast asleep as was likely at this hour? Or was there a chance he was thinking about her?

He'd seemed genuinely interested in her artwork. But she wasn't quite ready to talk about that yet.

She needed sleep. But it was no use. Huffing out a breath, Carli got out of bed and put on her slippers. She walked over to the window and lifted the blind. She could see the rooftop of the B and B from where she stood. From there, her imagination took over. She thought of Justin in his bed, under the covers. A man like him probably slept with only pajama bottoms. Or nothing at all.

She sucked in a breath at that thought and tried to force the image out of her head.

This was the closest she'd ever come to fantasizing about a real actual man in her life. Not even with ex-boyfriends had she done such a thing. But here she was, in the dead of night, unable to get Justin Hammond out of her mind. A curse escaped her lips on a whisper. Damn him for kissing her the way he did. And damn her for responding. What a mistake. She should have never gotten playful with him in the first place. Why, oh, why hadn't she just said hello to her nephew and then walked away when she'd seen him in the town square? If only she could go back in time and stop herself from throwing that snowball.

It was such a ridiculous thing to wish for that she couldn't help but laugh. To think, an ill-timed snowball fight had led to such turmoil within her. She would have happily gone on with her life, admiring Justin from afar. But now there was no turning back from the line she had crossed. And that's exactly what she'd done—crossed a line.

Well, maybe there was no turning back time or rectifying the mistake she had made. But she could certainly vow to be more cautious in the future. From now on, for the week or so that she and Justin were in Westerson, she would be the utmost professional. She wasn't one of those women to wallow in her mistakes, but she certainly made sure to learn from them.

Starting tomorrow morning, Justin would see nothing but the serious and accomplished career woman that she was. She'd make sure to steer the conversation toward business matters and details surrounding the store and its operations.

She just had to figure out how to do that exactly, while baking Christmas cookies with the man all day. Right. Easy-peasy. Carli sighed and walked over to the bookcase in the corner of her room. Plucking out one of her childhood favorites, she settled back onto the bed and opened the well-worn pages to one of her preferred chapters.

May as well read, she thought. There was no way she was going to fall asleep anytime soon.

The smell of newly baked muffins and freshly brewed coffee hit Justin as soon as he left his room. Betty was already pouring a cup when he reached the small dining room.

She handed it to him. "I heard you coming down the stairs," she told him with a bright warm smile.

Justin blinked as he took the cup and uttered a heartfelt thanks. He couldn't remember a time someone had listened for him in the morning just to have a cup of coffee ready. No doubt Betty was simply being an attentive innkeeper. Still, he felt oddly touched by the gesture.

She handed him a napkin as he sat down at one of the small linen-covered tables.

"I also baked more of those vanilla almond muffins that you liked so much," she told him offhandedly.

Justin felt his mouth water at that bit of news. He was going to gain so much weight this week. "But I thought those were only made on Saturdays?"

"Normally. But you seemed to enjoy them so much. I wanted to make them for you again."

Justin felt an odd sensation at the base of his throat. Perhaps Betty really was simply responding to the tastes of a paying customer. But this was a novel experience for him. The large chains and glamorous hotels he usually stayed in offered the utmost in glitz and luxury. But no one had ever gone out of their way to specifically make something just because he'd liked it.

Hell, no one would have even noted such a thing, even in one of the establishments where he was a regular, highly regarded guest. The notion left him with an unexpected sense of familiarity. "I know you must be busy, Betty, but do you have a minute or two to join me?"

She didn't hesitate and pulled out a chair. "That would be lovely, thank you. It will give me an excuse to put off the myriad of items on my to-do list this morning."

"Glad to oblige," he said, and gave her a conspiratorial wink.

"And what are your plans for the day?" she asked him.

Justin grabbed one of the muffins and split it open. Aromatic steam arose from the center. "Unbelievably, I'll be baking Christmas cookies."

Her smile grew. "Why is that so unbelievable?"

He swallowed. "It's nothing I've ever done before. Nor ever expected to do."

Betty's eyebrows drew together. "You've never baked Christmas cookies? Not even as a child?"

He wasn't aware it was so unheard-of. The truth was, his mother hadn't been the baking type. Heck, she hadn't really been the *mother* type in any way. There were always baked goods and pastries laying around in the various kitchens he'd been in over the years, but he'd be hard-pressed to say where they'd come from.

"Well, I imagine the Hammonds had plenty of people on staff to bake for them. I guess it makes sense that you never did so yourself."

Justin wasn't going to get into the whole Christmas conversation and tell this kindly woman that cookies were the last thing on his mind whenever the holidays came around. And then when he and his mother had left New England, it had just become another day.

Christmas celebrations were a family affair for most of the world. He had a brother, but he may as well have been an only child. And even the parent he'd grown up with had barely been around. Very different than the way Carli had grown up, for instance.

"So how'd you get corralled into it then?" Betty asked.

"A very persuasive four-year-old," Justin answered, hardly believing it himself. It was difficult to say no to that little nephew of Carli's.

She laughed at his answer. "I should have known. Ray can be quite persuasive when he wants something," she said, echoing his thoughts.

"He certainly had my number."

He didn't tell her that there was more to it. Or about how he knew he'd be spending this Sunday alone otherwise. How he'd jumped at the chance to be able to spend it with Carli. Even doing something as mundane as baking cookies.

Betty somehow seemed to read his thoughts yet again. "Mmm-hmm. And tell me, was Ray the only reason you agreed to do this?"

He lifted an eyebrow in question, though he obviously knew what she was getting at. The woman was very perceptive, it appeared.

"I just thought I'd give it a try."

She wasn't falling for it. "I see. And it had nothing to do with the way you were looking at Carli Tynan yesterday morning, I suppose."

Wow. Was everybody in this town so direct? He bit down on another piece of muffin as he tried to scramble for a way to respond.

"I'm sorry," Betty began, sparing him. "It's just that I've known that girl since she was knee-high. One of the sweetest, purest souls you'll ever meet. She doesn't deserve to have her heart broken."

Again. Though unspoken, the word hung in the air as clear as day between them. Then the older woman suddenly stood up with a soft clap of her hands. "Oh, dear. I hadn't realized how late it was getting. I really should get to those chores. Please excuse me."

"Of course." Justin stood, but she'd already turned away and was walking to the front desk.

Leaving Justin with the succinct feeling that, sweet old lady or not, he'd just been issued a gentle yet clear warning.

Carli opened the door to him with a yawn, then stepped aside to let him in. She was dressed in baggy gray sweatpants, an oversize flannel shirt and thick fuzzy socks. Her hair was pulled back in a loose ponytail at the base of her neck but several tendrils had made a blatant escape and framed her face haphazardly.

She looked downright adorable.

What was wrong with him? Justin thought as she took his coat and hung it. He'd been less attracted to women wearing scanty lace panties than he was to her right now. None of it made any sense.

He glanced around the empty house. "Where is everyone?"

She stifled another yawn and shook her head. "Sundays are pretty busy around here."

"I see."

"My parents are out running errands after services, the twins had breakfast plans with friends. And Tammy's due to drop Ray off. But she's always late, usually because it can be a military level challenge getting a four-year-old out the door. Particularly on a Sunday when *The Squigglies* are on."

"*The Squigglies*?"

"Ray's favorite TV show."

He followed her to the kitchen. "Can I get you some more coffee? Though I'm guessing Betty has already filled you up to the brim."

People in this town really seemed to know each other well. "Correct call."

"Just as well. I might actually need the full pot for myself," she said through yet another yawn.

"Long night?"

She didn't look at him as she poured her coffee. "I didn't get much sleep. Sometimes I have trouble sleeping right before a big storm hits."

For some reason, her statement didn't quite ring true. "I've never heard of that. Weather-induced insomnia."

She glared at him over the rim of her coffee cup, so intensely that he had to stifle a laugh. So what was the real reason for her insomnia? What were the chances it had anything to do with him? He was most likely just flattering himself. But it was an intriguing notion. Lord knew he'd spent more than a few waking moments overnight remembering that kiss. The way she had felt in his arms, the warmth of her body up against his. The way she'd tasted.

He cleared his throat. "So tell me, just how bad is this storm supposed to be? When is it due even?"

She swallowed the gulp of coffee and sighed with pleasure as it went down. The whole image sent a surge of longing through his chest. He gripped the granite counter in front of him just to give his hands something to do.

"Well, it's a nor'easter. Set to bring several inches of snow with high, gusting winds. And of course, out here on the Cape there's always the real risk of flooding."

Justin recalled nasty storms from his childhood in Metro Boston. The way he'd hide under thick blankets as the wind rattled the windows. But not much else. He must have blocked it out. Too bad there was no real way to block out everything.

"And it's due to hit sometime tomorrow night." Carli answered the second part of his question.

"No one seems terribly nervous."

She shrugged. "Winter storms are a way of life around

here. Some things you just can't change." She gave him a pointed look.

Wasn't that the truth? If he could, he would change the way he was starting to feel. Carli had awakened a longing within him that he hadn't known existed. More than his attraction to her physically, it was her warmth, her humor, the way she interacted with her family and friends. The combination was like a gravitational pull that seemed to suck him into her orbit. It made no sense; he would have to get over it. Carli deserved someone with the same sense of belonging and roots that she'd known all her life. He was too far removed from being such a person.

He'd remember kissing her for the rest of his life; that tender, sweet moment would live with him from now on. A cherished memory of a woman who could never be his.

"I guess not," he answered. Such a simple response. It warranted no further conversation. Nothing more needed to be said. On the surface anyway.

If he could tell her everything, if he could bare his soul, he'd admit that right now he wanted nothing more than to repeat the mistake he had apologized for. He wanted to pull her up against him, right here in her parents' kitchen and taste her plump soft lips. He wanted to run his fingers through her hair and feel her warmth.

No, he couldn't come out and say all that. But there had to be a way to somehow convey how impressed he was of the woman Carli Tynan was. Or how fond he'd grown of her in such a short time, even though it couldn't lead to anything more.

He was trying to come up with the words when they were interrupted by the shuffle of small feet running through the house toward the kitchen.

Any further revelations would have to wait.

* * *

Justin Hammond had no idea how to separate an egg. Carli had to hold in her laughter as she watched him crack it open then stare blankly at it in his hands, clearly trying to figure out how to get the yoke apart from the rest.

When he reached for a spoon to do heaven knew what, she figured she'd better intervene in the interest of avoiding a food-borne illness.

"Here, let me help."

He looked so grateful that she had to suppress another laugh. Between Ray and Justin, she'd be hard-pressed to decide which one of them was less useful in the kitchen. So far, she might have to say it was Justin. As if to challenge that conclusion, her nephew chose that moment to knock over a bowl of sifted flour, making a colossal mess on the floor.

"Oops."

Carli sighed. Something told her they'd be heading to the bakery or they'd have to do without Christmas cookies this year. Her parents were both still out on their errands. Tammy had begged to run to the nail salon while they watched Ray. Maybe she should just call one of them now and have them pick up a box from Patty's Pastries on their way home.

She was debating whether to pull out a broom and dust pan or a vacuum when Justin somehow managed to drop both parts of the egg right into the pile of flour Ray had just spilled.

"Oops." This time, both males said it unison.

Carli didn't know whether to cry or just run out of the room screaming. Let someone else deal with all this.

Of course, that wasn't an option. She grabbed a large kitchen towel and threw it at Justin. "You work on the egg that got on the counter. While I try tackle the mountain of flour on the floor."

An hour later, they hadn't even managed to put anything into the oven. Yep, no doubt about it. Someone was going to have to make a bakery run.

The entire kitchen was a disaster area. She'd seen neater construction sites in Metro Boston. But just to go through the motions, for Ray's sake, she walked into the pantry where her mother kept the holiday themed cookie cutters. As if any of their creations would actually be viable enough to hold any kind of shape. Except for perhaps one mound of sugar cookie dough, they were batting zero.

A loud clanging sound followed by Ray's horrified scream had her dropping the cutters and running back out into the main area.

"What happened?"

Ray's lip quivered as he looked up at her. Justin seemed at a complete loss. Half the counter and part of the floor were covered in a shiny puddle of green.

"I don't really know," Justin began. "We were trying out the food coloring, trying to decide which color to use."

"I dropped the whole bottle," Ray wailed. Large fat tears began to roll down his cheeks.

Carli immediately ran to him.

"It was my fault," Justin said, ramming his hand into his hair. "I shouldn't have let him play with it."

Ray climbed off the counter stool he'd been standing on and ran straight into her arms. "I made a mess, Aunt Carli. And now we have no cookies."

Carli didn't doubt that the latter statement was the real cause of all the tears. She brushed them off his wet, ruddy cheeks.

"Oh, buddy. It's okay. It was just an accident."

Justin swiftly crouched next to them both. "Ray, it was my fault. I should have known better. Please don't cry."

For an insane moment, Carli had the thought that Justin might need comforting even more than the child. He seemed really shaken. He'd clearly never been around a crying child before. Heaven help them, he didn't realize they did it all the time.

Or was there something else behind his inflated response to the minor disaster?

Ray hiccupped on another sob.

"Hey, we'll still have some cookies," she reassured him. "This is no big deal." She spoke over his head, looking straight into Justin's eyes.

Her mother chose that moment to walk in. Taking in the scene, she blew out a deep breath. Then she went over to her grandson. Ray pulled away and ran to his grandmother as soon as he saw her.

"I ruined the cookies, Nana."

"Mmm-hmm. And the kitchen is a mess," she said in an even, soothing tone. "But it's nothing that can't be fixed. Okay?"

Ray sniffed and nodded.

"Let's go get you cleaned up," she said, and picked him up.

"Thanks, Mom!" Her mother could comfort Ray like no one else could.

"Don't thank me," Louise threw over her shoulder as she walked out with her grandson. "Just get that mess cleaned up. Both of you."

"Yes, ma'am."

Poor Justin looked like he'd just run through a minefield. "So that went well."

He blinked at her. "Where do we start?"

She pointed to the one ball of dough on the counter

that had somehow survived, albeit it was the color of a mossy lake. "I say we try to salvage that dough so that we can throw at least one batch in the oven. Then we start scrubbing."

"You still want to bake? Using that dough?"

"Sure. Why not?"

"For one thing, it's green. Very green."

She shrugged. "So, we'll have green cookies."

"Uh-huh."

"Are you okay?"

He ran a hand through his hair. "I'm not sure. The little guy was pretty upset."

"He's four. It doesn't take much. He'll forget about the whole fiasco by bedtime."

"He will?"

"Of course."

"If that's true, it will be thanks to you. And the way you handled it. Your mom too."

"How else would I have handled it?"

He gave her a blank, confused stare. "You were just so… I don't know…gentle. And understanding." He took a deep breath. "And your mother was the same. Even as she agreed that the cookies were ruined, she calmed and reassured him."

"That's what one does when it comes to children. They're just learning their way."

"I guess I wouldn't know."

Carli grabbed a roll of paper towels and tore off a good amount. The green was starting to settle into her mom's granite counters. She handed a few to Justin, who followed her lead and began wiping furiously. "Maybe not. But you were a child once."

He snorted. "Trust me when I tell you, I don't ever recall any adult behaving quite so evenly after a major mishap. Or even in general."

Carli's heart nearly burst in her chest. How could that be? "You don't?"

Justin shook his head. "No. When I did something wrong, which was often, I got a thorough lashing of the tongue. Followed by some form of punishment. Then my mother would make sure my dad heard about what I did and what an awful handful I was, usually the moment he got home. That always led to loud, long arguments with plenty of door slamming."

"Oh, my God." She stilled. "Justin, that sounds terribly unfair."

"It's how I remember. I suppose a lot of it was my fault. I should have tried harder."

"You can't be serious. You were a child."

"Still, I was aware enough to realize my behavior was causing strife."

"Like every other child."

He shook his head. "Not really. Not James. I can't ever recall him acting out. It was always me."

"I'm sure James had his moments. It's just that some children are more active than others."

"Maybe. My behavior had ramifications for him too. He'd always turn tail and hide in his room whenever it started. I knew he was angry with me for causing so much trouble."

Carli's heart sank. She wanted to cry for the little boy Justin must have been. She doubted he was anything more than an energetic and curious child like so many others. Apparently, his parents used that as an excuse to vent their own issues and anger. To make it all worse, the two brothers had apparently turned on each other as a result.

He took another deep breath before adding, "So I know

he must have blamed me for the destruction of our parents' marriage."

"How can that be?"

"On some level, he's right."

"Don't say that. A mere child can't cause the breakup of a marriage. There has to be underlying issues at play."

"You're right. But I caused the final fight that led to my mother reaching her last nerve, so to speak."

"What happened?"

Justin was wiping the counter, not looking at her as he spoke. The events he was recalling happened years ago, but they seemed to have left considerable if invisible scars.

"It was Christmas Eve. The big tree had been set up in the main foyer. I couldn't stop admiring it. It was so majestic. Bright lights and shiny ornaments. And it was so tall, I could barely see the top."

Oh, no. Carli could guess where this was going.

"I remember one particular ornament. Just out of my reach. A Red Sox catcher's mitt. It looked more like a toy. I just wanted to play with it for a bit. I was going to put it right back. But when I jumped up to grab it, the whole tree fell over. Almost all the ornaments broke."

"Oh, Justin. You must have been so scared."

"You have no idea. I came so close to running out the door in that moment. Thought maybe I could just keep running and never go back."

Carli noticed he'd bunched up the paper towels into a tight ball, gripping it in his fist.

"But my mother came rushing down the stairs. She kept yelling over and over how I'd been told so often to leave it alone. And why couldn't I just listen. She called my father and demanded he come home right then."

Carli's gasped in horror at the woman's reaction. To a simple accident that could have very well severely injured her son. She'd never wanted so badly to give another adult a reassuring hug. To hold him and tell him he'd done nothing wrong all those years ago. If anything, he'd been the one who'd been betrayed and disappointed. But though her arms itched to hold him, she clenched her muscles instead. It was doubtful Justin would want her sympathy. He seemed way too proud for that.

"What ensued when he arrived is not a pleasant memory," Justin continued.

"I'm sure it wasn't." She figured he didn't have too many pleasant memories based on what he was revealing to her right now.

"I was young, but I remember the expression on James's face. He'd turned white as a ghost. I'll never forget what he said later that night. We could hear our parents having it out upstairs. He just walked over to me and gave me a hard shove. I couldn't blame him. He was so angry."

Carli was afraid to guess and almost didn't want to ask. But she had to. "What did he say?"

"He said he hated me."

She couldn't help it. Walking over to where he stood, Carli rubbed a soothing hand along his arm. He'd gone tight and rigid.

"That was the last time I saw him until we were well into our teens. Simply coincidentally at some boating event on the Charles. And didn't see him again after that for years."

What a burden to bear as a child, Carli thought. Justin had been too young to understand that his parents' tumultuous relationship hadn't been his fault.

"You can't believe you were the real cause of their divorce."

"I know that now. But for years I kept replaying that day in my mind. If only I had just left the tree alone."

"You were a child." She wanted to just say it over and over again until it somehow sunk into his psyche.

"Maybe. But I was old enough to know better."

"You can't honestly believe that. Sooner or later something was going to happen that triggered the same result—your parents didn't want to be together."

He gave her an indulgent smile. "Interesting theory. I always wonder though."

"Wonder about what?"

"What would have happened if I hadn't been their son. After all, I seemed to be the cause of all the animosity. If it wasn't for me, they probably would have been the perfect family who had everything. But then I came along."

Carli could no longer stop herself. Her arms automatically went up and went around Justin's wide shoulders in a tight embrace. They stood that way silently for several lengthy moments. There didn't need to be any words between them. Right now she just wanted him to feel her understanding and her support, wishing with all her heart that someone had done the same years ago when he'd been a small boy.

A boy who thought his family hated him.

CHAPTER TEN

JUSTIN WANTED TO kick himself. He hadn't meant to get into the whole sordid story of his childhood and what had led to him and James growing up on opposite coasts. But he'd just been so struck and so touched at how she'd gently dealt with Ray just now. Plus, it was so easy to talk to her. He'd be hard-pressed to say why that was. Never before had he divulged so much of his past to anyone, let alone a woman who he'd essentially just met.

He was usually much more restrained, more in control. But what little of it he had snapped like a stretched rubber band when she wrapped her arms around him and held him against her. This felt right; *she* felt right. He could smell the perfumed scent of her soft, delicate skin. Mixed with the hint of sweetness in the air, it shook his senses.

He had to taste her again.

Lifting her chin, he watched as desire shaded her eyes. She had the longest lashes. Her lips were lush and beckoning. He knew what he was about to do wasn't wise. He was technically in this town as her boss on a project. He had no business kissing her. Even as that thought ran through his head, he reached down and took her lips with his own.

She tasted as good as he remembered. No, even better. Like honey and forbidden fruit. He thought he might lose his mind when she responded. With a soft sigh against his mouth, she molded herself tighter against the length of him.

Unlike in the square, this time they were alone. The knowledge brought a heady sense of excitement that he found difficult to clamp down on.

Placing his hands against the small of her back, he pulled her even closer. He wanted her to feel his full reaction. She had to know how attracted he was to her. More than he'd felt for any other woman. Inexplicable on every logical level, but there it was.

But it was more than a physical attraction. He'd just opened up to Carli Tynan like no one else before. Her response had been to try to comfort him, to reassure him with both her words and her touch.

Her hands went up to his shoulders and she gave him a small nudge back, and he pulled away from the kiss.

"We really shouldn't be…" she whispered against his mouth.

"I know." But he guided her with his body up against the counter and kissed her again, deeper. She gasped in shock but didn't try to stop him.

If anyone had told him last week he'd be standing in a rustic New England kitchen kissing a Hammond employee, he would have laughed in their face.

The wisest thing to do would be to pull away. On top of everything else, they were in her parents' kitchen for heaven's sake. That reality was driven home when they heard the water turn off upstairs just as someone walked in through the front door of the house.

Carli jumped back and jerked out of his arms. She ran around to the other side of the kitchen island, clearly putting distance between them. Rubbing her lips, she averted her eyes.

Justin ran a hand down his face. How had things between them gotten so heated, so out of control? He'd just barely delivered an apology for the first time he'd kissed her.

"I don't know how that happened," he began before Carli held up a hand to stop him.

Her sister Tammy entered the kitchen at that very moment. She stopped in her tracks as soon as she took in the scene. Justin tried not to groan out loud as Tammy's gaze traveled from her sister to him, then to the mess in the kitchen before landing back on Carli's bewildered face.

"You have some 'splainin' to do," she addressed her sister.

"Yes, she does," another voice chimed in as Carli's mother walked in. "Carli Tynan. That food coloring is going to leave permanent green stains on my counter. Why in the world have you two not cleaned it all up yet?" she demanded to know and then gave Justin a scolding glare for good measure. He squelched an urge to actually step back.

And now he was standing in that same style kitchen being reprimanded by the Hammond employee's mother. The whole scenario could be straight out of a sitcom.

Carli looked like she didn't know whether to laugh or cry. He felt pretty torn himself.

"This is all my fault."

Carli actually stomped her foot. "No, it's not. It just happened. Ray spilled the food coloring by accident. No one is at fault." She emphasized the last word.

Tammy gasped while Carli's mother tilted her head. "I must not have made myself clear," Louise said. "All I care about is that it gets cleaned up. Now."

"Yes, ma'am," they both said in unison. Tammy's sisterly smirk was undeniable as she followed her mother out of the room.

Carli let out a deep sigh as she watched the other two

women leave. Grabbing the paper towels off the counter, she tore off a bunch before throwing the roll to him without warning. He caught it as it landed on his chest.

"Justin?"

"Yes?"

"You are really bad at making cookies."

Forty-five minutes later, Carli pulled the final tray of cookies out of the oven and set them on a rack to cool. They were definitely the greenest sugar cookies she'd ever seen.

Justin leaned over and gave them a long look. "They don't look like sugar cookies."

She didn't care. She just wanted this whole afternoon to be over. Also, she wanted to stop dwelling on the way Justin kissed.

"They look more like mint cookies," Justin added. He was right.

"Or perhaps spinach," she said, and earned a snicker.

They'd worked mostly in silence as they'd baked and cleaned. Everyone else seemed to have left. Traitors. No one had wanted to stay and help clean the mess. Not that she could blame them. Her mother's counter and a good portion of her floor tiles still held a greenish hue.

"All that matters is how they taste," she told Justin, poking one of the star-shaped cookies. Though it was still hot, she gingerly picked it up and tasted a small piece. "See, they taste great." She held it up to him. "Try it."

Justin's reached to take it from her. The touch of his hand on hers triggered another fiery tingle along the edge of her skin. Dear heavens, she was a fool. She had to fight this crazy attraction. He would be gone from New England and out of her life within a week. She worked for his family business. What was she doing kissing the man and then fantasizing about it afterward?

She had to get out of here.

"We should head to the store," she blurted out.

"The store?"

"Yeah, Hammond's Cape store. The reason you're here in town."

He gave a quick nod. "Of course. I was hoping to stop in there a bit today."

"It's a good time to go. Sundays are crafts days. Mr. Freider always has some kind of activity set up for the kids. I think it's gingerbread houses this time."

"Sounds fun. As long as it doesn't involve any baking," he quipped, then frowned as if realizing the lameness of the joke.

"I know Ray's been looking forward to it. We'll bring him with us. He should be up from his nap soon."

And he'd also make for a useful buffer between her and Justin, she added silently. They'd been in way too close proximity for the past several hours.

"Great idea."

Carli was right. By the time they got to Hammond's with Ray, the little boy had completely forgotten about the epic baking disaster and was back to his regular bouncy self. The prospect of decorating a gingerbread house proved an effective distraction.

If only Carli could find a distraction for herself. She was all too aware of Justin still. And all too quick to recall his kisses. Subconsciously, she ran a hand over her lips.

Stop it.

"This is a great crowd—" she made sure to point out "—despite the prospect of a major snowstorm that usually keeps people indoors."

"Point taken," Justin acknowledged.

She smiled with satisfaction. At least she had that much

going for her, despite the circus that this visit was turning into.

Ray saw a little friend and immediately ran over to
where the other child was setting up his craft area. He
tugged Justin along with him.

"Hi, Josh," he said to the other boy, pronouncing the end
of the name with a "th" sound. "This is my friend Justin,"
he added, and pointed up. "You know, like just in time."

Josh giggled and Ray looked pretty proud of himself.
Justin crouched to both boys' level. He stuck out his hand.

"Nice to meet you, Josh. I'm a good friend of Ray here.
You know, like ray of sunshine."

He said it with such a straight face that Carli had to
laugh. Now both boys were giggling.

"Do another one," Ray demanded.

"Sure, ray-nee day."

The two boys collapsed on each other in a fit of giggles now.

"Your friend is funny," Josh proclaimed, and laughed
some more. Justin was so naturally at ease with children.
No wonder Ray had grown so fond of him in such a short
time. Carli's eyes suddenly stung as she watched the three
of them. It broke her heart that Justin had never been afforded the opportunity to be that carefree when he was
little.

So different from the way she'd grown up. The Tynan
girls had been pretty fortunate as children. Things were
often crazy and hectic when you had four other siblings.
It was a fact of life that things could get very competitive
with five girls under one roof. Her younger twin sisters
were constantly trying to better each other.

But she'd truly been blessed with a caring family unit
and loving, doting parents. She couldn't deny that, no matter how betrayed she'd felt last year. Not only by Janie and

Warren, but by the way her family had reacted in response. Carli tried not to bristle at those thoughts. She loved every last one of her family members, she really did. With all her heart. But not a single one of them had shared in her outrage. Not even Tammy. Essentially, they'd all just expected her to accept it and move on. For the sake of family harmony, no doubt. No one bothered to try to put her feelings first. The betrayal still stung, even after all these months.

"Hello. Earth to Carli. Come in, Carli." She looked up to find Justin waving a hand in front of her face.

"Sorry, I was just admiring all the kids' handiwork."

He nodded, then glanced around the store as the boys continued. He had to be noticing the numerous people in the aisles and line leading up to the checkout area. He had to see how well the store was doing. She just had to make him realize that it had the potential to be this way throughout the year. She knew Mr. Freider could pull it off. Carli would do whatever she could to help.

She turned to Justin to tell him so, but just right then he leaned over Ray to help him mount the base of his gingerbread house. Her nephew's smile widened with appreciation. And she knew no matter Justin's thoughts on the store, she was glad he was here with them.

Ray's gingerbread house was a complete failure. Between that and the baking fiasco earlier, Justin had to admit that he didn't possess a creative cell in his whole body. It didn't help that Ray kept popping the candy corn and gum drops into his mouth rather than using them as decorations.

"Your parents are here," Carli said to Ray, then took him by a sticky hand toward where Tammy and her husband, Raymond, had just walked in. Tammy gave her sister a hug. Her brother-in-law did as well, then turned to shake Justin's hand.

"Thanks for taking care of the little tyke," he said to them both. "We saw the cookies at the house. Decided to make mint ones this year, huh?"

Tammy laughed out loud, and Carli gave her a useless punch on the arm.

"What did I say?" her brother-in-law asked.

"Nothing. Never mind."

He shrugged and picked up his son. "Guess we'll see you all tomorrow then. Unless this storm has everybody housebound, that is. Looks like a nasty one."

Justin watched as the three of them left the store. Tammy hooked her arm inside her husband's as he carried their son. It was such a touching domestic scene. So simple. So pure.

For an insane moment, Justin thought about himself as part of such a picture. An image of him and Carli walking arm in arm the same way sprang into his head. He shook it away.

Hammond men didn't do the whole family thing. Look at what a fiasco it had been when his parents had tried.

"We should get going," Carli said, interrupting his thoughts. He was reaching for his coat when Mr. Freider came rushing out to them. He held a framed photo in his hand.

"Wait. Justin, I have something for you." He held out the frame.

Justin reached for it, unsure what he was looking at. Then an unfamiliar sensation settled across his chest as he realized what it was.

"I don't understand."

"After you left yesterday, I remembered I had it. Thought you might want it as a memento."

"What is it?" Carli leaned over her arm to look.

"It's a newspaper clipping. Of a photo of me as a little boy." He held a toy truck in his hand, a big grin on his boyish face. He couldn't have been more than the age Ray was now.

Mr. Freider smiled. "That was the day of the store's grand opening. Your whole family came to cut the ribbon. This is from the write-up in the local paper."

Now that he studied the picture, Justin vaguely remembered the day. Even at that age, he could tell that his parents were simply going through the motions. But he and James had been excited nonetheless.

Unfortunately, the memory of it all had been overshadowed by the stinging fight that occurred within hours of them getting home. No wonder he'd blocked it out.

Until now. Justin found his mouth had gone dry. "I don't know what to say, Mr. Freider. This is such a thoughtful gesture."

"Nonsense. We picked up several copies of that issue all those years ago. Of course, the paper it's printed on has yellowed a bit. But not bad for twenty something years, huh?"

"No." Justin choked out the word over an achy lump that had formed in his throat. "It's not bad at all. I can't thank you enough."

Mr. Freider's smile grew wider. "Like I said, it wasn't that big a deal. Just thought it might recall some happy memories."

But it was a big deal. Bigger than Mr. Freider would ever know. He tucked the picture under his arm and went to shake the older man's hand.

But Mr. Freider had other ideas. He embraced Justin in a big bear hug. "You two have a good night now. That snow's about to come down at any minute. Much earlier than they said."

"You, too, Mr. Freider."

Out on the sidewalk, Justin couldn't help but glance at the picture once more.

"You were a very cute child," Carli said.

"Think so?"

She pointed to the frame. "No doubt about it. Look at those big round eyes, the thick wavy hair. Very cute."

It was childish, but her words pleased him to a ridiculous degree. "That was very nice of him."

"Mmm-hmm," Carli agreed. "He's one of a kind."

So are you. The words hovered on his tongue but he knew not to speak them out loud.

"No one's ever done anything like that for me before."

Carli looked up and studied the air. "He also seems to have been right about the snow." A big fat snowflake landed on her nose. He had to clench his fist to keep from brushing it off with his finger. Then kissing the spot where it had landed.

There were plenty more to follow. Suddenly, a flurry of white flakes blew like confetti all around them.

By the time they reached the inn, the snow was blinding. He couldn't believe the speed at which it fell, accompanied by a blinding cold wind he could feel down to his bones.

"Well, looks like you'll be snowed in at least for the night." Carli stopped in front of the glass door. "I'll call you later tomorrow. Make sure to charge your cell phone as soon as you get in. We're likely to lose power at some point." She turned to walk away. "I should be getting home."

He gently grabbed her by the arm. "There is no way I'm letting you walk back alone to your house." He could barely see her face in front of him for the white cloud of snow between them. "Not in this mess."

"I'll be fine," Carli assured him. But he wasn't buying it.

"No way," he insisted. "I'll come with you."

"And then what? You'd have to walk back here. And this is just going to get worse. Something tells me you won't be comfortable on my mom's lumpy couch all night if you get stranded there."

"I'll take my chances."

She looked ready to argue some more when Betty stepped outside. "What in the angel's name are you two doing out here? You'll both catch your death of a cold."

Without waiting for an answer, she physically ushered them both into the lobby. Carli looked ready to protest, but Betty stopped her with a no-nonsense look and thrust her hands on her hips.

"Carli Tynan. What kind of neighbor do you think I am? If I let you walk the rest of the way home in that?" She jutted her chin toward the window to indicate the snow.

"But Bet—"

"But nothing. I have plenty of extra rooms. You are staying here tonight. You can borrow something Leddy left here before heading away to college. And I don't want to hear another word about it. Now call your folks and let them know."

Another sleepless night. Despite all the homely comforts of the Sailor's Inn, Carli was getting no more rest tonight than she had the one before. The loud whooshing of the wind outside her window did not help the situation.

Sighing, she pulled off the covers and got out of bed. One more insomnia-laden night meant she was going to be a total wreck tomorrow. Warm milk. It had never worked for her before, but it was worth a try. Betty wouldn't mind if she checked the kitchen fridge and heated some for herself. Things were getting desperate here.

The well-placed outlet night-lights afforded just enough

illumination to make it downstairs without disrupting the other guests. There was at least one more couple staying at the inn. Within moments, she had a steamy hot cup of creamy milk in her hands. Not quite ready to go back upstairs, Carli made a detour through the lobby into the main sitting room. She'd always loved this room, even as a small child when her mother had come to visit Betty and dragged her girls along. Carli had spent hours sitting in front of the large fireplace with her book while her mother and Betty chatted over tea. She walked over to the hearth now. It was no longer a wood fireplace. The Mills had a newer, more convenient electronic model installed several years ago. But the rest of the room looked achingly familiar. Carli flipped the switch on the wall and a blue-tinged fire roared to life in front of her. She sighed with satisfaction as the heat spread over her skin.

"You can't sleep either, huh?"

Though he'd spoken softly, the unexpected sound of Justin's voice behind her made her jump. Warm milk sloshed over her cup and spilled onto her hand. She wiped it away on the side of her borrowed nightgown.

"Justin, you startled me."

"Sorry," he said, and made his way into the room. He came to stand next to her by the fire. "I thought I'd come down and watch the storm through the big bay window down here. It's something to behold. All this snow."

"We get at least one or two of these a year, and it never ceases to amaze me, the sheer magnitude of their power."

"It's beautiful, really. The entire town covered in sparkling white. Like an ivory blanket sprinkled with glitter."

She turned to look at him. "Wow. That was very poetic. We'll see how pretty you think it is when it's time to shovel tomorrow. And don't think my father won't ask you to. Guest or not."

He laughed, then surprised her by lowering himself to the floor and sitting cross-legged in front of the fire. "I have an electric fireplace too," he offered. "Back in my condo in Seattle."

Feeling awkward and rude at speaking down to him from her standing position, Carli felt no choice but to join him on the thick faux fur rug on the floor. "Yeah?"

"Yes. Funny though. It's not nearly as...cozy as this one is. It's designed to look like a pit. With fake charcoal and kindling. I like this one much better."

She wasn't sure what to say to that so she remained silent and took another sip of her milk. It wasn't doing a thing to make her sleepy, not that she had any hope of that with Justin sitting right next to her. He wore drawstring flannel pajama bottoms that somehow looked sexy on him. And a crisp white T-shirt that accented his solid chest and biceps. She could feel his warmth next to her along with the warmth of the fire in front of them, like a safe comfortable cocoon.

An empty yet easy silence settled between them. This was nice, Carli decided, allowing herself to relax into a peaceful lull. There were worse ways to sit through a storm than lounging in front of a fire watching the flames while listening to the sound of the wind.

So she wasn't prepared for what came next. When he spoke again, the next words out of Justin's mouth shocked her to her core.

"I need to ask you something. Are you in love with your sister's boyfriend?"

Justin hadn't meant to blurt it out that way. Subtle, it was not. Carli was clearly uncomfortable now, and he could have kicked himself for that. They'd been having such a pleasant and casual conversation. He'd just ruined the whole relaxed ambience with one question.

"Why do you ask?" She took a sip from her mug, not taking her eyes off the fire.

They were sitting so close together, his knee brushed against hers when he turned. Shadows from the flames fell across her face and highlighted the silky chocolate brown of her eyes. He fought the urge to pull her into his lap.

"Never mind. Forget I said anything."

"But you did."

"I shouldn't have. It's none of my business. I apologize."

Carli set the cup she'd been holding on the floor. "There's nothing between Warren and me," she said with a firm note of finality.

She was clearly uncomfortable talking about it. Which had to mean there was something there. A surge of emotion shot through his chest, a feeling he refused to acknowledge as jealousy. What he'd said earlier was true. It really was none of his business. In a few short days, he'd be back on the West Coast and likely not see Carli Tynan again for a good long time, if ever. There could never be anything real between them. Carli wasn't the type to have a casual fling, and there was no way he could give her anything more.

"He and I had a messy breakup about a year ago. I was angry and betrayed when he ended it."

Justin sucked in a breath. Hearing how much she'd cared for another man affected him way more than he would have liked, more than it should have.

"Because you were in love with him."

"I thought I was. But he fell for my sister. As I'm sure you surmised at dinner."

"I can't imagine that." He meant that with all his heart. How could any man prefer the quiet, albeit beautiful sister to the dynamic, intelligent woman who sat beside him now?

She looked off into the fire, the reflection of the flames dancing in her eyes.

"Why do I get the feeling there's more to the story?" Justin prodded.

She didn't look away from the fire when she answered. "Very perceptive, Mr. Hammond."

"So I'm right."

"Yes. But the summary is that I felt betrayed and deceived. The two of them were too afraid to tell me what was happening at first. Maybe for fear of hurting me, I don't know. But I just felt deceived. To make matters worse, I felt like my parents sided with Janie, at first."

"How so?"

She shrugged. "Little things. Warren was still always welcome at the house. I know that sounds petty. But I felt like he should have been made to feel at least a little out of place." Her chest heaved as she took a deep sigh. "Plus, Mom and Dad would make these quaint remarks about how things that are meant to be will happen. Or not. You know, que será, será."

He wasn't sure what to say to that. After witnessing how close the family was, he couldn't imagine what it must have felt like to think you were losing your place within it.

She wrapped her arms around herself, lost in her thoughts. Justin had never felt a stronger urge to comfort someone. He leaned closer to her, literally giving her a shoulder to lean on if she so wanted.

It thrilled him beyond words when she took him up on the offer and placed her head gently against him.

He could smell the sweet fruity scent of her shampoo. Her warmth settled over his skin. "I have to tell you something," he began.

"Hmm?"

"I think Warren is a fool."

Her first response was to snuggle in closer to him. "But you've seen my sister."

"So?"

He could feel her breathing; her hair tickled his chin. "So she's stunningly beautiful. Poor Warren can hardly be blamed."

He cupped her chin, turning her face to his. "I'll repeat. Warren is a fool."

Carli sucked in a breath, studied his face. She was so close, barely half an inch separated them. "Do you really think so?"

"Without a doubt. Janie's a pretty girl. But I never went for the frail, dainty type. I prefer women with unruly hair and inner strength. Like you."

She swallowed, and he couldn't resist leaning even closer. "You do?"

"Oh, yeah."

Justin didn't even know who moved first. He just thanked the heavens that suddenly her lips were on his. She tasted like sugar and cream, her mouth warm and soft against his. It was the slightest, gentlest of kisses.

But somehow he felt it through to his soul.

What time was it? Justin awoke disoriented and confused. The wind outside rattled the windows. There was a clear crisp chill in the air; the fireplace had gone out. The room was dark as hades. They must have lost power at some point, as Carli had predicted. But somehow he felt surprisingly warm. It took a moment for his eyes and senses to focus.

He realized with a shock why he wasn't cold. Carli was nuzzled against him, cradled along his length. Her back snug tight against his stomach.

They'd fallen asleep in front of the fireplace. Right there

on the faux fur rug. His traitorous body immediately re-acted.

Control.

But it was no use. He was only human, and he'd been wildly attracted to this woman from the moment he'd laid eyes on her. His arousal hit fast and strong. She'd be horrified if she woke up and became aware of the current state he was in.

"Carli, wake up."

Her response was to nuzzle her head against the bottom of his chin. The action did nothing to diminish his arousal. He bit out a silent curse.

"Carli. Hon. It's the middle of the night."

That attempt didn't work either. She moaned softly and shifted closer to him. Justin couldn't help but groan out loud. This was torture. He dared a glance at her face. Thick dark lashes framed her closed lids. She looked so peaceful, so content.

He couldn't do it. He couldn't force her awake. Just a few more minutes. Let her get some rest, she'd been yawning all day yesterday. Clearly she needed the sleep.

He would just have to suffer it out for a while.

Justin found himself second-guessing that decision three hours later when he heard footsteps approaching. Through some miracle, he'd fallen asleep despite his inconvenient reaction to having Carli in his arms. And now someone was about to find them in a very compromising position.

There was nothing for it, nothing he could do to try to rectify the situation. Way too late for that.

Making himself look up, Justin found Betty staring down at them with clear shock on her face. But was there also a ghost of a smile? She cleared her throat. Loudly.

Carli awoke with a start and jolted back in his arms.

A harsh flash of pain shot through his jaw as the top her head connected hard with his chin. He couldn't help his grunt in response.

"Good morning," Betty said, as if nothing was amiss.

Carli removed herself from his grasp. She opened her mouth to speak and then promptly shut it again. Clearly at a loss for words, she sat up.

"Hello, Betty," Justin managed to choke out. His jaw actually clicked. Just then the lights flickered and the power came back on. Something hummed back to life in the kitchen area, and the fireplace lit up.

"Well, thank goodness," Betty said, still staring at the two of them. She had to be referring to the lights coming back on, right?

"Mr. Freider has been trying to get a hold of you, dear." She addressed Carli. "I'm afraid he has some bad news."

Justin helped Carli to her feet and then stood himself, ignoring the aches and pains that came with sleeping on a hard floor all night.

"What's happened?" Carli asked, a little unsteady on her feet.

"It's the toy store. Apparently, the roof was too weak for the massive onslaught of snow in such a short period of time. It collapsed under the weight, snapping a water pipe as it came down." She took a breath. "I'm afraid the store has flooded."

Carli gasped. "Oh, no. How much damage?"

"I'm sorry, dear. That's all I know."

CHAPTER ELEVEN

IT WAS EVEN worse than she'd feared. The whole back corner of Hammond's Toys Cape store looked like a demolition zone. Carli bit back a cry of despair as she and Justin entered what was left of the store. Most of the damage had occurred in her favorite section, the Book Nook. Her heart broke when she saw the collapsed shelves, the scattered books with soaked and torn pages. A mountain of snow had piled up in the corner; thick icicles covered the shelves.

Mr. Freider was already there, trying to save anything that was salvageable. The poor man must have been freezing. Either that, or he was shaking from sheer sadness. Probably both.

"Oh, Mr. Freider." She walked over and gave him a gentle hug. "We'll find a way to fix all this." Though she couldn't imagine how. The store's very existence was already in jeopardy. Not that Mr. Freider had any idea. And now this.

He gave her a skeptical look. "Thank you for coming, dear."

"Would you like me to call the insurance company?"

For some reason, Mr. Freider's eyes started to tear up at the question. Then she understood. Technically, this would be considered flood damage. Something most insurance companies didn't cover.

This was devastating. What were the chances Justin would ever commit to keeping the store open now? It would take considerable cost and resources to repair all this and open up again.

"The alarm went off and alerted me at home around dawn," Mr. Freider told them. "I ran down as soon as I could to shut the water off. But by then…" He let the sentence trail off. "For it to happen this time of year."

Justin stepped over and placed a hand on the other man's back. "Why don't you take a break, Mr. Freider. Go home for a couple of hours. If you've been here since dawn, you're past due for some rest.

"Carli and I will take over for a while," Justin added when he hesitated. Finally he gave a reluctant nod and put down the book he'd been holding.

Carli watched him walk away and had an urge to hug Justin too—for the consideration and kindness he'd just shown. "That was very thoughtful of you."

Justin shrugged. "He looked ready to collapse. It was a no-brainer to send him home."

"Where do we start?"

"I'm going to find some boxes. He must have some empty shipping boxes somewhere."

"What for?"

"We can't do this out here. We'll freeze. It'll be easier and more effective if we work in batches. We'll carry a box or two at a time to his office and sort them out there."

"Great idea." Good thing one of them was thinking straight. "I'm sure there's some empty boxes in the storage area. Follow me."

Twenty minutes later, Justin had covered the exposed area with a heavy tarp he'd found in the storage room and the two of them were in the back office. They'd already made several piles, sorting through the various books and items depending on their level of damage.

Despite the unfortunate distraction with the flood, Carli couldn't stop thinking about what had happened this morning. Or last night. Justin had to be thinking about it too. How could he not? They'd spent the night in each other's arms. The fact that it had happened without knowledge or intent mattered little. He'd been the perfect gentleman; she had to let him know how much that meant to her.

"Thank you for helping me with this." Carli clutched the book she was holding against her chest like a shield. "And there's something else I should thank you for."

"What's that?"

"Last night. When you…uh…you know…didn't even try. I mean, all we did was sleep." She clutched the book tighter. Why was this so hard?

"Trust me, it wasn't for lack of wanting to." He blew out a breath. "If you only knew."

Electricity cackled between them. "You shouldn't say such things."

Justin visibly stiffened. "What exactly am I supposed to say to that?" He threw the question out like a challenge, a hard glint in his voice. Anger flashed in his eyes.

"Is something bothering you?"

"One of my family's retail locations has just incurred considerable damage."

She nodded, mustered a wealth of sarcasm into her voice. "Mmm-hmm. You've cared so much about the family business over the years, I can see how that would agitate you now."

She saw immediately that it was the wrong thing to say. He clearly didn't appreciate the sarcastic remark. Justin's mouth tightened into a thin line. But she wasn't buying that his sour mood was the result of the flood or the damage it had caused. So what else could it be?

"You know what's bothering me?"

A shiver ran through Carli at his tone and the tightness in his shoulders. But she decided to take the bait. "What?"

Suddenly, he'd moved in front of her. A mere breath separated them. Her heart pounded in her chest. She couldn't even tell if it was due to the proximity or because of the frustration blaring in his eyes.

"The way you're standing there thanking me for not touching you last night." With a finger, he lifted her chin. "When I make love to a woman, I can guarantee you it won't be when she's half asleep and tired after a restless night."

Her mouth went dry. She'd simply meant to thank him. "I didn't mean to imply otherwise." He had to know that.

"Right. I just have one question: Did you want me to?"

Well, he'd clearly gone and thrown the gauntlet down, hadn't he? She refused to lie. "I think you know the answer to that."

"Oh, no you don't. You're not getting off that easy. Answer the question. Did you want me to?"

Her breath caught in her throat. But she blurted out the only answer she could. "Yes."

She didn't know what she'd been expecting, but in the next instant, she found herself lifted up by the hips. Justin carried her the few steps to the desk behind them. Then he set her down and conquered her lips with a savage kiss.

Desire slammed through her as he ran his hands along her rib cage, then plunged them into her hair. She wanted him, all of him. The taste of him sent fire through her nerve endings, igniting wants and needs she could no longer hope to suppress. All that mattered was this moment and where it might lead to. She lay back on the desk surface, bringing him down with her. All the while, his hungry lips continued their sweet onslaught.

Something shifted under her weight and dug into the small of her back. The small nuisance was just distracting enough that Carli regained some semblance of sanity. On a regretful moan, she gave Justin a gentle push and he immediately pulled back. She straightened back to a sitting position.

"What the—" But Justin didn't finish. He appeared as shell-shocked as she felt.

Dear God, she'd nearly made love to him right there in the middle of the store office, on top of a metal desk. A man she hardly knew. What if someone had walked in? Or worse, what if one of her parents had come to the store to check on her? It was bad enough Betty had discovered them asleep in front of the fireplace this morning.

The thought of someone walking in on the two of them was too horrifying to further contemplate.

One thing she knew for certain. She'd become an unrecognizable version of herself since Justin Hammond had arrived in her life. She didn't like this incarnation of Carli. A woman who was too reckless and too unrestrained. It had to stop. All of it.

One way or another, they were going to have to resolve the question about the fate of the store. Then she was going to have to return to her previous life. And to her previous self.

Justin stepped away from Carli and rammed his hand through his hair. Damn it. What was it about her that made him lose control the way he did? He barely had a grasp on it now. She arranged her top and fixed the collar, breathing heavy all the while. Her lips were swollen from his kiss, her cheeks reddened from the stubble he had due to not having had time to shave this morning. He knew it was insane, but all he wanted to do was rub that stubble all over her soft, supple skin. Leave his mark on every inch of her body.

She may have done the sensible thing and pushed him away just now, but her eyes were clouded with passion and desire. For him. She wanted him as much as he wanted her.

But not here, not now.

The roar of a siren pulled them both out of a breathless stupor. The sound grew closer and within seconds could be heard right outside the wall. Damn it. He should have figured the fire marshal would want to come make sure the building was structurally sound.

"The fire department," he told Carli. Her clothes were in disarray, her hair a mess of tangles from the way he'd rammed his hands through her curls.

"I'll go greet them, if you want to…you know." He motioned to her.

"Yes, thank you. I'd like a minute or so."

Rubbing his chin in frustration and self-reproach, he left the office, the taste of her on his tongue still teasing his senses.

It took the fire marshal less than fifteen minutes to declare the building safe pending an electrician's assessment. Also, he told them that they'd been lucky to actually lose power as the flooding could have cause an electrical fire.

Justin saw the man off and went to tell Carli the news. His phone vibrated in his pocket before he got far. A text had arrived from Jackson. To call him as soon as he had a free moment.

Justin sighed. No time like the present.

He dialed the number and waited as Jackson answered.

"Mr. Freider called me," Jackson said. "How bad is the damage?"

"Pretty bad. It's going to take a huge amount of resources to restore and become operational again. My original conclusion makes even more sense now…" He paused, an idea suddenly occurring to him. "But if you're going to put money into restoration, it might be an opportunity to invest a bit more and take the unit into an expanded direction."

"I'd be very interested in hearing about that."

"I'll sum up the proposal and email it to you."

Justin ended the call and returned the cell phone to his pants pocket. He might have come up with a way to make the flood damage an opportunity in disguise.

Jackson sounded open to the idea. He had no doubt Carli would love it. He couldn't wait to tell her.

Justin had been gone for quite a while. Was the fire marshal taking that long to wrap things up?

Carli's curiosity got the better of her and she left the office to go find him. To her surprise, Justin was in the hallway speaking to someone on the phone. She immediately turned to give him some privacy until she heard a snippet of the conversation.

He was talking to Jackson.

"My original conclusion makes even more sense now…"

That was all Carli needed to hear. She felt like she had just taken a punch to the midsection.

Without her knowledge or her input, Justin was speaking to his father about the future of the store. And from the sound of it, he was making the argument that storm damage had only served to finalize his decision. He thought it should be shut down. She ran back into the office and slammed the door shut.

Justin had betrayed her.

He hadn't even bothered to mention anything to her before making his decision. He'd just gone straight to Jackson. Using the storm as an excuse to argue for what he'd originally planned all along.

Like a fool, she'd gone ahead and trusted yet another man she shouldn't have.

A knock sounded on the door. "Are you decent yet?" Justin asked from the other side.

With a huff of annoyance, Carli strode to the door and pulled it open to let him in.

Justin's smile faded from his lips when he saw the look on her face.

"Has the wrecking crew been called in then?" she demanded to know.

He blinked at her. "I beg your pardon."

"I suppose we'll need to auction or donate the remaining items."

"I'm afraid I still don't understand."

"You were talking to Jackson just now, weren't you?"

"Yes, I called him after—"

She cut him off with a dismissive wave of her hand. Her heart sank further. So Justin *had* been the one to initiate the phone call.

"I know why you called him. And you did it behind my back."

"What are you talking about?"

"You didn't have to courtesy to come to me first. Just went ahead and gave your decision to your father. I don't expect someone like you to understand just how wrong that was."

"Someone like me?"

"You've never felt a loyalty to anyone or anything, have you? That's why you don't give a damn about keeping this store open. You never felt the sense of belonging that a place like this affords to the people who love it. After all, you never really felt like you belonged or were a part of anything, did you? Not to a town. Not to a family. All you manage to do is ruin things for others."

"Wait just a minute—"

She didn't want to hear it. Not right now. She had no use for his explanation, which that would no doubt involve numbers and returns and all the factual things that men like him always cared so much about. She crossed her arms in front of her chest to quell the shaking that had suddenly gripped her and turned away. "Just go."

Justin had heard enough. Carli's anger was palpable. And why? All because he'd had the nerve to talk to Jackson without her knowledge. She didn't even care what the content of the conversation may have been. Her immediate assumption had been to think the worst.

You never really belonged...

Well, he had better things to do with his time than to try to explain himself to her.

He stepped closer to where she stood. Even now, with her anger directed straight at him, he couldn't help but long to pull her to him, to kiss her fury away until they both couldn't care less about some damn store and some ruined toys.

He clenched his fists at his side instead.

She paced around the desk, then turned to shoot him an accusatory look. A wealth of anger shone in her eyes. All directed at him.

Something snapped within his soul as he met her gaze. Somehow, some way, he'd done it again. He'd damaged something precious. Damned if he knew how or why. But it seemed to be a talent he had.

Served him right for ever thinking things could be any

different. And curse Carli Tynan for ever leading him toward that misconception in the first place.

Well, he'd heard enough. "I'm not sure why you're so worked up. But understand this—I don't need to run my intentions by you or anyone else."

She gasped, then lifted her chin. "You're absolutely right. I'm not sure why I thought you would have the decency to do so."

Justin didn't bother to reply to that. Without a word, he turned and stepped out of the office.

After all, what was there left to say?

Justin walked out of the rental agency and over to the late model SUV he'd just secured. He'd drive back to Boston, then arrange for a flight out of Logan. There was nothing left for him to do here.

In the interest of professionalism, he'd stop by Hammond's corporate office building and give his father a quick summary. Not that it mattered at this point.

Shame too. He actually may have figured out a way to save Carli's precious store and make some money for Hammond's in the process. Well, it was none of his concern now.

Getting into the rental vehicle, he started the ignition, then sighed and pounded the steering wheel with his fist. Damn it. None of this felt right.

Every inch of him wanted to delay leaving, despite what had just happened back at the store. Only one explanation for it.

There was no denying he had inexplicably, unwittingly developed deeply serious feelings for Carli Tynan.

Look where it had led. He didn't have it in him to have a healthy relationship. Certainly not with a woman like Carli who had a rich, fulfilling life. With family and friends who loved her.

Look how much havoc he'd caused her in the short time he'd known her.

Had it really been barely a week since he'd touched down at Logan Airport for the first time? It felt like years had gone by. The fact was, he'd be leaving a changed man. More so than he would have ever guessed.

He should have never come to New England. He'd known it was a bad idea from the beginning to come here, running to do Jackson's bidding like an eager errand boy. He should have known it wouldn't end well.

The conversation with Betty Mills had been awkward and uncomfortable when he'd gone to grab his belongings from the inn. She didn't buy the explanation that he had to leave early due to a pressing business matter back in his Seattle office. The woman was too perceptive by half. She'd told him to visit again as soon as he could. He assured her he would. A lie. Betty would most likely never see him again, as sad as that was.

He didn't have any business here in Westerson, regardless of how fond he'd grown of everyone he'd met during his short stay.

Now, sitting in the driver's seat of the rental, all he wanted to do was drive straight out of town and keep going until he reached Logan Airport.

Begrudgingly, he realized he couldn't do that. It would be a coward's way out. He had to at least talk to Carli like a man and tell her he was leaving. And somehow explain that he hadn't intended to mislead her in any way.

Not the easiest conversation.

He shifted into gear. Best to just get it over with. If he was lucky, Ray would be there at the house. He didn't want to leave without saying goodbye to the little guy. Justin realized with a start that he would genuinely miss him.

Carli was on the porch as he approached the driveway. Unfortunately, she wasn't alone.

Justin swore out loud. He just wanted to talk to her one-on-one, in private, to say all the things that needed to be said between them. For one final time. Unfortunately, it appeared that waiting for her to finish with whoever she was with was his only option. The last thing he wanted was a delay right now. He started to pull over across the street. After all, she wouldn't recognize the car.

But then he realized three of her sisters and her mother were surrounding her. They were all laughing, sharing snacks and a bottle of wine. The scene was the perfect picture of a close, tight-knit family. A family full of love and affection. It was a picture someone like him had no business interrupting. Or trying to be a part of. Not with his history.

Her angry words echoed in his head once more—*I don't expect someone like you to understand.*

An image of the Christmas tree crashing down in the Hammond foyer flashed across his vision. No, there was really no point in talking to Carli.

Justin drove on.

CHAPTER TWELVE

JUSTIN RODE UP the elevator to the top floor of the Hammond corporate office building. Still late afternoon. If he knew his father, the old man would still be at his desk.

He didn't intend to be here long. He wasn't going to leave Boston without personally notifying his father that as far as he was concerned, his responsibilities here were finished. Justin would email him the figures and ideas at a later time. Not that it mattered at this point. But the professional businessman in him wouldn't let it slide. Not even when it came to his father.

To his dismay, Jackson's office was empty. The lights turned off. Justin bit out a curse. He probably should have called first, but he'd been certain Jackson would still be at work.

"Justin? Can I help you?"

He turned to find Miranda, his old babysitter, in the hallway. "I was just looking for Jackson. Is he traveling?"

"No, dear. Believe it or not he's already gone for the day."

He had to admit he wasn't quite sure if he believed it. At his curious stare, Miranda gave a small shrug. "He's a different man these days. Ever since the Fryberg acquisition. Frankly, both your father and brother are behaving out of the norm."

Could nothing go his way today? He really didn't need to go back to that house. The Hammond mansion held no fond memories for him. "They have?"

She nodded. "No one can figure out why, but Jackson's been leaving earlier and earlier. Some days he calls to say he's working from home."

Justin didn't even know what to say to that. This was his father they were talking about, right? The same man he didn't see for days at times as a child because he came home late from work and left early the next day?

"Anyway, is there something I can help you with?" Miranda asked.

"No, thank you."

"Okay then." She turned to go, but Justin felt an uncharacteristic tug in his chest. He hadn't had a chance to say goodbye to anyone besides Betty back in Westerson.

And he had no idea if he would ever see Miranda again, for that matter. It surprised him that he cared. "Wait."

"Yes, dear?"

"I just want to say how glad I am that I got to see you again, after all these years. I'm leaving tonight. So I guess this will have to be goodbye." The words left his mouth in a swift torrent. He wasn't used to being so damn sentimental. What had Carli Tynan done to him? With some awkwardness, he extended his arm to shake Miranda's hand.

She ignored it and wrapped him in a big bear hug instead. He gingerly hugged her back. "Do you have to leave so soon?" she asked against when she finally let him go.

"I'm afraid so. I just need to wrap some things up with my father, and then I need to be on my way."

"I see. It's a shame James missed you entirely. I think it would have been good to have you two see each other again." She slammed a hand against her chest. "Silly me. Just look at me sticking my nose where it doesn't belong.

But it broke my heart to see you boys yanked apart all those years ago. I think about it a lot."

"You do?"

"Of course. It was wrong. So wrong. James just wasn't himself those first few years after."

"He wasn't?"

She studied him with wide eyes. "Of course not. I know you must have struggled too, dear. But I saw firsthand how hard it was for that little boy to have his mother and brother just disappear like that."

Justin had to admit, with no small amount of shame, that he hadn't really given James much thought over the years. After all, he'd been the son who'd gotten to stay home, able to grow up in the same house he was born in. He slept in the same bed, kept attending the same school.

Whereas Justin's whole life had been upended.

But of course, it couldn't have been easy for James either. Justin hadn't allowed himself to think about that. The reason was simple really: he knew James blamed him for all of it.

And he wasn't wrong to do so.

"I wondered a lot about how you were doing," Miranda added. "But I never doubted you'd grow to be a successful, decent young man."

Justin had to stifle a groan. A decent man would have tried harder to get Carli to understand. Instead he'd simply walked off. But she'd get over it, he was sure. Judging by what he'd seen on the porch, maybe she had already started to.

"I wish I could have watched you grow up," Miranda added, breaking into his thoughts. Tears shimmered in her bright blue eyes, which had grown dimmer and surrounded by more wrinkles over the years. This woman had genuinely cared for him. He'd been too much of a child to appreciate that at the time. The notion brought on a profound sadness. It might have made a difference all those years ago if he'd only known there was someone he could have turned to.

"Thank you. But I guess that ship sailed when my father made his choice."

"Your mother did the leaving, dear. She took you with her."

Justin had to laugh at that. Why was he getting into all this anyway? With a woman he barely remembered. Simply because she'd watched him a few evenings when he was a child. "Maybe so. But my father didn't exactly go out of his way to reach out me. No, he chose the son he wanted to keep with him just as much as my mother did."

Miranda patted his cheek. "But don't you see?"

"See what?"

"From where James stood, it was the exact same thing. As far as he was concerned, you were the favored one."

"I don't understand."

"Your mother chose you. And she never looked back. He was the one who was left behind."

With her words, Justin had to face a possibility he'd never let himself entertain before. His brother hadn't fared any better in the aftermath of their parents' breakup.

All these years, he and James had lived alternate versions of the same reality. Their lives were just flip sides of the same coin.

Where was Justin now? She hadn't heard from him, only knew that he'd left yesterday per Betty. Carli needed to get going too. This morning, the contractors had started reparations on the store. All that was left to do was to grab her bag and drive back to Boston. So why was she putting off the inevitable?

She glanced at her phone for the thousandth time, trying to decide whether to call him or not. He shouldn't have gone behind her back as he did. But throwing his lack of family in his face was clearly a low blow. Something she wasn't exactly proud of now upon reflection.

Carli swore out loud and threw her cell phone across her parents' living room. Luckily, it landed on the couch.

"Annoying spam?" A delicate voice startled her. She turned to see Janie standing in the doorway.

Carli squeezed her eyes in frustration. "I'm trying to decide if I should call Justin. I might owe him an apology."

"Oh?"

"Yeah… I may have said some things I shouldn't have."

"Then I think you should just bite the bullet and call. He might be waiting for you," Janie offered.

Carli blew out a puff of air in frustration. "More likely, he never wants to talk to me again. He couldn't wait to get out of town."

Janie nodded. "Yeah, Mom may have mentioned something about him leaving prematurely."

"Thanks to me."

"Wanna talk about it?"

The question caught Carli off guard. The truth was, Janie was the first person she'd always been able to talk to. That was part of the reason this whole past year had been so hellish. She'd lost a dear confidante when things had turned icy between them. All those times Carli had thought to reach out but had been too stubborn to do so. And for what? A relationship with a man who she'd never really believed would work out anyway.

"I made a huge mistake," Carli admitted on a low sob, not even certain if she was still referring to Justin or the wedge that had been sitting between her and Janie for the past year.

Janie rushed over to her. Soon they were both holding each other as the tears flowed like a sudden rain. "Me too, sis. Me too," Janie said, then handed her a tissue from the side table and grabbed one for herself.

"Are we okay?" Janie asked, dabbing her eyes. "Please say yes."

"We will be," Carli answered, realizing she'd known that all along. "But I just wish you'd told me. When it first started between you and Warren."

Janie nodded. "You're right. It was just so hard. Neither one of us wanted to hurt you. That was the only reason we kept it from you at the beginning. You have to believe that."

Carli gulped back a sob.

"I've missed you," Janie said, her voice a scratchy rasp from her crying.

"I've missed you too."

If only one of them had had the courage to admit that before so much time had passed. She wouldn't have had to do without her closest sister for all these months. Not to mention, maybe she would never have lashed out at Justin the way she had after the storm.

She'd felt let down and betrayed when he'd called his father. Just as she'd felt betrayed by Janie and Warren. And her response at the first sign of trouble had been to put the blame squarely on Justin's shoulders, exactly the way his parents had when he was just a mere child.

She had to make this right.

"I think you have a phone call to make," Janie stated. "I'll give you some privacy."

"Thanks, sis."

Janie gave her a tight hug and left the room.

Carli didn't give herself time to think. Grabbing her phone, she clicked on Justin's number. But his phone went straight to voice mail.

A lump formed at the base of her throat. With her luck, Justin might very well be on a plane back to Seattle.

She was probably too late.

Carli rubbed her thumb absentmindedly along the corner of her mother's granite counter where a stubborn green stain still marked it. In time it would fade. She hoped so anyway. There were a lot of things she was banking on having time fix.

Though none of the mountains of snow had melted, the late-morning sunshine brought with it a golden touch to the vast amount of white outside. Everyone had shoveled out for the most part. Life in town was back to normal. But it felt anything but for her. She felt like the world had somehow tilted on its axis. Nothing would ever be the same.

Her mother walked in carrying a load of freshly laundered kitchen towels. It occurred to Carli how content her mother was, how so very in tune with her existence. Louise had worked hard all her life to build a loving home and a strong family, foundations that Carli had depended on growing up.

Alas, it appeared very unlikely that Carli would ever be able to achieve the same for herself. Not at the rate she was going when it came to men.

Her mom did a bit of a double take when she saw her. "I thought you'd be on your way by now. I heard Justin already left."

"He did indeed."

Her mother put the towels down and studied her with concerned, motherly eyes.

"I'm surprised you haven't. You usually can't wait to scram out of here and head back to the big city after a couple of days of visiting."

That was Louise, her mother was always straight to the point.

"Are you trying to get rid of me, Mom?" Carli said with as much comical outrage as she could muster.

"Of course not." Louise came over and gave her small kiss on the top of her head. "But if you stick around, I'm very likely to put you to work. The pine needles that keep shedding off the Christmas tree and onto the floor need to be swept up. And heaven knows there's always more shoveling and deicing to do."

Carli held her hands up in mock surrender. "Okay. Okay. I was just leaving." But she didn't make a move out of her chair. "Can I just ask you something first?"

Louise's eyes narrowed; whatever she saw on Carli's face made her pull out a counter stool and sit across from her daughter.

"Shoot."

"It's about you and Dad."

Her mom lifted a finely shaped, dark eyebrow. "What about us?"

"You're just so, I don't know, strong together."

"I suppose. We've been together for over three decades."

"And then there's Tammy and Raymond. They're just so happy together with their new house and their son."

"They were high school sweethearts. They've known each other a long time too."

"I know." She sighed deeply before continuing. "And now Warren and Janie."

Her mother leaned over and gave her hand an affectionate pat.

"Janie and I just had a bit of a chat," Carli told her. "Finally."

"Are you okay?"

Surprisingly, she was. Despite the shattered mass that

now sat where her heart used to be, she genuinely felt no loss over Warren. Not anymore. "We are, Mom. I'm happy for them. I really am. I realize now they fit much better than Warren and I ever could."

"You may not have seen it at the time, but he wasn't right for you. You're too independent, too driven." She leaned closer before continuing. "He's the type who wants to stay in Westerson and plant more roots here. Just like Janie. You have to see now that those two belong together."

Carli sighed. "I do see that. Now. So do Tammy and Raymond. But you and Dad especially. I've seen you have arguments, but they never last. And you're both always so in tune." She took a deep breath; she had her mother's full attention now.

"Trust me when I tell you that wasn't always the case. None of you kids know this, but we almost broke off the engagement a month before the wedding."

Carli felt genuine surprise at that last comment. "You did? Why?"

"I was starting to get cold feet. And your father could tell. He didn't want to rush me into a commitment as serious as marriage if I wasn't totally ready for it."

"You? You were the one who got cold feet?"

"Believe it or not, there was a time I couldn't decide what I wanted or what path I needed to take in life to be happy. And your father was man enough not to put any pressure on me."

"Huh? I never knew."

"It's true. Now, every time I walk through this house, or hold my grandson—or even sit in the kitchen having a conversation with one of my girls—I know I made the right decision."

Carli felt the tears spring into her eyes. She was so lucky to be part of this family, to be this woman's daughter.

So what if her love life was in shambles. In a few years, she may even be able to get over the foolish way she'd fallen for a man who had turned and walked out of her life at the first sign of discord.

"Tell me," her mother began. "Do your questions have anything to do with Justin Hammond perhaps?"

Carli wasn't surprised by the question. Louise Tynan was very on top of things when it came to her children. It was one of the reasons she loved her parents so much.

"As well as the way you were looking at him?" her mother added when she didn't respond right away.

Carli bit down on a bitter chortle. "I guess. But it's over. Almost as soon as it began."

"What happened?"

"I let my guard down. I wasn't careful enough and didn't see the obvious. Kind of like with Warren." She gulped down on a low sob. "But this feels so much worse, Mom. This feels like the hurt might never end."

Her mother stood and gathered her in her arms. "You've fallen for him."

"I'm afraid so."

"And he's leaving?"

"Probably flying out at this very moment."

"I see." She rubbed Carli's cheek. "Do you know why Dad and I mostly stayed out of the whole situation between you, Warren and your sister?"

She sniffled. "Because you wanted us all to learn a valuable lesson on how thoroughly Carli could make a fool of herself?"

Louise gave her an affectionate smile. "Hardly. Because we knew you would figure out what was best for you. You've always been good at deciding what you want and going after it."

"I am?"

"Indeed." She gave her arm a tender squeeze. "From what I can see, you've determined what you want. Now are you going to go after it?"

Justin had decided to sleep in for the first time in his life. But whoever was calling his cell phone apparently had other plans. The screen read Hammond Ent, so he picked it up without delay fully expecting Carli to be on the other end.

Only it wasn't Carli calling.

A bolt of disappointment shot through him. Foolish, wishful thinking. Carli wanted nothing to do with him. He'd managed to earn her ire and scorn. Just as he'd earned his brother's all those years ago when his antics had finally pulled the family apart.

No, the deep baritone voice on the other end of the line belonged to his father. Looked like he had indeed blown his chance to rectify things with her. Justin sat up in bed and rubbed the sleep out of his eyes.

"Do you have a moment, son?"

Would he ever get used to hearing that word coming from Jackson? He glanced at the bedside clock on the bureau across his hotel room: 8:30 a.m. Much later than he usually slept, but he'd been restless and unable to fall asleep last night, reliving the events of the previous day repeatedly in his head.

"Sure." He just had to wake up fully first.

"I wanted to let you know I was very impressed with the initial plans you sent over. Once the repairs to the Cape store are completed, I'd like to begin implementing your ideas."

Justin sighed with relief. He'd been fully prepared to take matters into his own hands if he had to. "I'm glad to hear it. I'm sure Carli will be more than anxious to get started on it all."

His father was silent a moment on the other end. "That's one of the things I'd like to discuss with you, in fact. I don't know what your plans are, but would you be able to come in later this morning to go over some of this?"

He couldn't mean what Justin was beginning to suspect he meant. Did he honestly have someone else besides Carli in mind to run the project? Rubbing his eyes, he answered, "I can be there within the hour."

"That's great, son. I'll see you then."

"Wait, Jackson."

"What is it?"

"I just want to be clear. All those ideas I proposed, I had Carli firmly in mind as the project manager to carry them through. I think she's the best qualified given how well she knows the store and the town."

He could hear his father's pride in Carli when he answered. "I couldn't agree with you more."

Then what was this all about?

Jackson gave him a jolt when he answered the unasked question. "I believe she may need some help. I wanted to talk to you about perhaps clearing your calendar for the next several months. Perhaps even permanently, depending on what you're comfortable with."

Now he was awake. "Never mind what I said earlier. I can be there in half an hour."

It took only twenty minutes.

His father was standing in front of his office window, staring down at the traffic bottleneck along Boylston Street when Justin knocked on his door.

Jackson motioned to the chair in front of his classic executive desk, and then waited for Justin to sit down before taking his own seat.

"Thank you for coming in so quickly, son."

"I had nothing else to do. What's this about?"

"To put it mildly, I'd like you to come back. Back to the Boston area, the Cape specifically. Back as a Hammond working for Hammond's Toys."

Mildly? Justin would not have called that mild. Bluntly sharp was more like it. "Just like that?"

"I realize what it would mean. You have a life back in Seattle, but we can talk about relocation incentives."

Justin was too shocked to speak.

"You're a rightful heir of this company. You need to be here at the helm, along with your brother."

A jarring thought occurred to him. "Are you dying?"

Jackson's immediate response was a loud snort of laughter. "Not that I know of!"

"Then what's going on?"

"I've been doing some thinking. About both you and James. Your brother came to me before the holidays. Started a conversation we probably should have had years, perhaps even decades, ago."

Justin rubbed a hand down his face. If this was Jackson's attempt at some sort of reconciliation after all these years, he was totally unprepared for it.

"It made me realize how much I missed of you boys growing up. You especially."

Whoa. He definitely hadn't seen that coming. "I don't know what to say."

"Then I'll just do the talking for a bit." He took a deep breath as if to steady himself. "I know I should have tried harder to contact you. But your mother was a...a difficult woman. The time to cast blame or bad-mouth anyone is long gone. But she loved to remind me how much trouble you were."

"I remember."

"Only, you really weren't. I think you were a convenient way to prove to me that I was insufficient, that there was something I couldn't handle. I'm convinced she took you with her that night just to drive that point home. I couldn't handle you. So she left and took you with her."

Justin tried to process all he was being told. Given what he knew of his mother, it wasn't a terribly farfetched theory. But the idea that he'd simply been a pawn in his mother's argument stung more than he would have liked.

"That still doesn't explain why you chose to let her get away with it. Why you didn't make any kind of attempt to have some sort of contact, or even a relationship."

"I have no excuse, I'm afraid. Except that maybe on some level, I let her convince me of it too."

Jackson looked away then, studied a Bruins banner he had hanging on the wall to his left. "I know I should have tried harder to track you down. But she moved around so often. Support payments went direct to her bank account. And as the years grew longer, the prospect seemed more and more futile. But I'm trying now, if it's not too late."

A week ago, Justin would have told his father precisely that it was too late. But a lot had changed since then.

He'd met Carli Tynan.

Justin braced himself against the cold wind as he stood outside Carli's door on the footstep. He'd gone over various ways he might approach the conversation countless times in his head. But for the life of him, he still had no idea where he would start once she opened the door. He'd called earlier to tell her he would be stopping by. To say she was shocked would be an understatement. It had been unclear whether that was pleasant shock or the opposite. He supposed he was about to find out.

Taking a deep breath, he rang the doorbell, then waited. It opened within seconds and Carli stepped aside to let him. The apartment was just as festive as he remembered; Christmas decorations still adorned every wall and corner. Hard to believe that had only been a few short days ago.

"I'm surprised you're still in town." She looked different, tired. Dark smudges framed her eyes; her skin appeared paler. When she turned and walked to the sofa, there was unmistakably less of a spring in her step.

He had done that to her; he couldn't deny it. And he wanted to kick himself for his behavior. Well, it was the reason he was here.

"I decided to delay my return flight."

"I see. Can I get you anything? Coffee or something?"

This felt so wrong. Just a couple of days ago they'd spent the night sleeping in each other's arms in front of a cozy fireplace as a turbulent snowstorm raged outside. Now they were addressing each other as strangers.

"No, thank you."

She motioned to the loveseat he stood next to. "Have a seat."

He took off his coat and sat, trying once again to come up with the right words to say. He should have tried harder to make her understand at the store. Instead, he'd run.

Something he deeply regretted now.

He had to tell her that. But when he tried, they both started talking at the same time, awkwardly speaking over each other.

Justin ran a hand through his hair. "Please, go ahead."

"I was just wondering why you delayed your flight."

"Or why I'm here, for that matter?"

"That thought had crossed my mind, as well." She

pulled her feet under her and positioned herself into a ball on the couch. "I imagine it has to do with the Cape store?"

"In part."

"I don't understand."

"I was actually just hoping to try to clear the air between the two of us."

"I see."

"I should have had the courtesy of listening to you that day, Carli."

Her gaze shifted downward, and she hugged her knees.

"I mentioned something to you the first day I arrived. When I made the mistake of judging you, do you remember that?"

"I think so, something about how it had nothing to do with me and everything to do with Jackson."

Bingo.

He should have known she was sharp enough to recall exactly what he was referring to. She was one of a kind. What a fool he was, to have had a chance with someone like her and to have blown it the way he had.

"And apparently, I didn't learn my lesson the first time I messed up."

Women like Carli didn't come along twice in one lifetime. His mishandling of it all was just one more thing in a long line of missteps he was going to have to live with. He got the distinct impression it might be the biggest. He had only himself to blame.

To spare her the effort of summoning a response, he stood and grabbed his coat. "I should leave. Thanks for giving me a minute."

Carli jumped up too. "Wait, before you go." She walked over to the oak angled desk under the corner window and pulled out a sketch pad. Tearing off the top sheet, she handed it to him. "I just finished it."

It took Justin a moment to realize what he was looking at. Then he remembered the framed sketch he had seen mounted along her parents' hallway.

She had drawn *him*. The piece of paper had one large portrait of him as an adult in the center and then another drawn smaller in the corner. The smaller one portrayed him as a boy. She had clearly based it on the newspaper captioned photo Mr. Freider had given him back at the Cape.

The resemblance in both was amazing, detailed and nuanced.

But more than merely replicating his physical features, the charcoal portrait seemed to capture his aura, right down to his soul. Only someone who had looked beneath the surface to his very core could have been able to draw him the way she had. The effect rendered him speechless.

"Do you like it?" she asked in a nervous and hesitant voice. How could she possibly be insecure with talent like that?

"It's the nicest thing anyone's ever given me. Or done for me, actually."

Yeah, he thought as he stared at the picture. He had definitely blown it.

CHAPTER THIRTEEN

CARLI HAD FULLY intended to give Justin the sketch since the moment she'd started it after the heartfelt conversation with her mother. It just hadn't occurred to her that he would be there in person to accept it. She'd expected to have to mail it to him at some point. When they were both somehow past the fateful events of the last week.

She figured that would have put the ball squarely in his court. He'd beaten her to the punch, however, when he'd surprised her with a phone call earlier this afternoon.

"I planned on rolling it and packaging it for you," she told him. "But since you're here, it's yours to take."

He blew out a deep breath. "I don't know what to say. Except I thought you said you had stopped sketching?" His gaze never left the paper he held in his hands.

"Yeah. I had. But I was inspired." She wasn't going to tell him just how inspired she'd been. The sketch had taken hours, and she'd been working nearly nonstop. In fact, she'd been tidying up furiously after receiving Justin's call that he was coming by.

It had been shocking enough to discover he was still in town. But to have him actually want to visit her apartment was a whole other level of altered reality. She wasn't entirely sure she wasn't dreaming this whole thing up at this very moment.

"I can't help but feel honored," he admitted, and a silly rush of girlish pleasure shot clear through her toes. "Can I ask you something?"

"Sure."

"Why did you ever stop in the first place? You have an amazing gift for it."

She had a hunch the question may have been coming. This was the risk she'd known she was taking when she picked up the charcoal pencil.

"Let me guess, it's a long story."

"Actually, it's not. It's quite an old, regular story, in fact."

He quirked an eyebrow in question.

"It's hard to put your heart into a drawing unless you feel a true joy in doing so. I'd lost that for a while. Now it seems to be back."

Justin's eyes flicked over her face. "I must say I'm honored."

She wanted to tell him there was so much behind her rendering of his image. His face was the first thing she saw when she closed her eyes before going to sleep. Those hazel eyes of his haunted her dreams and even her waking moment. But what purpose would it serve? Some things were better left unsaid.

She followed Justin as he made his way to the door. Suddenly, he pivoted on his heel. Carli's heart thud against her chest. He couldn't leave just yet.

"I almost forgot. I emailed you a document with detailing some ideas. For the Cape store. Please take a look when you get a chance."

Just a request to look at a file. "Oh, I'll be sure to do that."

Without another word, he opened the door and left.

Carli stared helplessly outside her window as she

watched Justin walk briskly down the street, the sketch tucked under his arm. She felt torn and helpless. But what was there to do? They'd made their peace as best as could be expected.

So why did she feel like a boulder was sitting on her rib cage?

Just to give herself something to do, she flipped open her tablet and called up the email program. As he'd said, Justin's email sat toward the top. Clicking it open, she began to read.

It didn't take much time to come to a decision. She couldn't let Justin fly to Seattle and walk out of her life. She didn't even bother to grab her coat.

"Justin wait!"

Justin was almost afraid to turn around. What if he was simply imagining her voice? It was very likely he wanted to see her so badly that his mind was playing tricks on him. But when he turned around, there she was. Without a coat.

"Carli?"

He quickly went over to her; she was shivering. "You're freezing. And I don't even have a scarf to offer this time."

She laughed at that even as she rubbed her upper arms with her hands in an effort to get warm.

Justin didn't think about right or wrong at that moment. He simply went to her and put his arms around her shoulders, pulled her close.

"What are you doing out here? It's about twenty degrees."

Her teeth chattered as she answered him. "I think it's less than that."

He pulled her closer.

"I wanted to tell you I looked at the email," she said against the base of his neck.

"Okay. You could have simply typed a reply."

She shook her head. "No, that would not have worked."

"It wouldn't have?"

"No way. We clearly have to discuss all your suggestions in person."

A heady feeling of warmth began to spread through his chest. "I see."

With her in his embrace, he inhaled the scent of coconut shampoo and that soft subtle scent of hers that he'd grown so fond of. God, he'd missed it.

"There's no other way," she said, snuggled tight up against him. "You're going to have to have dinner with me."

"Is that so?" he asked, unable to stop himself from dropping a hint of a kiss to the top of her head.

"Uh-huh. You're just lucky my mother passed on her lasagna recipe to all her girls."

She had no idea. Justin hadn't realized he could be so lucky. Lifting her chin with his finger, he decided he needed to show her with a kiss.

How in the world had he been talked into this? Justin adjusted the scratchy fake beard and groaned as he looked in the mirror in his new room at the Sailor's Inn. The answer stood next to him. Carli Tynan could probably get him to do anything with that sweet smile of hers.

Also, she'd reminded him of all the times he'd uttered the words "I'll make it up to you, somehow" since he'd met her. But this was hardly playing fair.

She stepped up to him and placed the velvet red hat atop his head. "You know, for someone who insists he's not really that into Christmas, you make a pretty good Santa Claus."

"If you say so." The goose-down pillow that was supposed to be his fake stomach threatened to drop once more, and he tightened the belt that held it up. Carli had informed him this morning that the actor who usually played Santa at the Westerson snowman competition had backed out due to a nasty case of the flu. She thought Justin would be the perfect replacement as he was the stranger in town and therefore less likely to be recognized by the older children.

Frankly, he didn't think he was going to be able to fool anybody. For one thing, every time he tried to yell "Ho-ho-ho!" he sounded utterly ridiculous. Which was exactly how he felt.

"You'll do fine," Carli reassured him. "You just have to walk around the tree farm commenting on all the contestant snowmen and hand out a few toys along the way. Hammond's was very sweet to donate those, by the way. Not to mention the matching donation to Toys for Tykes."

He shrugged. "I'm surprised there wasn't any kind of donation program to that charity up until now."

"There wasn't one until you started it." She gave him a peck on the cheek.

"Uh-uh." He grabbed her gently by the waist, pulling her up against his length. "You're gonna have to do better than that. Seeing as you're the only reason I'm dressed in this ridiculous costume and about to make a complete fool of myself."

Taking him up on his challenge, Carli hooked her arms around his neck and brought his mouth down to hers.

"How's that?" she asked with a breathless sigh when he finally managed to pull away.

"I'd say it'll do. For now."

The truth was he'd never be able to get enough of her. They'd been spending most of the days together since that fateful morning he'd stopped by her apartment. To think he had almost simply emailed her then left town. Taking the chance to go see her had been the best decision he'd ever made.

Unlike the decision to agree to this whole Santa thing. That was a totally different story. Carli noted the time on her cell phone. "We should make our way down. It's officially about to start. We'll have to sneak you out the inn's receiving door in the back of the building."

"Just tell me I don't have to ride in a sled."

The tree farm was bustling with activity when they arrived. Justin hoisted the toy bag over his shoulder and was immediately surrounded by a slew of youngsters.

"Santa's here!"

Despite himself, Justin had to admit this was somewhat fun. The cheers and laughter from the children as he handed out toys buoyed his spirits. Or maybe that was just the effect of Carli's infectious laugh as she walked by his side. He even attempted a lame "Ho-ho-ho" once or twice. Eventually, the onslaught of children approaching them slowed to a steady trickle, with a single child here and there. Good thing. His bag of toys was nearly empty.

"Aunt Carli!" Ray's exuberant voice rang behind them, and they both turned around as the boy ran up.

"Ray!" Carli bent and embraced her nephew. "Would you like to say hello to Santa?"

Ray's response was a knowing giggle. "That's not Santa! That's Justin!"

Carli gave a frantic look around and put her gloved finger to Ray's mouth. Luckily, no other kids were near them at the moment.

"Shh, you don't want to spoil it for the other kids."

"Okay."

"But how did you know?" Carli asked the child as Justin crouched to give him a fist bump.

Ray shrugged as if it should be obvious. "Prolly 'cause his eyes. But mostly 'cause I know him. He's my friend."

"I see."

"And he's your boyfriend!" Ray added, nearly shouting this time as he clearly thought this was a hilarious thing to say.

Justin's eyes met Carli's over Ray's head. A surge of emotion shot through him. Her nose had gone a deep cherry-red in the cold. She wore a fuzzy elf's hat on top of her head with a small bell at the end. Her ears were adorned with the same snowman earrings she'd worn the night of her office party. The whole look was meant to appear whimsical and fun in the spirit of Christmas.

He didn't think any woman had ever looked more strikingly beautiful.

"You're right," Carli answered her nephew. "He is my boyfriend."

EPILOGUE

One year later

JUSTIN SCANNED THE large and ever-growing crowd in front of him. All of Westerson appeared to be here. He'd been an official resident for just under a year now, and it never ceased to amaze him the degree of loyalty the people of this town had for each other.

How he'd managed to snare one of their own as his fiancée he would never fully grasp. But he knew better than to ever take it for granted.

The object of his thoughts approached him from the side of the dais. "It's time to cut the ribbon," Carli prompted.

Mr. Freider came to stand next to her. He would be the one doing the actual cutting. After having managed the store for over two decades, and how hard the man had worked to bring the new version to fruition, he more than deserved the honor.

James and Noelle stood ready behind them near the podium. They'd flown in two days ago for the grand opening of the new and improved Hammond's Toys Cape store. A project that had been a year in the making.

"Ready?" he asked her.

"I think so. Funny, I know everyone here quite well. But I'm still nervous to speak in front of all these people."

"You'll do great," he assured her.

Carli leaned into the microphone and cleared her throat. "Thank you everyone for coming," she began. "We are so excited to unveil the new Hammond's Toys Cape store. Although the name has not changed, a lot inside the store has. For those of you who haven't had a chance to read the write-up in the *Westerson Eagle* or haven't otherwise heard, Hammond's now is so much more than a toy store. It's been expanded to include a teen center, an arts and crafts area, which will offer weekly lessons, as well as a state-of-the-art arcade. And so much more in the way of seasonal activities depending on the time of year." She gave him a smile that shot pleasure through his chest, then took a deep breath. "I can't tell you how proud it makes me to tell you that all this was the brainchild of my fiancé, Justin Hammond." She held her hand out toward him.

Justin's turned to the audience and took a mock bow. "That was the easy part," he yelled toward the crowd. As was the financing. Justin had found willing investors in a relatively short period of time once he explained his vision. The store was such a central point of the town, it only made sense to have it offer more reasons for the customers to visit and more for them to do once they got there. All those new attractions Carli mentioned would not only bring in their own revenue, they'd increase traffic to the actual toy store—resulting in higher sales.

Carli continued. "And now, without further delay, we would like to welcome you to the new Hammond's."

Cheers and raucous clapping erupted before she even finished the sentence. Once the applause died down, the five of them watched as Mr. Freider handled the comically large scissors to cut the wide red ribbon. Two newly hired employees dressed as elves pulled the double doors open to let the still cheering crowd into the renovated store.

His brother came to give him an enthusiastic handshake. "Well, done, man."

"Thanks." It was taking a while, but they were slowly starting to get to know each other. Bonding over the two women in their lives played no small role in their growing relationship.

"I can't tell you how much Noelle appreciates Carli's gesture," James told him, his gaze traveling to where the two ladies stood chatting by the doors. "She's really looking forward to being a bridesmaid."

What was one more? Justin thought. At this rate they were going to have the largest bridal party ever heard of. Not that he was complaining. Carli Tynan deserved to have the wedding she wanted, down to every detail. "I'm glad they're growing so close."

Right on cue, the two women shared a laugh at something Carli had said. Justin and James went to join them.

"You did great," he told her as James and Noelle entered the store.

"I'm glad that part's over," she replied. "Now we can finally start planning for the other big event."

"Oh? I'm not exactly sure what you might be referring to. There's a lot happening," he teased, and gave her a playful tap on the tip of the nose. She meant the wedding, of course.

"Very funny."

Justin pulled her to him and gave her a deep, lingering kiss. Something told him planning their nuptials was going to take just as much time and effort as opening the new store had. That's what happened when you had a family as large as the Tynans and everyone possessed input they had to share.

He wouldn't have it any other way.

The easiest decision by far had been picking the date.

Twelve months from now, Justin would be walking his Christmas bride down the aisle.

He could hardly wait.

* * * * *

Look out for the previous story in
THE MEN WHO MAKE CHRISTMAS *duet*

CHRISTMAS WITH HER MILLIONAIRE BOSS
by Barbara Wallace

And, if you enjoyed this story, check out these other great reads from Nina Singh

MISS PRIM AND THE MAVERICK MILLIONAIRE
THE MARRIAGE OF INCONVENIENCE

All available now!

MILLS & BOON®

Cherish™

EXPERIENCE THE ULTIMATE RUSH OF FALLING IN LOVE

A sneak peek at next month's titles...

In stores from 14th December 2017:

- **The Italian Billionaire's New Year Bride** – Scarlet Wilson *and* **Her Soldier of Fortune** – Michelle Major
- **The Prince's Fake Fiancée** – Leah Ashton *and* **The Arizona Lawman** – Stella Bagwell

In stores from 28th December 2017:

- **Tempted by Her Greek Tycoon** – Katrina Cudmore *and* **Just What the Cowboy Needed** – Teresa Southwick
- **United by Their Royal Baby** – Therese Beharrie *and* **Claiming the Captain's Baby** – Rochelle Alers

Just can't wait?
Buy our books online before they hit the shops!
www.millsandboon.co.uk

Also available as eBooks.

MILLS & BOON®

EXCLUSIVE EXTRACT

Snowed in together on New Year's Eve, their attraction explodes…! Leaving Italian billionaire Matteo Bianchi to wonder if he could finally open his heart and make Phoebe Gates his bride.

Read on for a sneak preview of
THE ITALIAN BILLIONAIRE'S
NEW YEAR BRIDE

He could still taste her, and he'd never felt so hungry for more. Every part of his body urged him to continue.

But he took a deep breath and rested his forehead against hers, his hand still tangled in her hair. Phoebe's breathing was labored and heavy, just like his. But she didn't push for anything else. She seemed happy to take a moment too. Her chest was rising and falling in his eye line as they stayed for a few minutes with their heads together.

Everything felt too new. Too raw. Did he even know what he was doing here?

"Happy New Year," he said softly. "At least I'm guessing that's why we can still hear fireworks."

"There are fireworks outside? I thought they were inside." Her sparkling dark eyes met his gaze and she smiled. "Wow," she said huskily.

He let out a laugh. "Wow," he repeated.

Her hand was hesitant, reaching up, then stopping, then

reaching up again. She finally rested it against his chest, the fingertips pausing on one of the buttons of his shirt.

His mind was willing her to unfasten it. But she just let it sit there. The warmth of her fingertips permeating through his designer shirt. He could sense she wanted to say something, and it made him want to stumble and fill the silence.

For the first time in his life, Matteo Bianchi was out of his depth. It was a completely alien feeling for him. In matters of the opposite sex he was always in charge, always the one to initiate things, or, more likely, finish them. He'd never been unsure of himself, never uncomfortable.

But from the minute he'd met this woman with a warm smile and thoughtful heart, he just hadn't known how to deal with her. She had a way of looking at him as he answered a question that let him know his blasé, offhand remarks didn't wash with her. She didn't push. She didn't need to. He was quite sure that, if she wanted to, Phoebe Gates would take no prisoners. But the overwhelming aura from Phoebe was one of warmth, of kindness and sincerity. And it was making his heart beat quicker every minute.

Don't miss
THE ITALIAN BILLIONAIRE'S
NEW YEAR BRIDE
by Scarlet Wilson

Available January 2018

www.millsandboon.co.uk